Lynne Graham was born in Northern Ireland and has been a keen romance reader since her teens. She is very happily married to an understanding husband, who has learned to cook since she started to write! Her five children keep her on her toes. She has a very large dog, which knocks everything over, a very small terrier, which barks a lot, and two cats. When time allows, Lynne is a keen gardener.

New York Times and *USA TODAY* bestselling author **Jane Porter** has written forty romances and eleven women's fiction novels since her first sale to Mills & Boon in 2000. A five-time RITA® Award finalist, Jane is known for her passionate, emotional and sensual novels, and loves nothing more than alpha heroes, exotic locations and happy-ever-afters. Today Jane lives in sunny San Clemente, California, with her surfer husband and three sons. Visit janeporter.com.

DA ROCHA'S CONVENIENT HEIR

LYNNE GRAHAM

KIDNAPPED FOR HIS ROYAL DUTY

JANE PORTER

MILLS & BOON

First Published in Great Britain 2018
by Mills & Boon, an imprint of HarperCollins*Publishers*
1 London Bridge Street, London, SE1 9GF

Da Rocha's Convenient Heir © 2018 by Lynne Graham

Kidnapped for His Royal Duty © 2018 by Jane Porter

ISBN: 978-0-263-93534-9

MIX
Paper from
responsible sources
FSC® C007454

Printed and bound in Spain
by CPI, Barcelona

DA ROCHA'S CONVENIENT HEIR

LYNNE GRAHAM

CHAPTER ONE

ZAC DA ROCHA, the Brazilian billionaire, powered towards his father's office on long muscular legs. He was in a rare state of surprise because his stuffy, rigidly formal half-brother, Vitale, the Crown Prince of Lerovia, had just matched the facetious bet Zac had made him earlier that morning. Zac enjoyed yanking Vitale's chain but he had not expected a retaliation. He raked his hand impatiently through the long, luxuriant dark hair falling onto his broad shoulders and grinned with sudden appreciation, flashing perfect white teeth in the process. Maybe Vitale wasn't such a narrow-minded bore after all. Maybe he had more in common with his half-sibling than he had assumed.

As quickly as that idea occurred to him, Zac suppressed it again because he wasn't looking for a family connection. He had never had a family. He had looked up his long-lost father, Charles Russell, out of pure curiosity and had lingered on the edge of the family circle out of pure badness, thoroughly entertained by the immediate animosity of his two half-brothers, Vitale and Angel. The emergence of a third son had shocked and unsettled them and Zac had made little effort to foster a sibling relationship. But then what the hell did he know about blood ties? He had never had a brother or a sister and, what was more, he had had a mother he had seen only once a year if he was lucky, a stepfather who hated him and a birth father whose identity he had only discovered the year before when his mother had finally told him the truth she had long withheld because she was dying.

Yet when it came to his birth father, for once in his life he had landed lucky, Zac conceded grudgingly, because he actually *liked* Charles Russell. Zac was more accustomed to people who tried to use him and he trusted very few people. His light grey-blue eyes hardened. Fabulously rich from birth and raised like a little prince, surrounded by fawning servants, Zac was very cynical about human nature. But from their first meeting, Charles had taken a genuine interest in his third and youngest adult son, despite the fact that, at twenty-eight and six feet four inches tall, that son was already a man grown.

After only a few hours in the older man's radius, Zac had realised how much better he would have done had his mother, Antonella, chosen to stay with Charles rather than choosing to marry the playboy fortune hunter, Afonso Oliveira, the love of his mother's life. Unhappily, while being engaged to Antonella, Afonso had got cold feet and dumped her for several weeks. Heartbroken, Antonella had succumbed to a rebound affair with Charles, then in the process of divorcing a wife who had been cheating on him throughout their marriage with another woman. But then, Afonso had returned to Antonella to ask for her forgiveness and Antonella had followed her heart. When soon after the wedding she had realised she was pregnant, she had fervently hoped that she carried Afonso's child and had refused to acknowledge that Zac might not be her husband's son. Sadly, for all of them, Zac's very rare blood group had become a ticking time bomb in his mother's marriage.

As Zac strode into his father's office he was rewarded by an immediate smile of warm welcome and acceptance. He might be a tattooed guy clad in jeans and biker boots with diamond studs in his ear but Charles, the grey-haired older man who greeted him in an immaculate business suit, treated him the exact same as his other sons.

'I did think of putting on a suit to surprise the brothers,' Zac murmured deadpan, his strikingly light eyes glittering with self-mockery against his bronzed skin. 'But I didn't want them to think I was conforming to expectations or competing.'

'No fear of that, I think.' Charles laughed, wrapping his arms round his very tall and vociferously different son in a whole-hearted embrace before stepping back. 'Any news yet from your lawyers about your chances of breaking the trust?'

The internationally renowned Quintal da Rocha diamond mines had been locked into a trust by Zac's great-great-grandfather to protect the family heritage. Since his mother's death, Zac had been in possession of the income from the mines but he would not have the right to control the extensive Da Rocha business empire until he produced an heir of his own. It was an iniquitous arrangement, which had sentenced previous generations to a deeply dysfunctional family life, and Zac had long been determined to break the cycle.

Sadly, the answer his legal team had given him was not the one he had sought.

He could not be truly independent or free until he had met the terms of the trust one way or another. Hedged by restrictions throughout childhood and adolescence, he had railed against the trust when he had finally understood how it would limit him. He was the last da Rocha and he enjoyed enormous wealth but until he fulfilled the conditions imposed by that trust he had no more rights than a child to control the diamond mines and the vast business empire built on the back of their profits. He felt sidelined, powerless and dispossessed by his current weak position and there was little he would not have given to be free of it.

'My lawyers tell me that if I marry and *fail* over time to produce a child they think there would be little problem breaking the trust,' Zac revealed grimly, his chiselled cheekbones taut. 'But that would take years and I'm not prepared to wait for years to run what is mine by right of blood.'

Charles expelled his breath in a slow hiss. 'So, you're going to get married,' he assumed.

Zac frowned. 'I don't need to get married,' he countered. 'Any heir will meet the terms of the trust, boy or girl, legitimate or otherwise.'

'Legitimate would be better,' Charles protested quietly.

'But the ensuing divorce settlement would cost me a fortune,' Zac responded with resounding practicality. 'Why marry when I don't have to?'

'For the child's sake,' Charles supplied with a grimace. 'To protect the child from growing up as both you and your mother did, isolated from normal life.'

Zac parted his lips as though he was about to say something and then thought better of it, swinging restively away. His grandfather had found himself married to a barren wife. He had then impregnated a maid in the household, who had given birth to Zac's mixed-race mother. Antonella had been whisked away to be raised at a remote ranch, separated from her mother and never acknowledged by her aristocratic father once her arrival had refuelled his wealthy lifestyle. She had been an heiress but one from the kind of humble background the rich and sophisticated delighted in despising.

Initially, Zac's stepfather, Afonso, had assumed that Zac was *his* child and he had married Antonella, willing to turn a blind eye to her embarrassing background if he could share her riches. When Zac was three years old, however, his need for a blood transfusion after an accident had roused Afonso's suspicions about his parentage and the truth had emerged. Zac still remembered Afonso screaming at him that he was not his child and that he was 'a dirty, filthy half-breed'. After that fallout, Zac had been transported to the ranch to be raised by staff, out of sight and out of mind while Antonella worked on repairing the marriage that meant so much to her.

'He's my husband and he comes first. He *has* to come first,' Antonella had told Zac when he'd asked to go home with her after one of her fleeting visits to see him.

'I love him. You can't come to Rio. It will only put Afonso in a bad mood,' she had argued vehemently years later with tears in her beautiful eyes.

Yet Afonso had enjoyed countless affairs during his marriage while Antonella struggled to give him a child of his own, suffering innumerable miscarriages and finally the premature birth that had claimed her life when she was already well beyond the age when child bearing was considered safe. Afonso had not even come to the funeral and Zac had buried his weak-willed but lovely mother with a stone where his heart should've been and the inner conviction that he would never ever marry or fall in love, because love had only taught his mother to reject and neglect her only child.

'I married two very beautiful women, neither of whom was the least maternal,' his father, Charles, told him heavily, pulling Zac suddenly back into the present. 'Angel and Vitale paid the price with unhappy home lives. Right now you're at a crossroads and you have a choice, Zac. Give marriage a chance. Choose a woman who at least *wants* a child and give her the opportunity, with your support, to be a normal mother to that child. Children need two parents because bringing up a child is tough. I did the best I could after the divorces but I wasn't around enough to make a big difference in my sons' lives.'

It was quite a speech and it came from the heart; Zac almost groaned out loud because he could see where his father was coming from. Although marrying would cost him millions when it inevitably broke down, that legal framework *would* provide a certain stability for the child. It would be a stability that he had never enjoyed but then, unlike his grandfather, he had always planned to be involved in his child's life, hadn't he? Even so, if he wasn't *married* to the mother of his child, his freedom to be involved would be dictated by her. He already knew those facts, had worked through all possible options with his legal team and preferred not to think about those facts because they only depressed him. After all, the odds of him having a good relation-ship with his child's mother were slim, he reflected impatiently.

Women *always* wanted more from Zac than he was prepared to give...more time, more money, more at-tention. But all he had ever wanted from a woman was sex and once that was over, he was done. He was an unashamed player, who had never been in a real rela-tionship, who had never pledged fidelity and who could not bear the sensation of being caged by anyone or any-thing. In many ways, he had been caged most of his life, raised on a remote ranch before being placed in a stiflingly strict boarding school run by the clergy and forced to follow endless rules. He hadn't known a mo-ment of true freedom until he reached university and it was hardly surprising that he had then gone off the rails for a while. In fact, it had been a few years before he got back on track and completed his business degree.

And what had brought him back? The discovery that at heart he was a da Rocha and that he couldn't run away from his birthright. A workers' dispute in which he was powerless to intervene on their behalf had per-suaded him to start attending business meetings and, although he still couldn't legally call the shots, he had discovered that the directors were very wary of mak-ing an outright enemy of him. Like Zac, they looked to the future.

'How long will you be away?' Charles prompted, aware that Zac was leaving London to check out the diamond mines in South Africa and Russia.

Zac shrugged. 'Five...maybe six weeks. I've a lot to catch up on but I'll stay in touch.'

Leaving his father's office, Zac headed back to The

Palm Tree, the small, exclusive and very opulent hotel he had bought in preference to an apartment of his own. His thoughts immediately turned in a more frivolous direction, escaping with relief from the serious ramifications of his father's sage advice. He had bet his brother that he couldn't find an ordinary woman and pass her off as his socialite partner at the royal ball to which he had also been invited. Unsurprisingly, Vitale, who didn't have a humorous bone in his entire body, had been unamused by the challenge but, on emerging from his meeting with their father earlier, Vitale had startled Zac by not only accepting the bet but also by making his own. And what had followed had had very much an 'own goal' feel for Zac...

Remember that little blonde waitress who wanted nothing to do with you last week and accused you of harassment? Bring her to the ball acting all lovelorn and clingy and suitably polished up and you have a deal on the bet.

Freddie? Lovelorn and clingy? That was the challenge to end all challenges when he couldn't even get her to join him for a drink! His even white teeth clenched hard in frustration. Zac had never before met with an outright rejection from a woman and it had infuriated him, his innate need to compete making him persist. But Freddie had interpreted persistence as harassment and had burst into tears in Vitale's presence, a fiercely embarrassing moment that had frozen Zac where he'd sat in all male horror at what he had unleashed on himself in a public place. Even more gallingly, Vitale had stepped straight in to defuse the scene with all the right soothing words until another waitress had arrived to rescue them. But then that was Vitale, all smooth, slippery and refined in a way Zac was distinctly aware that he himself was not. The most formative years of Zac's life had been the dropout years when he had belonged to a biker club, not rubbing shoulders with the rich and sophisticated in polite society.

In polite society, Zac was mobbed by women seduced by his great wealth and he avoided such women like the plague, well aware that they would've been equally enthusiastic even if he were old, bald and unpleasant. That he was none of those things simply made him more of a target. He had loved the male brotherhood in the club, the easy acceptance, the loyalty and the complete lack of rules that had enabled him to be himself. He had enjoyed women equally happy to enjoy him in bed, women without an agenda, only looking for pleasure. But after a while, even that had got old and as soon as the Brazilian media had discovered his hideout and exposed the story of the billionaire biker boy, he had moved regretfully on, knowing that phase of his life was over.

He revelled now in the anonymity of his life in London and had avoided his siblings' social gatherings out of a strong desire to preserve it. Spoiled, privileged young women with cut-glass accents didn't do it for him because they saw him as a prize trophy to be won. He had met with more sincerity and honesty in people his brothers would probably snobbishly deem to be vulgar and uneducated. And even conservative Vitale had conceded that Freddie was a real looker.

Zac only knew that he had never wanted a woman with such instantaneous lust. Lust at first glance, he conceded grimly, thinking it ironic that out of all the many women who wanted him back his libido had had to focus on one who not only did not want him, but also actively appeared to dislike him. He couldn't accept that he had done or said anything to incite that reaction from her and the injustice had outraged him, encouraging his damaging determination to change her attitude. *Meu Deus*, after her outburst, he would scarcely be looking in that direction again, which meant that Vitale had won the bet outright and as the loser he would have to hand over his cherished sports car. Exasperation and growing annoyance gripped him. He would now be gone for weeks in any case.

One last try...

When he got back to London next month, what would he have to lose? He could attempt outright bribery, Zac decided with sudden savage cynicism...*use* the power of money to persuade for once in his life. Freddie had refused his first generous tip and then had just as swiftly changed her mind and accepted it, he recalled with a sceptical curl of his full sensual mouth. She would turn out to be like every other woman he had ever met: she would surrender for money. After all, she wasn't working all day on her feet as a waitress for fun.

Freddie was having a dream about a man with eyes the colour of crushed ice, a wealth of silky blue-black hair and a full sensual mouth.

It was a wonderful dream until a little hand shook her arm and a little voice said, 'Bekfast? Auntie Fred... *bekfast*?' while one warm little body pushed for space in her single bed and another warm little body crawled up over the top of her.

With a groan, Freddie woke up and checked her alarm in case she had slept in. Some hope of that with her nephew and niece around, she thought ruefully, with three-year-old Eloise pinning her up against the wall and ten-month-old Jack lying on top of her in a happy baby sprawl.

'You *don't* lift Jack out of his cot,' she told her niece for the tenth time. 'He could get hurt. It's not safe if I'm still asleep—'

'You wake now,' Eloise pointed out cheerfully as Freddie scrambled over her with Jack in her arms and went to change him.

A vague recollection of her dream flushed her triangular face and her soft mouth tightened, her brown eyes sparkling with self-loathing. Loser alert, loser alert, she chanted inside her head in exasperation. Eloise and Jack's father, Cruz, had been a very good-looking guy as well, beautifully dressed and polite, but he had turned out to be a terrifyingly violent drug dealer and a pimp. Her older sister, Lauren, had died of a drug overdose within days of Jack's birth, utterly destroyed by the man she had loved, who had not only refused to acknowledge his children but had also so far escaped paying a single penny towards their support.

Zac whatever-his-name-was might not be either beautifully dressed *or* polite, but he had been staying for weeks in the very expensive penthouse suite in the exclusive hotel where she worked in the bar and, although he had been gone for over a month now, the suite was apparently being held for his return. How the heck was he affording that when as far as she could see he didn't engage in any normal form of work? He also mixed with some very flash, international, business-suited men. He was dubious and up to no good, of course he was, she told herself angrily, furious that the Brazilian had invaded her dreams. It had been bad enough, she acknowledged, when she'd had to see him every day in the bar. And now that he was gone, why hadn't she completely forgotten about him?

It was even more weird that he had shown such an interest in her in the first place, she reflected irritably. She had seen how attractive he was to women while she worked. Zac wasn't a mere babe magnet, more a babe tornado. She had seen desperate women do everything but strip in front of him in an effort to gain his attention. They nudged up to him at the bar, tripped nearby, tried to strike up conversations and buy him drinks. And he acted as if they didn't exist, behaving like a blind celibate monk in their radius. Weird and suspicious, *right*?

After all, Freddie *knew* she wasn't a show-stopper. She was way too undersized to be one. Barely five feet tall and slender, with only a very modest amount of curves. She had dark blonde hair that fell halfway to her waist and plain brown eyes. So why would a guy with Zac's attributes chase a waitress unless he was a weirdo? Or some kind of user who assumed she would be stupid enough to fall for whatever nefarious purpose he had in mind? Well, no, Freddie had never been stupid and she knew how to look after herself, particularly after having spent years watching her late sister make the very worst decisions possible.

Freddie made breakfast for the children quietly, striving not to wake up her aunt, Claire, who had come home in the early hours. Claire, her late mother's youngest sister, was only six years older than twenty-two-year-old Freddie, so they had never had the traditional auntie/niece connection, being far too close in age for that, but they had always got on well. Even so, just at present Freddie was worried about the other woman's mood. Claire was being evasive and quiet, not to mention going out a lot and using a babysitter without ever talking about where she was going. Freddie believed in respecting Claire's privacy but, at the same time, she couldn't help worrying herself sick that their little 'family' arrangement was somehow at risk.

At Freddie's instigation, Claire had applied to foster the kids after Freddie was turned down for the job. That had been after Lauren's death when the welfare services had wanted to remove the kids from Freddie's care and put them into a foster home with strangers. Freddie had been deemed too young and inexperienced to take charge of the children she had been looking after from birth—for that was the unlovely truth about her late sister's parenting skills. Lauren's world had had only two focuses: drugs and her violent, threatening boyfriend. Freddie had long been the only person available to care for Eloise and Jack while trying at the same time to dissuade her sister from her worst excesses.

And there she had failed abysmally, she conceded sadly, having found it impossible either to get Lauren off drugs or to persuade her to break up with Cruz. Grief still filled her when she thought of the loving, light-hearted big sister she had grown up with and clung to in foster care. Their parents had died in a car crash when Freddie was ten and there had been no relatives willing to take them in. Five years older, Lauren had been more like a little substitute mother than a big sister, at least, *until* she had fallen under Cruz's influence and every rule had been broken, every moral flouted, every evil permitted. Freddie had been stuck in the middle of all that horror from the day of Eloise's birth, knowing that if she moved out her niece would be lucky to survive that chaotic household where only constant vigilance protected the weak and vulnerable. Claire had urged her to walk away and turn her back but she had loved Eloise too much to do that.

So, when Claire had generously agreed to apply to be the kids' foster carer even though she wasn't really 'a kiddy person', as she put it, the agreement had been that Freddie would continue doing the lion's share of the childcare. That meant that Freddie stayed home days to see to the children and worked nights in a bar, having readied the kids for bed before she left Claire's tiny terraced home. Claire had confessed herself content to live off the foster-care payments but Freddie had had to find work to bring in some extra money.

And during Zac's stay at the hotel, his tips had virtually doubled Freddie's earnings. He had routinely tossed her two fifty-pound notes every time she served him and the first time, aware of his personal interest, she had taken umbrage and tossed them back, telling him she wasn't for sale, only to be ambushed by another waitress who had angrily reminded her that their tips went into a communal pot, so she had had to go back to Zac's table and apologise and pick up the discarded notes.

His unsought generosity had, however, reclothed Eloise and Jack, put some very nice meals on the table and now that little gold pile was almost gone it was time for a treat, she thought, determined to start being more positive and stop worrying about Claire, who, ultimately, would do what she wanted to do regardless of what anyone else wanted. Equally, why was she beating herself up about a stupid dream? Fantasies were harmless and, in the flesh, Zac was decidedly a fantasy, a traffic-stoppingly beautiful man whom women stood still to study until they recollected themselves and, blushing, moved on.

Of course, Freddie had done worse several weeks earlier when she had lost her temper with Zac and then burst into floods of tears. The stress of two sleepless nights with Jack running a fever had smashed all her defences flat. Claire had been so irritable about his crying disturbing her sleep and Freddie had been so exhausted, she had simply cracked down the middle and snapped when Zac had merely put a hand on her spine to steady her when she'd wobbled in the very high heels she had to wear for work. She had learned to be very averse to men touching her while she was living with her sister, whose home had overflowed with untrustworthy men. She had developed the habit of maintaining rigid boundaries and it had come back to haunt her at the worst possible moment.

But then, although she had been forced to apologise for the scene she had made to retain her job, she had still believed her hysterical outburst couldn't have happened to a more suitable person. Zac's very first words to her, after all, had been unrepeatably dirty and blunt, an invitation to spend the night with him but not one couched in polite or acceptable terms. She had had many such invites before but he was the first who had ever employed that kind of language to her face and she had felt soiled by it, besmirched by the simple fact she had to wear denim shorts, little tops and high heels to work in the hip hotel bar. After all, she was well aware that at least one of her colleagues took money to sleep with customers, and she had always been very careful not to give the wrong impression to the male clientele by being too flirtatious and she never ever gave out her phone number. In any case, for better or for worse, she had no time for a boyfriend in her life. Her life was full to overflowing from the moment she got up at six until she fell into bed worn out soon after midnight.

She checked into work punctually that evening, having earned several admonitions for being late when Claire failed to come home on time to take over charge of the children. Stashing her bag in the locker provided, she put on the shorts and the high heels that she had mercifully finally worn in and walked into the elegant black and white bar, with its eye-catching lighting and mirrored ceiling, to begin serving drinks. The black and white theme and the wonderfully opulent décor ran right through the boutique hotel, where no expense had been spared and where every comfort was on offer to those who could afford the high prices.

'Mr da Rocha is out on the terrace,' Roger, the bar manager, informed her.

'Who the heck is Mr da Rocha?' she asked.

'That guy you don't like. He's back,' Roger told her wryly and he lowered his head to whisper tautly, 'A fairly reliable source tells me that Mr da Rocha *bought* this place a couple of months ago, so I would watch my step if I were you because if he decides he wants you out, you'll be history.'

Freddie was drop-dead stunned by that piece of information and she stared wide-eyed after Roger as he moved off to attend to a customer at the bar. Zac *owned* the hotel? How was it possible that a foul-mouthed, tattooed guy in ripped jeans and biker boots had *bought* a hotel in one of the most exclusive areas of London? She clenched her teeth in thwarted disbelief. Yes, Zac was a huge mystery because, no matter what he wore or how carelessly he spoke, he emanated a force field of power and arrogance and contrived to appear totally at home in a very upmarket hotel. Practising her brightest smile, Freddie marched out to the terrace, which was unnervingly empty but for him.

And like a juggernaut parked in a too small parking space, Zac overfilled it, his devastating effect all the stronger because it had been so many weeks since she last saw him. He was wearing all black, which was a change from his usual denim blue jeans. Black jeans, black shirt, leather cuff on one arm, his St Jude necklace gleaming gold at his bronzed throat. Patron saint of lost causes, very appropriate, she thought inanely. But he was so outrageously gorgeous standing there that her mouth ran dry and her nipples tightened and her entire body leapt in a response that maddened her because it happened every time she saw him, like an alarm clock shrilling in her ear, reminding her that she was as weak and hormonal around him as every other young woman she saw staring at him with longing. While she might not stare, she was, at heart, no different from the rest of her sex, and the reminder rankled like a stone in her shoe she couldn't shake loose.

Lounging back against the boundary wall, Zac straightened the instant Freddie appeared, so tiny, so dainty she reminded him of a delicate doll. A doll he wanted to flatten down and spread on the nearest horizontal surface, he reminded himself, looking boldly into eyes that ranged from the colour of melted caramel to that of liquid chocolate. A wall would do perfectly well, he thought absently, so aroused at the sight of her he was threatening the fly in his new jeans, and the infuriating thing was that he didn't know exactly what it was about her that so turned him on every time she was within view.

'Mr...er da Rocha,' she pronounced, startling him with both the name and the undeniably false smile she had pasted on her lips because, most pointedly, she was careful never ever to smile at him.

And he knew right then that somebody had been talking and that she was somehow aware that he was not merely a hotel guest at The Palm Tree. Exasperation shimmered through him. He had bought the hotel for convenience, not for any form of recognition.

'I have a proposition for you,' Zac murmured huskily.

He had the most lethal electric sensuality Freddie had ever heard in a man's voice. He could make a drinks order sound like a caress that skimmed spectral fingers down her rigid spine.

'I think I've already heard that one, *sir*,' she tacked on tightly. 'And I'm going to pass on it—'

'No, you haven't heard this one,' Zac cut in with a raw impatience he did not even attempt to hide. 'I will give you a thousand pounds to spend an hour with me. And no, not in bed if that's what you're thinking. An hour *anywhere* in *any* place of your choosing.'

Her lashes fluttered up on utterly bewildered eyes. 'But why *would* you offer—?'

'I want to get to know you,' Zac lied. 'A conversation is all I'm asking for, nothing else. So, are you up for it or not?'

'Anywhere, any place?' she double-checked, because she didn't credit his desire to get to know her for a second.

'Anywhere, any place,' Zac confirmed.

Freddie straightened her stiff shoulders and thought fast. If he was fool enough to pay, she was bright enough to take advantage. 'Give me your phone number and I'll think about it,' she told him jerkily, barely able to credit that she was willing to sell her scruples down the river to spend even five minutes with him, never mind an hour!

'There would have to be no crude language and no touching,' she warned him carefully.

'I can handle that.' Zac gave her a huge charismatic smile that flashed white teeth and sent her heartbeat racing.

It was a crying shame that a man with his looks and presence should be so cynical and rough round the edges, Freddie reflected as he strode off the terrace, visibly satisfied with the result of his barefaced bribery. Of course, he didn't want to get to *know* her. He wanted to get into her underwear in the most basic way possible and her negative response had simply forced him to raise his game.

But how could she possibly turn down a thousand pounds with Eloise and Jack to consider? With that kind of money she could take them on a little holiday or finally establish a rainy-day fund for emergencies. Yes, she was being greedy and shameless to accept such an arrangement but, as long as he knew upfront that no sex would be involved, he only had himself to blame for his extravagance and his *huge* ego. And she knew that she was going to enjoy punishing him thoroughly for both flaws.

CHAPTER TWO

'ARE YOU WORRIED about something?' Freddie asked Claire gently, striving to redirect her anxiety about meeting up with Zac in an hour's time towards something hopefully less threatening to her peace of mind. 'You've seemed so preoccupied lately…'

Her aunt, a brunette with her hair tied up in a casual ponytail, shrugged a shoulder and almost squirmed in her seat beneath Freddie's troubled appraisal. 'Oh, you know…things get on top of me sometimes.'

'You must miss Richard,' Freddie said sympathetically, because Claire's boyfriend had recently gone out to Spain to help his parents set up the business they had bought out there. At the same time he was expected home within days.

'Obviously,' Claire muttered rather cuttingly, rising from the kitchen table with heightened colour in her cheeks. 'I've got some emails to catch up on. See you later.'

And there it was, the refusal to spill the beans again, Freddie reflected ruefully while wondering if she should simply mind her own business because the two women had never been best friends who shared everything. Furthermore, didn't she have enough to worry about?

Ever since she had made that agreement with Zac da Rocha, she had been regretting it. Her worst sin was impulsiveness. What if the guy turned nasty? From his point of view, she would be wasting his time and he would probably refuse to cough up the money he had offered, so all she was likely to do was embarrass herself and infuriate him. Was that wise when he could—possibly—be her employer? Ridiculous as it still seemed to Freddie, the rumour of his ownership of the hotel was spreading in spite of the fact that for some strange reason he apparently didn't want anyone to know.

Regret and uncertainty stabbing at her nerves, she had tried to take a rain check on the arrangement she had made with him by text, but Zac was set on denying her any wriggle room while adding that he was looking forward to seeing her, which, in the circumstances, only made Freddie feel worse because by no stretch of the imagination was it going to be a date.

Yet, for all that awareness, Freddie found herself taking more care with her appearance than she usually did on such trips. Her hair was freshly washed and she put on her best jeans and newest top while also ensuring that the children looked presentable. Eloise danced alongside the buggy containing Jack because she adored the park where she could swing and run about. Freddie approached the bench by the central fountain where she had arranged to meet Zac and breathed in deep and slow.

'Who we meeting?' Eloise demanded again.

'A man. A…a friend,' Freddie fibbed.

'Name?' Eloise pressed.

'It's Zac,' Freddie told her reluctantly, fairly sure that Zac would not last five minutes in their company once he registered that she had called his bluff in the most basic way possible. Did he even have a sense of humour?

Freddie stood up to pace the instant she saw Zac in the distance. He was so tall he was easy to spot. Jack grizzled to get out of the buggy and, with a sigh, she freed him, praying that she could keep him out of the water because she had not brought spare clothing out with her. Jack had confounded all expectations by getting up and walking at ten months old on his sturdy little legs. He had never crawled, he had just pulled himself up to walk and Freddie had discovered that her baby boy was suddenly a toddler with even less wit than the average toddler because he was still so young.

Eloise pushed the empty buggy along the path, Jack at her side. Freddie focussed on Zac's approach, her heart beating very, very fast until it reached such a pitch that even breathing became a challenge. It was nerves, she told herself. He strode with the innate fluidity of a predator and she was hyperaware of every facet of him: the blue-black hair blowing back from his bronzed and perfect features, the sheer beauty of his bold masculinity in the sunlight, those strikingly light eyes of his, the colour of which she was still unsure of, glittering with the same charisma as his wide slashing smile. Oh, heavens, he was going to *hate* her, she thought with a sudden sharp pang of regret that startled her.

Were those kids with her? Surely not, Zac reasoned, deeming her too young for such a role while glancing around hopefully for another adult and failing to see one in the vicinity. They were her kids? *She* had kids? And not just a modest single one, but *two*? *Inferno*, what had he got himself into? But Zac had always been a quick study and light on his feet and he was careful not to betray an ounce of his discomfiture while feasting his attention on the slender blonde by the fountain. It was her body, he told himself urgently, just something about those seemingly fragile little bones and tiny curves that hugely turned him on. Or maybe it was the hair, thick and streaky blonde and definitely natural in his opinion, long twirling strands with a slight wave shifting in the breeze. Or was it the face, the unexpectedly dark eyes that were so much more unusual with that hair colour than blue? Or that incredibly voluptuous pink mouth of hers that left him painfully turned on?

Meu Deus, she was finally smiling at him and it lit up her solemn little face like the sun. True, the smile was a tad awkward and stiff, which it ought to be, considering that she had set him up with two kids in tow. Involuntarily, Zac was amused for no woman had ever tried to block him with children before, and he also knew that if he had known in advance what her reservations related to he would have run a mile, because kids and the freedom he valued so highly didn't work together at all. And how the hell could she even *try* to fulfil the bet with Vitale for him with two little kids around? To his intense annoyance, the possibility of retaining his precious sports car seemed to move further out of his grasp.

'Well, you said you wanted to get to know me,' Freddie reminded him with more than a little desperation, for the silence had stretched far longer than she could be comfortable with. 'And *this* is my life pretty much... the kids.'

Zac watched her settle down on the bench while the

little girl hovered with huge dark eyes below her mop of blonde curls and the baby clung to her knees. 'What do you call them?' he asked.

'I'm Eloise,' the little girl informed him importantly while lifting up her dress to show off her underwear.

'Eloise, leave your dress alone,' Freddie interposed.

'And you're Auntie Freddie's friend, Zac,' Eloise completed, skipping over to him to grab his bare arm where a tattoo of a dragon writhed. 'What's that?'

'A dragon.'

'Like in my storybook?' Eloise screamed with excitement.

'And this is Jack,' Freddie supplied, her face pink with embarrassment.

'*Auntie* Freddie?' Zac queried, his hopes rising afresh while the little girl clambered uninvited onto his lap, the better to examine his tattoo.

'Get down, Eloise,' Freddie instructed.

Eloise ignored her. Zac lifted the child down onto the bench between them and extended his arm in the slender hope of getting some peace.

'I can't really talk about it here with little ears,' Freddie admitted awkwardly, wondering if ever a woman had been more punished for trying to outface a man. 'But my sister...er...passed last year.'

'And there's no one else?' Zac pressed, insanely conscious of the little girl's eyes clinging to his.

'Well, there's my aunt, Claire, who's twenty-eight and their official foster carer, but my agreement with her is that she's the official but I do the caring,' Freddie volunteered in a horrid rush that mortified her because she felt as if she were apologising for her unavailability. 'As you know I work evenings, so there's really no room in my life for anything else.'

'I'm not still trying to…gave up on that,' Zac lied.

He had so many tells when he lied, Freddie recognised, noting the downward shift of his outrageously long black lashes, the evasive gaze, the clenching of one hand on a long, powerful thigh. Yes, he was still interested in her but currently pretending not to be for some strange reason.

'So, why did you want to meet up, then?' she enquired, striving not to sound sarcastic because he had taken the presence of the kids like a gentleman, even if she was convinced that he was far from being one.

Jack wobbled over to him like a homing pigeon and clutched at both his knees, beaming up at Zac with a sunny Jack smile of acceptance. Zac unfroze and stood up with care, trying not to dislodge Jack. 'Let's walk,' he suggested. 'It'll occupy the children.'

It was well timed, with both her niece and nephew treating him like a wonderful and mesmerising new toy. When she had made the decision to meet Zac in the park with the children, it should have occurred to her that Eloise and Jack would be fascinated with him because they very rarely had any contact with men. Claire had complained bitterly about the way they hogged her boyfriend's attention when he came round.

'We'll move on to the playground,' she agreed, lifting Jack, who wailed in protest and putting him back into the buggy.

Finding himself in possession of a trusting little girl's hand, Zac strode along the path below the trees, trying and failing to slow his stride to match Eloise's tiny steps. Without further ado, he began telling Freddie about his bet with his brother, Vitale.

'My goodness, that's so childish…what age are you?' Freddie asked in sincere wonderment.

'Twenty-eight.'

'Really?' Her wondering gaze grew even wider. 'Maybe it's a boy thing, but I just can't imagine making such a crazy bet and risking losing something I valued out of pride.'

His nostrils flaring, Zac computed that far from complimentary comment and drew in a long steadying breath before continuing, 'Vitale was the guy I was with the day you had your…episode,' he selected finally, shooting her a sidewise glance.

'Oh, you mean when I screamed and shouted at you?' Freddie translated with unexpected amusement. 'Yeah, it was a rough day after too many rough days in a row… sorry about that. So, your brother was the nice guy?'

Zac jerked his chin in affirmation even while his temper rocketed at that unjust designation being bestowed on Vitale. What was so bloody nice about Vitale? His half-brother had hushed her like a sympathetic audience and every word he had spoken had been fake as hell! Hadn't she realised that? Was she blind or deaf? He wasn't fake or a smoothie like Vitale! But were those qualities what she found attractive in a man?

'And *the nice guy* who was present when you broke down,' Zac enunciated with raw precision, 'bet me that I couldn't bring you "all lovelorn and clingy", as he put it, to his precious royal ball at the end of this month.'

As Eloise released Zac's hand to race off ahead of them to the swings, Freddie stopped dead with the buggy, her face a mask of shock. *'Me?'*

'And suitably polished up to royal standards,' Zac said with even greater scorn.

'I don't do lovelorn and clingy,' Freddie muttered blankly, still struggling simply to accept that Zac could have a brother with some sort of *royal* connection. 'Are the two of you crazy competitors or something?'

'Or something,' Zac fielded non-committally. 'But I'm here today because I was wondering if, for a very generous *price*—'

'*No,*' Freddie slotted in flatly straight away. 'And don't embarrass me by quoting figures! I was annoyed with you last week when you offered to pay me for an hour of my time and I wanted to teach you a lesson by landing you with me and the kids, but this paying me nonsense *has* to stop now.'

Zac frowned, level black brows pleating, his bewilderment patent. 'But why?'

And he didn't get it, he *really* didn't get that it was offensive to try and buy people like products, she registered in frustration. 'Because it's wrong.'

His eyes were a very light, almost crystalline blue in the sunshine, she marvelled as he stared down at her, her brain momentarily a complete blank. 'You accept my tips,' he reminded her stubbornly.

'Because the tips go into a communal pot for *all* the staff and when I turned your tip down the first time, it naturally annoyed the other wait staff,' Freddie explained. 'That's why I returned and accepted it and didn't refuse again.'

Zac was furious at the explanation and immediately resolved to change the rules in the bar, so that Freddie got to keep her own tips: her sneakers were faded and had a hole in one toe. Even the buggy was threadbare—

in fact all three of them looked poverty-stricken in comparison to the children he saw around the hotel. Jack lurched out of the buggy again and headed straight for his knees and Zac let him cling, grudgingly impressed by the baby's huge smile. Jack definitely knew how to make friends. Zac's wide, full mouth compressed.

'Obviously… I mean, I assume,' Freddie stumbled, unable to read the sleek, taut lines of Zac's darkly handsome face and trying not to offend, 'you're not short of money but people who *are* short of money have pride too.'

'But if I've got it and you need it, it's a simple exchange and not offensive,' Zac incised with ringing, argumentative conviction.

'I won't take that thousand pounds under any circumstances because it is wrong and it would make me feel like a con artist! Or like a person you could buy, like a hooker or something!' Freddie declared vehemently.

Passion fired her eyes to glowing gold, Zac noted absently, the fit of his jeans tightening as a wave of desire washed over his body. 'But that's not how I think of you,' he objected in a driven tone, wondering why absolutely everything had to be so infuriatingly complicated with her and hating it. He was reminded of Vitale and all *his* many dos and don'ts, which prevented his half-brother from enjoying the freedom that Zac cherished.

'How could you feel like a hooker when I haven't even touched you?' Zac asked thickly, thinking about touching her to such an extent that even a vacant swing was pushing him into highly inappropriate fantasies.

Freddie's heart was hammering again. Those eyes of his filled her vision, full of glitter and a kind of wild rebellion that was strangely appealing to a young woman who always, *always* played safe. She so badly wanted him to understand her point of view that she wanted to shake him into properly listening, which she knew he wasn't doing.

'*Eu quero voce*… I want you,' Zac growled in English the instant he realised what he had spoken in his own language. '*Why* is that wrong?'

'I didn't say it was wrong!' Freddie gasped. 'I said it was wrong to try and use money to tempt me.'

Zac was on firmer ground now and he extended a hand to wind long brown fingers very slowly through the fall of her hair, his every hunting instinct on high alert in an adrenalin charge beyond anything he had ever experienced. 'But you already want me,' he contended with devastating assurance. 'You wanted me the first time you saw me, so why are we still arguing about it?'

And Freddie deflated as suddenly as a balloon that had had an unfortunate collision with a pin. Colour surged hotly up her face in a crimson tide. That *he* should know that with such appalling certainty, that he should feel in his bones what she had studiously denied even to herself, shook her rigid and utterly silenced her.

Zac tugged her closer and bent his arrogant dark head lower and lower until he finally found her mouth, where the sultry sweet taste of her released a surge of such powerful lust he trembled with it. He eased her up into his arms, ignoring Jack's pleas to be lifted, indeed forgetting the child's very existence.

Freddie had never ever had a kiss of that magnitude. Admittedly, life had ensured that she had not had the opportunity to have many kisses, but when she got her arms wrapped round Zac's neck for the merest fraction of a second she felt as if she never ever wanted to let go because she felt safe, safe for the first time since she had lost her parents, safe as if nothing bad could ever happen to her again. And that unholy kiss, the passionate pressure of that wide, sensual mouth on hers, the plunge of his tongue, that tiny provocative flick he performed across the roof of her mouth... All of a sudden, Freddie wanted what she had never wanted before and she wanted it so very badly, an ache stirred between her slender thighs, heat bursting in her pelvis, her nipples tightening so hard and fast it prickled and *hurt*.

Zac set her down on the ground again, vindicated in his every claim, rejoicing in her responsiveness, wishing he had had the chance to demonstrate their potential chemistry when he had first met her. Showing worked better for him than telling, he acknowledged, now in a good enough mood to scoop up a red-faced, crying Jack and hold him against his shoulder to console him for being ignored.

Freddie almost fell over when Zac returned her to earth. She was dizzy, disorientated, her brain refusing to function, her legs wobbling while her mouth felt swollen and hot. Her hands clenched into fists because she wanted to hit Zac for that lethal demonstration of power over her. Her pride was stung, her heart was still racing and for one unforgivable instant she had forgotten the children. Eloise was shouting to be pushed on the swing and Jack? Jack, astonishingly, she registered, was in Zac's arms, his little head laid down trustingly on Zac's shoulder as the need for his morning nap overcame his little body. Since Freddie could not think of a single thing to say, she rushed over to push her niece on the swing, leaving Zac standing.

Zac scanned her stiff and flushed little face with growing annoyance. What was wrong with her now? *This* was why he didn't date, didn't chase women, didn't ever make an effort. He thought about planting Jack back in the buggy and strapping him in and leaving, but Jack was clutching his jacket in one hand and emanating a rather endearing little snore of contentment, a contentment that would be shattered by any sudden movement. It would be good practice for him when he became a father some day, he told himself begrudgingly. His own child might be horrible; at least Jack was smiley with relatively simple needs.

Eloise, though, would be more demanding, he recognised as the little girl called for him to push her instead of her aunt and he studiously ignored the invite. And then the oddest memory occurred to him, a very early one as he cried for his mother's attention and failed to receive it. Before he knew what he was doing, Zac had stalked over to the swings, passed Jack over to Freddie, who was still acting like a frozen popsicle, and he had taken over pushing the swing. Sometimes children *should* get what they wanted, he decided generously. Just because *he* hadn't didn't mean others should be disappointed too.

Freddie defrosted while Zac pushed Eloise because he was being so unexpectedly helpful and it was very immature to want to punish him for making her enjoy a kiss. What was a kiss? Or what was it about a single kiss that made her dangerously crave another? It was too risky for someone in her position, she reasoned unhappily.

'I can't have a fling with you!' she whispered to Zac over the top of her niece's head.

'What's a "fling"?' Zac fielded in his usual speaking voice.

'Work it out!' Freddie urged impatiently.

'But why not?' he asked equally baldly. 'You're not married. You don't have a boyfriend.'

'We can't talk about it here,' Freddie incised, her colour rising again.

'And whose fault is that? *You* arranged this,' Zac reminded her harshly.

'You were *supposed* to walk away and lose interest!' Freddie flung at him accusingly, striving not to focus on that tantalisingly tempting mouth of his.

'I'm obstinate,' Zac declared with a sudden slashing grin of one-upmanship that emanated extraordinary charisma. 'It takes more energy to put one over me, *meu pequenino*.'

Freddie dropped her head, dark streaky golden hair semi-screening her troubled expression, because she abruptly recognised that on some level she was dragging out their meeting for her own purposes and there was no point in wasting Zac's time when she had no plans to let anything go any further. 'Look, it's time for us to go,' she declared, fighting her awareness of his compelling appeal with all her might.

'Or I could treat you to lunch.'

'No, Jack will scream if he's wakened,' Freddie muttered woodenly, wondering how Zac had contrived to travel from hateful to almost bearable in the course of an hour and hurriedly squashing the pointless reflection. 'We have to go home.'

Zac shrugged a wide shoulder and fell into step beside her as she gathered up Eloise and lowered Jack back into the buggy. 'Aren't you leaving?' Freddie demanded in surprise.

'I'll see you home,' Zac countered stiffly, angrily aware that his welcome seemed to have worn out, questioning why he should care when there were so many more available women around.

Freddie didn't know how to shake him off politely and she felt she had to be polite because, whether she liked it or not, he had been a good sport and at least he was no longer trying to stuff banknotes in her direction.

'You must have *some* social life,' Zac remarked drily, walking down the small dismal street of terraced houses.

'Not really,' Freddie mumbled, fumbling for her key and about to unlock the door when it opened without warning and framed Claire. 'Oh, hi, Claire!' she began.

'And who's this?'

Zac extended a hand and introduced himself and Claire invited him in, completely ignoring Freddie's frantic mute grimaces from behind him.

'Hot, hot, *hot*,' Claire whispered in surprising delight as Freddie passed by her into the cramped hall and Zac lifted in the buggy. 'I'll put on the kettle, shall I?' she added with enthusiasm.

Freddie took Jack upstairs to his cot and when she went down to the lounge, Zac was drinking coffee, comfortably ensconced like a welcome guest while Claire acted as hostess. Maybe he would be attracted to Claire, she thought abruptly and then killed the suspicion, taken aback by how something visceral inside her rose in rage at that idea.

'I'll babysit for you so that you can go out with Zac,' Claire announced, startling her with that unprecedented offer. 'I keep on telling Freddie that she *has* to make her own life beyond the kids. You're not working tonight, are you?'

'Well, no, but—'

'Thanks, Claire. I'll pick you up at eight,' Zac delivered, sidestepping Eloise's offer of her dragon storybook and vaulting upright to seize the moment.

Freddie chased him into the hall but he was too quick for her, already out of the front door and down the steps before she could reach him.

'Why did you do that?' she returned to ask Claire. 'I don't want to go out with him.'

'Of course, you do. He's gorgeous,' Claire parried crushingly. 'All work and no play will make Freddie a very dull girl and if I can help you to see that I'll be happier.'

Silenced by that assurance, reluctant to get into a disagreement with Claire, whose opinions tended to be strident, Freddie swallowed hard. She didn't want to spend more time with Zac when she found him so attractive and was finally admitting that to herself. But pursuing that attraction in any way would be futile. She didn't want a sleazy one-night stand with him and that was all he was after, a little recreational sex to fill a fleeting moment. That wasn't her, would never be her. After a frightening attack in her teens, her sister had gone on to have a lot of casual sex and that was ultimately how she'd ended up with her creepy boyfriend. Freddie was still a virgin because she had had little time for a social life, but she still knew that she wouldn't settle for a meaningless fling. She wanted feelings involved as well as mutual respect and consideration and Zac wasn't programmed to offer any of that. She needed more before she could give her trust and if that was old-fashioned, well, she was content to be old-fashioned.

Zac was equally discomfited at the prospect of the evening ahead. He had never been on a date, had never sought that kind of relationship and hadn't a clue how to go about it. But he had no problem in asking his other brother, Angel, for clarification when he met him out of his office for coffee that afternoon, because his Greek sibling didn't annoy him the way Vitale did. Angel had a much more laid-back and less judgemental attitude.

'Never?' Angel queried in some surprise. 'By the sound of it, your sex life is pretty basic.'

'Very basic,' Zac admitted without embarrassment. 'But I really want this woman.'

'Merry would probably be more help than me,' Angel acknowledged wryly, referring to his new wife. 'I screwed up very badly with her, so we never really dated as such. Take your lady for a drink or dinner, keep it casual.'

Zac's ego was mollified by Angel's confession, but he need not have worried because Freddie had agonised throughout the afternoon before finally texting him her suggestion that they try go-karting.

Zac was astonished by the suggestion because it seemed ridiculously boyish and competitive for a woman who struck him as ultra-feminine, but it appealed much more to his energetic nature than an evening that had to be based on conversation. It did not once occur to him that he was being managed.

Freddie was delighted by Zac's assent. The setting would ensure she wasn't silly and prevent him from getting too handsy. When Claire looked at her in almost comical surprise when she told her where they were going, Freddie simply laughed.

Zac arrived to pick her up on a motorbike, a big black and gold beast that disconcerted her when she had expected him to arrive in some flash sports car. He got off the bike and said very drily, as if he was offering her a huge compliment, 'I've never had a girl on the back of my bike before.'

'First time for everything,' Freddie quipped, putting on the helmet he handed her. 'I haven't been on a motorbike before.'

He flipped out the foot pegs for her, climbed back astride and voiced several terse instructions. With difficulty, Freddie hopped up behind him and wrapped her arms round him, belatedly appreciating that, while a car would have marooned them in dangerous privacy, a bike offered physical intimacy of a possibly more dangerous kind. Her palms rested against rock-hard abs, her fingers brushing against his belt, and then the bike started up and vibrations travelled through her from head to foot in an unexpectedly exciting way.

She rested her face against the back of his jacket, strands of his black hair whipping against her brow, and the scent of him engulfed her like a rip tide, sent to torment. He smelled clean and male with a hint of some exotic cologne and the combination was one to savour, she acknowledged absently, marvelling that such a reality could make her skin tingle and her body heat while she felt every flex of his powerful abdominal muscles shift beneath her clinging hands. Her fingers spread against the heat of him, her own body savouring the connection in the most astonishing way.

Zac wanted to push her hands down to where he really needed her attention below the belt where she was being so very careful not to touch him. Why was she so inhibited? What did she have against pleasure? He had to work that out before sheer sexual frustration drove him crazy. It had been weeks since he had had a woman and that was a new development for him and not one he appreciated. After all, sex was one of life's greatest free pleasures and a need he was accustomed to indulging in regularly.

Why was a single woman as attracted to him as he was to her refusing him? Something in her past? What else could it be? Had she been assaulted? *Abused?* His guts twisted at the suspicion because he despised men who used physical force against the weaker and more vulnerable. *Meu Deus*, could she be even more complicated than he had already recognised? Once again he asked himself angrily, *Why her?* Why was he chasing a woman for the first time in his life? Why wasn't he simply moving on? He swore furiously to himself then that if she refused him again, he would forget about her and seek his pleasure elsewhere...

CHAPTER THREE

As HE PEELED off the last of his protective gear, Zac glanced across at Freddie and his wide, sensual mouth quirked with concealed amusement. There she was, benched after being red-flagged for a safety violation, her face still a mask of angry mortification. Yet she had initially gone onto the track with all the risk-taking verve of a nervous elderly lady and then Zac had flashed past her, a manoeuvre that had evidently unleashed her competitive instincts, and the die had been cast as she raced into pursuit of him in flagrant disregard of her apparent lack of experience on the track.

'Go on...*laugh*,' she urged sulkily, her annoyed gaze challenging him to do his worst while even then noticing the natural animal rhythm of his fluid stride. He walked lightly for so large a man yet testosterone seeped from his very pores. Even in a crowded location, his stunning looks stood out and guaranteed female turned heads and interested stares. Her stiff cheekbones flushed on the sinking acknowledgement that she was woman enough to be proud of being seen with him.

'When you suggested it, I assumed go-karting was a favourite pastime of yours.'

'You must be kidding. I've only been once and that

was years ago…a birthday treat with the foster family we were staying with then.'

Zac took her breath away by simply lifting her off her feet and settling her down on the back of his bike. 'Foster family? *We?*' he queried with a frown.

'Never mind,' Freddie parried, seeing no reason to share her past with him when he was about to take her home.

Resting her cheek against his broad back as the bike glided through the traffic, Freddie closed her eyes, the oddest sensation of regret tugging infuriatingly at her while her body reacted with heat and awareness to the physical contact with his. The date, as such, was done and dusted and he had to now recognise that she was scarcely the sexy temptress of his dreams. He had enjoyed himself though, for Zac and speed were a perfect match, so hopefully there would be no hard feelings and her job would be safe because she really could not afford to lose her job, she thought fearfully.

Lifting her off the bike, Zac unclipped her helmet. As he herded her forward, he tossed his key fob to the doorman and addressed him in a foreign language. 'Where the heck are we?' Freddie demanded, cursing herself for having drifted off into her thoughts and failing to pay attention.

And even by the time she bleated that foolish question she knew exactly where she was and she cringed because she had never walked through the front entrance of The Palm Tree before. Staff had a side entrance and the bar was separate as well and employees were instructed to stay in their designated zone. Ahead of her and below the magnificent crystal chandeliers stretched a blur of mirrored reception counter that was dazzling and disorientating in the bright light.

Something remarkably like panic grabbed Freddie. 'I can't be in here... I *work* here!' she exclaimed in dismay, trying to pull away from Zac's controlling hand at her hip.

Zac grabbed her up into his arms as though she were Eloise and strode into his private lift before setting her down.

'Let me go, for goodness' sake!' Freddie launched at him furiously as he slid her down his long, lean body, ensuring that she missed out on not a single angle of his lean, muscular physique. 'I'm not coming up to your penthouse with you!'

'Yes, you are,' Zac countered without hesitation. 'I have food waiting for us.'

'I'm not hungry!' she protested contrarily.

'And I'm not an abuser of women and dislike being treated as though I am,' Zac replied very, *very* drily.

Colour ran in a hot tide up beneath Freddie's pale complexion and she collided with narrowed eyes the shade of crushed ice, glittering like a dangerous glacier in sunlight below a black lush fringe of lashes. 'That's not how I'm treating you.'

'It is,' he contradicted. 'And I don't like it. I would never touch you without your permission.'

A maddening need to apologise assailed Freddie and she fought it off, examining her behaviour, conceding that she might have come off a little hysterical in her rigid need to protect herself around a man. 'Look, I have to work here, and obviously I don't want to be seen inside *your* penthouse.'

'And maybe, just maybe,' Zac incised in a lethal

undertone, those eyes luminous and cold as polar stars, 'I'm tired of doing everything *your* way, *meu pequenino.*'

Freddie compressed her lips and studied her scuffed trainers in the rushing silence. Her muscles ached with the tension in the air and her tummy performed a nauseous flip.

'When were you in foster care?' Zac continued smoothly as he thrust open the door of what she assumed to be the penthouse suite, because a superb wall of glass overlooked the twinkling lights of the city skyline that bounded one side of the huge room.

Freddie was busy looking around herself at a level of luxury way beyond her experience. There was a tiny elegant kitchen alcove in one corner, not one to be taken seriously, for few who could afford the rates for the penthouse would wish to cook for themselves in a hotel renowned for its cuisine. Another couple of doors led off the main area, which was furnished with a massive wall television and buttery soft leather sofas, currently strewn with car magazines.

'Freddie?' he prompted, amused by her frank curiosity about her surroundings.

Freddie relocated her wits, still careful not to look at him. 'My parents were killed in a car crash when I was ten. I had a completely happy childhood up until then, not so much after that,' she admitted stiffly, food scents tugging at her nostrils, provoking an embarrassingly loud and needy growl from her stomach.

Freddie spoke quickly, fearful that he had heard her tummy grumble. 'What about you? Where did you grow up?'

'A *fazenda*…a ranch in Brazil.' Zac lifted the cover on the food trolley with a flourish. 'Help yourself,' he urged.

Grateful to have something to do with her knotted hands, Freddie reached for a plate while scolding herself for her nerves. Being alone with a man was no big deal and it was time she got over her hang-ups from the years spent living with her sister. In any case, Lauren had been the victim of the abuse, not Freddie, who had merely been a powerless shrinking presence. Zac had probably done her a favour by calling her on her attitude to him. After all, some day in the future, she might want a man of her own and she wouldn't want to scare him off by acting weird, would she? Her spine stretching out of the stiffness she had maintained, she struggled to relax her defences.

'I would never have picked you out as a country boy,' Freddie confided as she ate the convenient mini finger foods she had piled on her plate, perched on the edge of a too comfortable sofa.

Zac's beautifully shaped mouth quirked. 'I'm not, although I'm quite interested in breeding pedigree horses,' he admitted, startling her afresh.

Zac watched her ease back into the sofa as though it were a potentially dangerous manoeuvre. Her feet left the floor and she crossed her legs like an elf, making herself at home with him for the first time, and he got a rush out of that display of relaxation, which unsettled him. It was only that she was prickly, difficult and an unknown quantity and he loved a challenge, he told himself squarely. Maybe without really noticing he had got bored with the constant sexual come-ons and the easy conquests. And Freddie was different, so very different from the sort of women he usually bedded. She also looked ridiculously cute sitting there, he acknowledged uneasily, frowning at that aberrant thought.

'I also wanted to ask if you've thought any more about joining me in that bet I mentioned this morning,' Zac delivered, getting back down to business with a strong sense of relief.

Her vivid little face screwed up tight and she studied him in surprise. 'You're *still* on about that?' she questioned.

Zac shrugged a broad shoulder. 'I don't give up on anything easily.'

No, if she could peel him apart Freddie was convinced she would find the word 'determined' stamped through him as though he were a stick of rock. She parted her lips to protest and then closed them again, wanting to be civil. 'I have the children to look after,' she said finally.

'And I could easily hire a nanny,' Zac traded, once again refusing to take no for an answer. 'We could have a lot of fun at Vitale's royal ball. I'm sure you'd enjoy getting all togged up in a fancy designer dress as much as any woman.'

'No, sorry,' Freddie muttered, crushing down the temptation offered by that treacherous word, 'fun'. For a split second, she considered the offer of a nanny's help and then suppressed the idea again because, with Claire's current mood, she did not want to risk rocking the boat. It was out of the question. Certainly not while Claire was currently saddled with a boyfriend flying out to Spain whenever he could to help his parents set up their new business. It would be the worst possible time for Freddie to start demonstrating a desire to fly free on her own behalf.

Zac sank down beside her on the sofa, suddenly way too close for comfort, she told herself anxiously. Or was that prickling fullness in her breasts and the sudden tiny betraying burst of heat between her thighs a mortifying wish for him to get closer still? Colour bled up beneath her skin, heating her all over.

'But that's crazy,' Zac argued.

'You don't know when to quit, do you?' Freddie remarked in reproach. 'I don't want to talk about this.'

'But I do,' Zac parried with irrepressible enthusiasm, light eyes shimmering like stars in the dusk light. 'I'd like to spend more time with you and I can't understand why you would fight that when you want it too.'

Eloise and Jack, Freddie reflected without speaking. 'I *don't* want to spend more time with you, though,' she told him drily, running for her only possible escape hatch.

'Why do you lie about it?' Zac demanded with sudden lancing impatience.

Freddie breathed in deep. 'I'm not lying,' she told him, looking back at him steadily, literally *willing* him to believe what she was saying.

His big hands came up to cup her cheekbones, long controlling fingers sliding into her hair to fasten to her skull, and she couldn't move an inch, brown eyes dilating with an enervating mixture of excitement and dismay.

'Liar,' he growled again.

'Just because I won't say what you want to hear doesn't mean I'm lying!' Freddie proclaimed in desperation.

The silence between them smouldered as if someone had set it on fire, brown eyes clashing with volatile light grey condemnation, and then he took her mouth with a wild, seething passion unlike anything she had ever felt before. It was like being swept away by a tidal wave, like sticking a finger in an electric socket or hitching a ride on a rocket because one minute she was grounded, the next she was flying high on a hunger that consumed her with its ferocious urgency. Sensation roared through her trembling body with every delving exploration of his tongue. He lowered a hand to crush the slight pout of her aching breast and she almost spontaneously combusted inside the prison of her flesh, her body screaming for more while she kissed him back with both hands laced tightly into the luxuriant depths of his long black hair.

In a sudden movement, Zac tore himself free, breathing heavily and raking a hand roughly through his tousled hair as he sprang upright again. 'So, *why* do you lie about how I make you feel? What's your game?' he demanded rawly.

'G-Game?' she stammered blankly, focusing on the prominent bulge at his denim-clad groin, and then on the stray black hairs still caught between her greedily clutching fingertips.

'Your agenda, because obviously there *is* one,' Zac bit out. 'Evidently it's not money.'

'No, it's not,' she agreed, stricken, hastily unfolding her legs and sliding upright on knees that wobbled because sheer shock was still rocking her. Shock that *he* could make her feel like that and that he should be the one with sufficient control to back off, *not* her, as it should have been in all fairness, she acknowledged guiltily. 'I don't have an agenda, Zac.'

Zac shot her a chillingly angry appraisal. 'Oh, I think

you do. I think you're one of those archaic women who thinks the longer she says no, the keener I'll become!' he spelt out with derision, thinking of how she had become rather more encouraging since she had learned that he owned the hotel that employed her. 'That doesn't work for me. I don't do keen with women.'

'I didn't think you did,' Freddie told him, lifting her chin in a defiant signal of intent that Zac was unaccustomed to receiving from a woman. 'I've known from the start that all you want is a one-night stand and I certainly wouldn't waste my time or yours playing games with you. I don't want or need a man in my life right now but I don't mind admitting...just so you can see how *very* unsuited we are...that I would want more caring and commitment than a one-night stand. So, anyway, thanks for the evening out and the food.'

And with that, Freddie sidestepped him and stalked out of the door in high dudgeon.

Her eyes were stinging with tears and she furiously dashed them away in the lift. He had only confirmed what she had already guessed about the level of his interest and it was at rock-bottom level: sex. Talking about caring and commitment to a guy like that was undignified and humiliating, she censured herself angrily. Why had she bothered saying those stupid things? You couldn't ask or magically wish into being what wasn't being offered and Zac wasn't chasing a waitress for anything more lasting than a spirited toss between the sheets. Of course, there was also his crazy wager, which his stupid brother had involved her in by choosing her as the target of a bad joke. The royal brother had seen her hostility towards Zac and had known it would be a very tall order for Zac to bring her to the ball acting 'lovelorn'. Lovelorn, what a very outdated word, she thought wearily as she climbed on a bus home, planning the little white lie she would give Claire and certainly not the unlovely truth that she wasn't prepared to be quite as much fun as other young women her age.

Should she have considered a one-night stand? No, no, where was her brain travelling now? Yes, she had been very attracted to him but not enough to ditch long-held convictions. She would have felt used and foolish if she had slept with him; she also would have wanted more from him than he was prepared to give and that would have hurt her. And she might already be feeling hurt, but she rather suspected she would have felt even worse had she become intimate with Zac and then had to serve drinks to his next casual lover. It was better to play safe, she reasoned, wiser to stand by her beliefs and stay on an even keel.

When she got home, Claire was out and a babysitter was installed. Just managing to pay the babysitter with what she had in her purse, she was too restless to slide into bed and go straight to sleep the way she always did. Instead she went browsing on her aunt's laptop, snooping online to satisfy the curiosity that Zac had aroused. That exercise piled shock on shock! The Quintal da Rocha diamond mines in Russia and South Africa *belonged* to Zac and his brother was a Crown Prince. She recalled the diamond studs in one of his ears and his charismatic confidence and slowly marvelled that she had simply not worked out for herself that Zac's striking level of blazing assurance was only innate in someone of wealth.

Yet she, biased as she was against men, had immediately assumed he was some sort of chancer up to

no good when she'd first seen him, she conceded ruefully, condemning him on the slender facts that he was
breathtakingly good-looking and bold because Lauren's vicious boyfriend, Cruz, had had rather similar
characteristics. Annoyed by her misconceptions and
even more annoyed by the unhappiness dogging her,
she forced herself to go to bed. Her sole consolation
was that Zac would surely soon be off on his travels
again to attend his royal brother's ball. She had satisfied
almost all her curiosity with a series of searches. But
she also knew that she would find it easier to get back
to normal if Zac left the hotel for a while…or stopped
using the hotel bar.

When Freddie walked out on him, Zac punched the
wall with so much force that blood dripped down it
and then he swore in every language he knew even
though he knew that on one level she was right and
there was no way on earth they could meld their respective wants and wishes. Caring? Commitment? Zac very
nearly shuddered with distaste at the concept. He didn't
know how to do either and he had no desire to learn.
As he was, he was free as a bird and he had no plans to
change that pleasurable state, certainly not for a woman.
Women were always available, tall, short, curvy, thin—
he wasn't particular. At least he hadn't been until he had
met *her*. He would get drunk and wash her out of his
mind, he decided with grim determination.

What he could not understand was what he had found
so attractive about her in the first place! Possibly a man
reached a certain age and was programmed to crave a
different kind of woman. Maybe it could even be his
father's genes at play. Charles Russell was certainly a

man who liked to settle down with women in committed relationships. He had freely admitted that he would have married Zac's mother if he had got the chance and was currently seriously spending time with Angel's very glam grandma-in-law, Sybil.

Zac shook his head in bewildered anger while arrogantly marvelling at Freddie's resistance to him. Then he found himself wondering abstractedly if anyone would ever take the time to read Eloise that dragon story and, with another curse word of finality, rolled his eyes heavenward and consigned the whole Freddie debacle to history and oblivion. He would attend the ball alone…so what? No big deal, was it? He *liked* being alone; he *preferred* his own company.

CHAPTER FOUR

ONLY TWO DAYS LATER, Freddie's whole world imploded.

'I did warn you last year that I wouldn't *do* this for ever,' Claire reminded the younger woman briskly, having announced her imminent plans to move to Spain with her boyfriend. 'I've already given social services a month's notice, so they'll be looking for a new foster home for Eloise and Jack…although I got the impression they're actually hoping to put them up for adoption now. Cruz finally acknowledged paternity and signed off any interest in them. Oh, Freddie, for heaven's sake, *don't* look at me like I'm a monster!'

Freddie was trembling and biting her lip hard, determined not to vent any of the very emotional feelings flying through her head and brimming on her lips. 'I'm not. I'm shocked, that's all, but you did warn me before we got the kids,' she conceded, striving to be fair. 'It's just I thought our arrangement would last a bit longer—'

'And maybe it would've done if I hadn't met Richard,' Claire cut in with a grimace. 'I was in a bad place when I agreed to take on the kids with you but now my life's opening up again. Richard will be the chef in his parents' restaurant and I'll work front of house. We're getting the little apartment above the restaurant to live in…it's nothing fancy but it'll do us fine and it will be a fresh start for me.'

Freddie tried very hard not to be selfish and not to surrender to a heart that felt as if it were being torn apart inside her. When she had begun living with Claire, Claire had been getting over a broken engagement and she had been unemployed. Fostering the children had suited the brunette back then, giving her the breathing space she had needed to rethink her future, and then Richard had entered her life.

'Yes,' Freddie agreed, struggling to block out the up-setting images of Eloise's and Jack's distress at being parted from her, because they had never lived without her in their lives. It would be *her* job to try and pre-pare the children for the changes ahead, she warned herself sternly, *her* role to ensure that any move went as smoothly as possible.

Claire planted her hand firmly on the back of her niece's tautly spread fingers. 'They're not *our* kids, Freddie.'

'But they feel like it.' Tears were openly swimming in Freddie's eyes.

'To you, not to me, I'm afraid.' Claire sighed. 'They're Lauren's kids. She chose to have them.'

'I don't think she *chose* anything,' Freddie protested.

'She was an addict. She made her mistakes and I don't feel the need to make sacrifices in her memory and neither should *you*,' Claire emphasised stridently. 'Haven't you already given up enough for those kids? OK…grieve, but let them go and live your own life now.'

'That's the problem. I don't *want* to let them go!'

Freddie sobbed helplessly. 'I love them like they're my own!'

'But they're not yours *or* mine,' Claire reminded her single-mindedly. 'I don't even know yet if I want to have children! Why aren't you thinking about how Lauren's lifestyle destroyed yours? You should've gone to university, should've let her go but instead you hung in there trying to save someone who refused to be saved.'

'I know… I know,' Freddie gasped in grudging acknowledgement and sniffed into the tissue she had grabbed, struggling to master her turbulent emotions, for Claire's reminder had roused deep sadness for the once loving sister she had lost. 'But I couldn't turn my back on Eloise.'

'You'll have to learn how to step back now,' the brunette pointed out with the coolness of her pragmatic temperament. 'Let them go, Freddie, and move on with your own life like I'm doing.'

The day he got back from Lerovia, Zac wasn't looking for Freddie but he inevitably noticed her the instant she came on shift, walking strangely slowly, seemingly drained of her usual energy. He lounged back fluidly in his chair on the terrace, reminding himself that he no longer had an interest there. He watched while she took an order from a table of drunken men, city types, sharply suited, arrogantly convinced of their right to torment the cute little waitress with catcalls and comments. She kept her head down, doing her job by rote, her delicate profile set.

But when she returned with the tray, the guy on the outside seat ran his hand up the back of her slender thigh, fingers sidling up under the hem of her shorts. Zac stiffened, long, powerful thighs bracing. She stepped back, saying something, and the hand fell back; however, as she served the rest of the drinks the guy simply grabbed her, dragging her down onto his lap by force. Zac exploded out of his seat like a volcano. He was well aware that uninvited physical contact plunged Freddie into panic mode.

Freddie froze, trying to stay calm, recognising that the guy who had grabbed her was simply showing off, potentially not meaning any actual harm. And then suddenly she was plucked off the guy and set aside and her assailant was airborne, being shaken by someone much larger as a terrier shook a rat. And the customer was not a small man, yet he was being held off his feet and controlled like a dangling puppet and there were fear and consternation in his red sweaty face, his brash smart comments dying an immediate death.

'Let him down,' Freddie told Zac in shock once she realised who had stepped in to rescue her.

But sheer outrage had flushed Zac's perfect features, his light eyes bright as a silver sword blade in the dimness of the bar, his rage at the man's behaviour unconcealed.

'The waitress is here to bring you drinks, nothing else,' Zac informed the offending customer in a raw controlled undertone. 'You don't get to touch. She's not for sale like the drinks.'

'Put him down,' Freddie urged again, shaken by Zac's wrathful intervention and embarrassed by all the attention now coming their way, not to mention the bar manager and the burly bouncer now approaching them, eager to avoid an incident.

'If that's what you want,' Zac drawled grudgingly, slowly lowering the guy to the ground again.

'It is. Thanks,' Freddie proffered uneasily, keen to dial the tone down because Zac had looked as if he wanted to do a lot more than hold the guy in the air. Zac had looked as though he wanted to punch him and was barely restraining the urge to do so.

Zac stared down at her, noticing that her eyes were swollen and red rimmed. 'Bring me an espresso,' he told her casually, 'and whatever you want for yourself, and then you'll join me for a break.'

'It's not time for me to have a break.'

'It is now,' Zac told her without skipping a beat, pulling out the I'm-the-boss card without an ounce of self-consciousness, his assurance absolute.

Freddie duly collected two coffees from the bar and walked out onto the terrace into the bright sunlight to carry her tray to Zac's corner table. He ranged back in his seat like a panther forced into a reluctant retreat, luxuriant black hair feathering round his breathtakingly handsome bronzed features, only accentuating silvery pale blue eyes laced with lancing enquiry.

'What's wrong with you?' he demanded of her, because she looked as though a light had gone off inside her.

'There's nothing wrong,' she told him evasively.

Zac widened his stunning ebony-lashed eyes in scornful disagreement. 'Do I look that stupid?' he traded drily. 'Sit down and tell me what's happened.'

Freddie settled down into the seat opposite, her limbs heavy and clumsy to do her bidding because sleepless nights extracted a cost. 'I'm losing the kids,' she admitted with gruff abruptness. 'It's…painful…'

'Eloise and Jack? How can you lose them?' Zac questioned with a frown.

And she explained in as few words as possible about Claire and Richard's plans and shared the insights gained from her own general enquiries with the social services earlier that same day. 'I haven't got enough to offer...to foster or adopt them,' she admitted in pained conclusion. 'I'm only twenty-two, without a reliable income or a settled home. I can't offer them a mother and a father, so I wouldn't be a serious contender if they're putting my niece and nephew up for adoption.'

Zac breathed in deep, fascinated by her sudden rush of candour. 'How long have you been with them?'

Freddie's triangular face tightened, soft mouth tightening. 'Since they were born. My sister, Lauren, was a heroin addict. She wasn't capable of looking after Eloise and I stayed with her because someone had to do it.'

Zac gazed into her melted caramel eyes and dropped his scrutiny, unhappily encountering the soft pert swell of her unconfined breasts stirring as she shifted back into her seat opposite him, the light fabric of her top outlining the delectable contours of her delicate curves. He wondered how much of a bastard he was to notice her sexual allure in the middle of such a conversation but the heavy readiness at his groin was inescapable. Desire thrummed hungrily through his big powerful frame and with a very male sense of relief he celebrated the return of his libido, which had proved unsettlingly absent and inactive while he was in Lerovia. He wanted Freddie and substitutes, he had discovered, wouldn't do, no matter how beautiful and alluring they were.

'The children are very attached to you,' he remarked uncomfortably, wondering why he had even encouraged such a conversation in the circumstances. 'But perhaps *two* parents *would* be better for them than one.'

In dismay and hurt at that statement, Freddie gazed back at Zac's lean, hard-boned face, involuntarily mesmerised by the glow of those glittering light eyes below lush black lashes, her body suddenly turned taut and growing uncomfortably hot in places she didn't want to acknowledge. Even without trying, Zac contrived to emanate a powerful wave of electrifying sexual magnetism.

'I had only one parent and she was mostly absent during my childhood,' Zac divulged unexpectedly. 'I loved her but she wasn't up to the challenge.'

'Oh…' Freddie muttered awkwardly.

'She had good intentions but she put my stepfather first and he didn't want her to have anything to do with me because I wasn't his child,' Zac admitted curtly, already questioning why he was making such a personal admission. 'Having another parent around would have been a big improvement for me while I was growing up.'

Well, that was telling her, Freddie conceded unhappily, wishing the dialogue had gone another way so that she wouldn't have to feel that her powerful need to hang onto her sister's children was an entirely selfish urge. Zac quite clearly *did* believe that, if there was a choice, two parents would invariably be preferable to one.

'When do you have to give them up?' Zac prompted quietly.

Freddie lost colour and gave him a speaking look of reproach, her eyes burning with tears. 'The end of the month, before Claire leaves the UK. They'll go into foster care initially, unless the authorities identify a potential adoptive couple beforehand,' she told him painfully. 'And perhaps they will because they're attractive children, young enough to become part of a new family. It's probably horribly selfish of me to want to keep them with me when I don't have much to offer in terms of material things.'

Zac studied her swimming eyes and grimaced, feeling guilty without reason. 'You love them.'

'But, unfortunately, my love doesn't have a value in the same way because Eloise and Jack are still young enough to forget me and learn to love other people.' Freddie sighed in grudging acknowledgement of that reality. 'I would have to be contributing a lot more... and I don't have more yet there's nothing I *wouldn't* do to keep them!'

Zac watched tears trickle down her taut cheeks, tears she wasn't even aware that she was shedding because she was resolutely swigging the coffee she had got herself and keeping on talking earnestly, struggling to politely hide her anguish. He wished his mother had been capable of feeling even half as much after she had left him as a little boy marooned on the *fazenda* month after month, year after year, living in hope of visits or phone calls that had rarely happened. But, sadly for him, Antonella had craved her husband's child and no other and in all the years that had followed fate had only given her Zac and an endless stream of miscarriages and other disappointments.

There's nothing I wouldn't *do to keep them.*

The words echoed afresh in Zac's mind. And a subtle illuminating shift took place in his attitude at that point as a recollection of his father's advice surfaced simultaneously: choose a woman who at least *wants* a child. His lean, strong face tensed and shadowed. How was he to view a woman willing to make any sacrifice to keep children that were not even hers?

'You must love children,' Zac commented with forced casualness.

'I don't know about that,' Freddie demurred uncertainly. 'But I loved Eloise from the minute she was born...and Jack. He had to be weaned off drugs before he was allowed to leave hospital and I was so worried about his development at first but he's done so very well.'

'Jack's full of life,' Zac agreed lazily, deep in thought and struggling against so unfamiliar an exercise. He had skimmed along the shallow surface of life for a very long time, having learned far too young that caring too much about anything, wanting anything too much and setting hopes too high invariably hurt like hell. An intelligent man, therefore, should avoid optimistic goals, emotional entanglements and complications.

He needed a child. Freddie, however, needed a husband, willing to take on two children. The prospect of being a parent to *three* children shattered Zac and drew him up short in his ruminations. To adopt Eloise and Jack, he would definitely have to marry Freddie and meet all conventional expectations to satisfy the authorities involved and it would scarcely be an easy process. In all likelihood that process would also be hedged with regulations likely to curtail his every move. Was he prepared to go to such punitive lengths to solve his inheritance problem?

After all, he could choose virtually any woman to have his child. Zac had few illusions about his own worth on the matrimonial front. He was filthy rich and ambitious women targeted men who could provide a fantasy lifestyle. But in spite of being poor, Freddie didn't seem mercenary. In fact, she had infuriating principles set in stone that had held Zac to ransom and actually forced *him* into retreat. He didn't do caring and commitment, but he also knew that any child would require caring and commitment from him to thrive. He could *try* to meet those obligations though, couldn't he? He was not so divorced from humanity that change was impossible, he told himself stubbornly.

Zac focussed on Freddie, tousled dark blonde hair skimming her taut cheekbones, dark chocolate eyes surrounded by wet clogged eyelashes, which signally failed to diminish her appeal. Raw hunger rippled through him, hot as a river of lava, pushing and pulling at him even though he was far too shaken by the concept of becoming a father of three to really want to continue.

'When you finish work tonight, come up to the penthouse and we'll talk,' Zac murmured almost hoarsely through clenched teeth. 'There's a possibility that I could be able to help you retain custody of Eloise and Jack.'

Dumbfounded by that claim, which had come at her out of nowhere, Freddie stared in bewilderment back at him, her full pink lips parting in surprise to show pearly teeth. 'How?' she asked baldly.

'We'll discuss that later.' Zac dealt her a brooding appraisal. 'But I can tell you now that it'll come down to how much you're willing to give up to hang onto those kids.'

Freddie's gaze had widened. *'Anything.'*

'People often say stuff like that but they don't really mean it,' Zac dismissed with a sceptical glance. 'We'll talk about it and see if we can help each other.'

'Help each other?' she queried in wonderment.

Zac compressed his wide sensual mouth and finished his black coffee, refusing to expand on the topic.

In a complete daze, Freddie went back to work and watched Zac stride out of the bar twenty minutes later without even looking her way. How could he possibly help her? And how could she possibly help *him*? Her mind whirled with fantastical supposition, none of which made sense or seemed remotely likely. Meanwhile she was conscious of the stares of her co-workers and a new disturbing wariness in their attitude towards her.

'Obviously he's nailing her and you can't blame her, can you? I'd have him in a heartbeat!' one of the bar staff was opining when Freddie entered the locker room after work to change.

A horrible silence fell when her presence was noted and the other two women got very busy with their lockers before leaving in haste. Freddie's face was burning but such speculation was only to be expected. Of course, the staff was gossiping about Zac's apparent interest in her, and his intervention earlier on her behalf had only encouraged conjecture. Naturally everyone would assume that she was having sex with him. And if Zac had had anything to do with it, she thought ruefully, she would have been. No, it would have happened only once, she reasoned, unable to imagine that any more enduring relationship would have developed between them. Zac bore all the hallmarks of a man who got easily bored.

She slid through the door that communicated with the hotel foyer, her cheeks warm with discomfiture. She was shabbily dressed, a hoodie pulled on over her top and skinny jeans and sneakers in place of the shorts and high heels. She had put some concealer over her swollen eyes and she was depressingly conscious that she looked tired and washed out. She entered the lift Zac had used and a burly man in a suit stepped in straight after her and stuck a card in a slot.

'The penthouse?' he queried, looking her over doubtfully. 'Miss Lassiter?'

'Yes.'

'Mr da Rocha is expecting you,' he informed her as the doors closed. 'I'm Marco, one of his security team, and I work for him.'

Freddie realised that the private lift would not have worked for her without that all important card. When the lift stopped Marco led the way, opening the door to the penthouse and standing back for her to enter before closing the door on her heels. A door inside the suite opened and Zac strolled out, half naked, a pair of jeans hanging loose and unbuttoned on his lean hips.

'Oh, it's you. Make yourself at home,' he urged casually. 'Pour yourself a drink.'

And with that careless suggestion he stalked back barefoot into the bedroom, leaving her breathless because Zac half naked was an unforgettable sight: an expanse of ripped, incredibly muscled torso liberally inked with intricate designs leading down to a V of muscle that emphasised his flat, hard stomach and his narrow waist. Flustered and more nervous than ever, she tugged off her hoodie because she was too warm, and finger-combed her hair before approaching the well-stocked bar and choosing a juice. She was very grateful that he hadn't hung around long enough to notice that she had been welded to the floor and staring at him like an awestricken schoolgirl.

Annoyance that she was so easily overwhelmed by Zac's sheer impact licked at her. Yes, he was utterly, absolutely gorgeous but surely she was capable of acting normally around him? Had she *ever* acted normally around him? She didn't think she had. From that very first glimpse, he had unsettled her, then he had outraged her and from that point on she had become nervous, judgemental and oversensitive in his radius.

Zac reappeared fully dressed in a black shirt and jeans. His attention went straight to the glass in her hand. 'Tomato juice...*really*?'

'Alcohol would send me to sleep at this time of night,' she said defensively.

'I was teasing,' Zac assured her while he studied her and asked himself if access to her was worth what he would be sacrificing. Of course, it wouldn't be, his intelligence told him. No woman would ever be worth his freedom. But he had to be practical and work with the system, and if he married her and she didn't conceive his lawyers would be able to move to break the trust. One way or another marriage would be a step forward and he would move closer to his goal of complete independence and control of the diamond mines that were his family heritage.

'Why did you say that we might be able to help each other?' Freddie pressed tautly.

Zac settled down carelessly opposite her on the arm of a sofa and leant back, wide shoulders squared, long, powerful thighs spread and braced. 'I'm the heir to the Quintal da Rocha diamond mines. I receive the profits but I won't be able to control the business until I have produced an heir of my own. That iniquitous arrangement was laid down in a legal trust by my great-great-grandfather a long time ago and I deeply resent it.'

'You *have* to have a child?' Freddie whispered with disconcerted emphasis.

'Yes, and if you are willing to try and give me that child *I* am willing to marry you and attempt to adopt Eloise and Jack with you,' Zac completed smoothly.

The mention of marriage shocked Freddie so much that she took a great desperate gulp of her tomato juice and almost choked on it, coughing and then clearing her throat with a painful swallow while Zac continued to steadily watch her. 'You'd be willing to adopt Eloise and Jack?' she prompted shakily, careening wildly from one thought to the next, all her thoughts disjointed and incomplete.

'If you also agree to meet my condition by giving me a child,' Zac responded with measured cool.

'Do you have a criminal record?' Freddie demanded, disconcerting him with the staggering abruptness of that question.

Ebony brows drew together in perplexity. 'Of course not.'

Freddie went pink. 'Just asking. You probably couldn't be considered as an adoptive parent with a record.'

Zac was entertained by that tactless leap-frogging question that revealed that she was already considering his proposition. 'Have you ever been pregnant?' he traded in return.

Freddie stiffened and shook her head. 'Er...no, I'm afraid, no proven fertility record here.'

Zac lifted and dropped a fatalistic shoulder. 'Either of us could be infertile. At this point, it doesn't re-

ally matter because I have to go through the motions…
marry and *try* to have a child, and if it doesn't happen
for us I can then go to court and ask for the trust to be
set aside.'

'You would *truly* be prepared to adopt Eloise and
Jack with me?' Freddie prompted, sudden tears burning the backs of her eyes at the idea that there could
possibly be a solution that would enable her to keep her
sister's children.

'Yes, if you agree. You said you'd do anything to
keep them and I will also pretty much do anything it
takes to gain control of the da Rocha business empire,'
Zac admitted grimly.

As if she had been winded by a feverish sprint, Freddie coiled back almost bonelessly into the sofa and
snatched in a deep shuddering breath, striving to calm
down and think with clarity. She had to set down her
glass because her hand was shaking so badly. 'Do you
think we'd have a chance of adopting the kids together?'
she asked anxiously, refusing to plunge herself into the
turmoil of considering what it would be like to marry
Zac and have a child with him and instead concentrating on what was most important to her at that moment.

'I don't see why not if we present ourselves as a loving couple. I'm wealthy enough to buy us a home. I'm
also mixed race, like the children.'

'Are you?' Freddie studied him in surprise.

'My grandmother on my mother's side is black. My
grandfather was white,' Zac explained. 'Brazil is a huge
melting pot of ethnic diversity and if you're like me you
can't choose your genes when you reproduce. I'm telling you that now because any child we have could take
after either side of my family.'

Freddie nodded understanding.

'Not every woman could comfortably accept that possibility,' Zac admitted, involuntarily amused by Freddie's complete lack of reaction to his frankness.

His mother had been haunted by the spectre of her husband's racism and her fear of having a child of a darker complexion than her own while Zac had been relentlessly bullied at an almost exclusively white school for being the only child that was different. He had learned to fight to protect himself at an early age, but he had also had to learn how to back down when there were too many ranged against him. The trouble that had erupted around Zac then had led to him being labelled an agitator, a tag he had fiercely resented.

Silence fell while Zac surveyed Freddie, coiling tendrils of lust curling up hotly through him. He remembered the rounded little curve of her bottom in the shorts, the shapely length of her legs, and pictured her spread across his bed in various different positions, anticipation and hunger leaping through his veins. He could not remember *ever* wanting a woman with such fierce immediacy. Had her reluctance sustained his desire? Was he truly so basic that he needed the challenge she had represented? And why did the idea of getting her pregnant turn him on as hard and fast as a bullet? Wasn't that a little kinky? A hard line of colour suffused his exotic, high cheekbones and, sliding upright, he strode over to the bar to pour himself a drink.

'Not for me, thanks,' Freddie framed when he glanced at her enquiringly.

'You're very quiet,' he murmured warily.

'Shocked,' Freddie contradicted. 'Marriage...seriously, you and me?'

'Not a for-ever kind of marriage,' Zac qualified softly. 'But I would still continue to be involved in the children's lives, regardless of what happens between us.'

The marriage would not be permanent, Freddie interpreted, but he was still promising that he would go on being a father to the children. Obviously he was planning on an eventual divorce to regain his freedom, leaving her a single parent with three children. A child with Zac, *having* a child with Zac, she grasped suddenly, her face and body gripped by heat at the notion. She stared down at her feet, shutting out that silly flush of sexual awareness and exasperated by it, because just then it struck her as a trivial issue when compared to the awful threat of losing her sister's children, whom she loved and who had learned to love her. Sex was no big deal, she told herself urgently. Sex would *have* to be no big deal if they were forced to try and conceive a child because that could take months and months to achieve. The alternative would be to lose Eloise and Jack, whom she could not bear to imagine her life without. That recollection steadied her nerves and cooled her down. She had to keep on reminding herself of what the end result of such an arrangement would be.

'Is divorce a stumbling block for you?' Zac prompted with a frown.

'No. But this idea of yours…well, it's a lot to get my head around,' she confided ruefully, cheeks colouring as she encountered his pale glittering gaze, finally recognising how very intense he could be because she could feel the raw force of his volatile temperament in that assessing appraisal.

'You said you'd do anything,' he reminded her sibilantly.

'Marriage and a baby?' Freddie quipped. 'Not something I'd even got around to thinking about yet.'

'If we married, you would also be financially secure for life. You would never have to work again if you didn't want to,' Zac continued.

And even though she knew he was trying to tempt her, she was filled with anticipation of what her life could be like were she free to live it and have sufficient money to afford childcare. She had missed out on her place at college, where she had planned to train as a teacher, because after finding Eloise cold, wet and hungry in her cot, forgotten by Lauren, she had known that there was no way she could leave a baby alone with her sister. Not when Eloise needed her, not when Freddie loved Eloise as much as if she had given birth to her herself. Those were the truths that had reshaped Freddie's future and forced tough, unselfish choices on her.

'All I want is what's best for the children. That has to be my main aim,' Freddie declared. 'You'd have to start taking the time to get to know them properly.'

'I'll do whatever it takes. I want you—'

'For a while,' Freddie interposed ironically, brown velvet eyes flickering over his lean, darkly handsome features, her mouth running dry. 'And I come as a package with two children. I don't want them damaged in any way by *our* choices.'

'We're only human. We can't see the future but my motivation is good. I don't want anyone harmed by this arrangement.'

'But why did you pick me?' she asked baldly.

'I can be businesslike about this with you because you have as much to gain from the marriage as I do,' Zac stated. 'I like that because it gives us a better chance of making it work. *Com certeza*...of course, if I wasn't attracted to you, it wouldn't work on any level.'

Freddie reddened, lashes cloaking her gaze as she tore her attention from his lean, powerful figure, her body slowly heating. Her nipples prickled and tightened, her thighs pressing tightly together to ease the sudden compulsive ache between them. Wanting without any hope of satisfaction hurt, she finally acknowledged, but she still tensed at the prospect of giving way to that need.

But Zac was offering her what she wanted in return for what he wanted and she deemed it a fair bargain if he was willing to take on parenting her niece and nephew and any child they had of their own. She concentrated on the positives. Zac would give them security. Zac would be another parent to support her. After a while he would not be around on a daily basis as a father, but in a world where nothing was certain and marriages often broke down that was not unusual and at least he was being honest about his intentions from the outset.

She didn't have an alternative choice. Nobody else was coming to rescue her. And even Zac wasn't rescuing her, she reflected wryly. He was offering her a lifebelt on one hand and demanding his pound of flesh with the other. They would be equal partners in the marriage because both of them would be bringing something important to the table. Would she be able to conceive? How long would it take to accomplish that feat? And what would it feel like to have Zac as a husband and lover and then lose him again? But all those scary questions were for the future and not relevant to the present.

'Yes. I am attracted to you,' she said stiffly, reckoning that there was no longer any need to pretend otherwise.

A wide appreciative grin slashed Zac's mouth. 'No more lies, then.'

'No more lies,' she agreed ruefully. 'I'm saying yes to your proposition because you're the only hope I have of keeping Eloise and Jack and I'll do whatever I have to do to facilitate that.'

'*Venha aqui*…come here,' Zac urged.

Stiff as a plank of wood, Freddie rose from her seat and approached him. He swept her up like a doll and held her high with the kind of controlled physical strength that shook her. 'You won't regret this decision,' he told her and then he kissed her.

Hotly, extravagantly, passionately and with all the energy that drove him, he crushed her soft lips beneath his, both arms banded so tightly round her narrow ribcage that she could barely breathe. But she didn't want to breathe, she just wanted to fall deeper into that kiss. His tongue ravaged the tender interior of her mouth and a shower of sparks flew up inside her, tingling along every nerve ending in her slender body. His tongue teased and flicked and darted and with a gasp she closed her arms dizzily round his neck.

'We could get this project off to a flying start right now,' Zac suggested thickly.

And Freddie froze and let go of him, pushing him away until he had to let her down to stand on her own feet again.

'Problem?' Zac quipped very drily, his eyes luminous and coolly enquiring in the dim lights.

'I'm not getting into bed with you until we're legally married,' Freddie spelt out in a defiant rush as she fought for what little security she could retain, which to her meant staying safe and uncommitted to the last possible moment. 'You could still be shooting me a crazy seduction line. After all, you *are* the guy who bets sports cars away! I won't take the risk of getting pregnant until you've proved your commitment to our agreement.'

Zac stared at her in astonishment. 'You think this could be a scam?' he breathed incredulously, astonished by the level of her distrust. 'I've never had to seduce a woman in my life!'

Freddie backed away another few steps, embarrassed now that she had voiced her reservations. 'I'm naturally suspicious—'

'Of men,' Zac slotted in boldly. 'You don't trust my sex.'

'My past experiences have not been good,' Freddie conceded reluctantly.

'Then tomorrow we'll get this party started with a visit to my London lawyers. They'll make a start on the adoption application and advise us on how soon we can get married here. Bring your birth certificate and your passport and the children's,' Zac advised, his lean, hard-boned face set with purpose.

Freddie groaned out loud. 'Zac... I don't have a passport and neither do the children. In any case the authorities wouldn't allow us to take the children out of the UK without their permission.'

'You've never been abroad?' Zac asked in astonishment.

'Never,' Freddie confirmed.

'My lawyers will deal with all the details,' Zac pronounced with innate arrogance.

'And I'll have the children in tow,' Freddie warned. 'And they can't go on a motorbike.'

'Obviously not,' Zac fielded drily. 'Stop putting obstacles in my path, *meu pequenino*. When I want something, I allow nothing to get in my way…and I *want* you.'

Freddie went pink, disconcerted by that unequivocal statement of intent. And yet in the strangest way she found his determination to have her ridiculously flattering, because no man had ever wanted her with such stubborn, resolute intensity. Of course that wouldn't last, she told herself ruefully, not once he realised how inexperienced and ordinary she was. No doubt he was expecting fireworks in the bedroom. How would he feel when he instead wakened to find Eloise and Jack in bed with them at some ungodly hour of the morning? Family life, she thought heavily, was likely to be a big culture shock for Zac.

CHAPTER FIVE

'IT'S PERFECT,' ZAC pronounced as Freddie smoothed an apprehensive finger down over the knee-length, shimmering silver sheath dress.

'But what does it cost?' Freddie hissed in an anxious undertone, fearful of attracting the attention of the saleswoman, who was grander than a queen.

Zac dealt her a silencing look that was equally intimidating. Requesting prices was apparently a vulgar act in his radius. Apparently, prices were no longer her business but *his*. Freddie sucked in a steadying breath but it didn't work. From the instant she had agreed to marry Zac, her life had begun changing at warp speed.

The next morning, he had taken her straight into a meeting with his London lawyers. Freddie had tried to keep Eloise and Jack entertained in a corner while incomprehensible legal jargon interwoven with long voluble snatches of Portuguese had whirled round the room. Zac had made copious notes on his phone and dragged her out of there again, but only after she had filled in a sheaf of official documents. They had climbed back into the limousine that had picked them up that morning, a real genuine long black limousine complete with car seats for the children, and that was the first time

Freddie had actually come to terms with the idea that Zac was very rich.

New experience after new experience had bombarded her ever since and she felt dizzy from the shock of it all. Without the children around to ground her, she felt lost. Claire had agreed to keep Eloise and Jack while they went shopping for a new outfit for Freddie. Zac had wanted to hire a nanny and had been exasperated when he had finally grasped that only Claire was officially allowed to take care of the children. That was Zac, infuriated by red tape and rules, always impatient to move quickly past them to the next challenge.

A giant blue diamond solitaire ring weighed down Freddie's left hand and if she stirred even a finger it sparkled with blinding brilliance. It was a very beautiful and eye-catching ring.

'Play everything by the book,' Zac's legal team had advised him, and that seemed to entail doing stuff that Zac's unconventional heart rebelled against. He had been told to give her an engagement ring, introduce her to his family and play up his family connections, not one of which acts came naturally to him. So, Freddie could not feel flattered by anything Zac had done or arranged although she was grateful that he was willing to do it to facilitate their application to adopt Eloise and Jack.

'You do what you *have* to do,' Zac had enunciated through gritted teeth as he had slid that extraordinarily opulent ring onto her ring finger.

No, there had been no risk of Freddie suspecting that Zac cherished more romantic feelings for her than he was willing to share with her. And shopping with him even for one morning was a bit of a nightmare for a shy, introverted young woman. Evidently, he liked women clad in skimpy lingerie, and he had been wildly disconcerted by her mortification when he had discussed *his* preferences for what she was to wear with the saleswoman. More than ever, it had made Freddie feel as though she was just a body to Zac, a body for him to dress and impregnate at the same speed with which he did everything else. That very evening they were joining his family for what he had described as 'an informal dinner'. Yet the event obviously required her to wear a designer dress with all the trimmings.

'Those shoes,' Zac indicated to the hovering assistant with a careless sweep of one bronzed hand. 'That bag.'

'You *have* to get more into the spirit of this,' Zac censured as he herded her back out to the limousine like a wayward sheep, who might stray. 'You've got a fitting for your wedding dress tomorrow.'

Two days earlier, Freddie had chosen the dress in a breathtakingly impressive designer atelier while Zac had turned Jack upside down to keep him amused and strings of baby chuckles had filled the air and Eloise had stood by awaiting her turn.

'I don't see why it matters what I wear when I meet your family,' Freddie admitted. 'It's not as if you even want me to meet them!'

'I'm not close to my half-brothers but over time that could change, particularly when all of us have young children. I would like the connection for *our* children,' Zac admitted with emphasis. 'Growing up, I had virtually no family and it made me a loner. I want the kids to have a different experience. And it *does* matter what you wear when you meet my family.'

'How?'

'Angel's wife, Merry, and my father's girlfriend, Sybil, will look as if they walked straight off a Paris catwalk. I will not have you look *less* than them in any way,' Zac completed grimly, his pride on the line. No way would he allow Freddie to be patronised or labelled unfit for such exclusive company. Without effort she would outshine all of them, he thought with satisfaction, surveying her delicate triangular face and her warm brown eyes.

She would be the perfect wife for him, he savoured. She wouldn't be clingy or needy because she would be far too wrapped up in the children to worry about what he was doing. She wouldn't make demands or throw temperamental jealous or possessive tantrums. She would just get on with things the way he did without making a big song and dance about them. Freddie was wonderfully practical, so she wouldn't go falling for him or anything inconvenient like that either. She had already signed the pre-nuptial agreement without the smallest difficulty. 'A woman in a million,' one of his lawyers had commented afterwards and Zac had felt very real pride in his future wife, who was so gloriously free of avarice and ambition.

Unaware of the unspoken accolades coming her way, Freddie settled into a corner of the opulent limo and studied Zac's lean, darkly handsome face. He looked so different from the man she had first met. He had abandoned his jeans and worn sharply tailored suits for all their official appointments and, ironically, he wore a suit with the panache of one born to such formality. Exquisitely tailored in a fine grey wool and silk blend, his present dark grey suit outlined his broad shoulders and wide chest and enhanced his lean hips and long powerful legs to perfection. In jeans he looked incredibly masculine and sexy but in a suit he was to die for.

Her body was all of a quiver in his radius because it didn't matter how much he annoyed or confused her, he still fascinated her. Her temperature rose, her heartbeat quickened, her sensitive breasts feeling constricted by her bra. She pressed her slender jeans-clad thighs together tightly, struggling to contain the swelling heat at the heart of her.

'Don't look at me like that,' Zac husked. 'Not when you don't want me to do anything about it.'

Freddie turned pink, striving to look inviting and flirtatious rather than desperate to be touched. 'You can still kiss me.'

'No, I can't,' Zac contradicted. 'I won't start anything we can't finish. I've already had enough cold showers to last me a lifetime.'

That blunt response sent a tide of hot colour washing up over her disconcerted face. Her eyes evaded the allure of his glittering and all too compelling light grey gaze. Something tightened low in her pelvis, a contracting thread of very physical yearning that was strong enough to unnerve her.

'You can't *still* believe that I'm going to jilt you at the altar,' Zac intoned thickly.

Freddie swallowed with difficulty. 'Not any more,' she conceded reluctantly.

'Then come back to the penthouse with me tonight. I'm dying here.' Zac groaned that feeling admission without a shade of inhibition. 'I've never gone without sex for as long as this.'

'I'd prefer not to,' she muttered tightly, that gruff, innately sexual intonation making her body burn hotly from head to toe. 'Because it'll be my first time and I just think it'll feel more relaxed once we're married.'

Zac frowned, ebony brows drawing together. 'Your first time at what?' he queried.

'At sex,' Freddie framed, her soft pink lips compressing with embarrassment.

Zac looked back at her, stunned, the riddle Freddie had occasionally shown herself to be suddenly clarified. 'You're a virgin...a *virgin*?' he said again as if she now fell into the same unlikely category as a unicorn. 'Are you joking?'

'No,' she confirmed flatly.

'OK.' Zac rolled his eyes, attempting to compute this new information and utterly failing because he was so startled. 'But *why* are you still a virgin?' he persisted.

'I don't want to talk about that, right now,' Freddie told him hastily, hugely relieved to see that the limo had come to a halt near Claire's terraced home and that escape into the company of others, where even Zac could not continue such a conversation, was within reach.

'You can hardly blame me for being surprised,' Zac murmured in reproof. 'I had no idea.'

'It's not something I feel a need to talk about,' Freddie parried in frustration.

And Zac looked back to their very first meeting and barely managed to suppress a groan of frustration. Without even knowing it he had blown his chances with her right from the start by assuming that she would be as laid-back and casual about sex as he was. Now he knew differently, now he knew why her barriers went up the instant he got too close, but he still could not even begin to understand why she had retained her inexperience into her twenties. It was a complication he hadn't expected and he didn't know how he felt about it. But obviously, any plans to enjoy a sexual marathon to satisfy his currently rampant libido would be out of the question.

Eloise and Jack engulfed him in the narrow hallway. Jack clutched at his knees and Zac hoisted the baby high, ruffling Eloise's hair as she sucked her thumb and rested her head sleepily against his thigh. The kids were so trusting and openly affectionate with him that it touched even his hard heart. Claire had said enough for him to know that Freddie had dealt with a lot of stuff she shouldn't have had to deal with in an effort to shield the children from lasting damage at her sister's hands. But Zac was beginning to recognise the damage done to Freddie, who, like a victim of abuse, was very nervous around men and found it very hard to trust.

'I took them to the park,' Claire told Freddie. 'They're exhausted and ready for a nap.'

'I'll take them upstairs,' Freddie volunteered.

'Want the dragon story,' Eloise mumbled round her thumb, clutching at Zac's jacket.

Over the past two weeks, Zac had not left the house without having to read the dragon story at least once and he gave way with grace, shepherding Eloise into the lounge where she quickly produced her favourite book. Jack went to sleep on his shoulder while Zac read and then Eloise announced her desire to go to the zoo to see a real dragon. Zac explained that dragons flew so fast and high in the sky that zookeepers couldn't catch them. Eloise looked sad but cheered up when Zac reminded her that he was taking them to the zoo with Claire the next day while Freddie had her dress fitting.

Freddie watched and marvelled at the noticeable

bond even now forming between Zac and her niece and nephew. Their interaction was very comfortable. Both she and Zac had already had initial interviews with social services and character references and basic documentation had been lodged. With their wedding only forty-eight hours away, Freddie believed that everything was progressing as well as could be expected. Zac had also requested permission to apply for passports for the children and to take them abroad for a trip after the wedding.

Claire had said that they were crazy to jump into marriage so fast simply in the hope of adopting the two children. Freddie had kept Zac's need for a child of his own to herself, leaving the brunette to assume that Zac had fallen madly in love with her and she with him. And in truth, Freddie reckoned that she would've fallen for Zac had he not made such a disastrously bad first impression on her. Now when she saw him entertaining the children even for a few minutes, she blessed the quirk of fate that had brought him into their lives, for without him where would she have been? In despair at the threat of losing the children she loved.

Even so, she was nervous as anything at the prospect of meeting Zac's rich and fancy relatives and their undoubtedly high standards. At least the royal pair would not be present, she thought with relief. Apparently, Prince Vitale's mother had abdicated after a huge scandal and, now that Vitale was about to become King, he and his pregnant wife were much too involved in official business to spare the time for a family dinner in London.

With such grand people in the family, would Zac's lofty relatives criticise her the moment she was out of

hearing? Would they be shocked by his choice of someone like her? Would they try to persuade him to change
his mind at the last minute and *not* marry her? After
all, a waitress with two children in tow was no great
catch for a very wealthy and educated man. She would
never be his equal in the eyes of the world. Perhaps they
would simply shake their heads in surprise and remind
themselves that Zac needed an heir and that it might as
well be Freddie as any other woman. Perhaps they simply wouldn't care either way.

That evening, Zac long gone and the children readied for bed, Freddie got dressed for the dinner she was
dreading with Zac's father and his girlfriend and his
elder brother and his wife. It bothered her that he had
told her so little about himself and she worried that she
would stumble in conversation and reveal her ignorance.

Zac stood at the passenger door of the limo watching Freddie descend the steps, her tiny feet in pearlised
shoes, ultra-careful in the high heels, her clutch pinned
between white-knuckled fingers, her state of nerves patent. But she looked absolutely amazing, like a delicate
doll in silver, shapely legs as fragile as the rest of her,
big brown eyes anxiously pinned to him.

'You look fantastic,' he told her bracingly, wishing she weren't a virgin, wishing he could lower the
privacy shields and pounce on her in the car to live
out every fantasy she had awakened. But intelligence
warned him to hang onto his self-control. She would
trot out all sorts of excuses when he finally tackled
her but Zac had already reached his own conclusions:
she was *scared* of sex, *scared* of everything he made
her feel. The last thing she needed from him was *more*
pressure. He would have to be rather more subtle than

nature had made him if he didn't want to risk frightening her off.

'Thanks,' she said tautly, settling into the limo to fiddle unnecessarily with her clutch bag while studiously avoiding his attention. 'So, your father married twice and that's where Angel and Vitale come from but he had an affair with your mother and she was in love with someone else.'

Zac lounged back with a sigh. 'Both Charles and Antonella were on the rebound when they met in Brazil. If Afonso hadn't returned to my mother, Charles would've married her as soon as he was free to do so. My father seems to fall in love with every woman he sleeps with. He's a very tender-hearted man.'

'But your mother still loved your stepfather even though he treated her so badly? I mean, ditching her when they were engaged to go off with another woman?' Freddie prompted in surprise, stealing a glance at him, loving how elegant he was in his dinner jacket. Clean-shaven for once without a hint of his usual stubble, his perfect features were revealed from the smooth planes of his high cheekbones to the strong angle of his jawline. His deep-set heavily lashed light eyes gleamed and, caught staring, she reddened, her mouth running dry, all concentration evaporating simultaneously.

Zac shrugged. 'I never understood her obsession but Afonso Oliveira was *it* for my mother. She worshipped the ground he walked on and believed he had done a wonderful thing in overlooking her humble background to choose her as a wife.'

'How was her background humble when she was born into so much wealth?' Freddie asked in disbelief.

'She was the illegitimate daughter of a black maid

and some people, notably those of my stepfather's ilk, looked down on her for that. My grandfather ignored my mother's existence because he was equally snobbish. Afonso was from a similar aristocratic background. The Oliveiras had long since run through their family fortune but that was less important than their reputation and their impressive family tree.'

'Your mother had a sad life.' Freddie sighed reflectively. 'She didn't really fit anywhere.'

'Life is what you make of it. Her attachment to Afonso was toxic. Getting too attached to anyone is dangerous,' Zac pronounced grimly. 'Think of how attached you are to Eloise and Jack and the sacrifices you're prepared to make to keep them!'

Unexpectedly, Freddie smiled. 'But, loving them has enriched my life in so many other ways. Yes, I could have made different choices but they're my family and they make me happy. I have no regrets.'

The dinner was being held in a private room at an exclusive restaurant. Freddie remembered Charles Russell and his eldest son, Angel, joining Zac for coffee one morning. But the two women, one brunette and one elegant, much older blonde, were completely new to her. The blonde turned out to be Sybil, Charles' girlfriend and also, it seemed, Merry's grandmother.

Zac kept one arm wrapped protectively round Freddie's spine as he introduced her to everyone. Angel's wife, Merry, admired Freddie's ring, but although both women were charming Merry seemed a little uncomfortable around Freddie and Zac, while Zac's father treated Freddie for all the world as though she was his dream choice of bride for his youngest son.

They took their seats while Freddie noted what the

other two women were wearing and recognised that Zac had not brought her to the party overdressed. Merry and Sybil sparkled with jewellery and sported stylish outfits sprinkled with the kind of little handmade embellishments that screamed haute couture. Merry talked about her little girl and asked her about Eloise and Jack. Zac shared Eloise's current obsession with dragons. Charles was asking when he could hope to meet the children when Freddie rose at the last minute to follow the other two women out to the cloakroom.

'I just felt *so* awkward meeting Freddie!' Merry was exclaiming loudly in the corridor as she and her grandmother rounded a corner. 'I wish Jazz hadn't told me what Zac got up to at the royal ball.'

'What did he get up to?' the older woman asked as Freddie automatically speeded up in the hope of hearing the rest of the tantalising exchange.

'Apparently, Zac disappeared into a private room with two women that work at the palace. Obviously, they went in there to have sex. Jazz said he didn't even blush when he reappeared. He's shameless,' Merry contended in a pained voice. 'But that was only two weeks ago. How am I supposed to treat Freddie like a happy bride-to-be when I know that Zac was still playing away so recently?'

'Well, I think you have to give Zac the benefit of the doubt because only the individuals in that room know what actually happened there. I also think you need to remind yourself that you are very happy with a man who enjoyed an equally raunchy reputation *before* he married you,' the other woman commented wryly.

Snatching in a breath, Freddie had frozen where she stood as she listened. Merry and her grandmother were talking about Zac. Apparently, he had had sex with two women at the Lerovian ball that Freddie had declined to attend. *Two* women. Shock rippled like a lightning bolt through Freddie, jarring every bone and muscle. A wave of fierce jealousy ripped through her in the aftermath as she realised that, without ever thinking too deeply about it, she had come to look on Zac as *hers*. Yet while coming on to *her*, pretending to want *her*, he had still been having sex with other women. That knowledge cut into her like a knife and made her feel like a fool. How many other women had he dallied with since they met? Appalled and deeply wounded, she walked stiffly into the cloakroom as the other women were leaving and managed a vague smile even though she felt like a zombie.

How could she marry a man she couldn't even trust to be faithful? She had taken exclusivity for granted in their relationship but it was not something they had actually discussed. She had made stupid, naïve assumptions, she acknowledged painfully, and Zac had played on her lack of experience. Telling her that he had never gone so long without sex! Yet it was only two weeks since the ball. Was two weeks a long time for him? How did she know? And what did she care? How could she possibly care about a man that brazen?

Thankfully, she didn't *care* about him, she told herself resolutely. She was wildly attracted to him but that was all, because she was cautious with her feelings and careful to protect herself from unhealthy attachments. She had watched, after all, what love did to her sister, Lauren. Lauren had bent every rule there was to justify keeping Cruz in her life, refusing to break away from him, excusing his infidelities as a trifling 'man thing'.

Zac noticed how pale and quiet Freddie was when she returned to the table and decided that it was time to call it a night. She was probably tired, he thought wryly, knowing the kids woke her at the crack of dawn. He had seen the tiny room she shared with the children and marvelled that she could live in that confined space without complaint. He draped an arm round her as they said their goodbyes, but she pulled away from him on the pavement outside, slipping into the waiting limo like a little silvery ghost.

'Can we go back to the hotel first?' Freddie asked tautly. 'We have to talk.'

Angel had once joked that the four deadliest words in Merry's vocabulary were those words but Zac was nonchalant, cocooned as he was in his conviction that he was absolutely without a sin to his name. He wondered only absently what she wanted to talk about.

CHAPTER SIX

'No, THANKS,' FREDDIE said flatly in answer to the offer of a drink.

Zac was already revising his belief that nothing could be seriously amiss because Freddie was posed in front of him with all the accusing stiffness and tension of a miniature St Joan of Arc. All she lacked was a sword and a burning torch. 'What's happening here?' he demanded abruptly.

'I overheard a conversation tonight,' Freddie volunteered between gritted teeth, struggling to prevent herself from visibly trembling with rage. 'I heard how you entertained yourself at the royal ball.'

Zac put the evidence together and within seconds he had the whole picture clear in his mind. Vitale's wife, Jazz, had probably gossiped to Merry and then Merry had talked and somehow Freddie had got to listen. His macho pride had been his downfall, he registered, his teeth gritting. Losing the bet, not even being able to persuade Freddie to join him at the ball, had hit his ego hard and when his brothers had assumed he was partaking of a little al fresco sex, he had seen no reason to put the record straight.

Now Freddie had judged him and found him wanting and it was far from the first time he had endured the experience of others believing the worst of him. As a child he had come up with his own defence strategy and it had only hardened to steel as he matured. Never apologise, never explain. In point of fact he didn't owe Freddie any explanations as they had not been together at the time. He had done nothing he was ashamed of doing. He had told no lies, had caused no injury to anyone and he refused to apologise for something he hadn't done to keep the peace.

If Freddie was going to be his wife, she had to respect his boundaries. He loathed emotional blackmail and had no scruples about fighting fire with fire.

'Was it educational?' Zac countered softly, his sibilant Brazilian accent roughening his vowel sounds with the hint that he might not be as cool and calm as he appeared.

His apparent complete lack of reaction infuriated Freddie. He stood there, lean, powerful body balanced and strong in his beautifully cut suit, his eyes glittering like crushed ice below his luxuriant black lashes.

'Is that all you've got to say to me?' Freddie launched at him furiously.

'I don't know what else I can say since you still haven't clarified the issue,' Zac responded with sardonic bite.

Colour spattered her cheeks, chasing away the pallor induced by shock. 'You went into a private room at the ball to have sex with two women.'

'No, that's incorrect,' Zac contradicted. 'I went into the room first to make a phone call and two women followed me in.'

'If you think that *that* makes a difference to *my*

feelings—' Freddie began heatedly, incensed that he still seemed in absolute stress-free control. He wasn't embarrassed. He wasn't angry at being found out. He wasn't even defensive. And even worse, if he had a drop of guilt in him he wasn't showing it.

Zac threw his arrogant dark head back. 'That's how it happened, but I don't understand what your feelings have to do with it—'

'Oh, you don't, don't you?' Freddie broke in, almost bouncing on her high heels as she threw herself as tall as she could, slight shoulders squaring with hostility.

'No, I don't,' Zac repeated. 'We were not in a relationship at the time. In fact, forty-eight hours before the ball you walked out on me, making it clear that you wanted nothing more to do with me.'

That reminder flashed through Freddie like paraffin thrown on a bonfire and only sent the rage clawing up inside her climbing higher. 'You said you wanted *me* and then you went off and had sleazy sex with another woman the first opportunity you got!' she slung back at him in disgust.

'No, that wasn't the first opportunity,' Zac corrected with a reflective air and a cynical set to his sensual mouth. 'I was approached in the VIP lounge at the airport by a woman, propositioned by a stewardess on my flight and given at least two phone numbers after I landed in Lerovia. So, no, *not* my first opportunity to let loose.'

Freddie stared at him in mounting disbelief and horror. The one undeniable truth about Zac da Rocha was that he was gorgeous and many women didn't wait for him to demonstrate interest before going into pursuit. She had watched that happening in the bar when women became frustrated at failing to attract his attention and then made more aggressive moves. But the concrete proof that Zac was targeted by so many other women only sent Freddie plunging even deeper into panic mode. How could someone as ordinary as she was ever hope to hold onto the interest of such a spectacular male specimen? It was obvious that she could not and that getting out before she got in any deeper was her sole option.

'Fidelity is very, *very* important to me,' Freddie declared shakily, struggling to breathe evenly and stay calm even when she felt like an over-shaken cocktail of drama inside herself.

'Yet we're getting married the day after tomorrow and this is the first time you've mentioned it,' Zac pointed out, pouring himself a malt whiskey and tossing it back without hesitation because when it came to the issue of fidelity there was really nothing he wanted to say. He had never had to be faithful because he had never stayed long enough with any one woman for that to become a concern. But that confession would scarcely soothe Freddie.

'I just assumed…you know…' Freddie forced out the words because her throat was closing over and aching '…that I could trust you and now I've found out I *can't* trust you.'

Zac swung back to her, his lean, powerful limbs compellingly graceful in motion, stunning eyes like blazing polar stars, his anger unhidden now. 'We broke up before I even left for Lerovia. Anything I did there is my business. Obviously, I have a past. I can't change that.'

'This wasn't the past…this was only two weeks ago!'

Freddie condemned stridently, fighting the tears threatening her, refusing to show weakness and break down. 'I can't marry a man I can't trust!'

'That is, of course, your decision but, considering that our marriage was supposed to be more based on practicality than sentiment, I don't see where the problem arises.'

'No, and the fact you *can't* see it only proves that we shouldn't marry!' Freddie threw back at him vehemently. 'You said you had never gone so long without sex and yet you were with other women only two weeks ago.'

Zac decided that he wasn't going to get involved in such dangerous trifles when she was acting like a rocket about to go off and light the night skies for miles around. Never apologise, never explain, he reminded himself stubbornly, angry with her, disappointed in her inability to cool down, face facts and see his point of view. She was in no fit state to grasp any explanation while she was still screaming at him. 'You need to calm down and think this through,' he murmured grimly, his firm sensual mouth compressing with steely self-control.

'I don't have to think about anything,' Freddie told him woodenly, misery creeping over her like a toxic cloud that shut out all the light. 'I can't marry an untrustworthy, unreliable womaniser. There's no coming back from that.'

'All that speech is telling me is that you have never been realistic about our marriage. Not only have you not recognised the boundaries I set, but you have also decided to judge me for sins I haven't committed,' Zac concluded grittily. 'Even so, when you fall off your soapbox I'll be waiting.'

'And that's all you've got to say to me?' Freddie ranted back at him, because she was far from finished and he was shutting her down.

'This is not a productive dialogue,' Zac growled, yanking open the door for her departure. 'The car's waiting downstairs to take you home.'

And the pain didn't engulf Freddie until she climbed back into the car and slumped like a doll who had had the stuffing beaten out of her. She travelled from thwarted rage to devastated hurt in the space of seconds. So, it was over. She tasted the concept, reeled from it, wondered vaguely what else she had expected when she'd chosen to confront him. It had been too like a fairy tale anyway, she told herself... Zac coming along and seemingly offering her a lifeline when everything was falling apart.

When had anything that unexpectedly good ever happened to her before? She wasn't a lucky person, never had been. She hadn't been lucky when her parents died, hadn't been lucky when it came to getting Lauren off drugs and she had been even less lucky when it came to retaining custody of the children. And that was the moment when Freddie realised that she had forgotten where her niece and nephew fitted into their marriage plans. Aghast, she felt a chill running up over her entire body, driving out the heat of anger, bitterness and pain.

She would lose Eloise and Jack and they would lose Zac. Zac might be no good in the fidelity stakes but he was already demonstrating sterling traits as a father. And wasn't that why she was supposed to be marrying him?

Practicality rather than sentiment, Zac had reminded her lethally. A marriage of convenience for both of them, not a marriage based on love or the finer feelings, not even a marriage supposed to last for ever. Her tummy gave a nauseous twist. What had she done? *What had she done?*

She had reacted personally to what she had overheard in the corridor at the restaurant. She had reacted as if she were marrying for love and had behaved as though she had been betrayed. Deep down inside herself, she had been bitterly hurt by the idea of other women getting intimate with Zac, imagining them touching him and being touched by him. But was she entitled to such feelings?

On one score, Zac had been correct: they *had* broken up before the ball. Learning that he had had sex with someone else might upset her but he had not betrayed her and he had not broken any promises he made her. Soberly contemplating those facts filled Freddie with chagrin because she had faced Zac in a spirit of angry condemnation.

Yet they weren't in love with each other or even lovers as yet. *Practicality rather than sentiment,* she reflected with an inner shiver of recoil, for, now that she was actually thinking about it, that struck her as a very chilly recipe for a relationship. No wonder Zac had accused her of not taking a realistic view of their marriage. She had reacted emotionally and gone way out of line, driven by her overwhelming need to express her anguished sense of rejection and hurt. But he had neither needed nor wanted such feelings thrown at him. He was not responsible for what she felt, *she* was.

'I had a fight with Zac. The wedding's off as we speak,' she confessed chokily to Claire when she got home.

'Family get-togethers can put people on edge,' Claire

remarked with a roll of her eyes. 'Did someone say something that upset you?'

'Something like that,' Freddie mumbled.

'Well, you'd better get round to the hotel and sort it out first thing tomorrow morning with him. If you give the kids breakfast, I'll take over. You have to go for your dress fitting at noon anyway and Richard and I are organised to accompany Zac and the kids to the zoo,' the brunette reminded her drily.

Claire crept into bed, listening to Jack's little snuffles and Eloise's slow peaceful breathing. How could she have forgotten even for a moment what her marrying Zac would mean for the children? Shame dug talon claws of guilt into her tender flesh. She hadn't been willing to have sex with Zac. Was she to blame him for taking what some other woman offered after she had rejected him? Was she really that much of a hypocrite? And why, oh, why had she taken it all so personally when feelings weren't supposed to come into their agreement? She closed her eyes and cringed and wondered if he'd make her grovel and whether she *would* grovel if he made it impossible to do otherwise. It was hardly surprising that she didn't get a wink of sleep that night and was waiting with breakfast on the table before the children even got up.

When she walked into the hotel foyer that morning, Marco immediately approached her. 'The boss expecting you?' he asked.

'Er...no,' Freddie admitted.

'He's in a meeting right now. I'll check.' He spoke in his own language into his headpiece before returning to her side. 'That's fine, Miss Lassiter. Go on up,' he told her, showing her into the lift and putting the card in the slot for her.

Freddie breathed in slow and deep to gather herself. A young woman she didn't recognise opened the penthouse door and ushered her out onto the big balcony where Zac was clearly enjoying a working breakfast while checking over documents with a young dark-haired man. The woman hovered and then sat down beside the man. Zac was back in jeans and a shirt, black hair rippling back from his lean bronzed features, his big powerful body poised in a relaxed sprawl.

'Freddie…meet my personal assistants, Abilio and Catina,' Zac introduced, rising fluidly upright, his eyes a cool luminous pale blue as they always seemed to be in sunlight, roaming over Freddie's stiff little figure with no expression that she could see. If he was surprised at her arrival, he gave no sign of it.

Zac betrayed not an ounce of the relief he'd experienced when he'd heard she was in the hotel. She had worked it all out for herself and he wasn't surprised at that. The night before she had acted on impulse with a temper that was quick to rise but equally quick to subside. Practicality had triumphed. But what would he have done had she not come back? Would he have chased after her? No, he was done with that, he decided decisively. She had to marry him of her own free will, knowing and accepting the limitations of such a marriage. Nothing else would work. But the shadows beneath her eyes, the evidence of a sleepless night troubled him all the same. He was finally beginning to appreciate that nothing about getting married and living with another person was as simple as he wanted to make it.

Freddie shook hands with his companions and then Zac headed indoors, long lithe legs moving at a fast pace. 'We'll take this into the bedroom because we don't want to be interrupted and Abilio and Catina are about to leave.'

'I didn't know you had staff,' Freddie remarked, keen to fill the smouldering silence.

'I may not be running the family empire but I've made a lot of investments on my own behalf with the income,' Zac admitted, lounging back against the solid wooden dresser that sat between the twin windows.

Freddie looked everywhere but at him, her gaze wandering to the gargantuan bed where the sheets still remained tossed from his occupancy. With a flush she glanced hurriedly away. 'Like this hotel?'

'Exactly.'

Freddie shot him a tense troubled glance. 'I'm here to apologise. I was upset last night. I wasn't thinking things through. I still want to marry you.'

Zac jerked his chin in acknowledgement.

'I was so angry I didn't even think about the children and…what would happen if we split up,' she framed awkwardly.

'Everyone has a price and the children are yours,' Zac drawled softly.

Freddie's eyes flared gold. 'Not *everyone* has a price!' she snapped back at him, nerves taking over and forging past her self-control.

'What else am I supposed to think when you're evidently still prepared to marry an untrustworthy, unreliable womaniser?' he derided silkily.

Put on the spot, Freddie reddened to the roots of her hair. 'I shouldn't have said those things to you.

I haven't found you unreliable or untrustworthy and what you chose to do while you were single is none of my business,' she completed with dogged determination. 'But you had better stay faithful to our marriage while I'm still trying to get pregnant because I will *not* share you!'

His lean, strong face darkening, Zac dealt her a brooding appraisal. 'No problem,' he conceded to that condition without argument, because he could not imagine getting bored with her any time soon.

But he did not appreciate that she had only come back because she was terrified of losing the chance to adopt Eloise and Jack. That struck him as ironic when he knew the adoption was the only reason she was marrying him and willing to have a child with him. But something deep and visceral inside him still rebelled against that ego-zapping knowledge.

He studied her slight figure, sheathed in leggings, ankle boots and a jazzy fitted tunic. Her breasts and her hips and a good part of her legs were hidden so he could not understand why just looking at her soft full mouth and caramel-brown eyes made him so aroused. He wondered how long it would take for him to work out the secret of her irresistible attraction, how long it would take for him to get jaded and start living for the day he would get his freedom back. He had never stayed with a woman longer than a week and even then only on the most casual basis. Now, he recognised, he was facing a steep learning curve.

Conscious of Zac's scrutiny and his unsettling silence in the face of her retraction of her insults, Freddie grew increasingly tense, the tip of her tongue sliding out to moisten her dry lips as her breath shortened in her throat. 'So, where do we stand?' she prompted anxiously.

Zac moved forward, seething energy and hunger powering him. Glittering eyes settled on her tense little face. 'Where we started. Me wanting, you backing away...'

Her breath literally rattled in her throat because without even realising it she had taken a step back as he approached, and in dismay at that awareness she fell still where she stood.

'That's getting old, particularly the day before our wedding.' Zac lifted a lean brown hand to trail a finger along the taut line of her delicate jaw. 'What are you so scared of?'

'I'm not scared,' she told him tightly, but she knew she was lying. Her body was in a state of conflict, her adrenalin buzzing while little internal alarms shrilled inside her. She wanted him close and she wanted to push him away, because pushing men away came more naturally to her than touching one. Yet she *longed* to touch him, to unbutton the shirt stretched across his taut pectoral muscles and trace every rippling leashed line of him with her fingers. She wanted shameless things she had never wanted before and that unnerved her.

Yet the little tingles already ignited by his proximity warred with her alarm system. Her skin prickled, her breasts pushing against the restraint of her bra as her nipples tightened almost painfully. Her mouth ran dry, her breathing rupturing into little snatched spurts of air while her body struggled to combat the wave of heat rising from her pelvis.

'There's nothing to be afraid of,' Zac husked, coiling an arm round her with lazy strength, bending her back to trail a hungry kiss across her delicate collarbone and up the slender column of her neck.

A tiny gasp escaped her, her reactions plunged into overdrive and intensified when he lifted her up against him and then brought her down on the tumbled bed. Eyes flying wide, she gazed up at him in disconcertion and got lost in the blazing magnificence of his crystalline eyes.

'Trust me,' Zac murmured softly, reaching down to flip off her boots and toss them on the floor. 'But at least tell me why you're so scared. Were you assaulted? *Hurt?*'

'No...*no.*' Freddie tried and failed to swallow, fighting to gather her wits. 'But, you know, I saw things... when I was living with my sister...and it put me off... er...sex,' she mumbled as he embarked on her leggings, tugging them down to expose her legs.

'Anything you don't like, you only have to tell me,' Zac told her thickly. 'Any time you want me to stop, I will.'

'O-Okay,' she stammered, barely grasping how she had arrived on the bed and wondering if she should be moving away, reminding him that he had agreed to wait until they were married. Only that restriction seemed so petty now in retrospect that she couldn't make herself voice that reminder. Tomorrow they would be married and all such restraint would naturally be at an end.

Her leggings went flying and she gulped, feeling overpowered and out of her depth with her rather shabby cheap knickers on view. And she was with a guy who loved luxury lingerie, she recalled in intense mortification, yanking her tunic down to cover herself again.

'*Fique tranquilo*...don't worry,' Zac urged, convinced she was ready to flee at any moment. 'I'm worrying enough for both of us.'

Taken aback, Freddie gazed up at him in astonishment. 'What do you have to worry about?'

A flashing grin softened the taut line of Zac's mobile mouth. 'I've never been with a virgin before. I want to make it good for you but I don't know if that's possible.'

'Kiss me,' she heard herself say.

He pressed a soft kiss to her lips and she stopped breathing, her heart hammering a frenzied beat.

'Once more…with enthusiasm,' Freddie whispered uncertainly.

And Zac laughed and covered her mouth again with his to extract a forceful, demanding kiss. He nipped at her lips, stroked her tongue, flicked the roof of her mouth and she started trembling, liquid heat rising from the heart of her.

He lifted his head and, gathering her tunic in his hands, he lifted it up and off her. She crossed her arms over her bra. 'I'm not very big,' she warned him apologetically.

He released the catch at her slender spine and she bowed forward as if to hide herself from him but he pressed her back against the pillows as he whisked the garment away. Her hands fell away because she felt foolish trying to conceal her body from the man she was about to marry. She closed her eyes tightly, fearful of seeing disappointment in his gaze when he realised that she wore a padded bra and was in truth more fried egg than full English breakfast.

'You have very pretty breasts,' Zac husked appreciatively, scanning the pert swell of her dainty curves and the pale delicate pink nipples adorning them.

'You forgot to say little,' she muttered awkwardly.

'Not the first thing that comes to mind,' Zac confided, lowering his dark head to apply his mouth to a quivering pink bud and lash it hungrily with his tongue.

Freddie jerked, her hips rising involuntarily, her whole awareness suddenly centred solely on what he was doing to her. Long skilled fingers skated a pattern over the stretched-tight fabric between her legs and she held her breath as he freed her of that final barrier. She shivered as he explored her with gentle fingers, stroking, teasingly probing, setting off screaming nerve endings and tingles wherever he dallied. She hadn't known she would be so sensitive that the gathering tide of pleasure would almost hurt with its intensity, and then he was rising over her and peeling off his shirt.

Nervous tension tugged at her because he was so much bigger and stronger than she was, his biceps bulging, his splendid torso a masculine vision of sleek bronzed and inked skin stretched over a solid wall of muscle. He rolled off the bed to remove his jeans, peeling them down, exposing the intimidating bulge at his groin outlined by his boxers. Then the boxers went and his long, hard length jutted out, clearly primed and ready for action, and she gulped, wondering how he was planning to fit *that* inside her without hurting her.

Freddie lay rigid, assuming they were in the final phase of intimacy and that it would all be over soon. Zac came back to her and kissed her with a devastating off-the-charts hunger, his tongue delving and teasing, mimicking a far more basic action. Her body softened in the momentary hard embrace of his and then he was sliding down over her, toying with her on the way, a tongue flicking a straining nipple, a kiss bestowed on her belly button, his hands closing over her thighs to part them.

'What are you doing?' she gasped when he kept on moving.

'Trust me,' Zac urged thickly. 'You can't have sex without foreplay. The more ready you are, the less it will hurt.'

Shut up, shut up, she told herself in feverish embarrassment. After all, he knew stuff she didn't. There had been nothing delicate or seductive about the sleazy encounters she had unwillingly witnessed when she was young and impressionable. She shut her eyes tight, surrendering control, banishing the images that had frightened her off sexual experimentation. Contrary to her expectations, Zac was being neither rough nor crude.

His tongue swiped over her and her hips lifted off the mattress in response. Nothing had ever felt so shockingly good and the ache deep inside her intensified its grip. Her legs trembled in his hold as he continued and the building tide of warmth and excitement made her shake. A bone-deep hunger was coalescing at the heart of her and surging higher and higher until at last she reached the pinnacle and the world exploded in glorious colour, leaving her quaking and breathless, absolutely wrecked by the intensity of her first orgasm.

'You are very, very sexy,' Zac growled as he came over her, all virile power and strength, his eyes luminous in the sunlight falling over the bed. 'But we have to go slow now...'

Freddie wasn't quite sure what planet she was on at that moment or what they were to go slowly with but that mental blankness evaporated as he spread her wide and sank into her, slowly stretching her with his fullness. A pinch of discomfort made her grimace and he froze.

'Don't move,' he told her raggedly, his big powerful body arrested over hers as he struggled to resist his need to plunge deep and hard.

Wide-eyed, she stared up at him, her face hectically flushed as he pulled back from her and then shifted forward to sink deep. A hot slice of pain pierced her for an instant and then faded away again.

'Think that's the worst over,' she mumbled.

'And now for the best,' Zac grated, circling his hips to stretch her with a hungry groan about how tight she was and then moving with a fluid rhythm that her body seemed to know as if it had been born for it.

There was no more pain, only gathering passion and increased sensation. She arched up in response as he plunged deeper with every thrust, sending pulsing, voluptuous waves of pleasure surging through her laced with mounting excitement. Her heart pounded so loudly she thought she could hear it and the edgy building tension in her pelvis was rising again until she couldn't hold it back any more and she reached another climax. He thrust into her weak, unresisting body one final time and then stilled with a deep masculine growl of satisfaction.

By the time that Freddie registered that the main act was over, Zac was already out of the bed and striding towards the bathroom. 'Do you want a bath?' he called over a muscular brown shoulder.

Freddie watched his bare bronzed body disappear from view, the intimacy strangely shocking even after what they had just shared.

'Do you?' Zac prompted.

'Yes.' Finally recalling the question and registering that it was broad daylight, she retrieved her brain, but still could not help feeling that it would have been lovely if Zac had held her close for a while after the sex.

But that was being silly, wasn't it? Practicality, not sentiment, she reminded herself in reproof, fearful of attaching any deeper significance to what they had shared. Sex didn't mean anything special to Zac, she told herself firmly. It was nothing more to him than a brief physical release. He had given her pleasure and she should be grateful for that and expect nothing more complex.

Yet insecurity still dogged Freddie. Having gathered up her discarded clothing, she crept into the bathroom and snatched a towel off the rail to wrap it round her.

'Umm…' She fumbled as Zac straightened. 'Was it OK for you?'

Zac shot her a heart-stopping smile of surprise and laughed, his darkly handsome lean features compelling. 'It was wonderful and now you can stop worrying about it.'

'I wasn't worrying… *Zac!*' she yelped in disconcertion as he twitched her out of the towel's folds and lifted her to settle her down into the bath he had run for her. She was taken aback by how natural it felt to be with him in such circumstances while the tender ache between her thighs reminded her of how physically close they had been. Physically close, *not* mentally close, she conceded ruefully.

'I hope you don't get pregnant *too* quickly, *meu pequenino,*' Zac confided, running his bright silvery eyes over her flushed and beautiful face. 'I'm looking forward to having a lot of fun with you in the short term.'

Sex as a simple fun activity was beyond Freddie's imagination but she could see that it was very much Zac's approach and that daunted her. He strode into the shower, evidently in the best of moods, and to console herself she counted her blessings. The sex had been acceptable, their wedding was still on and the adoption application was progressing.

Short term, he had been careful to remind her, she mused, her shoulders drooping a little. Fun in the short term. Could she do that? She *had* to do it. Too much would be lost if she failed to maintain a good relationship with Zac. She had to at least try to do things his way even if it felt foreign and threatening to embrace such beliefs. Only if they were reasonably content as a couple would the children thrive.

In the shower, Zac was weighing up the use of birth control against his legal need for a child and marvelling at the unexpected direction his thoughts were wandering in. Freddie could conceive immediately, which would kill the fun angle because he knew from his mother's experience that pregnant women got sick, tired and hormonal. If he used condoms, however, they could enjoy carefree sex for as long as they liked. He was already wondering how soon he could enjoy her again. He couldn't wait to see that dreamy, dizzy expression of bliss on her face again and revel in her honest, innocent openness because he had never had that connection with a woman before.

Freddie was a rare find, he conceded with satisfaction. Should he have told her the truth about that night at the ball? He grimaced. He didn't believe in baring his soul and he didn't want to risk hurting her. If he told her the truth she would misinterpret it and make feminine assumptions that would not fit the frame. Wouldn't she assume that she meant more to him than she did? He didn't want to do that to her. Inevitably what he felt would wear off and he would want other women and the freedom to enjoy them anywhere, any place, any time. He knew his own flaws. He was not a for-ever kind of guy and there was a limit to how honest he could afford to be.

CHAPTER SEVEN

It was a breathtaking dress, Freddie reflected, dizzily studying her appearance in the mirror in Claire's bedroom. Getting ready in her own room had proved impossible because there simply wasn't enough space.

The sleek handmade lace bodice with a low back clung from shoulder to hip, playing up her small curves and making her look taller. The skirt fell in intricate cobweb-fine lace folds shimmering with beadwork. At her throat glittered a diamond pendant, a wedding gift from Zac. Her hair was up in an elaborate coronet to support the diamond-studded tiara that Zac had told her had belonged to his late mother, along with the diamond earrings and bracelet she wore.

'Do I look like a Christmas tree?' she asked her aunt worriedly.

'Like I should have that problem!' Claire quipped enviously. 'But diamonds are the family business, so I suppose you have to put the finest on display. Your life will be *so* different, Freddie. It'll be champagne and caviar all the way now.'

Freddie swallowed hard at the thought because she still couldn't imagine it. A hair stylist and a beautician might have come to the house to prepare her for the wedding, but that had seemed more of a necessity than a luxury when she was marrying Zac and she needed to look like the sort of woman that he would marry. Heaven forbid that he would ever look at her and feel embarrassed by her and, thanks to that family dinner, she already knew that even those closest to him could be both critical and judgemental.

Zac, waiting at the church, forced a polite smile when Vitale came to join his two brothers. 'Your majesty,' he said, acknowledging that his half-brother had become the King of Lerovia since his mother's abdication even though the formal coronation would not be held for several months. 'I should be bowing, right?'

'No...not within the family,' King Vitale declared. 'And I intend to have a modern court, so there'll be a lot less bowing and scraping in Lerovia as well. By the way, our wedding present, which is car-shaped, is on its way back to you.'

Zac frowned at that reference to the prized sports car he had lost in that ill-judged bet with his half-brother. '*Back* to me?'

Vitale shrugged. 'Nobody won that bet. You may not have brought Freddie to the royal ball but now you're *marrying* her—'

'You won fair and square,' Zac began inflexibly.

Angel frowned with the air of a man who would have liked to knock both his stiff-necked brothers' heads together. 'He'll be delighted to accept his car back.'

With a stark exhalation of breath, Zac accepted that loaded hint and murmured through gritted teeth, 'That's very generous of you, Vitale...thanks.'

'And within the family circle there will be neither

bows *nor* any more bets,' Angel suggested with quiet emphasis.

Zac sank back into brooding silence, disturbed that he was so tense. People got married every day, he reminded himself. *He* didn't, though, and the surroundings and the stifling traditions made him feel constrained. The whole event was much more formal than he had expected.

The bride made quite a picture walking down the aisle with Jack, loveable with his hair in corn rows and clad in a miniature suit toddling along beside her and Claire. Eloise was walking very carefully behind her aunts clutching a basket of flowers and clad in the pink flouncy princess dress that was the summit of her little-girl dreams. Zac discovered that he couldn't take his eyes off that little tableau. His family, his *new* family, he realised suddenly as Jack beamed trustingly at him and Eloise waved from behind her aunts as if afraid that he might not notice her.

Without the smallest warning, the enormity of the responsibility he had taken on engulfed Zac. He tried to concentrate his attention on Freddie, who looked stunning, sexy and cute as hell, but all the while his brain was running at a mile a minute, telling him that freedom of any kind would be an unattainable luxury with one woman and two…eventually *three*…children depending on him to be a good husband and a good father. He lost colour, his spectacular bone structure tautly delineated below his bronzed skin as the ramifications of such a marriage finally sank in on him: he would *never* be totally free again because parenting was *for ever*, with no get-out clause. It was a sobering moment, most particularly when he was willing to admit that he didn't know the first thing about how to take care of anyone but himself.

Freddie's hands almost crushed her bouquet of white and pink roses when she glimpsed the cool bleak light forming in Zac's gorgeous eyes and the absence of his trademark grin. Her heart sank like a stone. He was disappointed in her. Did she not look the way he had imagined she would? Had he believed a designer dress and all the trimmings, not to mention the family diamonds, would transform an ordinary waitress into something rather more special? Or did he have cold feet about getting married? Whatever it was, he did not look happy, which he should have been, considering that their marriage was supposed to provide what he most wanted as well.

A child. *Their* first child to add to the mix of Eloise and Jack, whom Zac had insisted must share their day with them because he wanted them to have that first memory of the four of them becoming a family. Zac had never had that family experience, although Freddie had happily enjoyed it for the first ten years of her life. Zac, however, had known only rejection from those who should have given him love and support. By the time he got to know his real father, who *was* a caring man, it had been a case of too little too late. Of course, Zac was damaged by such a loveless childhood but wasn't it her role to ensure that he realised that together they could make things different for their own children? Or was that too tall an order for a new bride, who wasn't loved, to take on? She was rather afraid that it might be…

Her anxiety about Zac shielded her from the pressure of the church packed with rich, smartly dressed guests. Zac had many business acquaintances and his father, still keen to show off his newly discovered son, had invited his friends to share their day as well. His brothers were attending with small parties, further pushing up the numbers. Freddie, however, had only had a few friends to invite because her social life had been very much curtailed by the children.

The priest welcomed them to the altar and gave a serious opening speech about the responsibilities of marriage. When she reached for Zac's hand, it was ice cool in hers. She had a sudden disturbing and panic-inducing vision of him walking out on her at the last possible minute and, instinctively, she held on tight. The ceremony began and Jack escaped Claire to cling to Zac's knees like a limpet and loudly wail in disappointment when someone lifted him away. Zac raised Freddie's hand and slid the twisted platinum ring onto her wedding finger.

They had picked it together but there hadn't been much choice because her extravagant engagement ring took up so much space that there was little left to spare for the wedding ring she would wear. Zac had laughed heartily at the time, teasing her about her little hands and short fingers, and without warning tears stung her eyes at that memory. He had been so laid-back and light-hearted that day only a week earlier and his current change of mood unnerved her. He had wanted to marry her, *he* had asked *her* to marry him, she reminded herself to bolster her spirits.

They signed the register with his brother and Claire as witnesses and by the time they walked down the aisle at speed it was obvious that Zac could not wait to get out of the church.

On the steps, as the guests held up phones to photograph them, he expelled his breath in a hiss. '*Meu Deus*...glad that's over!'

Eloise clung to the foot of his jacket and Jack held out his arms, almost toppling out of Claire's hold.

'Tough, isn't it, Jack?' Zac derided, reaching out to take the over-eager baby into his arms, recognising that his shenanigans had taxed Claire's low patience threshold.

It was a challenge for Freddie to hold onto her bridal beam in Zac's radius, particularly after she saw Angel and Vitale exchanging meaningful looks across the disenchanted bridegroom. Getting into the limousine even with the children clambering over them was a relief because at least there were no watching eyes and listening ears there.

'What's wrong, Zac?' Freddie asked levelly.

'Nothing's wrong,' Zac intoned. 'I'm just not cut out for this kind of stuff.'

'You insisted on this being what you called a *normal* wedding,' she reminded him.

His strong jaw line clenched and his wide sensual mouth compressed, his crystalline eyes sombre below his semi-lowered lashes. 'We all make mistakes,' he said very drily, thinking that he should have opted to avoid the traditional hoopla and travel a simpler route.

Freddie froze. *'Am I a mistake?'* she suddenly demanded loudly.

Zac groaned long and low. 'You know I didn't mean it like that...*inferno*, I don't know what I meant! But that priest lecturing us on our marital duties reminded me of being at school,' he bit out impatiently.

Freddie embraced silence all the way to The Palm Tree, where the reception was being staged. Zac had dispensed with a greeting line as being too official and instead the guests mingled over drinks when they arrived. The hotel nanny was at their disposal and the children were borne off for lunch and a nap. Zac vanished into the bar before they sat down to their meal, reappearing just in time to make a very short speech in the wake of his father's. He ate little and drank a lot, responding to Freddie when she spoke but initiating no other conversation. He seemed bleakly set on just going through the motions and getting through what he clearly saw as an ordeal.

Somehow it infuriated Freddie that, even in a mood, Zac should still look utterly gorgeous, dark stubble beginning to shade in the angles and hollows of his beautiful bone structure, black lashes low over his brooding glittering gaze as he lounged back with careless elegance in his seat.

Exasperated by her susceptibility to him, Freddie tore her attention from him and went into the cloakroom to freshen up. She was grimacing at her downcast expression when a woman appeared in the mirror beside her.

'I hope Zac treats you better than he treated my daughter,' she remarked curtly.

Blinking, Freddie turned her head to look at the ageing blonde, studying her with pursed lips. 'Sorry?' she said blankly.

'Two years ago my daughter was working as a chalet girl in Klosters. Zac told her that she was the most beautiful girl in the world...well, actually she *was* a runner-up in the Miss World competition the year before,' the woman digressed with pride. 'Anyway. She was with him a week and then she never heard from him again. He broke her heart.'

Freddie straightened her slight shoulders and lifted her chin. 'And you're telling me this because…?'

'He loses interest once the chase is over. I thought I should warn you.'

'Thank you,' Freddie replied with equal insincerity, laced with a tight determined smile as she walked away.

Merry greeted her when she returned to their table to find Zac's chair empty.

'He's doing shots in the bar with Angel,' Angel's wife confided with a visible wince of embarrassment.

The guests were waiting for the bride and groom to open the dancing. Freddie persuaded the new King and Queen of Lerovia to do the honours instead and cut the cake with her new father-in-law's help because she was resolutely set on not chasing after Zac to nag at him to do anything he didn't want to do. Feeling suitably martyred, she sat with Merry and Jazz and got to know the two other women better while little Elyssa, Merry's daughter, played at their feet and Jazz shared the news that she was expecting twins, although her willowy frame showed little evidence of that reality.

Freddie and Zac were scheduled to leave the hotel at five and as soon as the kids had had an early supper Freddie went up to the penthouse to get changed. She put on silky wide-legged trousers and a floaty top for their flight to the South of France and only then went off to locate her new husband.

'Zac's waiting in the limo. His bodyguards took him out the back entrance,' Angel told her warily. 'He's drunk. Blame me.'

'Oh, I'm not blaming anyone!' Freddie said a tinge shrilly, her face as hot as hellfire.

'I think...' Charles Russell interposed anxiously, 'Zac was celebrating too hard.'

Freddie raised both brows, feeling like the original toxic bride with everyone trying to placate her. 'I don't think he was celebrating getting married. I think he was drowning his sorrows.'

'Zac can be a little unpredictable,' Angel volunteered, contriving to look both guilty and sympathetic. 'And he doesn't normally drink this much.'

Freddie shone a bright smile at their anxious faces, her pride badly stung by his family's concern on her behalf. And just behind that lurked her depressing recollection of the woman who had accosted her in the cloakroom to tell her that Zac lost interest in a woman once the chase was over. Since his dogged pursuit of her had ended in his penthouse bedroom the day before, she reckoned that there could be some truth in that disturbing allegation. Now that he had discovered that she was just like every other woman he had slept with, he evidently didn't even have enough interest left to stay sober for their wedding night, she thought with a mixture of anger, hurt and exasperation.

After all, as one of the former bar staff, she knew rather more than Zac's family did about his drinking habits, she reflected ruefully. Zac usually drank more coffee than alcohol, so if he had drunk a lot it could only be because something had upset him. And considering this was their wedding day, what else was she to blame for his mood than their new marriage?

Freddie didn't speak a word on the drive to the airport but Zac was too preoccupied to notice. He followed his bodyguards out of the car while she hung back with the children and they were rushed through VIP channels out to the da Rocha private jet. Zac boarded, sent her a careless glance and murmured, 'I'm going to lie down for a while.' And off he went, leaving Freddie to deal with Isabel, the young smiling nanny, waiting to help her with the children, the nanny Zac hadn't even thought to mention he had engaged.

Mercifully it was a large jet and there was a second sleeping compartment already prepared for the children's occupancy. Jack was already asleep but Eloise was very reluctant to go to bed at the same time as her little brother, and the nanny entertained her at the rear of the main cabin while Freddie took the time to eat a light evening meal and flip through the glossy magazines provided for her. She was absolutely enraged with Zac and holding it in was like trying to contain a screeching storm.

Zac emerged shortly before they landed and lifted Eloise, who, like Jack, was fast asleep. They would have been wiser to stay in London the first night and travel by day, Freddie acknowledged ruefully, but Zac had not consulted her. Having landed, they transferred to a helicopter, which took off with a lurch that sent Freddie's stomach plummeting. The racket of the rotors woke Jack up and he burst into frightened sobs. Finding himself with a stranger, he was inconsolable and Freddie reclaimed him with relief as soon as the helicopter landed again.

A weathered stone building loomed ahead of them, every tall window brilliantly lit up in welcome. Zac removed Jack from Freddie's arms. 'I'll take him. You look exhausted.'

Zac had returned to planet earth again, she registered irritably, feeling that she could have done without being told that she looked so tired. She wasn't vain but she had lived through a disastrous wedding day polished up to her very best and had received not a single compliment from her uninterested bridegroom. She said nothing as they trudged up the path towards the brightly lit frontage of the massive house.

The house reminded her of a postcard of a fantasy Provencal retreat, replete as it was with regimented lines of painted smoky blue shutters and flowers and terracotta vases ornamenting every window and door. But even with the light fading fast she could see the bulk of the house stretching back, recognising that it far outstripped in size any normal house. The number of staff waiting to greet them in the marble-floored hall was another reminder that she had married a man who was unaccustomed to looking after himself in any way. He handed Jack straight over to a young woman. 'This is Jennifer, Freddie. She will be helping Isabel with the kids.'

Jack screeched at physical contact with yet another stranger and almost threw himself out of the unfortunate Jennifer's arms. Freddie grabbed him back. 'It's all right. I'll see to settling the children down tonight. They're overtired and nervous of strangers,' she said apologetically.

Jennifer showed the way upstairs to the rooms readied for the children and Freddie heaved a sigh of relief at the freedom to do something familiar even if it was in an unfamiliar place. *Two* nannies? Was he crazy? Was he expecting Eloise and Jack to be kept out of sight by staff as children had been for centuries in well-off families? Who did he think he was to make such arrangements without involving her?

She wanted to strangle Zac and scream at him and it was an effort to smile gratefully at the nannies as she sat down to rock Jack back to sleep in what was undoubtedly the nursery of a little boy's dreams, with a cot shaped like a race car. By the time she got Jack ensconced in his cot and went into the bedroom next door, Eloise was already sleeping peacefully in a miniature four-poster bed draped in pink. All the luxury surrounding her, all the fancy toys piled up waiting to be played with, felt surreal and foreign and alienating to Freddie, and for a moment she wanted desperately to be back in the safe confines of the tiny bedroom she had shared with her niece and nephew.

Instead she had a housekeeper introducing herself as Mariette in broken English and offering to show her to the master bedroom suite. Once again, Zac was nowhere to be seen and at that moment, feeling totally isolated, Freddie didn't care. She wanted normal and for her that meant a shower and a bed and the renewed strength that would come from a good night's sleep. She had barely slept at all the previous night, lying awake dreamily thinking about Zac, her first sexual experience and their future together. Now the chances of them achieving some rosy perfect state of coupledom struck her as both pathetic and unlikely.

Zac walked into the master suite at one in the morning, the need to make amends having finally overcome his fierce pride, but he was too late. Freddie was already dead to the world, curled up in a tight little ball hugging a pillow on the far side of the bed. He studied her, the flush of sleep on her delicate features, the tousled dark blonde hair playing across the pillow, the relaxed line of her lush pink mouth. So lovely and so fragile, he acknowledged reluctantly, and he had hurt her. Getting married was fast proving to be a learning experience and the first lesson was that his behaviour affected her as well. Pretty basic one that, he acknowledged grimly, but then Zac had never had another person's needs and wishes to consider before.

In the morning, he would make everything right, he assured himself. Quite how to go about achieving that objective escaped him, but he was fairly sure that some serious thought would give him the answer. But why the hell had he brought her to the Villa Antonella, a place haunted by his earliest bad memories? The place where his short-lived but once normal family life had disintegrated into messy broken shards overnight?

He couldn't answer that question either.

CHAPTER EIGHT

FEELING ALMOST REJUVENATED by a night of unbroken rest, Freddie bounced out of bed and then looked at the time and almost laid an egg. What about the children? She should have been up two hours earlier to look after them! And then she remembered the nannies and the guilt ebbed, but only very slowly because feeding Eloise and Jack still felt like *her* job.

After another shower, she applied the lightest possible make-up from the new stash that had been part of her makeover and selected a cool cotton sundress from the new wardrobe of summer clothing Zac had ordered on her behalf. Only then did she feel ready to greet the sunshine blazing through the tall windows.

Zac was always *giving* her stuff. He was very generous, she acknowledged ruefully, but it didn't cancel out his stubborn go-it-alone attitude. She headed to the children's bedrooms first but both were empty. Jennifer was coming upstairs as Freddie went down and informed her that Eloise and Jack were with Zac out on the terrace. She was disconcerted by that news, for she had uncharitably assumed that the hiring of *two* nannies indicated that Zac wanted the kids kept out of his hair as much as possible. Mariette showed her out to the wide stone terrace that ran along the rear of the house to take advantage of the truly spectacular panoramic view across the rural valley behind it.

Freddie came to a sudden halt to appreciate the landscape. Olive trees with silvery foliage crowded terraces ringed by ancient stone walls and lavender fields stretched over the furthest hill, the brilliant purple furrows of blooms seeming to perfume the fresh air. The terrace was shaded by an ornate ironwork pergola lushly wrapped in grape vines and wisteria.

'Auntie Freddie… Auntie Freddie!' Eloise came running down the terrace to show her a picture of a dragon, or was it two dragons? 'See…they getting married.'

'Very nice,' Freddie assured her niece, trying not to notice that the larger dragon shape was adorned with what looked very like a tattoo. Eloise was already demonstrating a natural artistic ability that far outstripped her age group.

Tension laced Freddie's slight frame when she saw Zac rising from the table at the far end while Jack literally tried to run to her.

As she hastily scooped up Jack before he fell, for while he could walk he could not yet run, she noticed that Zac had forsaken his business suits in favour of close-fitting jeans and a white linen shirt against which his skin glowed. He looked, Freddie thought resentfully, like a health advert, not at all like a man who should've been nursing a monster hangover. She moved towards him stiffly, face tight, eyes evasive as she set Jack down to play with the toys scattered across the terrace.

'Mariette is bringing your breakfast,' Zac murmured casually.

'I didn't ask for any.'

'I ordered for you.'

'But you don't know what I wanted,' Freddie pointed out thinly.

'I ordered a selection,' Zac assured her with a steely glint in his brilliant eyes as he surveyed her. 'You suit blue. You look lovely.'

'I seriously doubt that,' Freddie countered with an angry flush, thinking of how her perfectly groomed self the day before had failed to attract such interest.

'Let's not argue in front of the kids,' Zac urged warningly.

Resenting that reproof, Freddie breathed in so deep that she was vaguely surprised she didn't explode like a bag of hot air, because suddenly she was so angry with him that she could barely breathe and hold the furious words in.

'These are for you…' Zac announced, lifting an elaborate and very large bouquet of flowers in a vase up onto the table. 'And this…'

'This' was a jewellery box, and she didn't want to open it. Flowers, and presumably diamonds. He had utilised a whole host of brain cells to come up with those as an apology, she thought nastily, but neither gift hit the right spot. She glanced at him, reading the wary light in his glorious crystalline eyes, the wariness of a man dealing with an unknown quantity and wondering how she would react.

Mariette arrived with an entire trolley of food and a maid to serve. Freddie felt embarrassed accepting only fruit, a croissant and a cup of tea. But even the melting tenderness of the pastry fought to make it past her tight throat. Did she give Zac the benefit of the doubt and move on past the debacle of their wedding day? Even if she didn't feel the smallest bit forgiving? As a rule she didn't sulk or hold spite, but he *had* to explain himself at the very least, she decided. She lifted the jewellery box so that he couldn't call her bad mannered and flipped up the lid on a diamond-studded gold watch.

'Wow...thank you so much,' she said generously, determined to be gracious, glancing across at him. Momentarily those lean, darkly handsome features surrounded by his blue-black luxuriant hair and accentuated by those bright pale blue eyes literally blew her concentration to smithereens.

'How can you drink tea instead of coffee in the morning?' Zac asked inconsequentially, watching her with an intensity that made her skin tighten over her bones and set up a disturbing throb between her thighs.

'It's what I'm used to,' she muttered, recognising that he planned to gloss over the whole wedding day thing without even making an actual apology aside of the flowers and the watch, and recognising too that she could never look herself in the face again if she allowed him to use his electrifying sexuality to derail her.

Jennifer and Isabel arrived to collect the children to take them out into the garden. An unearthly silence fell across the terrace after their departure and Freddie swallowed hard, still picking nervously at shreds of her croissant.

Entranced, Zac watched her pluck another shred of pastry and place it between her moist pink lips and his jeans tightened. He thought about sex. She clasped the watch round her slender wrist. He thought about more sex. He discounted her tension, reckoning that what they both needed was a good rousing tumble in bed to find each other again.

'Are you planning to say sorry?' Freddie asked, shattering both his expectations and his mood. 'Even *thinking* about it? Or is it just a case of not being able to get the words out?'

'You know that I regret my attitude yesterday,' Zac told her tautly. 'It's obvious, isn't it?'

Freddie nodded. 'But you can't expect flowers and a designer watch to do the job for you.'

'They always have in the past.'

'Then you've been mixing with the wrong kind of woman,' Freddie responded acidly. 'And to be frank, sorry wouldn't even begin to cover it.'

Zac sprang out of his chair, the legs of it scraping harshly across the stone tiles beneath. 'I got drunk. I didn't kill anyone!' he flashed back at her with sudden anger.

'You pretty much opted out of our entire wedding day,' Freddie declared, shaken by that anger but persisting. 'You weren't there to start the dancing with me. You weren't there even to cut the cake. It was humiliating and hurtful and, obviously, people noticed your absence. All I need you to do now is explain *why...*'

'I'm no good at those kinds of explanations.'

'But you could, at least, *try*,' Freddie said gently.

'*Meu Deus*...what do you want from me?' Zac demanded rawly. 'An apology? You already have it.'

'I need to know why—'

'No, you don't!' Zac fired back at her, his broad chest heaving as he dragged in a deep sustaining breath. 'You *don't*. I don't have that kind of conversation with women.'

'I'll forgive and forget if you just tell me why,' Freddie exclaimed in appeal. 'I need to understand.'

Rage glittering in his glorious eyes and the sense of being trapped intensifying, Zac compressed his lips hard. 'I won't argue with you. I'm going out for a while,' he told her, turning on his heel and striding down the terrace at speed.

For a startled moment, Freddie simply stared after him and then she chased after him, only to be greeted by the slam of the front door and a look of curious enquiry from Mariette. Her face colouring, she returned to the terrace, now blind to the wonderful view. He had walked out sooner than talk—not a very productive approach to a new marriage. But was she expecting too much from him too soon? Their marriage was not supposed to be a meeting of hearts and minds.

Practicality not sentiment.

The words rang like a falling tombstone of foreboding at the back of her mind.

Zac backed away from conflict, reluctant to get that involved with anyone. She couldn't live like that, she thought fearfully, never really knowing where she stood with him. But he had told her where she stood before they married, hadn't he? Practicality covered everything and emotions didn't have to be considered. But what if she already felt more than she should for him? Freddie grimaced at that suspicion but there it was, feelings she couldn't avoid, feelings he wouldn't want her to feel. It hurt when he walked away, refusing to answer her questions, refusing to shed a glimmer of light on what went on in that complex head of his, because hopefully if she understood better she could forgive more easily. Tears prickled her eyes as she sat there and listened to the roar of a powerful motorbike firing up and then the quieter sound of his security team following in a car.

Was she so unreasonable? Had she driven him away? And when would he return?

* * *

Zac travelled quite a distance before he cooled off. Angel had asked him, if he had the time, to check out the work he was having done on his yacht and report back to him. He drove down to the Saint Laurent du Var Marina and paused at a waterside café to order an espresso, avoiding the glances of a group of youthful tourists giving him inviting looks from nearby. Angel and Vitale seemed to have taken to marriage like ducks to water, Zac reflected resentfully, so why was it all going wrong for him? He had asked Freddie to marry him, had *wanted* her to marry him. He had chosen her and would still have chosen her even when she was almost shouting at him, he acknowledged grudgingly. But she wanted more from him than any other woman ever had. The flowers and the watch hadn't cut the ice.

What had come over him at the wedding? He was accustomed to responsibility but not to being responsible for other people, with the exception of employees with whom he had no personal ties. From childhood he had learned to hold people at bay to ensure they couldn't hurt him. If he didn't let anyone get close he was safe. But Freddie and the children weren't going to hurt or betray him. He was more likely to hurt them by failing to live up to their expectations, he reasoned impatiently. What if she fell in love with him? He would have to warn her off on that score. The very last thing he wanted to do was hurt Freddie, he acknowledged without hesitation. Or Eloise, or Jack. He was getting attached to the three of them even if he wasn't supposed to do so.

Practicality not sentiment, he reminded himself with a groan of frustration. But practicality didn't take any account of emotions or emotional women. And Freddie was emotional, all wide, accusing, hurt eyes and quivering lips. Eloise looked at him in much the same way when he refused to read the dragon story twice over at the same sitting. Jack? Jack was simple in his demands, content solely with attention.

Freddie's emotional outlook, however, was infinitely preferable to the kind of brassy, avaricious females who littered his past, Zac conceded wryly. She stood up for herself too. She wasn't a doormat eager to agree with everything he did and said. Freddie hadn't wanted the watch, she had wanted words, only what was he to do when the words wouldn't be the ones she wanted to hear? Honesty at any cost? What woman really wanted that?

The day went past very slowly for Freddie because Zac was such an unknown quantity. For all she knew he could have flown back to London or Brazil or even gone off with another, less demanding woman. 'Unpredictable', Angel Valtinos had labelled his half-brother, and now for the first time she was seeing that in Zac and it unnerved her that a simple request for an explanation could infuriate him to such an extent. She bathed the children and saw them into bed, promising that Zac would be back soon and praying that she was right.

She was shocked when she walked out onto the terrace and saw him simply standing there looking out over the valley.

'Zac...' she breathed with irrefutable relief. 'Where have you been?'

'I went to Nice, checked out the work being done on Angel's yacht...he asked me to,' he told her with a fluid shrug as he slowly turned round to face her. 'How are you?'

'I wasn't sure you'd come back,' she whispered tightly.

'I may storm off but I'll always come back,' Zac murmured with wry amusement. 'I don't like losing my temper with people.'

'I'm not people, I'm your wife,' she protested as the sun went down behind him in a crimson and golden blaze of colour, the light picking up the straight angle of his dark brows above his deep-set eyes and the wide sensual line of his mouth and sending a shiver of awareness travelling through her. 'But I'm not sure you were really ready to take on a wife.'

Zac raked long brown fingers through his black hair and breathed in deep. 'For a split second when I saw you and the children in the church, I felt trapped. I had no excuse to feel like that because I asked you to marry me. Even so, the sudden awareness that I was going to be a husband and a father to two, possibly *three* kids, knocked me sideways. Being free—the ability to get up and go where I like when I like and do as I like—has always been very important to me. The idea of being tied down filled me with—'

'Yes, I get it,' Freddie broke in tightly, ramming down her pain at that honest admission, ironically not wanting him to expand on it. 'It's a massive change for you and maybe you hadn't quite thought it through when you asked me to marry you. But if you want out now, it's *not* too late.'

Zac frowned in bewilderment at that statement. 'It's way too late. What about the adoption?'

Freddie's spine stiffened. 'I would rather give up the children than force you to go through with a marriage you don't want,' she told him starkly, because if they were both unhappy it would only make the children unhappy as well and she owed them a better future than that.

Zac went rigid, every muscle in his lean, powerful body pulling taut. 'That's a crazy offer to make, *meu pequenino*. I wouldn't do that to you.'

'Strictly speaking, we're not fully and legally married yet because we haven't shared a bed. Right now, we could still get an annulment.'

Without warning, Zac was being plunged into a much bigger crisis than he had expected and he wished he had lied about feeling trapped and had skipped the very self-indulgent drinking episode that had followed. 'I don't want an annulment. I don't want to lose you or the children,' he admitted in a driven undertone. 'I behaved badly. You suffered for it. Now I'm thinking more clearly and there is no one else I want to marry, no one else I want to be married to... I can only face sharing those kinds of ties with you,' he completed doggedly.

Freddie finally managed to breathe again. She had believed she *had* to make the offer because she didn't see how she could keep him if he didn't want to be with them. That would be a recipe for disaster. Now, fear and insecurity still pulling at her, she stared up at him anxiously. 'I don't want to make you unhappy.'

'Freddie...in my whole life, nobody ever cared whether or not I was happy!' Zac exclaimed in wonderment. 'Can we go indoors now? Standing right at this spot brings back unfortunate memories of the accident I had here as a child.'

'You came here as a child? And got hurt?'

'Antonella bought this place almost thirty years ago. My mother and stepfather liked to entertain friends here in the summer,' he told her flatly as they traversed the marble foyer. 'I was three and very adventurous. I clambered down the slope and fell and cut my leg badly. Luckily…or unluckily as it later proved…there was a doctor among the friends staying and he saved my life because I had lost a lot of blood.'

Zac had turned pale, his voice roughening as he walked up the imposing staircase. 'They rushed me to hospital, where it transpired that I have a very rare blood group. Charles's blood group. Apparently it had been mentioned at my birth but Afonso didn't pick up on the significance. Afonso believed I was his son and he couldn't understand why he or Antonella couldn't give me blood. His best friend, the doctor, explained that I couldn't possibly be Afonso's child and that's the day my life fell apart as far as family goes.'

Freddie had stopped dead on the stairs to work through what he was telling her. 'Oh, my goodness…' she framed sickly.

'I only remember two things about the whole experience. One was my mother having hysterics for days, the other was Afonso, the man whom I believed to be my father and whom I loved, pushing me away in disgust and calling me a "filthy half-breed",' he concluded heavily. 'Of course, he was upset and furious that he had accepted me as his son.'

Freddie winced and placed a soothing hand on his arm. 'Still no excuse for saying *that* to you. It wasn't your fault.'

'It wasn't anyone's fault. My mother had never admitted to my stepfather that she had had an affair with another man after he broke off their engagement. That was her little secret and she preferred to assume that I was Afonso's child. She went to pieces when the truth came out.'

Freddie's heart was breaking for him. She was imagining how lost and hurt he must have been at only Eloise's age, confronted with such a massive rejection and, indeed, hatred. 'And then what happened?'

'My mother took me back to Brazil and put me on the horse-breeding ranch with servants to look after me. It was over a year before I saw her again. I didn't see Afonso again until last year when he approached me with a business opportunity. I said no.'

'And their marriage survived all that? They stayed together?'

'Afonso enjoyed the da Rocha lifestyle but he was enraged that, as his wife's firstborn, I would inherit rather than any child *he* had with her,' he completed grimly. 'But Antonella refused to accept that reality and she kept on trying to give him a child even after the doctors warned her that she was risking her life. She only finally told me who my father was on the day she died. She was ashamed of it...and of me being illegitimate like she was.'

Freddie struggled to accept that Zac had been punished for his paternity by exclusion and virtual abandonment by his own mother. Simultaneously he had lost the man he'd believed to be his father. In one dreadful day, he had lost his whole family. She remembered how utterly lost she had felt after her parents died and how much she had clung to Lauren for comfort and security. Zac, however, hadn't had the consolation of a sibling.

'I'm surprised you still own this house,' she remarked as he paused in the ajar doorway of Eloise's bedroom to glance in. Illuminated by the night light she couldn't sleep without, Eloise was a small bump in a sea of cuddly toys. Zac's taut dark features perceptibly softened.

'My mother rented it out for years. I don't think she ever came back here and, as social services didn't want us to take the children out of Europe, it made sense for us to use the villa as a base. I was planning to put it on the market when we left. I didn't even realise that I still had memories of this place until I walked through the door,' Zac confessed, strolling on to Jack's room and walking in slowly when he saw a little leg dangling out between the cot bars.

Jack was fast asleep in the corner. Freddie leant down to gently rearrange his warm little body into a more comfortable position.

'He feels like he's mine even though I know he's not,' Zac said softly. 'And it doesn't matter that he's not.'

Freddie's tender smile swept the tension from her triangular face. 'Even people who don't like kids very much warm to Jack's sunny nature.'

'It was very generous of you to offer me an out but I freely choose to stay married to you,' Zac breathed gruffly outside the door. 'Can we start again as if yesterday didn't happen?'

Freddie nodded vigorously, caramel eyes welded to his lean bronzed face, her breathing feathering in her dry throat. His hand closed over hers and the buzz of awareness awakened by that contact sent her every nerve ending into overdrive. A slight quiver ran through her taut frame as they entered the master bedroom she had slept in alone the night before.

'I need a shower.' Zac peeled off his shirt and stripped

with the careless ease of a man without a single self-conscious bone in his body.

Freddie watched him walk naked and bronzed into the shower while she removed her make-up and washed her face. He caught her up into his arms while her face was still buried in a towel and she yelped in surprise when he lifted her and carried her back into the bedroom.

'*En quero voce...* I want you,' Zac growled, standing her up to extract her from her dress and smiling appreciatively when he discovered that she wore only knickers beneath.

His hands swept up to capture her breasts, his thumbs grazing over her sensitive nipples before he took her mouth with passionate force. Every rational thought she had evaporated at the same moment. Her fingers tightened convulsively on his muscular shoulders as his aroused body pressed against hers and excitement sizzled through her as the anxiety of the day finally melted away.

Zac tumbled her down on the bed and pinned her beneath him, luminous eyes glinting with amusement below black velvet lashes. 'I wanted to do this this morning. How would that have gone down?'

'Like a lead balloon,' Freddie framed with difficulty, insanely conscious of the hard pressure of his arousal against her stomach and even more insanely conscious of the heat and moisture gathering between her legs.

'Now I want you a hundred times more,' Zac husked. 'Because you stood up to me.'

'That's weird,' she told him, quivering as the tip of his tongue traced her delicate collarbone, setting up unexpected reactions in other places.

'No, it's not. I don't want a yes-woman.'

'You did this morning,' she countered with a grin.

'That's sex, that's different,' he dismissed lazily, skilled fingers outlining the entrance concealed between her damp folds, making her tremble and jerk. 'Every guy wants a yes-woman when it comes to sex.'

His honesty made her laugh and he ran teasing fingertips up over her ribcage, discovering where she was ticklish. Freddie made her own exploration over his warm, hard abdominal muscles, fingers straying playfully closer to his bold, hard shaft until frustration forced him to grab her hand and close it round him.

Surprise darted through her at the smooth, hard length of him and she stroked and cupped and shaped and then dropped her head down in an experimental mood, only to be dragged up again.

'I can't take that right now! I need to be inside you,' Zac bit out raggedly as he rearranged her to his satisfaction and plunged into her without ceremony, a guttural sound of satisfaction wrenched from him. '*Voce me excita*…you excite me so much.'

This time there was no discomfort, only the compelling sensation of her body stretching to capacity to accept his. Her hips lifted instinctively in welcome and then he moved and a wave of pulsing excitement was unleashed, her body thrumming like a new engine raring to go. She gasped as his hands cupped her hips to lift her and deepen his penetration.

'You feel like hot satin,' Zac groaned, provocatively withdrawing and then slamming back into her again while her hips squirmed and the heat in her pelvis rose with the tightening, building surge of pressure. 'I thought about this at least once every ten seconds today.'

'Tell me something that surprises me,' Freddie urged, her breath catching in her throat as the hard, virile thrust of his body made her writhe beneath him.

'You do...every time,' Zac groaned, claiming her reddened mouth in a hot, driving kiss.

His heart was thundering against her and she rose up against him one last time, her internal muscles clenching hard as an explosive climax gripped her. Her head fell back against the pillows, her hair in a wild tangle as ripples of melting bliss engulfed her sated length.

Zac reached his own completion with her but bliss seemed to be the last thing on his mind as he reared back from her and swore in Portuguese. '*Inferno*... I forgot to use a condom!' he bit out in exasperation.

'Why would you want to do that?' Freddie asked in dreamy bemusement.

Zac stared down at her, crystalline eyes deadly serious. 'I thought maybe we needed a breathing space to get this marriage up and running and that you might prefer a delay in the baby department.'

'No,' Freddie said decisively. 'Because it could take months and months for me to conceive, so it's easier just to go on as we began. If it happens, it happens.'

Zac released her from his weight and Freddie moved onto her side and draped an arm and a leg across him as he began to move off the bed. 'Where are you going?'

'My room's next door.'

'I thought this was *our* room.'

'I'm used to sleeping alone.'

'Time for a rethink,' Freddie whispered sleepily, fingers toying with his gold necklace of St Jude. 'Why do you wear this?'

'It belonged to my mother. She gave it to me before she died.'

'I want you with me at night,' she admitted.

'Why?' Zac demanded baldly.

'Cosier that way,' his wife mumbled, her arm clamping round him like a chain. 'And if you can shag Miss World chalet girls in Klosters and break their hearts without a blush, you can manage to share a bed with your wife…'

Zac froze and gazed down at her in complete consternation.

'Wasn't going to mention that…it just slipped out.' Freddie sighed regretfully as she snuggled up against him, impervious to all loaded hints.

'I don't want to break your heart,' Zac told her levelly, rather than demanding to know her source.

Freddie opened her eyes and looked languorously up at him. 'I don't fall for players, so you're safe. Anyway, my heart's fully wrapped up in the children.'

'*Que bom*…that's good,' Zac assured her, wondering why he should almost feel affronted by that comforting assurance. 'Love's a complication we definitely don't need when we're not staying together.'

Not staying together.

That reminder rocked through Freddie like an earthquake and sliced into her heart. Too proud to show any reaction, she fell still, instructing herself firmly to go to sleep. She had got too comfortable with him for a moment and had forgotten about the limits of their relationship. Perhaps she shouldn't have asked him to share the bed with her. Now she had plunged them into an intimacy that he had plainly told her was inappropriate. Of course, it was, she told herself uncomfortably. Their marriage was a sham because it was temporary and she had agreed to that condition, hadn't she?

Zac let most of his tension bleed out of him again. The innate urge to push her away had receded. She wasn't doing him any harm. She was just overly affectionate, which was a good trait for a mother of three to have, he conceded reflectively. He could share the bed, of course he could, but he still believed it would have been wiser to keep some constraint between them. After all, what they had wasn't permanent and the less they shared now, the easier it would be to part.

On the other hand, he could wake her up slowly in a few hours and revel in the benefits of sharing space, he thought with reluctant amusement. In a week or so, she might be happy to throw him into a room of his own.

CHAPTER NINE

'*No*, JACK!' ZAC thundered as the toddler's fingers wandered too close to an electric socket.

Startled, Jack fell back on his bottom and burst into floods of tears. Zac scooped him up to comfort him while Freddie traced a piece of carving on the wooden panelling with awe-inspired admiration.

'That was dangerous,' Zac told Jack ruefully as the little boy gazed at him with hurt dark eyes and a trembling lower lip. 'And drop the pathetic look, you little chancer!'

'So, what do you think of this house?' Freddie asked with fake casualness.

Zac had been with Freddie long enough to recognise a trick question. Indeed, house-hunting with Freddie was an education. For such a practical woman, Freddie was very impractical when it came to houses. Only belatedly had he worked out that Freddie's dream house was ancient, in need of a great deal of tender loving care and somewhere buried in the country. He had the penthouse suite for convenience and business meetings in the City but it was anything but a comfortable base for raising two young children.

He had given Freddie brochures for houses that were

immediately available for occupation but not a single 'wow' had escaped her lips until she had gone browsing on her own and discovered Mouldy Manor in Surrey. It was actually Molderstone Manor, he conceded grudgingly, but he preferred his own label for a property built on a shoestring in the Middle Ages and having since benefitted from a long line of penniless owners, who had been unable to afford restoration or modernisation.

'This house…it's different,' Zac selected tactfully. 'But it would be months before we could move into it.'

'But the north wing is liveable because it was rented out,' Freddie pointed out cheerfully. 'And we'd have plenty of bedroom space there. Jen and Izzy need their own space too.'

Their nannies had become Jen and Izzy, very much part of the family. Zac gritted his teeth at the reminder. He had forgotten about them. They needed more bedrooms than he had initially calculated and he didn't want to share their living space with staff round the clock. He watched Freddie caress the carved newel post of the staircase and almost groaned. 'We'll take another look at the north wing and see if it could be made habitable.'

'You realise that eventually you'll be living here alone?' Zac remarked, trudging round the two-storey north wing a second time, seeing every flaw in the tired décor and the paucity of bathrooms while Freddie waxed poetical about how quickly new bathrooms could be installed and how truly wonderful it was that the splendid plasterwork in the ceilings and walls had been preserved.

A sharp little silence fell and Freddie paled at that careless comment, that unwelcome reminder of the future that lay ahead in which Zac would walk away from her and the children. When he came back it would only be to maintain contact with the children. She wouldn't be his wife any more. She would only be the ex-wife in charge of the children and everything would be so very different. The reflection sobered her.

Only when he entered the extensive rear courtyard did Zac appreciate that Mouldy Manor could have unexpected possibilities. The stable block was enormous and the outbuildings were very good condition. 'I could ship over horses from the ranch and set up a breeding operation here,' he said then with surprising enthusiasm. 'We sell most of our most prized stallions to the Middle East.'

It was a gloriously sunny day and, determined not to spoil the day with anxious thoughts, Freddie unveiled the picnic she had brought in the overgrown garden, spreading a rug below a gnarled oak tree. At that point, Zac recognised that a brutal opinion of Mouldy Manor would be deeply unwelcome. The children were running wild in the garden with Izzy following patiently in their wake, and Freddie was beaming as she cast long languishing looks back in the direction of the house every chance she got.

'It just says family to me,' she told him with enthusiasm. 'Even though it's big, it's got cosy spaces and I could do so much with those rooms. And look at Eloise and Jack enjoying the freedom to run wild outdoors...'

Zac duly looked, to discover that unsurprisingly the kids were doing their best to resemble storybook-perfect kids passing through a flower-strewn meadow in aid of Freddie's arguments. 'And we won't be tripping over staff here,' she pointed out, having already accepted that

Zac would not live without, at the very least, a house-keeper and a cook.

Raised with domestic staff, Zac could imagine no other way of living. He didn't want his wife preoccupied with the necessities of life when he or the children wanted her attention. But Freddie found live-in staff intrusive and was only slowly adapting to her new luxury lifestyle.

'You could breed horses here,' she reminded him, relieved that he had found something to be positive about on the property.

They had been married for exactly eight weeks, having flown back from France on three separate occasions to attend adoption assessment sessions with the children. After the initial ructions, those seven weeks at the Villa Antonella had been blissfully happy. Zac had settled down and he hadn't shown any disappointment when her period had arrived within days of their wedding, confirming that she hadn't yet conceived.

That he wasn't impatient on that score was a plus, she reflected fondly. Yes, she *was* fond of him, she conceded, but fondness and love were two different things. She was fond of vanilla ice cream and even fonder of being wakened in the early hours by an insanely sexy masculine presence in her bed, but love she kept strictly focussed on the children. Zac was gorgeous and great company and many, many things she admired in a man.

He was amazingly patient with Eloise and Jack and, when Freddie had come down with a two-day virus, he had been kind in a way she had not expected him to be because those who rarely got ill usually weren't very sympathetic towards those who did. She had definitely made the right decision when she married him, she told herself happily. Of course, it would be a wrench when the time came for Zac to walk away, particularly if she didn't manage to give him a child and uphold her side of their bargain, but, knowing what lay ahead, she could prepare herself for that development. Practicality, not sentiment, she reminded herself resolutely, and there was no reason why she shouldn't enjoy their time together as a family, although sometimes she felt guilty at just how much she was enjoying being married to him.

'If you want this house, I'll buy it,' Zac breathed reluctantly.

'It's not your style, though.'

'I like the stables and I'm prepared to be persuaded,' Zac informed her, snaking out a strong arm as she knelt beside him and tipping her down onto his lap.

Freddie, demonstrating how much she had changed after two months of marriage, kissed him passionately and his arms tightened around her as he rocked her over the prominent bulge at his groin. A faint groan of frustration was wrenched from her as his arousal connected with the most intimate part of her.

'We could go back into the house and—'

'*Yes*!' she gasped with an eagerness she couldn't hide, and her cheeks reddened because just recently she couldn't seem to keep her hands off Zac and she was starting to wonder if that was quite normal or a sign that she was a little oversexed.

Zac laughed with rich appreciation. 'You really, *really* want this house.'

She gazed into his pale glittering black-lashed eyes, feeling her heart race at speed and her entire body heat to an embarrassing degree. 'I want you,' she contradicted without hesitation.

Being married wasn't so bad, Zac conceded, tugging his wife across the overgrown lawn to the house with one powerful hand. True, he had had to make explanations to Eloise about why he regularly forgot to wear pyjamas, and Jack, since he had learned how to climb out of his cot, allowed no such niceties to hold him back from a full-scale assault on the marital bed. Meal times had got messy but bath time was fun and bed time from an adult point of view was even more fun-filled, Zac acknowledged as he pinned Freddie to a wall and kissed her breathless, feeling as sexually voracious as a man who hadn't indulged in months, which would have been very untrue. But then Freddie acted on his libido like an aphrodisiac. Once was never enough and, now she was no longer as shy or nervous, she had become his dream lover, as enthusiastic and seemingly as sexually obsessed with him as he was with her. What was there not to like in that magical combination?

The skirt of her dress was up round her waist and there was a ripping sound as Zac impatiently dispensed with her skimpy silk knickers. She reckoned he preferred silk because it tore easily. Excitement sent her heart racing and her body pulsing as he unzipped, braced her back against the wall and suddenly he was there where she most needed him. She gasped and gasped again as he locked her legs round his waist to sink deeper into her slick, tender flesh. As he ground against her, possessing her with potent strength, carnal sensation pounded through her body in wave after wave until the pleasure rose to an unbearable crescendo and sent her flying high.

'You'll have to carry me back to the car,' she muttered after she had regained her voice, her head drooping down onto a broad shoulder for support. 'I'm done.'

'You can't be. You had an early night last night and you slept late this morning. I had to wake you for breakfast,' Zac reminded her, settling her down onto her own feet and bending down to retrieve her underwear and stuff it in his pocket.

Freddie swallowed back a yawn. 'You exhaust me... but in the nicest possible way,' she completed with a cheeky grin.

Zac made her pause before he opened the front door, long fingers combing through her tumbled hair to tidy it. But it made no perceptible difference. Her face was still pink from her climax and her eyes shone like stars. 'You still look like you've been thoroughly—'

'Pleasured is the word,' Freddie slotted in hastily, because Zac was trying to clean up his speech since Eloise had picked up a bad word after listening to him and if she had repeated that word once, she had repeated it a thousand times, making every adult in her radius cringe.

Zac looked down at Freddie and wished there were a bed within reach. 'Were you?'

'Thoroughly,' she told him, revelling in his spontaneous smile.

'By the way, there was something I've been meaning to discuss with you,' Zac told her in the back of the limo, Jen and Izzy and the children travelling in the car behind them. 'Who told you about the chalet girl in Klosters?'

Freddie grimaced. 'Her mother on our wedding day. I saw her with your father's party. He must have brought her, obviously not knowing how she felt about you.'

'I did first meet her in Dad's office with her mother

and then she miraculously took a job at his ski retreat the week I was staying there with Vitale and Angel. She was a desperately pushy girl and I hate being hassled. I didn't sleep with her because if I had she would have clung like a limpet.'

'OK, so she lied to her mother and made you out to be the bad guy.'

'What did her mother say to you?' Zac demanded angrily.

'Pretty much that once you slept with a woman you lost interest.'

Zac's bright eyes gleamed with amusement. 'Well, you know that's not true where you're concerned.'

But it *would* be true in the future, Freddie thought unhappily, wondering why half the gloss had seemed to fall from her image of the house once she tried to imagine living there alone with the children. When it happened, it would be the end of their marriage and change was always scary, which was probably why her mind was so stubbornly refusing to stop thinking it. She wasn't even pregnant yet, she reminded herself, and who knew how long that would take? Or how long Zac would be willing to be patient? He never forgot what they shared was temporary but she forgot it over and over again.

Her face drenched with colour as she thought about the way they had made love in the house. Zac had few inhibitions but she had encouraged him. Should she really be demonstrating that much enthusiasm with a man who was planning to *leave* her? Shouldn't pride make her a little cooler? But how was she supposed to act cooler in that department when their main objective was for her to conceive? Torn apart by those conflicting thoughts, Freddie buried them. When their marriage was over, she told herself firmly, she would have to make her peace with reality.

The following day, Zac announced that Molderstone Manor was theirs with immediate possession and that he was throwing in a local construction firm to upgrade the north wing to his standards, which would allow the main house to be renovated at a more leisurely pace.

Freddie was thrilled and she hugged him and persuaded him that a second trip had to be made down to the manor. By the time surveys came back on the property, revealing that the manor was in much better order than Zac had anticipated, he was resigned to his future home and planning a helipad in the grounds for faster access. Freddie, however, immersed herself blissfully in paint colours and upholstery fabrics, leaving Zac to choose bathroom fittings and loudly veto some of her décor choices.

Another two weeks rattled past in that manner, by which time Zac was thoroughly bored with floral fabrics that sent Freddie into paroxysms of delight and convinced him that beige was the only way to go.

'Bland…bland…bland,' Freddie contradicted. 'It's not your fault. You're too used to living in hotels.'

She was sitting on the bed with a giant pile of fabric swatches. She had dug herself into the project of turning the big house into a home to lift her mood. As summer wore into autumn, the anniversary of her sister's tragic death loomed and she was keen to visit the cemetery where Lauren had been laid to rest, even though she knew it would reanimate sad memories. Tomorrow definitely, she decided ruefully, feeling guilty that she hadn't been back there since the funeral.

Zac swept the fabric swatches off the bed and pounced on her. 'You're not allowed to bring those to bed with you.'

'It's only eight o'clock in the evening. I'm not technically *in* bed,' Freddie pointed out, gazing up into black fringed stunning eyes that were the colour of grey ice in that light.

Zac wound his fingers slowly through the silky thickness of her hair. 'But I can put you there, *meu pequenino*,' he traded, in a dark deep drawl that sent tiny shivers of awareness down her spine. 'And keep you there.'

'Arrogant much?' Freddie mocked with dancing eyes.

And his mouth crushed hers in answer. He tasted of coffee and hunger and he smelt divine. It was one of those truly perfect moments that she cherished. The bedroom was an oasis of peace for her once the children were in bed but it was also a wildly exciting but safe place to be with Zac. Her arms closed round him as his tongue tangled with hers. She decided he deserved one beige room. She could live with beige in very small quantities.

The next morning, Freddie slept in yet again and got out of bed in a rush, wondering why on earth she should be so tired when she was doing so little. Throwing on clothes in haste and only a smidgeon of make-up, she brushed her hair and went to join Zac for breakfast. The minute she entered the big reception room the smell of fried food assailed her nostrils and her stomach performed a virtual somersault, which left her cramming her hand against her mouth and racing back to the bathroom, grateful that Zac was out on the balcony and shielded from the sight. There she was very sick and, sobered by the experience, she leant on the vanity counter studying her perspiring face with wide, troubled eyes. Now that she thought about it, and she really *hadn't* been thinking about it, she began counting days very carefully back to her last period. She was almost two weeks overdue! Could she be pregnant?

Of course you could be pregnant, you idiot, she scolded herself in exasperation. After all, they had been doing everything possible to get her pregnant since the day after they had married. A faint wave of warning dizziness engulfed her when she walked briskly back into the bedroom and she sat down with a still-swimming head on the end of the bed. Pregnant? *Pregnant!* She had thought it would take months to get pregnant, she had *assumed* it would take months but, possibly, not always. She headed back into the bathroom to clean her teeth and freshen up. She could be carrying Zac's baby right now.

How long would he stay with her once she told him? That single question sliced through every other thought in her head. Of course, she would have to check that she was pregnant first because she didn't want to sound a false alarm. And if she mentioned her suspicion to Zac, Zac would take over and she would be rushed off to see some fancy doctor when she could easily buy a pregnancy test and find out for herself. Would he stay with her at least until the baby was born? Freddie's lips quivered and her eyes prickled like mad. She didn't know what was wrong with her. Maybe it was her hormones. Would he even stay with her until the baby was a few months old? She sucked in a deep breath like a drowning swimmer, struggling to compose herself.

What Zac chose to do was not her business, she

warned herself fiercely. They had an agreement. He had agreed to adopt Eloise and Jack with her and she had agreed to try and give him a child to enable him to take control of the da Rocha business empire. Obviously he couldn't leave her until the adoption was finalised, she acknowledged on a tide of sudden overpowering relief that even she couldn't ignore. And there was a couple of months yet to run on the adoption process.

Why did the prospect of Zac *leaving* fill her with horror and a deep and terrifying sense of abandonment? Practicality not sentiment, she rhymed to herself. Oh, to hell with that cop-out, she decided without hesitation. He was planning to desert her with two kids and another on the way and escape all the work and hassle of a newborn! How was *that* fair? Freddie hurtled at insane speed from misery to rage at the injustice of his plans.

This was the man she slept wrapped around every night. This was the man who enjoyed her body several times a day. This was the man planning to maroon her in the country with a house that needed a heck of a lot of work and someone with Zac's drive and energy to ensure it got done! That Molderstone Manor happened to be her dream house should carry no weight in the argument, she told herself, determined to be a martyr in every way.

'What's up?' Zac enquired lazily as Freddie tilted her nose in the air and walked to the far end of the balcony, turning her slender back to him.

'Nothing's up,' she responded, taking in a great gulp of fresh air to close out the faint aroma of fried food still on the table.

'Aren't you joining me for breakfast?'

'I'm not hungry. Where are the children?'

'Izzy took them to the park.' Zac appraised her as she turned. She looked very pale and the tip of her nose was pink as if she had been crying. 'Have you been crying?'

'Why would I have been crying?' Freddie asked stiffly. 'I've got some shopping to do.'

'I'm meeting Dad for lunch but I can do shopping as long as neither paint nor fabric choices are involved.' Zac sprang upright, every long, lean line of his powerful body defined by the beautifully tailored navy suit he wore teamed with a forest-green shirt and a silk tie. 'You're like a headless chicken when you shop. You can never make your mind up about anything.'

'I'd rather go alone,' Freddie muttered, biting at her lip. 'Because afterwards I'm planning to visit the cemetery where my sister is buried. It's the anniversary of her death.'

'Why am I only hearing about that now?' Zac queried, relieved to have grasped what had probably caused the tears he suspected. 'You know, you hardly ever mention her.'

'Doesn't mean I don't miss her. She was so good to me when I was a kid. But everything went wrong for her,' Freddie responded tightly, suddenly dangerously on the edge of tears again.

'She'd be proud of what you're doing for her children.'

Freddie said nothing because sadly her last memories of her sister only reminded her that Lauren would have sacrificed anything and anybody for her next fix. Lauren had been too lost in drugs to care about her children.

'I'm definitely coming with you to the cemetery,' Zac decreed. 'Give me a time and we'll meet up.'

Freddie gave way on that point and headed straight

out to buy a pregnancy test at the pharmacy only down the road. She then retreated back to the hotel cloakroom to get the test done. Well, actually, the *three* tests done because she didn't want to get all worked up about a possible mistake, did she? And, one after another, each test put up an unmistakeable positive and tears rolled down her cheeks. And she hated herself but she hated Zac even more for getting her pregnant so quickly. She should be happy that she had conceived and somehow that aspect had been stolen from her by their situation.

Why was that? she asked herself. Shouldn't she be rushing back up to the penthouse in the lift and sharing her good news? Zac would want to celebrate. He would be surprised it had happened so quickly for them. As he had said weeks back when she had realised that she hadn't conceived. 'We're not in a hurry.' Of course, he had had to say that, hadn't he? He didn't want her to feel stressed out about the conception plan, having already mentioned that stress wouldn't aid that goal. How had *he* known that? Had he been reading up about pregnant women?

She looked down at her flat tummy and tried to imagine a little jumping bean like Jack nestling inside her and warm acceptance spread through her at last. A little Zac or a little girl, she didn't care, only that it would be *his* child. And that was the point when it finally dawned on her that she was head over heels in love with her husband. She had broken the rules! She had gone and fallen for him in spite of all his warnings and against all common sense. The tears bubbled up again and she blinked them angrily away.

She was happy about the baby but terrified of losing Zac, and her pregnancy had to mean the beginning of the end for their marriage. There, now she knew what was wrong with her. It was fear of the massive changes ahead of her, of rebuilding a life that would seem empty without him. No more Zac. No more smiles or jokes or kisses. No more unexpected gifts. No more envious looks from other women. No more stories about Brazil. She would never visit Brazil now. Zac had been planning to take her there once the adoption was finalised but it wouldn't happen now. She had missed that boat.

She would never see the horse ranch where he had spent his early years. She would never meet his grandmother on the Amazonian rubber plantation where the old lady still lived in her retirement. She would never attend the carnival in Rio with him or see the beautiful women strolling along Copacabana beach in scanty swimwear, whom Zac had admitted fantasising about as a teenager. He had shared so much with her about his background and homeland but now he would never take her to Brazil because she was pregnant and what would be the point? From now on he would see everything through the prism of the reality that he would soon be splitting up with her.

Dear heaven, would he expect her to be all jolly and friendly about the divorce? Well, she would look like an idiot if she got upset and he realised she had become extremely attached to him. She remembered the young woman in Klosters whom he had shunned for fear that, given encouragement, she would cling to him like a limpet. Freddie had no desire to be Zac's limpet in life. She would be strong and sensible. She wouldn't let him guess how she felt.

Zac was waiting at the cemetery gates for her with

his bodyguards. He told her off for not using the limo or taking her bodyguard out with her.

'I felt like a walk alone,' she mumbled, walking through the gates with only the hum of a mower and the traffic beyond the walls infiltrating the emptiness.

'It was such a waste. She was so young,' she told him as she laid down her flowers and backed away to sit on a bench nearby.

Zac didn't voice any of the empty clichés that were often utilised in such moments. He settled down beside her and closed a soothing arm round her taut shoulders.

'I still feel so guilty,' Freddie admitted convulsively. 'I kind of used to blame her for falling into drugs but, the last year of her life, she told me something that has haunted me ever since. I wish she had told me a lot sooner and then I would've understood better, but she thought I was too young and she didn't want to upset me.'

'What did she tell you?' Zac prompted when the silence dragged on.

'We were put in a care home the first few weeks after our parents died.' Freddie struggled to control her turbulent emotions. 'When Lauren was pregnant with Jack, she told me that she was raped there but she didn't report it because she was threatened and she was scared something would happen to me. It's so ugly.'

'But not your fault. You were a child,' Zac soothed.

'You see, she changed but I didn't know why. Wherever we were she looked after me like a mother hen and then, when she got old enough to leave foster care, she fell in with a bad set of people and everything went downhill after that. She couldn't cope with life on her own.'

'You did everything you could to help her,' Zac interposed. 'Freddie... I've lost friends to drugs and not everyone is capable of what it takes to get clean. I think you need to believe that she's gone to a better place and forgive yourself for not being able to save her.'

'Yes,' she mumbled tearfully, loving him so much at that instant that she almost sobbed all over him.

'And perhaps we could get her a nicer headstone,' Zac suggested lightly.

'It was the best we could afford at the time. Claire paid for everything. Gosh, I still owe her the money for that.' Freddie sighed.

'I'll take care of it. Shall I wait at the gates for you?' Zac asked. 'Maybe you'd like to spend a few minutes here on your own.'

Nodding jerkily, Freddie watched the love of her life stride away, tall and straight and full of innate power and confidence. Lauren had said that Cruz was 'the one' for her and Freddie, who had never been in love, hadn't really understood the strength of such emotions, had not grasped that her sister simply didn't have the power to break away from her toxic boyfriend. But she understood now.

And for the first time she saw a clear path in front of her. One of the elements she most valued in her relationship with Zac was the level of honesty with which they dealt with each other. She had to tell him that she was pregnant immediately, she decided heavily. She couldn't keep secrets from him. But she *could* act on her own behalf like a strong, independent woman and walk away first.

It would hurt like hell, she knew it would, but at least it would cut out any 'will he, won't he?' scenarios in which she hoped for more from him than he wanted to give. If she made the first move, there would be no humiliating emotional scenes between them and their relationship would remain stable in the future, which was very important from the children's point of view.

Zac, after all, hadn't shifted an inch in his attitude towards their marriage. It wasn't even fair for her to expect more from him. He was good to her, *really* good, but he didn't love her, nor did he want to keep her for ever. Sadly, she wasn't 'the one' for Zac da Rocha, because if she had been he would surely have said something after two months of marriage. Instead he was still reminding her that what they had was a temporary marriage.

Her mind made up, Freddie rose from the bench to leave the cemetery.

CHAPTER TEN

'I HAVE NEWS for you,' Freddie announced with false bravado when she climbed into the limousine with Zac. 'I'm pregnant.'

'How do you know? I mean...' perplexed, Zac stared at her, black brows drawn together '...are you certain?'

'Well, I haven't seen a doctor yet, but I've done *three* pregnancy tests,' she told him.

Zac continued to stare at her, evidently astonished by her announcement. 'We'll make an appointment for today.'

'Maybe for tomorrow. That would be time enough. I'm only about six or seven weeks along at most,' she pointed out. 'So, there you are, we've done it!'

'I wasn't prepared for it to happen so soon,' Zac admitted tautly. 'But it's wonderful news.'

'Yes,' Freddie agreed. 'Hopefully by the middle of next year, you'll be sitting in the CEO chair of the da Rocha business empire. Bearing that in mind, I think it's time that we take stock of our situation and make plans for the future.'

Their *situation*? Zac didn't like that description of their marriage. He studied Freddie's flat stomach, striving to imagine a baby in there. *His* baby! He was transfixed by the concept until he recalled the many pregnancy complications that had assailed his mother. Every time he'd seen her, she had either been pregnant or just getting over another heartbreaking loss. Something very like panic attacked Zac as he looked at Freddie's fragile little body and thought in horror of all that could go wrong. *Run*, don't walk, to the doctor, he decided instantly.

'I would very much prefer you to see a doctor today, *meu pequenino*,' Zac told her squarely, wanting her tested and screened and scanned within an inch of her life at every stage of her pregnancy.

'Once we've decided what comes next,' Freddie agreed for the sake of peace as they walked back into The Palm Tree. 'Could we go into the bar for a while? I'd love a cappuccino.'

Zac glanced at her in surprise because she normally avoided the bar where she had once worked. But Freddie wanted a public space free of children in which to talk to Zac and the bar was the most convenient option. It was even better that he would soon have to leave to meet his father for lunch.

Within minutes they were seated out on the quiet terrace, free of the lunchtime crowds.

Zac was already on his phone, talking to Angel about which obstetrician Merry was seeing while she was in London. Obtaining the number, he rang and made an appointment for late afternoon. Only then did he give Freddie his full attention.

'I think we need a little distance from each other now,' Freddie informed him with a resolutely cheerful smile. 'I want to move straight into Molderstone and supervise the work there. I know the adoption application is still ongoing but you can visit whenever you like and you've got to admit that the penthouse is hopeless for the kids.'

Zac felt as if someone had crept up behind him with a large plank and bashed him on the head without warning. Her proposal had zero appeal for him. 'But—'

'It's what I want. My own space with the kids. I've hopefully met the terms of our agreement and our marriage is on the way out now.'

'It didn't feel like it was on the way out last night,' Zac was goaded into protesting.

Her colour rising at the reminder, Freddie gave him a steely appraisal. 'But we have to put that kind of stuff in the past now and work on establishing a friendly, platonic relationship.'

Zac tried hard to credit that this version of Freddie was still *his* Freddie. Native caution kept him silent. The minute she conceived, she wanted to ditch him, deprive him of the kids and move miles away to her dream house, which was probably anything but a dream house, full of workmen as it currently was. What had come over her? But she *said* this was what she wanted. Zac was in shock.

'You were keen for us to maintain a good relationship after we parted,' Freddie reminded him ruefully.

That was true, Zac conceded as he struggled to breathe evenly with a constricted chest.

'You want your freedom back,' Freddie continued.

That was true, *wasn't it*? Zac's mind was a blank at that definitive moment. All he could see in his brain was Freddie versus freedom in block capital letters although he wouldn't be moving with them.

'And just think of how free you'll be with all of us

out of your hair!' Freddie invited with yet another bright smile, as if she could hardly wait to get on the road and away from him.

A ghastly suspicion occurred to Zac then. Maybe right from the start Freddie had craved exactly this conclusion; maybe she wasn't as uninterested in his wealth as she had pretended. She had money now, a new home, and Eloise and Jack were well on the way to becoming theirs. She had kept her part of the bargain and now it was time for him to hold up his end of the deal. He didn't like the idea of *his* baby being part of a deal, but when she was so eager as to call time on their marriage the very same day that she found out she was pregnant, it was clear that she wanted *her* freedom back and had no hesitation in demanding it.

He was so angry with her that he didn't trust himself to speak. He could barely credit that only the night before they had been arguing about colour schemes for the house she was now planning to occupy without him. Or maybe her motivation was even more basic, he reasoned. Maybe she didn't like him or being married to him, which made her a heck of a good actress and him a sentimental idiot, he conceded grimly.

'Zac...?' Freddie prompted.

'We'll see Merry's obstetrician this afternoon and you can leave first thing in the morning,' Zac drawled stonily, his jaw line clenched, the exotic slant of his cheekbones flushed below eyes as cold as Siberian ice.

Freddie hesitated and weakness shot straight into the gap in her concentration.

'This is what you want as well, *isn't it*?' she pressed.

'It's pretty much what we agreed,' Zac conceded carelessly, and then he drained his expresso in one unappreciative gulp and sprang back upright, all leashed vitality and masculine restlessness. 'Look, I'd better make a move if I don't want to keep my father waiting. He hates it if you're late.'

'Give him my love.'

Zac froze and turned a chilling look on her. 'Bit pointless now, isn't it? You're on the way out of the family.'

Freddie sucked in a great shuddering breath as he strode off the terrace. She had believed he would be happier about both the pregnancy and her plans to move back out of his life. Instead he seemed angry, hostile, almost bitter. Was that because she had taken him by surprise when she had taken the lead for a change in making a major decision? She supposed it must be. Zac liked to do things at his own pace in his own way and he had been disconcerted and annoyed by her sudden decision. She wanted to weep into her cappuccino like a limp weed of a woman but she didn't. Instead, she went back upstairs to lunch with the children and pretend that she had not a care in the world.

Late afternoon, Zac reappeared to take her to the obstetrician's appointment. A lot of tests were carried out before she was ushered into Mr Simonides's presence. He confirmed her pregnancy and gave her a scan. Freddie stared rigidly at the screen, both she and Zac behaving rather like two strangers forced to share a waiting room. She wasn't used to Zac being quiet or cold and it unnerved her. The steady beat of their baby's heart broke the silence and her eyes welled up with helpless tears of awe as she concentrated on the screen showing nothing as yet recognisable as a baby.

'That's it?' Zac stood up to move closer and asked

several questions, demonstrating more interest and knowledge than she had expected.

When she walked back out onto the street, Zac wiped his damp eyes and said gruffly, 'That was fascinating. I won't miss a single appointment,' he swore.

And then, his cold façade having cracked for that split second, he got down on his knees with Eloise and Jack and patiently explained that they were moving to the house in the country where they had had the picnic but that, although he wouldn't be moving with them, they would still see lots of him. Jack didn't understand a word of that explanation but Eloise burst into tears, and Zac shot Freddie an accusing glance and hugged the little girl. A few minutes later, Zac stood up, announced that he was going out and didn't know how late he would be back but that he might not see them before they left in the morning.

Freddie was shocked by that news. It was as if Zac was rushing out of the door to reclaim his precious freedom while she was stuck for the evening with a grieving Eloise and a nauseous tummy that nothing would settle. She didn't sleep a wink that night.

The north wing was in a huge mess with builders' supplies stacked everywhere, but the required number of bedrooms and bathrooms and a temporary kitchen space were functional and Freddie gritted her teeth and got on with settling in. It was very unfortunate that she had never learned to drive because Jen had to take her shopping in the nearest town. Driving lessons were a must, she registered, and she was lucky she had the children to keep her focussed. Unfortunately, however, the name 'Zac' was flung at her by Eloise and even Jack multiple times a day, and just forty-eight hours after leaving London Freddie was struggling to cope and stay strong.

Leaving Zac had cut her in two. She had not appreciated how much she depended on him until he was gone from her life. All the sunshine in her world had evaporated. There was nothing to look forward to but the baby and the baby was making her very, very sick. The children were miserable and so was she. She fought to keep busy and tried to stop dwelling on the loss of him. After all, he would have left her anyway, and at least this way she had chosen the timing.

Zac lounged back in his usual seat on the bar terrace and drank his coffee because he was definitely feeling a little the worse for wear. Two late nights on the town in succession had drained him and coming home to the empty penthouse hadn't helped.

Freddie occupied every one of his thoughts and it was driving him insane. He remembered his first glimpse of her in the bar, the instant lust she had inspired in him. He pictured her delivering drinks, the fluid glide of her walk that by late evening would be stiff because her feet were hurting her, the cheeky grin that lit up her face when someone made her laugh, the warmth in her eyes when she looked at him. No, that was a much later memory, he reminded himself. There had been no warmth those first weeks, only distrust and wariness, and that was hardly surprising when he considered the crude way he had first approached her.

Regret and frustration coursed through Zac in violent waves. A woman had never walked out on him before. Could it really have been that his money was his sole attraction in her eyes? But the minute he considered that idea, he dismissed it again. Freddie was the woman who had offered to set him free the day after their wedding, even though that could well have meant that she lost the children and it would have seriously reduced any financial support she was entitled to receive from him. Freddie didn't have a greedy bone in her body. She had put his needs before her own that day, he finally acknowledged with regret.

What if she was doing that again? Giving *him* what she thought *he* wanted and needed?

That idea shot a bright clarifying light through Zac's dark brooding thoughts and a moment later he was on his feet and heading back up to the penthouse. It was a dull, overly silent and depressing space without Freddie and the children. He hated it. He hated waking up alone in bed as well. He hated lying about why she and the children had left London. To say that Freddie was supervising the builders was a joke because Freddie knew as much about building as he did about cooking, but for the sake of the adoption they had to keep up the illusion that they were a perfectly happy married couple...which meant that when he turned up, she wouldn't *dare* turn him away from the door!

Energised by that certainty, Zac went for a shower, decided not to waste time shaving and packed a bag, including several gifts he had bought earlier that day. He didn't want to be that kind of father though, one who visited rarely and brought presents to grease his passage. He enjoyed the daily hurly-burly of young children, recognising only now how very unnatural his own lonely upbringing had been on the ranch. He had spent half his life fiercely resenting the inheritance trust that would force him to have a child, only to discover late in the day that he liked children and that the sight of that tiny life on the screen at the doctor's had filled him with longing.

And now that he had a pregnant wife, he *should* be with her to look after her. What craziness had persuaded Freddie that she could dispense with him at such an important and dangerous time? But then Freddie wasn't very practical, Zac conceded, although she liked to think she was and he wasn't going to be the one to disabuse her of that false conviction. Freddie was a romantic, an idealist, and she had a heart as big as the planet, always looking out for others ahead of herself. He hoped she had some space left in that heart for the deeply flawed husband she had deserted. There was nothing he wouldn't do or say or utilise to get her back. Zac smiled for the first time in three days. He had always done well with a steep challenge...

As Zac climbed into a helicopter to travel to Molderstone Manor, Freddie was freaking out because the water had gone off just as she'd stepped into the shower and she badly needed to wash her hair. She'd clambered out again to find that Jack had emptied the bathroom cupboard and spilled everything everywhere while Eloise happily sprayed herself with Freddie's expensive perfume. Jen was in bed with the flu and it was Izzy's day off. Zac would have asked Izzy to pick another day but Freddie, knowing that the nanny hadn't seen her boyfriend for two weeks, couldn't bring herself to inflict that disappointment on the young woman.

Getting dressed again in her jeans and a clean tee shirt, Freddie wound a scarf through her hair to tie it out of her way and marvelled at how fast her sartorial standards had fallen. There was no Zac to dress for any more, no need for silk lingerie that only reminded her of things she would sooner forget. Gathering up the children, she went to check on Jen and found her asleep, which would probably do more to speed her recovery than anything else.

She had set up the big room off the kitchen, which was intended as a reception room, as a playroom for the kids, a safe space where neither could come to harm. She busied herself making chicken nuggets and chips for the kids and felt very guilty about it, but she needed Jen hale and hearty to drive her to the supermarket and she had to manage with what was in the freezer. If only she could manage herself half as well, she thought wretchedly, because she was so tired she could have lain down and slept on the tiles under her bare feet.

At least the fried food wasn't upsetting her to the same extent any longer and the nausea did tend to come in the morning and the ginger tea did seem to help a little. She winced as someone began hammering at a wall again and then the sound of a saw started up and she gritted her teeth. It was *her* choice to be here while the work went on, although in truth she couldn't follow the plans the master builder liked to spread in front of her every morning without fail while he shared his plans and acknowledged the problems he was having.

When Zac walked into the kitchen, she was munching on a half-cooked oven chip, and in shock at his sudden appearance she almost swallowed it whole. He looked so achingly familiar in black jeans and a dark green shirt that accentuated every lean line of his muscular physique. And *she* looked such a mess. Stupid to care about that, a little voice sniped inside her, but she did care at being caught without make-up with her hair in her mess and wearing her oldest clothes.

'I thought it was time I came for a visit,' he told her, his gaze roaming over her very slowly as though he didn't quite recognise her, and probably he didn't because she looked dreadful.

'You should've phoned, given me some warning. I hope you've eaten already because we're out of food,' she told him shakily, battling to steady herself and rise to the challenge of greeting Zac as if he were merely an old friend.

'How can you be out of food?' he demanded, and she explained about her not being able to drive and Jen being ill and Izzy off while his lean, darkly handsome face grew more and more grim.

About then she noticed the silence and peered out of the door. 'Where are the builders?'

'I told them to pack up for the day.'

'Oh…' Freddie could think of nothing to say to that, beyond, 'Maybe the water's back on!'

And mercifully it was, she discovered by dint of turning on a tap. By then Zac's presence had drawn Eloise and Jack and they threw themselves at him as if he had been absent for weeks rather than days. He produced a bag from the hall behind him and dug into it to bestow a fluffy unicorn on Eloise, her latest craze, and some kind of robot ball that was self-propelled, and which Jack immediately went off to chase round the room.

'I want to forget about the agreement we made before we married,' Zac informed her.

'But why?' she asked uncertainly.

'Because I've changed and I'm hoping you've changed too.' Zac rested his stunning eyes on her, thinking that she looked frazzled and feeling guilty because he had allowed that to happen when he was responsible for her well-being.

'What way have you changed?' she asked nervously.

'You changed my priorities. I don't want my freedom back. I've had ten years of complete freedom and it didn't bring me half as much happiness as you and the children have in two months. Two months of you wasn't enough,' he added, in case she had still not caught his drift because she was staring back at him with an expression as blank as a clean page.

'So...er...' Thoroughly confused by that speech, because her tired brain was malfunctioning, Freddie fumbled for words. 'You don't want a divorce any more?' she checked.

Zac lunged at the oven as the smell of burning assailed him, and grabbed up a dishcloth to pull a smoking selection of burning nuggets out of the oven.

'Auntie forgot them again,' Eloise told him forlornly. 'I'm hungry but now they burnt.'

'No problem.' Zac dug out his phone and spoke to his bodyguards. 'We'll order in tonight. What would you like, *meu pequenino*?'

'Anything,' she framed, too tied up in noticing that he hadn't answered her question about the divorce he had originally planned. 'But there isn't much choice of takeout round here.'

'Marco will find us something. We won't go hungry,' Zac declared, gathering Eloise up in his arms. 'Now, why don't you go and get some rest while I look after these two?'

'I can't do that.'

'Yes, you can. You're ready to pass out standing up and you shouldn't be in that condition,' Zac told her censoriously. 'You're supposed to be looking after yourself but, by the looks of it, you're not doing it very well.'

'Always the soul of tact!' Freddie snapped back at him, her colour roused, her brown eyes angry. 'I have bad days and good days and this has been one of the bad ones.'

'Which is why you need to lie down and let me take care of things,' Zac interjected impatiently.

The nagging tiredness that Freddie realised was a feature of early pregnancy, and which reduced her brain to mush, pushed Freddie up the stairs to the bedroom. He would ensure the kids ate and for one night it really didn't matter if they went to bed in the wrong pyjamas or he let them eat unhealthy stuff. But, exhausted as she was, she still trudged into the bathroom. She turned on the shower to check that both water supply and heating element were functioning before she washed herself from head to toe, slowly mulling over what Zac had said. Did the three of them make Zac happy? Had he missed them? Or had he simply missed the constant supply of sex? Was it possible that he had changed?

She fell into bed with hair that was still damp and thought about how she had changed. She had been so sure that she could keep control of her emotions and yet she had failed dismally. *She* had changed, learning what it was like to love someone even if she hadn't realise that she had loved him at the time and then learning what it was like to lose him again. She must've loved Zac when she'd offered him that annulment because she hadn't been able to bear the idea of him feeling trapped and unhappy in their marriage. Unable to reach a conclusion, she let sleep take over.

When she wakened again, it was dark outside and the bedside lamp was lit. Zac rose from the chair in the corner. 'Are you hungry?'

'Yes, but—'

'I'll bring you something.' And he was gone and clattering down the stairs before she could say another word.

She checked her watch. She had been asleep for hours. It was after eleven now and Zac was still on the premises, which meant that he was definitely staying the night. Her hopes rose exponentially and by the time he came back upstairs with a tray she was able to smile more normally at him. She looked down at the perfectly presented steak and salad in surprise.

'Marco. He used to be a chef,' Zac explained. 'He couldn't find a decent takeout place, so he bought food and cooked it for all of us, including Jen.'

Freddie picked up her knife and fork. 'Do you or do you not still want a divorce?' she demanded bluntly.

Zac leant back against the wall by the door. '*Don't...* don't want to lose you,' he extended with precision.

'And when did this change take place?' Freddie asked helplessly, because she was afraid to believe in what he was saying. 'Only a few days ago, you were telling me that—'

'I didn't know I'd changed until you walked out. I wasn't exactly on the ball with that,' Zac conceded with a sardonic twist of his mouth that could have signified embarrassment. 'I was just sailing along from day to day with you, perfectly happy, and then you exploded me out of my comfort zone.'

'By telling you that I was pregnant?' Freddie prodded.

'No, by *leaving me*,' Zac emphasised. 'I want you back. I have this big Freddie-shaped hole in my life and nothing other than you will fill it. I'm sorry that it took me so long to realise how I felt about you, but I was enjoying myself far too much with you to waste my energy psychoanalysing my...er...emotions.'

Freddie tried hard not to smile. 'And how long did it take you to work out that little speech?'

'The whole trip here,' Zac admitted with a grimace.

Freddie bent down to set the tray on the floor, her appetite having receded. She rested back against the pillows and surveyed him. He was nervous, long brown fingers clenching and unclenching, his glorious eyes intent on her. 'And how do you feel about me?'

'I love you. I've never said that to a woman before. I've never felt what you make me feel and I want to hang onto it with both hands,' he confessed in a driven undertone. 'I have a question for you.'

'No, if you tell me you love me, you have to throw yourself on the bed and kiss me passionately,' Freddie instructed gently. 'Then you can ask all the questions you like.'

An unholy grin lit up Zac's unusually sombre features and he stalked as fluidly as a jungle cat across the room to throw himself down on the bed with alacrity. 'This is why I love you. You always say the right thing at the right time...like asking me to do what I want to do anyway.'

Freddie leant primly forward, keeping the duvet

locked beneath her arms, as if making it clear that a kiss was all she was offering. His big hands spread across her cheekbones, his beautiful eyes full of tenderness. 'You don't believe me yet, do you?' he guessed.

'I'm working on it,' she mumbled, and then he kissed her and she fell into that kiss like ice cream sliding down a hot griddle, both hands clutching the front of his shirt as if she would never let him go again. She tasted him and savoured him, her head falling back as he ravaged her mouth with all the hunger she welcomed.

'So that question...' Zac dragged out the last word, his attention welded to the lush, inviting line of her swollen mouth. 'Did you walk out because you assumed that that would make me happy? Or were you teaching me a lesson?'

'I thought it would make you happy and cut out the emotional awkwardness of you having to tell me you wanted a divorce at some point. I really wasn't trying to teach you a lesson.'

'Even though I deserved it after all the times I told you *not* to fall in love with me? Please tell me you didn't listen. Please tell me that you feel the same way and that I can keep you for good,' he breathed raggedly.

'Yes, I love you, of course, I do,' she soothed him, running a gentle fingertip along the tense and vulnerable line of his full lower lip. 'I really, *really* love you and I want to be with you for ever.'

'For ever and ever and ever, like in a fairy story. You're too good for me. I've never been good. I'm often selfish. I suffer from tunnel vision. I married you sincerely believing in everything I said about our agreement and then you made me want so much more. In fact you *gave* me so much more I couldn't get enough of it or you,' he confessed in a shaken undertone. 'Your warmth, your open heart, your kindness, your sense of fun.'

'Getting a hugely swollen head here!' she warned, tears of happiness running down her cheeks.

'Why are you crying?' Zac demanded.

'Because I'm happy and I was *so* unhappy without you!' she confided convulsively on the back of a sob. 'I truly believed we were over.'

'Never. I missed you and Eloise and Jack far too much to stay away. I was lonely. I've been lonely all my life but I'm not lonely when I have you three as my family. The children are in bed, by the way,' he added. 'But Eloise insisted on wearing her princess dress to bed and Jack screamed the place down when I tried to separate him from that stupid toy I brought him, so I switched it off so it won't fire up and wake him in the middle of the night,' Zac told her. 'It plays the most horrible tunes over *and* over again.'

'He'll be bored with it by tomorrow,' Freddie forecast. 'Do you really want the children as well as me? I mean, I could never turn my back on them but you didn't sign up for that.'

'I fell in love with them too and it's largely getting to know Eloise and Jack that has encouraged me to feel that I can hardly wait to meet our baby,' Zac admitted reflectively, spreading his fingers across her flat stomach, the heat of his skin burning through the loose tee she wore to bed. 'They've taught me the basics. I'll be more useful by the time the third arrives.'

He had let the last of his barriers down and now he trusted and valued them enough to love them. She wanted to tell him that he had a warm, loving heart too, but sensed he wouldn't accept it yet though she saw that generous acceptance in his attitude to Eloise and Jack.

'I have one more confession to make,' Zac declared abruptly, resting back from her and withdrawing his caressing hand. 'And I should've made it months ago when you confronted me about it.'

'The two women at the royal ball?' Freddie exclaimed, frowning. 'I don't want to talk about that *ever*. It was your lowest moment.'

Zac winced. 'Even if nothing happened?'

'Nothing?' Freddie looked at him in open disbelief.

'I saved face at the expense of your feelings,' Zac admitted guiltily. 'Nothing happened because I didn't want either of them. I only wanted *you* and I only get turned on by you. I was too proud to tell you that at the time but I hurt you and I'm sorry for it.'

Freddie flung herself on top of him, finally convinced that he loved her because he had broken through his macho conditioning to tell her the truth. She wrapped both arms round his neck and Zac took it from there. He made love to her with all the passionate tenderness and smouldering sexiness she had learned to crave from him, but it was so much sweeter an experience when he was telling her that he loved her and holding her close in the aftermath, without feeling the need to pretend that she was the one forcing affection on him.

The toy ball woke Jack up in the middle of the night and his screams wakened the whole household, and the following day it was clear that Jack was scared of the ball because he wouldn't go near it and it had to be put away. Eloise arrived at dawn with her unicorn and her new unicorn story book and settled herself carefully between her future parents for over an hour. She was still wearing her princess dress and only gave it up when Freddie threatened to put her in the bath in it.

EPILOGUE

ON THE LAWN of Molderstone Manor, Jack, who was two and a half now, was playing ball. He was turning into an athletic little boy, Freddie mused, smiling as Eloise sat down to play with her little sister, Antonella, who was trying to crawl on her rug and not getting very far. It was a glorious sunny day and it was her youngest daughter Antonella's first birthday.

As she basked in the heat the past eighteen months played through Freddie's memory in fast and colourful images, crowded with milestones of happiness. To celebrate the adoption of Eloise and Jack, they had travelled to Brazil and had enjoyed a fabulous holiday, while also visiting Zac's elderly grandmother, Maria. Antonella had been born before that summer really took off and she was an adaptable baby with a nature as sunny and smiley as Jack's. Her hair was dark, her skin the colour of milk coffee and she looked very much like her namesake.

Zac had fussed a lot over Freddie during her pregnancy and she had been relieved that she had suffered none of the crises or complications that his late mother had endured. In fact her pregnancy had been relatively easy and the delivery straightforward. She suspected that if they decided to have another child, Zac would be considerably less prone to panic the second time around. Regardless, she was happier than she had ever hoped she could be, the shadows of past loss and pain finally laid to rest by both of them.

After their daughter's birth Zac had become CEO of the vast da Rocha business empire and during the months that followed he had flown from one end of the globe to the other, settling into his new role. Eventually he had taken Angel's advice and had hired several executive managers so that he could spend more time at home, or at least base most of his work in London. Molderstone Manor had blossomed since their first viewing and they were all now comfortably accommodated in the main house, where Zac enjoyed every comfort he craved amidst the floral fabrics he had learned to live with. His office, however, was strictly beige and functional.

The breeding stables he had established with the support of the Brazilian staff he had brought in were already doing very well. Freddie had taken a Montessori diploma course during the months that Zac was travelling most, knowing it would be useful to her when she was raising three children. Her aunt, Claire, had married her boyfriend earlier that year and Zac and Freddie had flown out to the wedding in Spain.

Jazz, now the Queen of Lerovia, strolled out of the house with her twins, Abramo and Chiara, tucked into a double buggy and walked over to join Freddie with the lack of ceremony that Freddie liked most about Zac's family. They all visited each other's homes, they all relaxed in those homes as if they were their own and, in making that effort to stay in regular contact, their husbands were getting closer and their children were growing up together.

'Where's Merry?' Freddie enquired sleepily.

'She decided to take a nap while Cosmas is down for his,' Jazz told her, for Merry's second child was a newborn and had not yet settled into a regular sleep pattern. 'And Vitale and Angel are hanging around the barbecue with Charles acting like grilling a hamburger is rocket science. Sybil's with them too.'

Merry's grandmother was Charles's girlfriend and rarely strayed from his side.

'It's so wonderfully peaceful here.' Jazz sighed, sinking down into a seat in the shade.

'Famous last words!' Freddie laughed as the racket of a helicopter disturbed the peace.

'Zac?'

'I hope so.' Freddie peered up at the sky but couldn't read the logo and then the craft circled and lowered, making identification unnecessary.

'Go and meet him,' Jazz urged. 'I'll watch Antonella.'

Freddie pelted at speed across the grass towards the helipad. Zac had been touring the mines in South Africa and Russia for two weeks and each week had felt like a month. Late-night phone calls hadn't made up for his absence. Zac sprang out of the helicopter and she raced into his arms.

'Missed you so much!' She gasped as he grabbed her up into his arms, the familiar scent and feel of him washing over her like a healing drug.

'And I missed you too,' Zac groaned, staring down at her smiling face with a wealth of love and appreciation.

He tasted her ripe pink mouth with sexy, hungry

brevity and gazed down at her with devouring crystalline eyes.

'No, we can't,' she told him as if he had asked a question, scanning his lean, darkly handsome features with a heady combination of longing and admiration. 'Later.'

'Why do we have two nannies?' Zac breathed in exasperation.

'We have your family here. Right now, we're hosts and we are not sneaking off like randy teenagers,' she declared. 'Lift a beer and be sociable round the barbecue instead.'

'I want you so much,' Zac husked in Portuguese and she could feel her bones turning to water, but at the same time she was also remembering the cracks the last time they had disappeared at such an event and the ensuing embarrassment. Sadly, Zac didn't get embarrassed about stuff of that nature. 'And I promise to make you very, *very* happy.'

'You always do,' she muttered as they returned to Jazz and the three babies.

'I was expecting you two to disappear,' Jazz told them cheerfully. 'You're famous for that.'

'Well, we've grown up a bit,' Freddie told her sister-in-law piously.

'You may have,' Zac said levelly. 'But I *haven't.*'

And with that statement, Zac swung Freddie up into his arms and carried her indoors, impervious to Angel taunting him from the barbecue. Ignoring her protests, he carried her upstairs to their bedroom and fell down on the bed with her, lamenting that she would need to go on a diet before he would try that again. Freddie thumped him with a pillow and then, suddenly, he was flattening her to the mattress and gazing down at her with an urgency that sent heat coursing through her lower limbs.

'I love you so much, *meu pequenino*,' he told her with raw sincerity. 'It's hell being away from you for so long.'

And at that admission, Freddie melted, breathlessly telling him how much she loved him while frantically tearing him out of his jeans in a generous invitation that Zac greeted with all the potent virility he could demonstrate. Freddie showered him with love and he never tired of her warmth.

'I think we should have a marriage blessing to make up for our catastrophic wedding day,' Zac told her afterwards, lying with Freddie wrapped in bliss in his strong arms. 'I've also torn up the pre-nup agreement. It wasn't fair enough to you and you signed it under duress.'

They both had a healthy appetite by the time they joined the barbecue. Zac was mobbed by the kids because he always played with them and expectations ran high.

'Freedom was never this much fun,' Zac told her before he ran off to play football with Eloise and Jack.

And with a contented sigh, Freddie cradled Antonella and sat with the new family she had gained, while marvelling in Zac's energy levels, because he had travelled for hours to get back in time for his daughter's birthday. But then that energy went into everything Zac did, she conceded, including his persistent pursuit of her. And she couldn't stop smiling at the acknowledgement that what had most annoyed her about Zac when they first met was truly his saving grace.

* * * * *

KIDNAPPED FOR
HIS ROYAL DUTY

JANE PORTER

For Kelly Hunter, Carol Marinelli,
Abby Green & Heidi Rice.

Thanks for the inspiration
and excellent company last summer!

This one is for you!

PROLOGUE

THE BRIDE WAS GONE, hauled from the chapel the way a victorious warrior carried the spoils from war.

Poppy's wide, horrified gaze met Randall Grant's for a split second before swiftly averting, her stomach plummeting. She'd been trembling ever since the doors flew open and the Sicilian stood framed in the arched doorway like an avenging angel.

She gripped her bridesmaid bouquet tighter, even as relief whispered through her. She'd done it. She'd saved Sophie.

But it wasn't just Sophie she'd helped; she'd helped Randall, too. Not that Randall Grant, the Sixth Earl of Langston, would be grateful at the moment, because he was the groom after all, and no man wanted to be humiliated in front of two hundred of England and Europe's most distinguished, their guests having traveled far and wide to Winchester for what the tabloids had been calling the wedding of the year, and would have been the wedding of the year, had the bride not just been unceremoniously hauled away by a Sicilian race car driver. Correction, *former* race car driver.

Poppy doubted that the Earl of Langston would care about the distinction right now, either, not when he had a church full of guests to deal with. Thank goodness he wasn't a sensitive or emotional man. There would be no tears or signs of distress from him. No, his notorious stiff upper lip would serve him well as he dealt with the fallout.

But she also knew him better than most, and knew that he wasn't the Ice Man people thought. She shot Randall another swift glance, strikingly handsome and still in his morning suit, the collar fitted against his strong, tan throat, accenting the lean, elegant lines of his physique, and the chiseled features of his face. He looked like stone at the present.

Detached. Granite-hard. Immovable.

Poppy swallowed quickly once more, trying to smash the worry and guilt. One day Sophie would thank her. And Randall, too, not that she would ever tell him her part in the disaster. He wasn't just Sophie's groom—*jilted* groom—but her boss of four years, and her secret crush. Although he was a very good boss as employers went, and rather protective of her, if he thought she had something to do with this wedding debacle, he'd fire her. Without hesitation. And that would break *her* heart.

But how could she not write to Renzo?

How could she not send the newspaper clipping? Sophie didn't love Randall. She was marrying him because her family had thought it would be an excellent business deal back before she was even old enough to drive. It wasn't a marriage as much as a merger, and Sophie deserved better.

So while Poppy's conscience needled her, she also remembered how Renzo had shown marauder.

It had been thrilling and impressive—

Well, not for Randall. No, he had to be humiliated. But Sophie… Sophie had just been given a chance at love.

CHAPTER ONE

SHE KNEW SOMETHING.

Dal Grant could see it in Poppy's eyes, the set of her lips and the pinch between her brows.

She'd worked far too long for him not to know that guilty as hell expression, the one she only got when she did something massively wrong and then tried to cover it.

He should have fired her years ago.

She wasn't irreplaceable. She'd never been an outstanding secretary. She was simply good, and rather decent, and she had the tendency to keep him grounded when he wanted to annihilate someone, or something, as he did now.

Most important, he'd trusted her, which had apparently been the absolutely wrong thing to do.

But he couldn't press her for information, not with two hundred guests still filling the pews, whispering giddily while Sophie's father looked gobsmacked and Lady Carmichael-Jones had gone white.

Thank God he didn't have close family here today to witness this disaster, his mother having died when he was a boy, and then his father had passed away five years ago, just before his thirtieth birthday.

Dal drew a slow, deep breath as he turned toward the pews, knowing it was time to dismiss the guests, including Sophie's heartsick family. And then he'd deal with Poppy.

"What did you do?" Randall demanded, cornering Poppy in the tiny antechamber off the chapel altar.

Poppy laced her fingers together uneasily, Randall's words too loud in her head, even as she became aware of his choice of words.

He hadn't asked *what she knew*, but rather, *what did she do*? *Do*, as in an action. *Do*, as in having responsibility.

She glanced over her shoulder, looking for someone who could step in, intervene, but the chapel was empty now, the guests disappearing far more rapidly than one would have imagined; but maybe that was because after Randall announced in a cold, hard voice, "Apologies for wasting your time today, but it appears that the wedding is off," and then he'd smiled an equally cold, hard smile, the guests had practically raced out.

She'd wanted to race out, too, but Randall pointed at her, gesturing for her to stay, and so she had, while he waved off his aunts and uncles and cousins, and then exchanged brief, uncomfortable words with Sophie's parents before shaking each of his groomsmen's hands, sending every single person away. Sending everyone but her.

How she wanted to go, too, and she'd even tried to make a belated escape but he'd caught her as she was inching toward the vestibule exit, trapping her in this little antechamber typically reserved for the clergy.

"What did you do, Poppy?" he repeated more quietly, eyes narrowing, jaw hardening, expression glacial.

Her heart thumped hard. He was tall, much taller then she, and she took an unconscious step backward, her shoulders bumping against the rough bricks. "Nothing," she whispered, aware that she was a dreadful liar. It was one of the things Sophie said she'd always liked best about her, and the very thing that had made Randall Grant, the Earl of Langston, hire her in the first place four years ago when she needed a job. He said he needed someone he could trust. She assured him he could trust her.

"I don't believe you," he answered.

Her heart did another painful thump as her mouth dried.

"Let's try this again. Where is my bride? And what the hell just happened here, and why?"

Poppy's eyes widened. Randall Grant never, ever swore. Randall Grant was the model of discipline, self-control and civility.

At least he'd always been so until now.

"I don't know where she is, and that's the truth." Her voice wavered on the last words and she squirmed, hating that he was looking at her as if she'd turned into a three-headed monster. "I had no idea Renzo would storm the wedding like that."

His dark eyebrow lifted. "Renzo," he repeated quietly, thoughtfully.

She went hot, then cold, understanding her mistake immediately.

She shouldn't have said his name. She shouldn't have said anything.

"Poppy."

She stared at his square chin and bit her lower lip hard. It was that or risk blurting everything, and she couldn't do it; it wouldn't be fair to Sophie.

Instead, she tugged at her snug, low-cut bodice, trying not to panic, which in her case meant dissolving into mindless tears. She actually didn't feel like crying; she just felt trapped, but whenever trapped, Poppy's brain malfunctioned and she'd lose track of her thoughts and go silent, and then those traitorous tears would fill her eyes.

It had happened in school. It had happened during her awful summer camps before Sophie rescued her and invited her home with her for the summer holidays. Poppy had thought she'd outgrown the panic attacks, but all of a sudden her chest constricted and her throat closed and she fought for air. Her incredibly tight, overly fitted bridesmaid gown, the icy-pink shade perfect on women like Sophie with porcelain complexions and gleaming hair, but not on short, frumpy secretaries who needed a pop of color near the face to lift a sallow complexion, suffocated her.

"I think I might faint," she whispered, not quite ready to actually collapse, but close. She needed fresh air, and space…and immediate distance from her furious employer.

Randall's black brow just lifted. "You don't faint. You're just trying to evade giving an honest answer."

"I can't get enough air."

"Then stop babbling and breathe."

"I don't babble—"

"Breathe. Through your nose. Out through your mouth. Again. Inhale. Exhale."

He couldn't be that angry with her if he was trying to keep her calm. She didn't want him angry with her. She was just trying to help. She just wanted the people she loved to be happy. Good people deserved happiness, and both Sophie and Randall were good people, only apparently not that good together. And Poppy wouldn't have sent that note to Renzo about the wedding if Sophie had been happy…

Her eyes prickled and burned as Poppy's gaze dropped from Randall's gold eyes to his chin, which was far too close to his lovely, firm mouth, and then lower, to the sharp points of his crisp, white collar.

She struggled to keep her focus on the elegant knot of his tie as she inhaled and exhaled, trying to be mindful of her breathing, but impossible when Randall was standing so close. He was tall, with a fit, honed frame, and at the moment he was exuding so much heat and crackling energy that she couldn't think straight.

She needed to think of something else or she'd dissolve into another panic attack, and she closed her eyes, trying to pretend she was back in her small, snug flat, wearing something comfortable, her pajamas for example, and curled up in her favorite armchair with a proper cup of tea. The tea would be strong and hot with lots of milk and sugar and she'd dunk a biscuit—

"Better?" he asked after a minute.

She opened her eyes to look right into Randall's. His eyes were the lightest golden-brown, a tawny shade that Poppy had always thought made him look a little exotic, as well as unbearably regal. But standing this close, his golden eyes were rather too animalistic. Specifically a lion, and a lion wasn't good company, not when angry. She suppressed a panicked shiver. "Can we go outside, please?"

"I need a straight answer."

"I've told you—"

"You are on a first-name basis with Crisanti. How do you know him, Poppy?" Randall's voice dropped, hardening.

He hadn't moved, hadn't even lifted a finger, and yet he seemed to grow bigger, larger, more powerful. He was exuding so much heat and light that she felt as if she was standing in front of the sun itself. Poppy dragged in a desperate breath, inhaling his fragrance and the scent of his skin, a clean, masculine scent that always made her skin prickle and her insides do a funny little flip. Her skin prickled now, goose bumps covering her arms, her nape suddenly too sensitive. "*I* don't know him."

His eyes flashed at her. "Then how does Sophie know him?"

Poppy balled her hands, nails biting into her palms. She had to be careful. It wouldn't take much to say the wrong thing. It wasn't that Poppy had a history of being indiscreet, either, but she didn't want to be tricked into revealing details that weren't hers to share, and to be honest, she wasn't even clear about what had happened that night in Monte Carlo five weeks ago. Obviously, something had happened. Sophie didn't return home on the last night of the trip, and when they flew out of Monte Carlo, Sophie left Monaco a different woman.

Maybe most people wouldn't pick up on the change in Sophie, but Poppy wasn't most people. Sophie wasn't just her best friend, but the sister Poppy had never had, and the champion she'd needed as a charity girl at Haskell's School. Sophie had looked out for Poppy from virtually the beginning and finally, after all these years, Poppy had found an opportunity to return the favor, which is why her letter to Renzo Crisanti wasn't about sabotaging a wedding as much as giving Sophie a shot at true happiness.

Dal battled to keep his temper. Poppy was proving to be extremely recalcitrant, which was noteworthy in and of itself, as Poppy Marr could type ninety-five words a minute, find anything buried on his desk or lost in his office, but she didn't tell a lie, or keep a secret, well at all.

And the fact that Poppy was desperately trying to keep a secret told him everything he needed to know.

She was part of this fiasco today. Of course she hadn't orchestrated it—she wasn't that clever—but she knew the whys and hows and that was what he wanted and needed to understand.

"Go collect your things," he said shortly. "We're leaving immediately."

"Go where?" she asked unsteadily.

"Does it matter?"

"I've plans to go on holiday. You gave me the next week off."

"That was when I expected to be on holiday myself, but the honeymoon is off, which means your holiday is canceled, too."

She blinked up at him. She seemed to be struggling to find her voice. "That doesn't seem fair," she finally whispered.

"What doesn't seem fair is that you knew about Crisanti and Sophie and you never said a word to me." He stared down into her wide, anxious eyes, not caring that she looked as if she might truly faint any moment, because her thoughtlessness had jeopardized his future and security. "Collect your things and meet me in front of the house. We're leaving immediately."

Poppy was so grateful to be out of the antechamber and away from Randall that she practically ran through the Langston House entrance and up the huge, sweeping staircase to the suite on the second floor that the bride and attendants had used this morning to prepare for the ceremony.

The other bridesmaids had already collected their things and all that was left was Sophie's purse and set of luggage, the two smart suitcases packed for the honeymoon—and then off to one side, Poppy's small overnight bag.

Poppy eyed Sophie's handsome suitcases, remembering the treasure trove of gorgeous new clothes inside—bikinis and sarongs, skirts, tunics and kaftans by the top designers—for a ten-day honeymoon in the Caribbean. A honeymoon that wasn't going to happen now.

Suddenly, Poppy's legs gave out and she slid into the nearest chair, covering her face with her hands.

She really hoped one day Randall would thank her, but she sensed that wouldn't be for quite a while, but in the meantime, she needed to help Randall pick up the pieces.

She was good at that sort of thing, too.

Well, pretty good, if it had to do with business affairs and paperwork. Poppy excelled at paperwork, and filing things, and then retrieving those things, and making travel arrangements, and then canceling the arrangements.

She spent a huge chunk of every day booking and re-booking meetings, conferences, lunches, dinners, travel.

But Poppy never complained. Randall gave her a purpose. Yes, he'd been Sophie's fiancé all this time, but he was the reason she woke up every day with a smile, eager to get to work. She loved her job. She loved—no, too strong a word, particularly in light of today's fiasco, but she did rather adore—her boss. Randall was incredibly intelligent, and interesting and successful. He was also calm, to the point of being unflappable, and when there was a crisis at work, he was usually the one to calm her down.

She hated humiliating Randall today. It hurt her to have hurt him, but Sophie didn't love Randall. Sophie was only marrying Randall because her family had thought it would be an excellent business deal back before she was even old enough to drive. It wasn't a marriage as much as a merger and Sophie deserved better. And Randall definitely deserved better, too.

"I came to find out what was taking so long," Randall said from the doorway.

His voice was hard and icy-cold. Poppy stiffened and straightened, swiftly wiping away tears. "Sorry. I just need a moment."

"You've had a moment. You've had five minutes of moments."

"I don't think it was that long."

"And I don't think I even know who you are anymore."

She blanched, looking at him where he remained silhouetted in the doorway. "I'm not trying to be difficult."

"But at the same time you're not trying to help. I don't want to be here. I have my entire staff downstairs trying to figure out what to do with the hundreds of gifts and floral arrangements, never mind that monstrosity of a wedding cake in the reception tent."

"Of course. Right." She rose and headed toward Sophie's luggage. "Let me just take these downstairs."

"Those are Sophie's, not yours. She can make her own arrangements for her luggage."

"She's my best friend—"

"I don't care."

"I do, and as her maid of honor—"

"You work for me, not her, and if you wish to continue

in my employ, you will get your own bag and follow me. Otherwise—"

"There's no need to threaten me. I was just trying to help."

"Mrs. Holmes manages my house. You manage my business affairs," he answered, referring to his housekeeper.

"I just thought Mrs. Holmes has quite a lot to manage at the moment. She doesn't need another worry."

"Mrs. Holmes is the very model of efficiency. She'll be fine." He crossed the room and pointed to a small, worn overnight case. "Is this one yours?" When he saw her nod, he picked up her case. "Let's go, then. The car is waiting."

Poppy's brow furrowed as she glanced back at Sophie's set of suitcases but there was nothing she could do now, and so she followed Randall down the sweeping staircase and out the front door.

Mrs. Holmes was waiting outside the big brick house for them.

"Not to worry about a thing, sir," she said to Randall, before turning to Poppy and whispering in her ear, "Poor lamb. He must be devastated."

Poppy wouldn't have described Randall as a poor lamb, or all that devastated, but Mrs. Holmes had a very different relationship with Randall Grant than she did. "He'll recover," Poppy answered firmly. "He's been caught off guard, but he'll be fine. I promise."

Randall's black Austin Healey two-seater convertible was parked at the base of the stairs in the huge oval driveway.

He put Poppy's overnight bag in the boot, and then opened the passenger door for her. The car was low to the ground and even though Poppy was short, she felt as if she had to drop into the seat and then smash the pink gown's ballerina-style tulle in around her so that Randall could close the door.

"This is a ridiculous dress to travel in," she muttered.

She'd thought she'd been quiet enough that he wouldn't hear but he did. "You can change on the plane," he said.

"What plane?" she asked.

"My plane."

"But that was for your honeymoon."

"Yes, and it can fly other places than the Caribbean," he said drily, sliding behind the steering wheel and tugging on his tie to loosen it.

"Speaking of which, should I begin canceling your travel arrangements?"

"My travel arrangements?"

She flushed. "Your…honeymoon."

He gave her a look she couldn't decipher. "I may have lost my bride at the altar, but I'm not completely inept. Seeing as I made the reservations, I will cancel them."

Her hands twisted in her lap. "I'm just trying to help."

"I'm sure you are. You are a singularly devoted secretary, always looking out for my best interests."

She sucked in a breath at the biting sarcasm. "I've always done my best for you."

"Does that include today?"

"What does that mean?"

"What do you think it means, Poppy? Or have you suddenly become exceptionally good at playing dumb?"

Dal wanted to throttle Poppy; he really did. She knew far more than she was letting on but she was determined to play her role in whatever scheme she and Sophie had concocted.

He was disgusted, and not just with them, but with himself. He'd always believed himself to be an excellent judge of character, but obviously he was wrong. Sophie and Poppy had both betrayed his trust.

He hated himself for being oblivious and gullible.

He hated that he'd allowed himself to be played the fool.

His father had always warned him not to trust a woman, and he'd always privately rolled his eyes, aware that his father had issues, but perhaps in this instance his father had been right.

Dal's hand tightened on the steering wheel as he drove the short distance from Langston House to the private airport outside Winchester. There was very little traffic and the sky was blue, the weather warm without being hot. Perfect June day for a wedding. This morning everything had seemed perfect, too, until it became the stuff of nightmares.

He gripped the wheel harder, imagining the headlines in tomorrow's papers. How the media loved society and scandal. The headlines were bound to be salacious.

Unlike Sophie, he hated being in the public eye, detesting everything to do with society. In his mind there was nothing worse than English society with its endless fascination of classes and aristocrats, and new versus old money.

He'd spent the past ten years trying to avoid scandal, and it infuriated him to be thrust into the limelight. The attention would be significant, and just thinking about having cameras or microphones thrust in his face made him want to punch something, and he hadn't wanted to fight in years.

Dal had been a fighter growing up, so much so, that he'd nearly lost his place at Cambridge after a particularly nasty brawl. He hadn't started the fight, but he'd ended it, and it hadn't mattered to the deans or his father, that he'd fought to defend his mother's name. To the powers that be, fighting was ungentlemanly, and Dal Grant, the future Earl of Langston, was expected to uphold his legacy, not tarnish it.

The school administrators had accepted his apology and pledge, but his father hadn't been so easily appeased. His father had been upset for weeks after, and then as usual, his anger finally broke, and after the rage came the despair.

As a boy, Dal had dreaded the mood swings. As a young man, he'd found them intolerable. But he couldn't walk away from his father. There was no one else to manage the earl, never mind the earldom, the estates and the income. Dal had to step up; he had to become the dutiful son, and he had, sacrificing his wants for his father's mental stability, going so far to agree to marry the woman his father had picked out for him fifteen years ago.

Thank God his father wasn't alive today. His father wouldn't have handled today's humiliation well. God only knows what he would have done, never mind when. But his father wasn't present, which meant Dal could sort out this impossible situation without his father's ranting.

And he would sort it out.

He knew exactly how he'd sort it out. Dal shot a narrowed glance in Poppy's direction. She was convenient, tenderhearted and malleable, making her the easiest and fastest solution for his problem.

He knew she also had feelings for him, which should simplify the whole matter.

Dal tugged on his tie, loosening it, trying to imagine where they could go.

He needed to take her away, needed someplace private and remote, somewhere that no one would think to look. The Caribbean island he'd booked for the honeymoon was remote and private, but he'd never go there now. But remote was still desirable. Someplace that no one could get near them, or bother them…

Someplace where he could seduce Poppy. It shouldn't take long. Just a few days and she'd acquiesce. But it had to be private, and cut off from the outside world.

Suddenly, Dal saw pink. Not the icy-pink of Poppy's bridesmaid dress, but the warm, sun-kissed pink of the Mehkar summer palace tucked in the stark red Atlas Mountains… Kasbah Jolie.

He hadn't thought about his mother's desert palace in years and yet suddenly it was all he could see. It was private and remote, the sprawling, rose-tinted villa nestled on a huge, private estate, between sparkling blue-tiled pools and exquisite gardens fragrant with roses and lavender, mint and thyme.

The spectacular estate was a two-hour drive from the nearest airport, and four hours from the capital city of Gila. It took time to reach this hidden gem secreted in the rugged Atlas Mountains, the estate carved from a mountain peak with breathtaking views of mountains, and a dark blue river snaking through the fertile green valley far below.

He hadn't been back since he was an eleven-year-old boy, and he hadn't thought he'd ever want to return, certain it would be too painful, but suddenly he was tempted, seriously tempted, to head east. It was his land, his estate, after all. Where better to seduce his secretary, and make her his bride?

The jet sat fueled and waiting for him at this very moment at the private airfield, complete with a flight crew and approved flight plan. If he wanted to go to Mehkar, the staff would need to file a new flight plan, but that wasn't a huge ordeal.

Once upon a time, Mehkar had been as much his home as England. Once upon a time, he'd preferred Mehkar to anyplace else. The only negative he could think of would be creating false hope in his grandfather. His grandfather had waited patiently all these years for Dal to return, and Dal hated to disappoint his grandfather but Dal wasn't returning for good.

He'd have to send word to his grandfather so the king wouldn't be caught off guard, but this wasn't a homecoming for Dal. It was merely a chance to buy him time while he decided how he'd handle his search for a new bride.

CHAPTER TWO

POPPY CHEWED THE inside of her lip as the sports car approached the airstrip outside Winchester.

She could see the sleek, white jet with the navy and burgundy pinstripes on the tarmac. It was fueled and staffed, waiting for the bride and groom to go to their Caribbean island for an extended honeymoon.

She'd only learned that Randall owned his own plane a few weeks ago, and that he kept the jet in a private hangar at an executive terminal in London. Poppy had been shocked by the discovery, wondering why she hadn't known before. She'd handled a vast array of his business affairs for years. Shouldn't she have known that he owned a plane, as well as kept a dedicated flight crew on payroll?

"We're back to London, then?" she asked Randall as the electric gates opened, giving them admittance to the private airfield.

"Will there be press in London?" he retorted grimly.

"Yes," she answered faintly.

"Then we absolutely won't go there."

His icy disdain made her shiver inwardly. This was a side of him she didn't know. Randall had always been a paragon of control, rarely revealing emotion, and certainly never displaying temper. But he'd been through hell today, she reminded herself, ridiculously loyal, not because she had to be, but because she wanted to be. He was one of the finest men she knew, and it could be argued that she didn't know many men, but that didn't change the fact that he was brilliant and honorable, a man with tremendous integrity. And yes, she had placed him on a pedestal years ago, but that was because he deserved to be there, and just because he was short-tempered today didn't mean she was ready to let him topple off that pedestal. "But won't there be press everywhere?" she asked carefully.

"Not everywhere, no."

"You have a place in mind, then?"

He shot her a look then, rather long and speculative. It made her feel uncomfortably bare, as if he could see through her. "Yes."

Her skin prickled and she gave her arm a quick rub, smoothing away the sudden goose bumps. "Is it far?"

"It's not exactly close."

"You know I don't have my laptop," she added briskly, trying to cover her unease. "It's in London. Perhaps we could stop in London first—"

"No."

She winced.

She knew he saw her expression because his jaw hardened and his eyes blazed, making her feel as if he somehow knew her role in today's disaster, but he couldn't know. Sophie didn't even know, and Sophie was the one hauled away on Renzo's shoulder.

Randall braked next to the plane and turned the engine off. "You can cry if you want, but I don't feel sorry for you, not one little bit."

"I'm not crying," she flashed.

"But knowing you, you will be soon. You're the proverbial watering pot, Poppy."

She turned her head away, determined to ignore his insults. She'd take the higher ground today since he couldn't. It couldn't be easy being humiliated in front of hundreds of people—

"I trusted you," he gritted, his voice low and rough. "I trusted you and you've let me down."

Her head snapped around and she looked into his eyes. His fury was palpable, his golden gaze burning into her.

Her heart hammered. Her mouth went dry. "I'm sorry."

"Then tell me the truth so we can clear up the confusion of just what the hell happened earlier today."

"Renzo took Sophie."

"I got that part. Witnessed it firsthand. But what I want to know is *why*. Why did he come? Why did Sophie go? Why are they together now when she was supposed to be here with me? You know the story. I think it's only fair that I know it, too."

Poppy's lips parted but she couldn't make a sound.

His narrowed gaze traveled her face before he gave his head a shake. "I appreciate that you're loyal to Sophie. I admire friends that look out for each other. But in this instance, you took the wrong side, Poppy. Sophie was engaged to *me*. Sophie had promised to marry *me*. If you knew she was having a relationship with another man, you should have come to me. You should have warned me instead of leaving me out there, stupid and exposed." And then he swung open his door and stepped out, walking from her in long, fast strides as if he couldn't wait to get away from her.

Poppy exhaled in a slow, shuddering breath. He was beyond livid with her. He was also hurt. She'd never meant to wound him. She'd wanted the best for him, too. And beautiful Sophie would have been the best if she'd loved him, but Sophie didn't love him. There had been no love between them, just agreements and money and mergers.

Shaken, Poppy opened her door and stepped out. She needed to fix this, but how? What could she possibly do now to make it better?

She wouldn't argue with him, that was for sure. And she'd let him be angry, because he had a right to be angry, and she'd be even more agreeable and amenable than usual so that he'd know she was sorry, and determined to make amends.

Poppy went around to the back of the car to retrieve her bag, but a young uniformed man approached and said he would be taking care of the luggage and she was to go on board where a flight attendant would help her get settled.

Poppy wasn't surprised by the brisk efficiency. Randall's helicopter was always available and his staff was always the epitome of professional but it still boggled her mind that he had a helicopter *and* a private plane. It had to be a terrible expense maintaining both of these, as well as his fleet of cars. Randall loved cars. It was one of his passions, collecting vintage models as if they were refrigerator magnets.

"What about the car?" she asked him.

"I'm driving it back to Langston House," the young man answered with a quick smile. "Do you have everything?"

"Yes."

"Good. Enjoy your flight."

Poppy boarded the plane self-consciously, pushing back dark tendrils of hair that had come loose from the pins. She felt wildly overdressed and yet exposed at the same time. She wanted a shawl for her bare shoulders and comfy slippers for her feet. But at least she wasn't the only one in formal dress. Randall still wore his morning suit, although he'd loosened his tie and unbuttoned the top button on his crisp, white dress shirt.

A flight attendant emerged from the jet's compact kitchen galley and greeted Poppy with a smile. "Welcome on board," she said. "Any seat."

The flight attendant followed Poppy down the narrow aisle, past a small conference table to a group of four leather armchairs. The seats were wide and they appeared to be the reclining kind with solid armrests and luxuriously soft leather.

She gingerly sat down in the nearest chair and it was very comfortable indeed.

"Something to drink?" the pretty, blonde flight attendant asked. "A glass of champagne? We have a lovely bottle on ice."

"I'm not the bride," Poppy said quickly.

"I know. But the wedding is off so why not enjoy the bubbles?"

"I don't think that's a good idea. I don't want to upset Randall."

"He was the one who suggested it."

Poppy laughed, nervous. "In that case, yes, a small glass might be nice. I'm shaking like a leaf."

"From the sound of things, it's been quite a day. A little fizz should help you relax."

The flight attendant returned to the galley and moments later Randall and the pilots boarded the plane. The three men stood in front of the cockpit, still deep in discussion. The discussion looked serious, too. There wasn't much smiling on anyone's part, but then, Randall wasn't a man that smiled often. She wouldn't have described him as grim or stern, either, but rather quiet and self-contained. The upside was that when he spoke, people listened to him, but unfortunately, Randall didn't speak often enough, tending to sit back and listen and let others fill the silence with their voices. Sophie thought his silence and reserve made him rather dull, but there were plenty of women who found him mysterious, asking Poppy in whispers what was the Earl of Langston *really* like?

Poppy usually answered with a dramatic pause and then a hushed, *Fascinating*.

Because he was.

He had a brilliant mind and had taken his father's businesses and investments and parlayed them into even bigger businesses and more successful investments, and that alone would have been noteworthy, but Randall did more than just make money. He gave his time generously, pro-

viding leadership on a dozen different boards, as well as
volunteered with a half dozen different charities, including several organizations in the Middle East. Randall was
particularly valuable to those latter organizations since he
could speak a staggering number of languages, including
Egyptian, Arabic and Greek.

The Earl of Langston worked hard, very hard.

If one were to criticize him it would be that he worked
too much. Sophie certainly thought so. Poppy had tried to
educate Sophie on Randall's business, thinking that if Sophie was more interested in Randall's work and life, the
couple would have more in common, and would therefore
enjoy each other's company more, but Sophie wasn't interested in the boards Randall sat on, or his numerous investments. Her ears had pricked at the charity work, because
Sophie had her own favorite charities, but the interest didn't
last long, in part because Randall failed to reciprocate. He
took Sophie for granted. He didn't try to woo her, or romance her. There were no little weekends away. No special
dinners out. It was almost as if they were an old married
couple even before they married.

Sophie deserved better. She deserved *more*.

Poppy hoped that Renzo marching down the aisle of
Langston Chapel would ultimately be a good thing for Sophie.

But even if it was a good thing, it would be scandalous.
It would always be scandalous.

Heartsick, Poppy closed her eyes and found herself wondering about Sophie. Was she okay? Where had Renzo
taken her? And what was happening in her world now?

"Guilty conscience, Poppy?"

Randall's deep, husky voice seemed to vibrate all the
way through her.

She opened her eyes and straightened quickly, shoulders
squaring so that the boned bodice pressed her breasts up.

He was standing over her, which meant she had to tilt her head back to look up at him. He was tall and lean, and his elegant suit should have made him look elegant, too, but instead he struck her as hard and fierce, and more than a little bit savage, which was both strange and awful because until today she would have described Randall Grant as the most decent man she'd ever met. Until today she would have trusted him with her life. Now she wasn't so sure.

"No," she said breathlessly, worried about being alone with him. It wasn't that he'd hurt her, but he struck her as unpredictable, and this new unpredictability made her incredibly anxious.

The flight attendant appeared behind him with the flute of champagne. "For Miss Marr," she said.

Randall took it from her and handed it to Poppy. "We're celebrating, are we?" he said mockingly.

Her pulse jumped as their fingers brushed, the sharp staccato making her breathless and jittery. She glanced from his cool, gold eyes into the golden bubbles fizzing in her flute. "The flight attendant said you were the one that suggested the champagne."

"I was curious to see what you would do."

Her eyes stung. Her throat threatened to seal closed. "Take it back, then," she said, pushing the flute back toward him. "I didn't want it in the first place."

"I wish I could believe you."

The hardness in his voice made her ache. She'd thought she'd done the right thing by writing to Renzo, but now she wasn't sure. Had she been wrong about Randall and Sophie?

Did Randall actually love her? Had Poppy just inadvertently broken his heart?

It didn't help being this physically close to Randall when her emotions were so unsettled, either. Nor did she know how to read this new Randall Grant. He wasn't anything like the quiet, considerate man she'd worked for, a man who always seemed to know how to handle her.

"You like champagne," he said carelessly, dropping into the seat opposite hers. "Keep it. I have a drink coming, too."

"Yes, but I shouldn't drink, not when working. I don't know what I was thinking."

"You were thinking that you're a bundle of nerves, and a little bit of alcohol sounded like the perfect tonic."

"Maybe. But we don't drink together. I don't think you and I have ever had a drink, just the two of us. If there was wine, or champagne open, it's because Sophie was there and Sophie wanted a glass and we never let her drink alone."

"No, we never did. We both looked after her, didn't we?"

Poppy's throat thickened. "Please don't hate her."

"It's impossible to like her right now."

Poppy stared down into her glass. "Maybe it's better if we don't discuss her."

"Four hours ago she was to be my wife. Now I'm to simply forget her? Just like that?"

She looked up at him, struggling to think of something she could say, but nothing came to her and she just gave him a look that she hoped was properly sympathetic without being pitying.

"I'm shocked and angry, not broken. Save the sympathy for someone who needs it."

"Do you want her back?"

"No."

"I didn't think so."

"Why?"

"Because even if she did decide she'd made a mistake, I don't think you'd forgive and forget. At least not for a long time."

The corner of his mouth curled. "I don't like being

played for a fool, no," he said, giving her a long, penetrating look that made her squirm because it seemed to imply that he also thought *she* had played him for a fool. And if that was the case, then spending the next week working together was asking for trouble. He wouldn't be in a proper state of mind.

The flight attendant appeared with a crystal tumbler. "Your whiskey," she said, handing him the glass. "Captain Winter also wanted you to know that the new flight plan has been approved, and we'll be departing in just a few minutes."

"Thank you," Randall said, giving the attendant a warm smile, the kind of smile he used to give Poppy, the kind of smile that had made her put him on a pedestal in the beginning.

And just like that, tears filled her eyes and she had to duck her head so he wouldn't see. Because if she did look at him, he'd see more than she wanted him to see. Randall was startlingly perceptive. He paid attention to people and things, picking up on details others missed.

"I knew it wouldn't be long before you got weepy," he said, extending his long legs, invading her space. "Before this morning, I would have said you are nothing if not predictable, but you surprised me today. You're not at all who I thought you were."

She drew her legs back farther to keep her ankles from touching his, and told herself to bite her tongue, and then bite it again because arguing with him would only make the tension worse.

He gave his glass a shake, letting the amber liquid swirl. "Did you know about Crisanti?"

Poppy continued to bite her tongue, because how could she answer that without incriminating herself? Clearly in this case, the best answer was no answer.

"Poppy."

The flight attendant was closing the door and locking it securely, and the deliberate steps made Poppy want to jump out of her chair and race off the plane. She should go now, while she could do. She needed to escape. She needed to go. She couldn't stay here with Randall—

"My bride was carted off from the church today, and she didn't even make a peep of protest," he continued quietly, almost lazily, even as his intense gaze skewered her. She didn't even have to look at him to know he was staring her down because she could feel it all the way through her.

Poppy swallowed hard. "I think she peeped."

"No, she didn't. And neither did you." He growled the words, temper rising, and she jerked her head up to look at him, and the look he gave her was so savage and dark that Poppy's pulse jumped and her stomach lurched.

"You weren't surprised to see Crisanti marching down the aisle today," he added, lifting a finger to stop her protest. "Enough with the lying. It doesn't become you. You forget, I *know* you. I've worked with you, worked closely with you, and I saw it in your face, saw it in your eyes."

"Saw what?"

"Guilt. But I also saw something else. You were happy to see Crisanti arrive. You were *elated.*"

"I wasn't elated."

"But you weren't devastated."

She placed the flute down on the narrow table next to her. "I'd like to take my vacation time, the time you promised me. I don't think it's a good idea to work together this next week. I think we both need some time, and time apart—"

"No."

"I can take the train back to London."

"No."

"I don't enjoy you like this—"

"Perhaps it's not about you anymore, Poppy. Perhaps it's now about me."

"I don't understand."

"I want to know what happened today. I want to know everything."

His voice was deep and rough and it scratched her senses. She dragged her attention up, her gaze soaking in his face. She knew that face so well, knew his brow and every faint crease at the corner of his eyes. She knew how he'd tighten his jaw when displeased, and how his lips firmed as he concentrated while reading. If he was very angry, his features would go blank and still. If he was relaxed, his lovely mouth would lift—

No. Not lovely.

She shouldn't ever think his mouth was lovely.

Even though she'd vanished, he still belonged to Sophie. He'd always belong to Sophie. They'd been engaged since Sophie was eighteen, with the understanding that they'd be married one day happening even earlier in their lives.

The fact was, Randall and Sophie had been practically matched since birth, an arrangement that suited both families, and the respective family fortunes, and Sophie insisted she was good with it. She'd told Poppy more than once that she hadn't ever expected to marry for love, and wasn't particularly troubled by the lack of romance since she liked Dal, and Dal liked her, and they complemented each other well.

A lump filled her throat because Poppy didn't just like Randall, she truly cared for him. Deeply cared. The kind of feelings that put butterflies in her stomach and made her chest tighten with tenderness. "It's not my place," she choked. "I wasn't your bride!"

"But you were part of today's circus. You took part in the charade."

"It wasn't a charade!"

"Then where is Sophie?"

His question hung there between them, heavy and suffocating, and Dal knew Poppy was miserable; her brown eyes were full of shadows and sorrow, and usually he hated seeing her unhappy. Usually he wanted to lift her when she struggled but not today. Today she deserved to suffer.

He'd trusted her. He'd trusted her even more than Sophie, and he'd planned on spending the rest of his life with Sophie.

Dal shook his head, still trying to grasp it all.

If Sophie had been so unhappy marrying him, why didn't she just break the engagement before it got to this point?

It was not as if he didn't have other options. Women threw themselves at him daily. Women were constantly letting him know that they found him desirable. Beautiful, educated, polished women who made it known that they'd do anything to become his countess, and if marriage was out, then perhaps his mistress?

But he'd been loyal to Sophie, despite their long engagement. Or at least he'd been faithful once the engagement had been made public, which was five and a half years ago. Before the public engagement was the private understanding, an understanding reached between the fathers, the Earl of Langston and Sir Carmichael-Jones. But for five and a half years, he'd held himself in check because Sophie, stunning Sophie Carmichael-Jones, was a virgin, and she'd made it clear that she intended to remain a virgin until her wedding night.

He now seriously doubted that when she'd walked down the aisle today she'd still been a virgin.

Dal swore beneath his breath, counting down the minutes until they reached their cruising altitude so he could escape to the small back cabin, which doubled as a private office and a bedroom.

Once they stopped climbing, he unfastened his seat belt and disappeared into the back cabin, which had a desk, a reclining leather chair and a wall bed. The wall bed could easily be converted when needed, but Dal had never used it as a bedroom. He preferred to work on his flights, not rest.

Closing the door, he removed his jacket, tugged off his tie and unbuttoned his dress shirt. Half-dressed, he opened the large black suitcase that had been stowed in the closet and found a pair of trousers and a light tan linen shirt that would be appropriate for the heat of the Atlas Mountains.

Hard to believe he was heading to Mehkar.

It'd been so long.

No one would think to look for him in his mother's country, either, much less his father's family. Dal's late father had orchestrated the schism, savagely cutting off his mother's family following the fatal car accident twenty-three years ago.

It was on his twenty-first birthday that his past resurrected itself. He'd been out celebrating his birthday with friends and returned worse for the wear to his Cambridge flat to discover a bearded man in kaffiyeh, the traditional long white robes Arab men wore, on his doorstep.

It had been over ten years since he'd last seen his mother's father, but instead of moving forward to greet his grandfather, he stood back, aware that he reeked of alcohol and cigarette smoke, aware, too, of the disapproval in his grandfather's dark eyes.

Randall managed a stiff, awkward bow. "Sheikh bin Mehkar."

"As-Salam-u-Alaikum," his grandfather had answered. *Peace be to you.* He extended his hand, then, to Randall. "No handshake? No hug?"

It was a rebuke. A quiet rebuke, but a reproof nonetheless. Randall stiffened, ashamed, annoyed, uncomfortable, and he put his hand in his grandfather's even as he glanced away, toward the small window at the end of the hall, angry that his mother's father was here now. Where had he been for the past ten years? Where had his grandmother gone and the aunts and uncles and cousins who had filled his childhood?

He'd needed them as a grieving boy. He'd needed them to remind him that his beautiful mother had existed, as by Christmas his father had stripped Langston House of all her photos and mementos, going so far as to even remove the huge oil family portrait only completed the year before, the portrait of a family in happier days—father, mother and sons—from above the sixteenth-century Dutch sideboard in the formal dining room.

Perhaps if Dal hadn't spent a night drinking, perhaps if Dal's phone call with his father the evening before hadn't been so tense and terse, full of duty and obligation, maybe Dal would have remembered the affection his mother had held for her parents, in particular, her father, who had allowed her to leave to marry her handsome, titled, cash-strapped Englishman.

And so instead of being glad to see this lost grandfather, Dal curtly invited his grandfather in. "Would you like tea? I could put the kettle on."

"Only if you shower first."

And Randall Grant, the second-born son who shouldn't have become the heir, the second son who had never flaunted his wealth or position, snapped, "I will have my tea first. Come in, Grandfather, if you wish. But I'm not going to be told what to do, not today, and certainly not by you."

Dark gaze hooded, Sheikh Mansur bin Mehkar looked his oldest living grandson, Randall Michael Talal, up and down, and then turned around and walked away.

Randall stood next to his door, his flat key clenched in

his hand, and watched his grandfather head for the steep staircase.

He should go after him.

He should apologize.

He should ask where his grandfather was staying.

He should suggest meeting for dinner.

He should.

He didn't.

It wasn't until the next morning that Randall discovered the envelope half-hidden by the thin doormat. Inside the envelope was a birthday greeting and a packet of papers. For his twenty-first birthday he'd been given Kasbah Jolie, his mother's favorite home, the home that had also been the Mehkar royal family's summer palace for the past three hundred and fifty years.

He wouldn't know for another ten years that along with the summer palace, he'd also been named as the successor to the Mehkar throne.

But both discoveries only hardened his resolve to keep his distance from his mother's family. He didn't want the throne. He didn't want to live in, or rule, Mehkar. He didn't want anything to do with the summer palace, either, a place he still associated far too closely with his beloved mother, a mother he'd lost far too early. It was bad enough that at eleven he'd become Viscount Langston following his older brother's death. Why would he want to be responsible for Mehkar, too?

Poppy glanced up and watched as Dal approached. He'd changed into dark trousers and a light tan linen shirt, the shirt an almost perfect match for his pale gold eyes. He looked handsome, impossibly handsome, but then, he always did. She just never let herself dwell on it, knowing that her attraction was unprofessional and would only lead to complications. Gorgeous, wealthy men like Randall Grant did not like women like her. Why should they when they could have the Sophie Carmichael-Joneses of the world?

"Your turn," Randall said shortly. "And once you change, please throw that damn dress away. I never want to see it again."

"Where is my bag?"

"In the closet in the back cabin."

Poppy located her worn overnight bag in the closet but when she opened it, she had only her nightgown, travel toiletries, a pair of tennis shoes and her favorite jeans. The jeans and tennis shoes were good, but she couldn't leave the cabin without a shirt.

Poppy sat back on her heels and tried to remember where she'd put the rest of her clothes. Had they gotten caught up in Sophie's things? Or had she left them at the hotel when they checked out this morning?

Suppressing a sigh, she returned to the chairs in the main cabin.

The flight attendant was in the middle of setting up a table for a late lunch, covering the folding table with a fine white cloth before laying out china plates with thick bands of gold, crystal stemware, and real sterling flatware.

"You didn't change," Randall said, spotting her.

"I don't have a blouse or top or…or bra…for that matter."

"You could borrow one of my shirts, and braless is fine. It's just me here. I won't stare."

There was nothing provocative in his words and yet her face and body flooded with heat. "Then yes, thank you. Because I'm ready to get out of this dress, too."

He rose from his seat, stepping around the table, and she followed him back to the cabin. The private cabin was small, and felt even tinier when Randall entered the room with her.

She stepped back so he'd have room to open his suitcase and find a suitable shirt for her.

"What are you wearing on the bottom?" he asked.

"Jeans."

He rifled through his clothes, selecting a white dress shirt with blue pinstripes for her. "This should cover you," he said.

"Thank you."

He nodded, and he turned to leave and she took a step to give him more room but somehow they'd both stepped in the same direction and now he was practically on top of her and he put out a hand to steady her, but his hand went to her waist, not her elbow, and his hand seemed to burn all the way through the thin silk fabric, and she gasped, lips parting, skin heating, her entire body blisteringly warm.

In the close confines of the cabin, she caught a lingering whiff of the cologne he'd put on this morning and it was rich and spicy and she wanted to step closer to him and bury her face in his chest, and breathe him in more deeply.

He smelled so good, and when he touched her, he felt so good, and it was frightening how fast she was losing those boundaries so essential to a proper working relationship.

"Looks like we're tripping each other up," he said, his deep voice pitched so low it made the hair on her nape rise and her breasts tighten inside her corset, skin far too sensitive.

"I'm sorry," she said breathlessly. "I didn't mean to get in your way," and yet she couldn't seem to step away, or give him space.

His hands wrapped around her upper arms and he gently but firmly lifted her, placing her back a foot, and then he exited the small cabin without a glance back.

Poppy exhaled in a rush, shuddering at the extreme awkwardness of what had just taken place. She'd walked into him, and then stayed there, planted, as if she'd become a tree and had grown miraculous roots.

Why?

Poppy carefully closed the door and then pressed her shoulder to the frame, wishing she could stay barricaded in the cabin forever. It was one thing to have an innocent crush on your boss, but it was another to want his touch, and Poppy wanted his touch. She wanted his hands on her in the worst sort of way. Which raised the question, what kind of person was she?

Poppy had always prided herself on her scruples. Well, where were they now?

CHAPTER THREE

POPPY STRUGGLED WITH the minute hooks on the pink dress, freeing herself little by little until she could wiggle out of the gown. The dress had been so tight that it had left livid pink marks all over her rib cage and breasts. It was bliss to finally be free and she slid the shirt on, buttoning the front. The fabric had been lightly starched and it rubbed against her nipples, making them tighten. She prayed Randall wouldn't notice. Things were already so awkward between them. She'd always thought they had the ideal relationship, professional but warm, cordial and considerate, but today had changed everything.

Today he overwhelmed her, and her brain told her to run but there was another part of her that desperately wanted to stay.

And be touched.

That was a very worrying part of her.

She'd have to work hard to keep that part in check, because elegant, refined Randall Grant was one thing, but dark, brooding Dal Grant was something else altogether.

Poppy finished changing, stepping into the soft, faded jeans that now hung on her hips thanks to four months of determined dieting, and after pulling the pins from her hair, she slipped her feet into her tennis shoes and headed back to her seat.

While she was gone, the flight attendant added a low arrangement of flowers to the center of the table, the lush red and pink roses reminiscent of the bouquet Sophie had carried this morning. The flowers made Poppy heartsick and guilty all over again.

"You look more comfortable," he said as she slid into her seat.

"I am."

"Tell me your sizes and I'll have some basics waiting for us when we land."

"I can shop for myself, thank you."

"There won't be shops where we're going."

"Where are we going?"

"Jolie."

The flight attendant appeared with the salad course, and Poppy waited for Randall to reach for his fork before she did the same. "Is it a country house?" she asked.

He didn't pick up his fork, or answer right away, instead he glanced away, his long black lashes lowering, accenting the high, hard lines of his cheekbones.

She'd always thought he had the most impressive bone structure, with his lovely high cheekbones, strong jaw and chin coupled with that long nose. Sophie had always disdained of his nose—not refined enough—but Poppy had disagreed, thinking he had the nose of a Roman or Greek.

"Something like that," he finally answered, his dark head turning, his light gold gaze returning to her, studying her for a long moment, making her feel strangely lightheaded. And breathless. Far too breathless.

Poppy inhaled slowly, trying to settle her nerves. She'd had a crush on him for four years and she'd managed to keep her feelings in check. There was no reason to let herself get carried away just because he was suddenly single.

And free.

Her heart did a funny little beat, the kind of beat that made her feel anxious and excited, but neither emotion was useful. She needed to settle down and be calm and steady and strong.

"You're not doing much to clarify things." She tried to smile, a steady, professional smile. "Where is it exactly?"

"Out of the country."

Did he just say out *in* the country, or out *of* the country? It was a tiny preposition, but a significant difference. "Where is the nearest airport?"

"Gila."

She touched the tip of her tongue to her upper lip as her mouth had gone dry and her stomach was doing a wild free fall. "I'm not familiar with Gila."

"The capital of Mehkar?"

For a moment she still didn't understand, unable to process what he was saying, and then everything inside her did a horrifying free fall. "We're going to *Mehkar*?"

"Have you been before?"

"No."

"It neighbors Morocco—"

"I know where it is, but we can't go to Mehkar!"

"Of course we can. We're en route now."

"But how? Why? It's hours away and I have no passport, just an overnight bag with virtually nothing in it at all."

He shrugged carelessly. "Sophie had nothing when she left the church, did she?"

Poppy's throat sealed closed and she stared at Randall, heartsick. He stared right back, his light gold gaze hard, so hard that it made him look like a stranger.

"You're not worried about her, are you?" he added, his voice dropping, deepening, an edge of menace in his tone.

A shiver raced through her. In the past hour Randall Grant had gone from chivalrous to dangerous.

"Answer me," Randall demanded, leaning forward, his anger altogether new. The Randall Grant she knew was impossibly calm, impossibly controlled.

"I didn't agree to leave the country," she said, voice rising, tightening. "I didn't agree to go to Mehkar. I'd like to return to London immediately. I have work to do—"

"You work for me."

"But the work I need to do for you is all there," she said, making a jabbing motion behind them. "So, please ask your captain to turn around and take me back to Winchester, or to London, so I can take care of the one hundred and one things that need to be done by Monday."

"You can do them in Mehkar."

"But I can't."

"You can, and you will, because it's your job to handle this crushing mountain of work I've tasked you with."

"I never said it was crushing."

"You make it sound crushing."

"I do have a lot of responsibility, and I take my work seriously. Nor do I want to let you down."

His firm lips quirked, but it wasn't a friendly smile. "I don't think that's true at all." His gaze slowly traveled across her face, as if examining every inch. "In fact, I know it's not true."

Heat rushed through her and she felt every place his gaze touched grow uncomfortably warm. "No?"

"No." He was about to add something else, but the flight attendant appeared to remove their salad plates even though neither of them had barely touched the greens.

Randall remained silent the entire time she was gone, and stayed silent while their next course was placed before them. Poppy stared down at her seafood risotto, feeling increasingly queasy. Seafood risotto was Sophie's favorite, not hers. Poppy didn't like seafood, or risotto.

She looked up at Randall to discover that he was watching her intently, his dark head tipped back against the pale leather seat, lids lowering, lashes dropping, concealing part of the golden glimmer. "If you valued your position with me, Poppy, you would be loyal to me. Yet, you're not."

For a second it seemed as if all the oxygen in the plane disappeared and she stared at him, lips parting, but no air moving in or out of her lungs. No air, and no words, either, because what could she say? How could she defend herself?

"Have you found a new position, Poppy?"

She shook her head, eyes stinging.

"Are you interviewing?"

She shook her head again.

"Résumés out...inquiries...networking?"

Poppy's stomach twisted. "No. I am not job-hunting. I like my job."

"Is that so?"

"Yes."

"Then maybe it's time you showed me some loyalty, Poppy Marr, and tell me what you know about Sophie and this Crisanti fellow."

She deserved that. Because she had taken sides, hadn't she? She'd taken Sophie's. Sophie was her best friend. Her only friend. If Sophie was queen, Poppy would be her lady in waiting. "I would like to help you," she said, stomach still churning, nerves and nausea. It didn't help that the smell of the risotto was making her want to gag. She carefully pushed her bowl away. "But I don't really know much of anything."

His set expression indicated he didn't believe her. "But you know something," he said. "So let's start with that. How long has Sophie known Crisanti? Where did she meet him?"

"I don't want to do this, and it's not fair of you to ask me when you know Sophie is the only one who has ever looked out for me—"

"Are you saying I haven't?"

He'd spoken lowly and yet his words vibrated all the way through her. She clutched the edge of the table, panicked and overwhelmed, not simply by what he was asking, but by the unreality of their situation.

She'd harbored the crush for years, falling for him almost from the very start as he was handsome and intelligent and wildly successful and best of all, he was kind to her, and always so very thoughtful, mindful of her feelings even when things were stressful at work.

It was on one of those terribly stressful days that Poppy had overshared with him, blurting out her fears and insecurities that she'd always be single, because men wanted women like Sophie, women who were strong and confident, women that made men feel like men.

Randall had sputtered on muffled laughter and then he shook his head, eyes smiling. "You can't compare yourself to Sophie. That's not fair of you. Sophie is Sophie Carmichael-Jones for a reason. There's only one of her, but also, there is only one of you. The key, Poppy Marr, is to be you."

"I don't think that's enough," she answered tearfully.

"Trust me, it's more than enough."

And as he'd looked at her, his gold eyes still smiling, she'd melted into a puddle of aching gratitude, want and wishful dreams. *Imagine* having Randall Grant as your champion. Imagine him in your corner, as your partner. Poppy had never been more envious of Sophie in all her life.

Poppy swallowed hard now, a lump in her throat. "You've always been very, very kind to me. Probably better than I deserve."

"So why only protect Sophie? Why not try to protect me?"

"But I did!" she choked. "I wasn't just trying to help Sophie. I was trying to help you, too!"

"So how did you help us?" he asked softly, silkily. "What did you do?"

He'd done it. He'd trapped her, cornered her, and she'd all but confessed.

Horrified, Poppy tried to run, but Randall caught her by the wrist as she attempted to leave the table. His fingers tightened around her slender bones, and he pulled her toward his side.

"Tell me," he said quietly, tugging her closer to his chair. "Let's have the truth."

She tried to pull free, but he was so much stronger than she was, and then he began to stroke the inside of her wrist with his thumb, lightly running the pad of his thumb over her wildly beating pulse. It was the most electric sensation, her nerves jumping, dancing, sending little rivulets of feeling everywhere.

"Sit," he said, drawing her toward him, and then pulling her down so that she perched on the arm of his chair. "Talk. The truth now."

But how could she think, much less say anything coherent, when his thumb was caressing her wrist, making her tingle all over?

She looked up into his eyes and her breath caught as she saw something in his eyes she'd never seen before.

Heat. A fierce, raw, masculine heat that was completely at odds with the man she knew.

But then his thumb caressing her pulse was equally at odds with Randall Grant, the Earl of Langston. The Earl of Langston was elegant, disciplined, restrained. The Earl of Langston did not want *her*.

"I can't think when you're doing that," she said under her breath.

"And I can't have you running off every time the questions get uncomfortable." He moved his hand, sliding it from her wrist up over the flat of her hand so that they were palm to palm, his long fingers pressing against hers, parting them.

She shivered at the press of his hand to hers. It felt wildly indecent.

"I would say this is far more uncomfortable than any of your questions," she whispered, trying to slip her hand out, but only succeeding in dragging her palm down his, sending sparks of sensation up her arm, through her breasts and into her belly below.

His fingers laced through hers, holding her still.

She looked down at their joined hands because there was no way she could look into his face right now. "I don't think this is proper."

"It's a little late to worry about propriety, Poppy. So tell me what you did. You don't need to tell me why. I think we both know the why."

She closed her eyes, mortified, not sure if he was suggesting what she thought he was suggesting.

She prayed he wasn't suggesting...

She prayed...

Just then the plane lurched and dropped, caught in a violent stream of turbulence, and Randall clamped his arm over her thighs, his hand locking around her knee, holding her steady. "I have you," he said.

And he did, she thought wildly, eyes opening as heat and desire rushed through her.

He'd touched her before—a hand to her elbow as he assisted her across a gravel car park, or a touch to her shoulder when entering a crowded lift to nudge her forward—but never like this. Never anything like this, and she was suddenly riveted by the sight of his hand on her knee, his fingers as lean and strong and elegant as the rest of him.

She'd imagined this, though, hadn't she?

Poppy smashed the little voice but it was too late, the little voice wouldn't be silenced. It was beyond inappropriate to have feelings for him in the first place. Randall Grant was Sophie's fiancé and her employer, and Poppy would rather cut off her right arm than embarrass Sophie, or Randall. But that didn't mean the feelings weren't there, suppressed. Buried.

She worked hard to keep them mashed down, too. And

one of the ways she contained her feelings was by keeping a proper distance from him.

She didn't let herself stand too close, or bend too low.

She didn't look him in the eye more than was necessary.

She dressed conservatively, even frumpishly, so no one could accuse her of trying to play up her assets—not that there were too many of those.

And she called him Randall, not Dal like his other friends, because she wasn't his friend. She was his secretary and on his payroll, and those were key distinctions.

She couldn't ever risk forgetting herself.

She couldn't risk dropping her guard, letting him see that beneath her professional demeanor was a real woman…a woman who wanted nothing more than to see him happy. Because Randall Grant was many things—brilliant, wealthy, strategic, successful—but he wasn't happy. In fact, he didn't seem to allow himself to feel emotions at all.

Perhaps that was what troubled her most. He would give the shirt off his back to someone in need, but he never asked for anything in return.

He never took anything from anyone, or wanted anything for himself.

He just existed in his space and sphere, brilliant and handsome and impossibly solitary.

Sophie had never seemed to notice. In her mind, Dal was just one of those introverts…a loner…and content to be alone, but Poppy didn't agree. Of course she kept her opinion to herself. But instinct told her that Randall Grant hadn't always been so alone, and that his isolation was perhaps the result of his being raised by a difficult father.

"I think you should let me go, Randall." Her voice was soft, almost broken.

"Maybe, but I don't think I shall. I quite like having you close. You have no defenses right now, making it impossible for you to lie."

"You're more of a gentleman than that."

"Oh, Poppy, you don't know me at all."

"That's not so. I know you quite well—"

"You've made me into someone I never was. Your impression of me is sweet, and flattering, but absurdly false. I am no gentleman, and am anything but chivalrous."

"I'd like to return to my chair now."

"Why? Isn't this what you always wanted? Haven't you wondered what it would be like to be Sophie, engaged to me?"

Poppy stiffened. She couldn't move, or blink, or speak. She couldn't do anything but sit frozen while shame suffused her heart. *He knew?* Dear God, did he really know? All these years she'd thought she'd been so good at hiding her feelings, hiding her attraction, and yet apparently she hadn't hidden anything well at all.

But then she forced the thought back, not willing to go there, not willing to be stripped emotionally bare before him. "How much whiskey did you drink?" she flashed, praying he hadn't heard the wobble in her voice.

"The one glass. I'm not drunk." He leaned back against his leather seat, infuriatingly relaxed. "And you can play it cool, and pretend you don't know what I'm talking about, but we both know the truth. I'm not trying to shame you—"

"It certainly feels like it, and I don't appreciate it. I was supposed to be going on holiday in the morning. I haven't had a proper vacation in years and this should have been the start to a vacation and instead you have me trapped on your plane, listening to your insults."

"It's not an insult."

"For you to imply that I've been dying for you to kiss me, yes, that's an insult because until five hours ago you were marrying my best friend."

"I never said Sophie knew. You were remarkably good at concealing your feelings when she was around."

"I don't have feelings for you!"

His expression of amused disbelief made her want to throw up.

"Can we agree on soft spot?" he suggested with the same insufferable smile.

Poppy shuddered. She averted her face, trying to hide behind her shoulder. "I miss the old you, the nice you. Can you please bring Randall Grant back?"

"Randall Grant is dead."

Her head jerked up and her gaze met his.

He nodded, expression almost sympathetic. "Yes, dead, because he never existed. I am Dal Grant, and have always been Dal. You made me into this Randall who was good and kind and considerate, but that's not me. It never has been."

"Fine. You're Dal Grant. Congratulations." She yanked on her hand, struggling to free herself, struggling with a new, feverish desperation. "Now, let me go."

"Not yet."

"Why not?"

"Because we need to finish establishing a few things—"

"I think we've established quite a lot already. You're Dal, not Randall. You're not a nice man and you never have been. You think I betrayed you—"

"I *know* you betrayed me."

"And you want me to betray Sophie."

"But you don't want to do that."

"Of course I don't. And I won't."

"Because she was your champion. She protected you from the time you were just a charity case at Haskell's—"

"Stop, just stop."

"I understand more than you think I do. I know more than you think I do, too. I know you grew up poor and insecure, and how you believed that you had to be perfect, or close to perfect, because one misstep and you could lose it all. Your scholarship at Haskell's. Your friendship with Sophie. And then later, your job with me. Sophie once said that the reason you were so dependable was because you knew life was precarious and fraught with uncertainties. You'd told her that the best way to survive, and maybe the only way to survive, was by being necessary to those around you. So you became Sophie's rock. And then my rock."

"You were Sophie's rock, too," he continued, "but she's gone now, and that leaves just you and me."

She flushed deeply, even as her body throbbed with awareness. Randall's arm still lay across her thighs, and his hand continued to cup her knee, and her pulse was beating so hard that her head felt woozy. "I don't like the way you make that sound."

"How am I making it sound?"

"As if there is something…illicit…between us. But there is nothing illicit. There is just a work relationship, and this—" she broke off, gesturing to the chair and the place she sat "—is not proper or professional and I'm asking you to let me go so that I can return to my chair."

"Did you not invite Renzo to my wedding today?"

Her stomach rose and fell and she stared into Randall's golden eyes, stricken. Had Renzo contacted Randall? Had there been communication of some sort between the two men?

But no, that couldn't be. There was no way.

He was making wild guesses, trying to unsettle her, and it was unsettling, but he didn't know anything and she could not, absolutely could not, give him details. Let him speculate all he wanted, but it would be disastrous if she confirmed her part in today's debacle.

Stay calm, she told herself. *Don't panic.*

And don't feel, and don't think about how warm Randall's hand is, or how heat seemed to radiate from him to her, seeping into her skin, making her aware of how large his hands were, and how the pressure of his forearm across her thighs made her feel tingly, and tingly wasn't good. Tingly was dangerous.

"It's not disloyal to care for us both," he added after a moment.

"I won't say more. I'm done talking."

"I could get you to say more. I could get you right now to tell me everything." He must have seen her expression because his mouth eased and his eyes warmed. "One kiss—"

"For God's sake, stop!" Tears filled her eyes and reached up to wipe them away before they could fall. "I know you've had a bad day. I know this has to be one of the worst days of your life, but why must you torture me? I love Sophie, and I love you—"

She broke off, horrified to have said so much, to have admitted the depth of her feelings. She closed her eyes, teeth biting into her lower lip to keep it from trembling, and yet she couldn't stop the tears from falling, one after the other, but she gave up trying to catch them, or stop them.

It didn't matter.

Nothing mattered anymore.

"I quit," she whispered. "I'm done. Consider this my formal resignation. As of now, I no longer work for you and the moment we land, I'm gone."

CHAPTER FOUR

DAL RELEASED HER, and Poppy returned to her chair, but Dal was fully aware that she didn't eat anything, choosing to simply stare out the window, the very picture of martyred innocence.

But she wasn't innocent. She was responsible today for his being on this plane, now, a single man, and he wasn't just holding her accountable. He fully expected her to solve his problem, saving him from failing his father.

Dal had never been close to his father but he'd made a vow to his father when he was dying, and he fully intended to keep the promise.

Which meant, he needed a wife. Quickly.

Thank goodness Poppy was available. She wasn't the wife his father had wanted for him, but she'd definitely do in a pinch.

Sadie, the flight attendant, appeared to check on them and when she saw that neither of them had eaten the risotto she asked if there was something else she could bring.

"The cheese plates," Dal answered. "And whatever chocolates you might have. It's an emergency."

Poppy muttered something unflattering beneath her breath and Dal looked at her, eyebrow rising. "You once said chocolate helps everything."

"Well, not *this*."

"I think you're wrong. I think once you eat some proper food and then have some excellent chocolate you'll calm down and realize you don't want to walk away from me in Mehkar, at the Gila airport—"

"Why not? It's supposed to be a gorgeous country."

"Without a passport, or money, or bra. Mehkar is not as

conservative as some of our neighbors but it's still an Arab country with a traditional culture."

"I can't believe you felt the need to mention the bra."

"Men are men."

"Well then, once we land, and you get out, send me back to England in your plane. That way I won't be stranded and my lack of undergarments won't create alarm."

"And what will you do once you're back in London?"

"Go on the holiday. Sleep in. Enjoy the freedom of being unemployed."

"And then when you're properly rested you'll begin looking for a new job."

"Yes."

He studied her thoughtfully. "But won't it be hard to get a decent position without references? I'd think you'd need me to put in a good word for you. You did work for me for four years after all."

"That's not fair."

"What happened today in the chapel wasn't fair, either."

"Sophie always did say she knew you better than I thought. Clearly, she was right."

His secretary was so disillusioned that he almost felt sorry for her. "It will be better tomorrow."

"What will be?"

"The disappointment. You'll realize it's just a temporary setback, and life goes on."

Poppy glared at him, her brown eyes flashing. "Thank you for that extremely deep and insightful philosophy lecture."

Sadie returned with two cheese plates, each plate filled with cheeses, crackers and fruit, along with a bowl of chocolates. She set the plates down, centered the bowl of chocolate and disappeared.

Dal watched Poppy try to ignore the chocolates and cheese plate. It was almost comical because he knew how much she loved both things. "You really will feel better if you eat something."

She refused to look at him, her smooth jaw set, lips pursed, expression mutinous. He'd never seen this side of her. She had a temper. He was pleased to see it, too. He'd worried that she had no backbone. He'd worried that Sophie had taken advantage of her generous nature.

"There is no reason to continue the starvation diet," he said. "The wedding is over. No one is going to compare you to Sophie's stick friends."

Poppy gave him an indignant look. "They're not sticks. They're models."

"They're annoying."

"You really think so?"

"You've never noticed that they live on their phones? For them, social media is more important than real human interaction."

"It's because they get paid for their Instagram posts. The more likes they get, the bigger the bonuses."

He rolled his eyes. "I find that very hard to believe."

"It's true. I didn't know it until one of them explained that modeling has changed. Lots of their jobs are pictures for their Instagram accounts."

"I'm still not impressed."

"Are you being serious? You really didn't like them?"

"Did you?" he retorted.

He seemed to have caught Poppy off guard and she paused to think about her answer. After a moment her shoulders shrugged. "They were nice enough to me."

"But?"

"I wasn't one of them."

"Of course not. You weren't an actress or a model—"

"Some of them are just horsey girls. They live for polo."

"You mean, rich men who play polo."

"You don't sound very complimentary."

"I knew I was marrying Sophie, not her social scene."

Poppy regarded him for another long moment, her wide brown eyes solemn, her full mouth compressed, and he was glad she was nothing like Sophie's other friends. He was glad she was short and curvy and fresh-faced and real. She was Poppy. And she was maybe the only person in his life who could make him smile.

"But maybe that was part of the problem," she said now, picking her words with care. "Maybe you needed to like her world better. Sophie is quite social. She likes going out and doing things. She was never going to be happy sitting around Langston House with you every weekend."

"It's a wonderful house."

"For you. It's your house. But what was she supposed to do there all day?" When he didn't answer she pressed on. "Have you ever looked at her? Really looked at her? Sophie is one of the most beautiful, stylish women in all of England. *Tatler* adores her—"

He made a dismissive noise.

Poppy ignored him. "Everyone in the fashion world adores her. Sophie is smart and glamorous and she is very much admired, but you…you only saw her as the woman who would beget your heirs."

When Dal's mocking smile disappeared Poppy felt a stab of pleasure, delighted that she knocked his smug, arrogant smile off his smug, arrogant, albeit handsome, face, but then when he rose and walked away, the pleasure abruptly faded.

Chewing the inside of her lip, she watched him walk to the back, heading for his private cabin in the rear of the jet. After he disappeared into the cabin, the door closing soundlessly behind him, she sank back into her seat, deflated, as if all the energy had been sucked from the cabin.

So much had just happened that she couldn't process it all.

Poppy didn't even know where to begin taking apart the conversations and the revelations, never mind examining the intense emotions buffeting her.

Randall—Dal—knew about her infatuation, and had implied that Sophie probably knew, too. And then Poppy, in a burst of uncharacteristic temper, had quit.

Poppy sighed and rubbed her brow, gently kneading the ache. Was she really going to leave him, after four years of working for him? After four years of trying to deny her feelings?

And did it matter that he knew her secret?

On one hand it was incredibly uncomfortable that Randall—Dal—knew, but on the other, so what?

She had feelings for him. Why should that make her feel ashamed? Why were feelings even considered shameful? She'd been emotional in her entire life. From the time she was a little girl, she'd felt things intensely. Her sensitive nature had made her a target for the girls at Haskell's. They'd enjoyed teasing her about being a charity case. They'd enjoyed mocking her lack of coordination and athletic ability. They'd enjoyed her discomfort at being forced to remain at school for holidays because her parents couldn't afford to bring her home.

And then wonderful, lovely, courageous Sophie stepped in and made the teasing and bullying stop. But she didn't just make the teasing stop; Sophie changed Poppy's life when she confessed that she respected Poppy's kindness and good heart. Suddenly, Poppy wasn't embarrassing but someone that Sophie Carmichael-Jones admired.

So of course Poppy had never acted on her feelings for Randall. She would never, ever be disloyal to Sophie. At the same time, what harm had there been secretly caring for Randall? Her devotion made her a better assistant. Her dedication making her more sensitive and attuned to his needs.

But now her secret was in the open. Did it have to change everything? Did she *want* it to change anything?

Did she want to say goodbye to Randall?

Poppy didn't know the answer to the first two questions but she knew the answer to the third. She didn't want to leave Randall. And the way she felt about him, she'd never want to leave him, but how could she continue working for him like this?

It wouldn't be the same. She'd feel self-conscious and he'd be awkward. Better to end things while she still cared about him. Better to say goodbye while she wanted the best for him.

But just admitting that she had to go broke her heart.

Dal closed his computer, rose from his desk and put away the computer in his briefcase. The jet had just begun the final descent for Gila and he'd not only canceled the essential pieces of the honeymoon but had also created a short list of possible countess candidates to share with Poppy when he returned to the main cabin.

The list was for show. There was only one woman he was considering to be his wife, and that was his secretary, but if he told Poppy she was the one and only name, she'd be terrified. Far better to ease her into her new reality, and it would be her reality because Dal had to be married by the time he turned thirty-five, and his birthday was just sixteen days away.

Which meant he had sixteen days to find a new bride and marry her as he wasn't going to lose Langston House, or the earldom, or any of the other Grant estates, because he'd failed his father.

He'd grown up with enough abuse. He wasn't going to let his father win, even if he was in the grave.

So he'd marry Poppy and prove his father wrong and then Dal would finally be free of this burden he'd carried that he wasn't his brother Andrew, and that he wasn't fit to be the Earl of Langston, and he didn't deserve the Langston House and estates.

Now he just needed to convince her that she was the perfect future countess.

Dal left the back office and returned to his seat in the main cabin. As he took his seat, Poppy stirred sleepily in her chair. Her lashes fluttered open for a moment before closing again. "You," she murmured crossly.

"Yes, me," he answered, his gaze sweeping her, studying her for the first time in an entirely different light.

She wasn't his secretary anymore, but his future wife, which meant not just overseeing Langston House and the thousand different domestic tasks that encompassed, but also bearing him the necessary Grant heirs.

It wouldn't be difficult taking her to his bed. She was pretty and tidy and wholesome, although at the moment she looked flushed and rumpled from sleep, her brown hair down tumbling to her shoulders while a rebellious tendril clung to her pink cheek.

His dress shirt overwhelmed her small frame, but it was refreshing seeing her in something other than her conservative navy and brown skirts, which she paired with equally conservative cardigans. In warm weather she swapped the jumpers for trim white blouses with oval collars and half sleeves. Her work wardrobe was neither well cut nor flattering, and while the pinstripe shirt wasn't flattering, it revealed her curves. Poppy Marr was voluptuous with hourglass curves. Full breasts, tiny waist, rounded hips. He suddenly wished she wasn't wearing jeans so he could see her legs. He'd very much like to see her in nothing but his shirt, and then without the shirt altogether.

"What do you want now?" she demanded, stretching and covering a yawn.

"We should be landing soon."

"Good."

He'd never noticed how firm her chin was until now. It matched her new backbone. He liked the spirit. Spirit was sexy and strong and his future countess would need to be strong.

"I'm not sending you back to England," he said casually. "You owe me two weeks after giving notice. It's in your employment agreement. You can't just quit and walk away."

Her dark lashes slowly lifted and she stared at him, clearly unhappy. "You're going on holiday. You don't need me."

"I'm not on holiday, and I do need you."

"For what?"

"To help find your replacement. I can't possibly interview for a new secretary and a new wife at the same time."

She stared at him blankly. "You're already trying to replace Sophie?"

"She's gone, isn't she?"

"Isn't that rather…callous?"

"Did you expect me to mourn her?"

"She was loyal to you for five and a half years!"

"But she decamped at the last possible second, and the fact is, I need a wife, quickly."

"You've never needed anyone, and yet now you must have a wife, immediately."

"It does sound ridiculous put like that, but that pretty much sums it up."

"I don't understand."

"It's a very convoluted story so I'll give you the short version. I must be married by my thirty-fifth birthday or I lose the earldom, the house and everything attached."

She was still for a moment before she sat upright in her chair. "Your birthday is July sixteenth."

"Correct."

"That's just…a few weeks away."

"Correct again."

She impatiently shoved hair behind an ear, away from her flushed cheek. "This sounds like something from a novel."

"I'm fully aware of the ridiculousness of my situation, but my father set up the trust that way. When he died just after my thirtieth birthday, I inherited the title, but there were provisions."

Silence followed his words. Poppy looked absolutely appalled.

Dal shrugged, adding. "My father thought he was being clever. Exerting control from beyond the grave, and so forth."

"When did you find out? At the reading of the will?"

"No, although wouldn't that have been a shock? Surprised my father didn't think of that. But no, I've known since my early twenties, and did my best not to think about it until I was nearly thirty."

"Did Sophie know this?"

"Sophie was part of my father's plan. He hand-selected her for me."

"This just keeps getting worse."

"She didn't ever tell you?"

"Heavens, no. But probably because she knew I'd disapprove. No wonder she ran at the last second. I would run, too. Poor Sophie."

"Sophie benefitted from the arrangement...until she didn't." He shrugged carelessly. "But now there is a serious time crunch. I have to be married in sixteen days. It's hard enough closing a big deal in two weeks, but to find a wife in the same amount of time? It's not going to be easy."

"And there is no way out of this?"

"No. But trust me, I tried. I've spent a fortune in legal fees and finally accepted that marriage really is the only solution."

She bit her lip and looked away, a sheen of tears in her eyes. "I am so upset."

In his shirt, with her thick hair loose and her slim legs curled up in the seat of her chair, she exuded youth and a sweet, innocent sensuality that teased his senses.

"Don't be," he answered her, forcing his attention from her lips to the sweep of her cheekbone and the strands of dark hair framing her pale oval face. "There is no point in both of us being upset."

"I know I shouldn't say it, but the more I learn about your father, the more I dislike him."

"He was a very tortured man."

"It sounds as if he did his best to torture you."

This was not a comfortable conversation. Dal couldn't even remember the last time he'd discussed his father with anyone. "I'd like to believe it wasn't intentional. I'd like to think he just…couldn't help himself."

She rubbed her eyes and drew a deep breath and turned to look at him, focused now on the goal. "So you need a wife."

"Yes."

"Have you given thought to possible women you could see…proposing to?"

"Yes. I've thought about it carefully and made a short list." He reached into his pocket and pulled out the sheet of paper where he'd scrawled the names, handing it to her.

He sat back, studying her face as she skimmed the list. For a moment her expression was blank and then her head shot up, her rounded eyes matching her dropped jaw.

"I don't appreciate the joke," she said shortly, folding the sheet of paper in half and thrusting it back at him. "Take it."

"I couldn't be more serious."

"Obviously you don't really mean to marry in the next two weeks."

"Why not? You don't think any of the three could be suitable?"

"Perhaps the first two," she said bitingly, "but not the third. She's not rich or a Sloane Ranger."

He unfolded the sheet of paper and glanced down at the three names.

Seraphina Woolton
Florrie Goodwin
Poppy Marr

"But number three is smart and generous and easy to like," he answered, rereading the names.

"That would be very nice if you were a vicar, or a primary school teacher, but you're not. You're from one of the oldest, most prominent families in England and you need an appropriate wife, someone sophisticated, respected and connected."

"I do?"

"Obviously. It's what your father dictated, and it explains why you and Sophie had all those contracts and agreements."

"Yes, but that was with Sophie, and exclusive to my engagement to her. There is nothing that stipulates who my replacement bride should be."

"You started with a very small list, and it's just grown shorter as we're crossing number three off."

"Are we?"

"Yes. Poppy Marr is not an option, which means we'll need to focus on Seraphina and Florrie."

"But Poppy Marr *is* an option. All three names on that list are options. I thought quite seriously about each possible candidate—"

"Please don't use the word *candidate*. It's dreadful. It's as if you're trying to hire a woman to fill a position."

"Being the Countess of Langston is a job."

"Then definitely take Poppy Marr off your list. She's not interested in that position."

"Why not? We work well together."

"Because this new *job* requires skills that are outside my area of expertise." Her cheeks flamed and her eyes glowed bright. "Nor have I any interest in acquiring the skills necessary to be the Countess of Langston."

Heat surged through him, and he hardened as he pictured her fulfilling her marital duties. His trousers grew uncomfortably tight as he imagined introducing her to those duties. "I would teach you."

"No."

"I'd be patient."

"We're ending this discussion now. It's not going to happen. It's not even a remote possibility. I'm not interested in jumping from your office to your bedroom. I like the you in your office."

"Randall," he said dismissively.

"Yes, Randall. Polite, controlled, chivalrous. I don't trust Dal at all."

"That's probably wise."

"Excuse me. Who are you? I don't even know you anymore!"

"I suspect it's because you never did."

"If that's the case, does anyone know you?"

His wry smile faded. That was an excellent question, and he had to think about it for a minute before answering. "Probably not."

More silence followed, and then Poppy broke it with a heavy sigh. "You have no idea how sad that makes me."

"And you, my dear Poppy Marr, have just moved into melodrama."

"Just because I feel things doesn't mean I'm being melodramatic."

"I have found that emotions unnecessarily complicate things."

"Probably because you were taught that emotions were bad things."

"No one has ever told me anything about emotions. My views are based on firsthand experience. Excessive emotion is toxic and damaging."

"What about good emotions? What about love and joy and—"

"That's Gila in the distance," he said mildly, cutting off her impassioned stream of words. "You can see the skyline on the horizon."

She shot him an indignant look, letting him know that she didn't appreciate him interrupting her, before craning her head to see out the window.

He watched as the city loomed nearer, surprisingly eager to see how much he recognized of the Mehkar capital. He'd heard that elegant, historic Gila had become a new, modern, urban city, but the change hadn't registered until now when he saw the dozens of new skyscrapers dotting the skyline.

As they approached the airport, they flew over lakes and glittering pools, and oases of green amidst the marble and glass. The captain turned just before they neared the historic neighborhoods, the ones Dal knew best as it was home to the royal palace, the place where his mother had grown up.

His mother loved to show off her hometown when they used to visit every year. They never went to Kasbah Jolie without first visiting their grandfather and family in Gila. One of their grandfather's drivers would take them out in one of the classic cars he loved, and they'd travel the wide, pristine boulevards lined with stately palm trees, boulevards that led to museums and palaces as well as her favorite shopping district.

To a boy, Gila represented family and history and culture. It never crossed his mind that it was a playground to others—sensual, sexy, hedonistic. It wasn't until he was at Cambridge that his friends talked about going to Mehkar on holiday, that Gila with its white marble and endless man-made lakes, was nonstop entertainment. His friends never understood why Dal wouldn't want to go on holiday to an exotic desert country famous for its hotels, restaurants, shopping and nightlife.

"I had no idea Gila was so big," Poppy said after a moment.

"There has been a lot of new development in the past twenty years. The people of Mehkar love their sports, and their toys."

"Sophie's friends used to come here for the polo tournaments."

"But not Sophie?"

"No. She always said she wanted to visit. Mehkar was on her bucket list." Poppy gave him one of her reproving looks. "But you should have known that, though. You were her fiancé, and engaged forever."

"Not forever, just five and a half years."

"Which is pretty much forever to a twenty-six-year-old." She continued to frown at him. "If you didn't discuss travel, and bucket lists, what *did* you discuss?"

He didn't immediately reply. The jet was dropping lower, and faster, a rapid descent, which meant they'd be on the ground soon before making the quick transfer to his helicopter, and Poppy would be making the transfer with him, too.

"Sophie and I didn't talk a lot. But I think you know that," he said as the wheels touched down in an impossibly smooth landing. They were still streaking down the runway, but soon they'd begin to slow.

"You can't blame her," Poppy answered. "Sophie wanted to be closer to you. You just wouldn't let her in."

And that was also probably true, he thought, but he didn't want to continue discussing Sophie. Sophie was part of the past. She'd chosen a different path, a different future, and it was time for him to focus on his future.

The jet turned at the end of the runway and began the slow taxi toward the small, sleek, glass and steel terminal.

"Women feel close through word and language. We bond through talking—"

"I'm not ready for another lecture on emotions," he interrupted firmly in the authoritative voice he used when he needed to redirect Poppy, and he needed to redirect her now.

"I'm trying to help you."

"That may be the case, but I'm not in the right frame of mind to be presented with my overwhelming failures as a man."

"You're not a failure. But you could work on your emotional intelligence—"

"Poppy!"

She pressed her lips together, her expression defiant, and he drew a deep breath, trying to hang on to his patience.

"I thought you said you had only sixteen days to find a wife," she said in a small but still defiant voice.

Where had this new Poppy come from? She was beyond stubborn, and while he appreciated persistence, now was not the time. She had no idea how unsettled he felt. It was difficult returning to Mehkar. He was already dreading getting off the plane and transferring to the helicopter. Mehkar represented his mother and his carefree summer holidays with his brother at Jolie. He'd never truly dealt with their deaths. He'd just stopped thinking about them and now he was thinking about them and it wasn't a good day to be feeling overwhelmed.

Dammit.

Why had he thought that going to Kasbah Jolie was a good idea?

How had he thought this could be positive?

He shouldn't have come. He should have stayed put at Langston House and weathered the media storm and focused on wooing Poppy there. Instead, he was here, jumping from the proverbial fire into the frying pan.

Dal could see the helicopter ahead. He also saw the cars and the crowd and the royal security details. The black helicopter wasn't just any helicopter but the royal Mehkar helicopter, the elegant gold crest as familiar to him as his mother's face and name. His heart thudded, his chest tight and hard as he battled memories and a past that gave him nothing but pain.

Maybe one day he'd be able to remember his mother without feeling the grief. Maybe after he'd spent a week at Jolie he'd be more peaceful when he thought of Mehkar. In his teens he used to dream of the summer palace and gardens, and when he woke up, his lashes would be damp and his stomach cramping as though he'd swallowed glass.

All through his twenties he'd continued to miss his mother profoundly. He'd missed his brother, too, but it was his mother that he had been closest to. His mother had been the anchor when his father struggled. Andrew had somehow been able to block out their father's volatility, but Dal, the sensitive second son, hadn't been able to unplug from the drama and chaos.

Dal wasn't proud of the boy he'd been. Sensitive boys were no good to anyone and it took his father ten years to stomp the sensitivity out of him, but Dal survived, and became a man, and a relatively successful, stable man.

The jet came to a stop. His flight attendant, Sadie, rose from her seat to open the door. But Dal didn't move, not yet ready.

He turned to Poppy, who was reaching for her seat belt. "So we're in agreement, then? You give me the full two weeks I'm due, and then if you still want to leave, I'll personally put you on a plane home. But I need the two weeks, and I need you available, round the clock if need be."

Poppy's gaze met his. She held his gaze, too, not afraid to let him see the full measure of her disapproval. "Round the clock sounds excessive. I'm not your nursemaid, I'm your secretary. And at the end of the two weeks, I will most definitely still go, so don't just focus on finding your wife. Work on the replacement for me, too."

"I trust you to find me a suitable secretary."

"You're leaving the entire task to me?"

"You know what I like, and what I need."

Her brows arched over her clear brown eyes. "You might regret this."

"Possibly. But I'm in a bind, Poppy, and you're the only one that can save me."

"Now you're laying it on a tad thick."

The corner of his mouth lifted. "You like to be needed."

Two spots of color burned in her cheeks. "But I draw the line at becoming a business transaction."

He said nothing and silence stretched and yet she never once looked away.

"I don't think I've ever refused you anything," she said after a moment, "but I am now. I won't be manipulated. You have two weeks and then I'm gone."

It had taken every bit of Poppy's courage and strength to stand up to Randall—Dal—and define her terms, because if she didn't make it absolutely clear, then she'd find it very hard to resist him.

It had nearly melted her when he'd said he needed her. She liked being needed, and once upon a time, she would have given everything to hear him say that he needed *her*.

But things had changed, circumstances had changed, and she couldn't continue in his employment, not when he knew she had feelings for him. He'd use the knowledge to his advantage. He'd be able to manipulate her far too easily.

As it was, he was intimidating. Not frightening intimidating, but thrilling. He was so very handsome, and so very polished and so very accomplished.

Every time he entered a room, he seemed to light it up. She loved the way he moved, and the way he frowned and the way he'd focus on whatever he was reading.

She loved the way he held his teacup—

Oh, heavens, she loved him. She did. And it had been excruciating trying to manage her feelings and her attraction when he'd been engaged to Sophie. How could she possibly manage her envy and jealousy as he began to court someone new? She'd hate the new woman. She'd resent her far too much. It wouldn't be comfortable for any of them.

Poppy rose from her seat and smoothed her men's shirt, and then her hair, tucking it behind her ears to control the thick wave.

Dal was leaving the jet, descending the stairs, and she kept her eyes on his broad shoulders as she followed him down the five steps and onto the wide red carpet banded by gold. The brilliant crimson carpet was something of a shock, but even more surprising was the sheer number of people gathered on the tarmac.

There were rows of robed men, and then rows of armed men, and even a couple of men with what looked like musical instruments.

Dal, for his part, did not look pleased by the welcome. From the set of his shoulders and the rigid line of his back, she knew he was tense and angry. She fully expected him to step onto the carpet and proceed toward the helicopter. Instead, he turned to her and offered his hand, to aid her down the last few steps.

She felt a little silly accepting his help when she was

wearing jeans and tennis shoes, not the staggeringly high heels Sophie preferred. But his fingers closed around hers, and he gave her hand a quick, reassuring squeeze as she stepped from the stairs onto the carpet.

And then he let her hand go and he started walking down the carpet, which stretched from the plane to the side of a huge black helicopter with a gold emblem on the helicopter's door. The same gold emblem filled the middle of the crimson carpet, and two rows of men in long white robes and headwear stood on either side of the carpet.

It was intimidating as hell, she thought, swallowing nervously, picking up her pace to catch up to him. "Dal," she whispered, taking in the men farther back, the armed ones, with their big guns and vests and helmets. "Who are all these people?"

"The welcoming committee," he answered.

Well, the welcoming committee was bowing now to Dal, every head nodding as he passed. A shiver coursed through her as she trailed after him. It was the strangest greeting she'd ever seen, and beyond formal, reminding her of the ceremony reserved for England's royal family.

Poppy didn't know what Randall had done to earn such a welcoming, or what the emblem of sword, lamb and crown represented, but clearly the government of Mehkar was aware of his arrival today, and clearly the government of Mehkar wanted Dal to know they respected him.

At the helicopter Randall stopped and clasped hands with a robed man that looked close to Randall's age. The man said something to Randall in a foreign language, and Randall answered in the same language, and then they shook hands, and the handshake became a swift hug, and then the hug became a longer, warmer embrace.

When Randall stepped back, there was a sheen in his golden eyes, and a flicker of emotion that Poppy had never seen before. But then the emotion was gone and Randall's

features were hard, and his expression remote. He assisted
Poppy into the helicopter and she glanced back at the men
Randall had called a welcoming committee, and it was only
then that she noticed the rows of cars farther back, black
limousines with tinted windows.

"That was quite impressive," she said, sliding into the
seat by the far window and reaching for the harness.

"It was," he agreed as the pilot shut the helicopter door.

She felt dazed by the pomp and ceremony. "Who do you
have to know to get a welcoming like that?"

"The king."

Her eyes widened. "He's one of the men you work with?"

"In my international work? No. My relationship with
King Hamid is personal. I've known him my whole life."
Randall hesitated. "King Hamid is my mother's father."

It took her a second to put the pieces together. "He's
your *grandfather.*"

Randall nodded once. "My mother's father."

"That's why you received such a royal welcome."

"Here in Mehkar I am not Randall Grant, the Sixth Earl
of Langston, but rather Sheikh Talal bin Mehkar."

It had been a day of shocks and surprises and this one
was just as stunning. Poppy stared at him, bewildered.
"You're a…*sheikh*?"

CHAPTER FIVE

POPPY'S HEAD THROBBED, the thumping at the base of her skull making her feel as if her head would soon explode. He was a sheikh *and* an earl? How was it possible?

Furthermore, how could she not know? Did *anyone* know?

It was one thing not to know that he had a private jet stashed in London, but another not to know his mother was a princess from Mehkar!

But thinking about it, Poppy realized she'd never read anything in the papers about his mother's family. There was very little in the society magazines about who she was, or where she came from, and Poppy knew because she used to read everything she could on Dal, and there were stories about his father, and his father's family, and lots of stories about Langston House itself, but very little about his mother. Some articles did briefly mention the tragic car accident that took the life of his mother and brother, but that was all that was ever said.

Now Poppy wondered if it was the Fifth Earl of Langston who'd kept his wife's name from the papers, or if it had been the royal family of Mehkar?

Poppy glanced at Dal. He was giving that impression of stone again, the same look he'd had this morning in the chapel. Detached. Immovable. It wasn't really a good look. It made her worry even more. "Dal?"

"Mmm?"

"Are you okay?"

"Never better," he answered mockingly.

She sighed and looked out the window, her stomach doing a little free fall when she did.

She'd been in helicopters before. She'd traveled with Randall in his helicopter dozens of times over the years, accompanying him to meetings, taking notes, pulling together his travel details, but the London-based helicopter was small compared to this one, and that one never flew over jagged mountains marked by narrow, deep ravines.

She tried not to look down. She didn't want to see just how close they were to the mountains, or how far from civilization, either.

There was nothing here.

Just scrub brush. The occasional flock of sheep. What seemed to be a sheepherder's hut made of mud and stacked stone.

Poppy exhaled softly, fingers curling into her palms, telling herself to relax. Not worry. But how could she not be concerned? The Randall Grant she thought she knew was gone, and this new man was even more complex and mysterious. "I know you said you didn't want to discuss Sophie anymore," she said carefully.

"Right."

"But I've been thinking about what you said, and how you feel betrayed by both Sophie and me, and I want to explain—"

"I wanted to hear earlier. But that was earlier. I've realized it doesn't matter. It won't change anything."

"But won't you always wonder?" When he didn't answer she drew a shaky breath. "Sophie met him in Monaco, during her hen party. It was on the last night. I don't know all that happened, only that he was there, and then he wasn't."

"She went with him?"

She couldn't meet his eyes. "I didn't know then that she had. I thought she'd maybe gone to get air, or maybe popped up to the room to freshen her makeup. We waited for her in the casino. We were drinking bubbly and playing roulette and I kept looking for her as I'd saved her seat as it was next to mine."

"She didn't return."

"She was back in her bed when I woke up the next morning."

"But she wasn't there when you went to bed."

Poppy drew a deep breath. "No."

"What time was that?"

She hesitated, debating telling him the details, wondering whether or not the details mattered now, after everything else that had happened.

"Late."

"Midnight? One? Two?"

Later than that, she silently answered, seeing herself in the opulent hotel room, sitting in the upholstered chair closest to the door, holding her phone, keeping vigil.

The other girls had all gone to bed.

Poppy couldn't, imagining the worst. Poppy was just about to dress and go down to the hotel reception and ask if she should contact the police when the text arrived.

Am fine. With Renzo. Go to sleep.

After getting Sophie's text, Poppy pressed the phone to her brow and squeezed her eyes shut, heartsick instead of relieved.

The fact that Sophie knew she'd be worried was small comfort.

Everything had changed.

Poppy continued her vigil until four-thirty when she finally fell asleep in that overstuffed chair. She was still curled in the chair when she woke an hour later and discovered the room dark, and Sophie tucked into her bed, pretending to sleep.

"We never discussed it," Poppy said carefully, and that

much was true. As they packed for their return to London, Sophie acted as if nothing had happened. And maybe nothing did happen. Maybe nothing would have happened. Maybe Sophie would have married Randall Grant this morning if Poppy hadn't sent the newspaper clippings to retired racecar driver, Renzo Crisanti, letting him know just who he'd taken to his bed five weeks before her wedding to the Earl of Langston.

On one hand, it was a terrible thing for Poppy to do.

On the other, it wouldn't have signified if Renzo hadn't stormed into the church and carried Sophie away with him.

Clearly, Sophie meant something to Renzo, and clearly Sophie had some interest in Renzo, too, because she hadn't kicked and screamed on the way out of the church.

It had been quite a scene, and profoundly uncomfortable, but the morning's events reassured Poppy that she'd done the right thing. She'd given Sophie not just a chance at love, but passion, too—

"Convenient," Dal said drily, sardonically. "Whatever you do, don't discuss the one thing that needs to be discussed."

The helicopter dipped and she grabbed at the harness straps connected to her lap belt and gave it a desperate tug. Thankfully, she was still secure, even though she felt as though her entire world had turned upside down.

Dal's gaze met hers, but he said nothing. He didn't need to, though. She could feel his fury.

Poppy looked away, out the window, fighting the emotion that threatened to overwhelm her as it crossed her mind that her note to Renzo hadn't just wrecked Sophie and Dal's wedding, but it'd wrecked her life, too.

Dal clenched his hand. He was so angry. So incredibly angry. He longed to smash his fist into Renzo Crisanti's face. He'd like to follow that blow with a series of hard jabs. Crisanti had no right. But then, Sophie had no right, either.

Jaw gritted, Dal glanced from the jagged red mountain range beneath them to Poppy's pale, stricken face and then he couldn't even look at her because she would marry him.

She didn't know it yet, but she didn't have a choice.

They traveled the rest of the way in tense silence, and then they were landing, heading for a sprawling pink villa. Tall, rose-pink walls surrounded the estate, while inside the walls it looked like a miniature kingdom complete with stables and barn, orchards and garden, and three different pools. They swooped lower, still, and her stomach dropped, too.

While the Gila airport transfer had been formal and choreographed, the arrival at the Kasbah was loud and joyous and chaotic. People were everywhere, and there was so much noise. Shouts and cheers and laughter and song.

Dal hadn't expected such a welcome, and from the look on Poppy's face, neither had she.

Poppy kept her smile fixed as she was greeted by one bowing, smiling woman after another, the women in long robes in bright jeweled colors. She was aware that the women greeted her only after first bowing to Randall. He, of course, received the biggest welcome, and it was a genuine welcoming, every staff member clearly delighted to see him. Several of the older men and women had tears in their eyes as they clasped his hand. One small, stooped woman kissed his hand repeatedly, tears falling.

Randall, so stoic in England, seemed to be fighting emotion as he leaned over to kiss the elderly woman's wrinkled cheek and murmur something in her ear.

Poppy got a lump in her throat as she looked at Randall with the tiny older woman. He wasn't affectionate with any of the staff in England, which made her even more curious about the elderly woman, but before she could ask, he brusquely explained the history as they walked toward the villa, shepherded by the jubilant staff.

"Izba was my mother's nanny," he said. "She used to look after me when we would visit Jolie. I hadn't expected her to still be alive."

"She was so emotional."

"She raised my mother from birth, and was closer to my mother than her own mother. Izba would have followed my mother to England, too, if my father had permitted it."

"Why wouldn't your father allow it?"

Randall shot her a mocking look. "He wanted my mother's wealth, not my mother's culture or family."

"It's not right to speak ill of the dead, but your father was—" She broke off, holding back the rest of the words.

"He was hard to love," Dal agreed. "And while he and I didn't have a good relationship, he was loving toward my brother. Andrew was his pride, his joy. My father was never the same after he died."

Poppy knew there had been a brother, but she'd never heard Randall speak of him, not in the four years she'd worked for Randall.

She shot him a troubled glance now, but before she could ask another question, they were climbing broad stairs and then passing beneath a graceful pink arch to enter a walled courtyard dominated by a huge blue fountain. White and purple bougainvillea covered the walls with pots of blooming lemon and orange trees in the corners of the courtyard. Two dark wooden doors were set in one of the long walls, and Randall opened one of those doors now.

"This is your suite," he said, leading her into a living room with a high ceiling covered in a dark carved wood. Windows lined one wall with the rest painted a warm golden khaki that made the floor-to-ceiling green-gold silk drapes shimmer in relief. The couch was covered in a vivid turquoise velvet; the two armchairs facing the sofa were covered in a luxurious silver silk. The lamps were silver, too, as was the giant sliding screen door that Randall pushed open to reveal the bedroom.

Again, one wall was nearly all floor-to-ceiling windows with views of the mountains and valley below. The bed dominated the large room, the bed itself enormous and low, covered in pristine white with two rows of plump white pillows. A long leather ottoman was placed at the foot of the bed while two silver nightstands were at the head of the bed. The ceiling had the same dark carved detail as in the living room, while a huge antique silver chandelier hung from the center of the ceiling, making the room glitter with soft iridescent light.

The space was expansive, furnishings were simple and yet the overall effect was sophisticated and glamorous. Poppy had slept in some beautiful rooms, but nothing came close to this understated luxury. Silks, satins and velvet. Furniture and wood covered in silver and gold.

"You're sure you want me in here? This looks like a room reserved for family."

"All rooms at the Kasbah are for family, and our special guests."

Something in his tone made her pulse jump. "When did I become a special guest?"

"When your job shifted from performing routine, mundane tasks to aiding me in a critical mission."

"Finding you a new secretary is a critical mission?"

"Absolutely. I'm a very busy, very important man. Surely you know that by now?" And then he smiled, his mocking, self-deprecating smile, and she felt a funny flutter in her chest. He was making fun of himself, teasing her in his self-deprecating manner, and she'd never been able to resist him when he made her smile.

"Can we please start with the search tomorrow? I'm beyond exhausted."

"Is this your way of saying you're not up for a big banquet tonight with live entertainment and a stream of visiting dignitaries?"

Poppy grimaced, unable to imagine a worse ending to what had been an absolutely horrendous day. "We're not really doing that, are we?"

"I am Prince Talal."

She saw the gleam in his golden eyes and the ache was back in her chest.

But then, she'd never been able to resist much about him. Even on the first day of work, she'd felt giddy in his presence. She'd thought that eventually she'd outgrow the juvenile reaction. Instead, she just developed deeper feelings, and a stronger attachment. "If you are indeed the prince, then you can excuse me from the lovely, but possibly lengthy, festivities."

"What if the festivities were short?"

"I've rather had it. I just want to go to bed and stay there forever."

"In that case, go to bed after dinner. Tomorrow is going to be a busy day. We have work to do, and since you're only here for fourteen days, we can't afford to waste any time."

"I'll be up early," she promised, unable to imagine life without him. It would be hard not seeing him almost every day. After she was gone, there would be no bounding out of bed, eager to get her day started.

"I'll have a tray sent to you," he said. "In the meantime, you'll find all the basics you'll need for the Kasbah in here." He opened one of the doors of the huge wardrobe. "I'm sure one of the dresses should fit, and then tomorrow one of the ladies' maids can adjust the others, and if need be, I can bring in a seamstress to make up anything else you might need."

"I don't need a lady's maid. I'm quite used to fending for myself."

"It would offend them if you refused assistance."

"Can you not explain that I'm English and eccentric?"

"Oh, I'm sure they'll realize just how eccentric you are, but please don't reject them. They've been trained by Izba, and Izba will want you happy."

Poppy sighed and rubbed at her forehead. "Fine. But there is no need to bring a seamstress in. I'm only here a short time and tunics are sort of a one-size-fits-all kind of dress. I should be fine without alterations."

"Sounds good. Sleep well, and I'll see you in the morning." Then he was gone, leaving her alone in the spacious suite.

Poppy had just opened the wardrobe to look for a nightgown when a light knock sounded on the door and then her door opened.

"Good evening," a young woman greeted Poppy in careful, stilted English. "May I please help you?"

"Thank you, but—" Poppy broke off, remembering Dal's warning and not wanting to offend anyone, much less within twenty minutes of arriving. "Yes, thank you. I was going to take a bath and then go to bed."

"I shall make your bath."

"Oh, no, I can start it myself. But I would like something for dinner. Perhaps salad or a sandwich?"

The young woman stared at Poppy clearly not understanding. "No bath?"

"Yes, I'll have a bath, but I can start it myself. I'd prefer if you could check on dinner."

"Please, more slowly." The girl's face crumpled. "My English is not so good."

So that was it. The poor girl didn't understand her. Poppy managed a tired smile. "Okay. Yes, I'll have a bath. Thank you."

* * *

Dal slept deeply, sleeping through the night and then until late in the morning, the blackout curtains in his room keeping the light out, allowing him to sleep far later than usual.

When he woke he was disoriented for a moment—the blackness of the room didn't help—and then it all came back to him.

The wedding.

The flight to Mehkar.

The helicopter ride to the Kasbah.

Dal left the bed and drew the heavy blackout curtains open, revealing brilliant sunshine. He could feel the heat trying to penetrate the thick glass windows. Thank goodness for thick stucco walls and triple glazed glass. The Kasbah remained cool even when temperatures soared outside.

He walked around his room, looking at it properly. This wasn't his room, at least, not the room he'd had as a boy. This room had been his grandfather's. It was the room reserved for the head of the family.

Apparently, here at Jolie he was the head of the family.

He felt like a disgrace.

He should have called his grandfather personally to let him know he was returning. He should have gone to the palace in Gila and met his grandfather for coffee or tea. He should have invited his grandfather here…

Dal opened the door to one of his terraces and stepped outside. Despite the heat, the air smelled fragrant, sweet.

He'd wondered if Jolie would still smell the same. It actually smelled better than he remembered—lavender and thyme, jasmine and orange blossoms.

He glanced down at the patio far below, and then at the tower off to his right. Past the tower he could see one of the tall external walls.

The Kasbah had been in the family hundreds of years, originally built as a fortress with thick external walls and tall towers offering vast, panoramic views ensuring that no one approached the Kasbah unseen.

The external walls were over fifteen feet tall and the same soft rose-peach hue as the palace itself, but once inside the huge gates, the hard surface of the walls disappeared, becoming a living garden, the plaster covered with flowering vines and lush scarlet, pink and white bougainvillea.

The Kasbah had been designed to protect the royal family in the event of a siege, with everything necessary for survival, but for a young boy that hadn't been its charm. Dal loved the towers and the secret rooms, the cool cellars and sunlit terraces with low couches piled high with silk pillows. He loved the clay pots used to cook his favorite dishes, chicken and lamb fragrant with saffron, fruit and spices.

The staff at Jolie was friendly, too, and in his mind, the staff had felt like family, always nodding and smiling and greeting him with warmth and pleasure.

Langston House was different. Even as a young boy he was aware of the difference and how no one smiled at Langston House. At Langston House the staff did not feel like family. They were servants. Menial. It was how his father liked things, the separation between classes, the distance between upstairs and downstairs. His father was the Fifth Earl of Langston, after all, raised with a clear sense of distinction and entitlement.

Dal's chest tightened up again, and he shifted in his seat, wishing he could just walk away from his past, and his father, but that would be the ultimate failure. His father had never expected Dal to succeed at anything, which is why Dal intended to keep his promise to his father—that he'd marry by thirty-five.

It was the only promise he'd ever made to his father and he'd honor the vow because then he'd be free.

And Dal longed to be free, not just of his father but the past.

With no time to waste, he rang for coffee and Poppy.

Poppy had thought her suite of rooms was lovely, but they were nothing compared to Dal's magnificent suite, which literally took up the entire second floor of the villa, bordered on all sides by sundrenched terraces and patios and fragrant, private gardens.

Like her, he had a living room and bedroom suite, but he also had a dining room, and office, all four rooms with the same floor-to-ceiling windows and doors that filled her suite with light.

He had papers, a notebook, pen and computer on a table outside, the area shaded by an elegant pergola covered with blooming jasmine.

"Is it too warm for you out here?" he asked, gesturing for her to sit in the chair by the laptop.

"It's comfortable now," she said, "but it'll definitely be quite hot later."

"I promise we'll move inside to an air-conditioned room before you melt."

She sat down in the low wooden chair with the teal pillows. "What am I to call you here? Dal? Prince Talal? Izba referred to you as Sheikh Talal, as well as His Highness. You have so many names."

"Not that many. My staff at the Kasbah will either call me Prince Talal, or Sheikh Talal. My family in Mehkar calls me Tal, although when we were in Gila, at the airport, my cousin addressed me as His Highness due to protocol."

"Your cousin? Which one was he?"

"The last man on the carpet."

"The one you hugged."

"Yes." Randall's mouth curved but his eyes were shuttered. "The last time I saw him he was just six years old. Now he's a man."

"How old were you the last time you were here?"

"Ten."

"You've both grown up."

"We have," he said, but there was no joy in his voice, just loss, and regret. And then his broad shoulders squared and his voice firmed. "Now to your question, you may call me anything you want, provided it's not Randall."

"You dislike your proper name that much?"

"My father is the only other person who has ever called me Randall."

She felt a shiver of distaste. No wonder he didn't like it. "I wish you'd told me that earlier."

"I tried. But you insisted Dal was too personal."

"I'm sorry."

"It's fine. Clearly, I survived the horror."

She shot him a swift look and was relieved to see that faint ironic smile of his. A smile she was learning that he used to hide hurts and needs, and all those emotions he viewed as weak. "But this is exactly what I mean. You have to talk. Tell people things. If I knew that the only other person who called you Randall was your father, and your father and you were not close, and it wasn't a positive or comfortable association—"

"You're getting a little carried away. You haven't inflicted any damage. I'm no more scarred than when you first met me."

She must have looked sufficiently startled because he grimaced. "That was supposed to make you smile."

Her brows pulled. "Do you think you're very scarred?"

"I was being amusing. Don't read too much into it."

But she couldn't help reading into it. She'd heard some horror stories about Randall's father, the Fifth Earl of Langston, and she'd long suspected that Dal's isolated nature was due to his father's volatility. Poppy carefully chose her next words. "Were you close to your mother?"

"Yes."

"What did she call you?"

"Tal."

All these years she'd thought she'd known him. She'd prided herself on knowing him better than anyone, but as it turned out, she didn't know the real Dal Grant at all. "Who are you?" she asked, smiling unsteadily.

His smile faded and he glanced away for a moment and when he looked back at her, his expression struck her as rather bleak. "Interesting question, Miss Marr. I'll have to get back to you on that one."

And then just as quickly, the darkness was gone and he was back to business. "Let's get started, shall we? I know you follow all of Sophie's friends, so how about we start by pulling up Seraphina's Instagram page—"

"No."

"No?"

"I'm not going to pore over Seraphina's social media. Or Florrie's. I promised I'd help find a new secretary, not a replacement for Sophie."

"I'd like your input on both."

"This makes me uncomfortable."

"It should. If you hadn't interfered yesterday, I'd be a married man today."

"You just think I did something, but you have no proof."

"And when I have proof? What then? How will you make it up to me?"

She shook her head, lips compressed.

"Poppy, I made my father a promise, and I'm not going to break that promise."

"Then perhaps you need a better list," she said, picturing Seraphina and Florrie. Both had been at Langston House yesterday for the wedding. Florrie was single at the moment—in between polo player lovers—and Seraphina was dating someone. It was in the early stages of the relationship but she apparently liked him and had told everyone he could be the one. Although that wasn't the first, or second, or even third time she'd said such a thing. "Only Florrie is currently single. Seraphina is seeing someone. She brought him to the wedding yesterday."

"I didn't notice."

"I'm not surprised. It was a tad hectic." She studied Dal, who looked handsome and rested this morning, his crisp white linen shirt the perfect foil for his black hair and golden eyes. "So tell me, how do you intend to proceed with your wooing?"

"I'll make a phone call, explain that I'm in need of a countess, and ask if she's interested."

"That's it?"

"Should I ask her to fill out an application and give five references?"

"Dal, this isn't the way to a satisfying relationship."

"You're a relationship expert now?"

She ignored the jab. "I'm not the one rushing into marriage, and I know it's been difficult these past few days, but you can't truly want a shallow, materialistic woman who is only marrying you for the title and money?"

"But that's exactly what I'm offering, and all I'm really offering—"

"That is not so. She gets you. *You*. And yes, you're a horrible, ridiculous, stubborn, awful man, but you're still you. Why give yourself to someone who doesn't care about you?"

"Because she'll be happier with the title and houses and bank account than she will with me."

"I don't know why you're saying these things."

"Why not let her enjoy herself? As long as she gives me heirs, she can do what she wants."

"I don't want to hear any more."

"It shouldn't upset you. You crossed yourself off the list of candidates. Who I marry, or how I choose my wife, shouldn't trouble you in the least."

"But of course it does! I care about you. I care about your happiness, or lack of happiness. I care that you lock yourself away from the world and just work, work, work. I care that you lost Sophie, and now you're in this position, but at the same time, I'm glad you didn't trap Sophie in a cold marriage. That wouldn't have been fair to her. She deserves so much more. And you deserve more, too, but you won't demand more and that absolutely baffles me."

She lifted the computer, rose and walked away.

Dal didn't stop her, letting her march away with the laptop as if she was the injured party.

She wasn't injured. She was lucky. She would soon have everything she wanted, and more.

A husband, a family, financial security, as well as respect. Once she was his wife, she'd have power and prestige. People would fall all over themselves wanting her approval, trying to ingratiate themselves.

She would be fine. He, on the other hand, was not. Normally, he was quite good at compartmentalizing emotions and suppressing anger, but he felt barely in control at the moment. He was being tested as his past, present and future collided together in a sickening crash of memories and emotions.

When he'd pictured Kasbah Jolie yesterday, he'd pictured a remote estate, someplace peaceful, and he'd imagined he'd arrive with very little fanfare, but the transfer in Gila had been anything but understated. The royal carpet, the line of dignitaries, the military guard behind, the royal helicopter itself. He hadn't wanted any of it. His flight crew had contacted the executive terminal at Gila and arranged for a helicopter for the Earl of Langston, but at no time had they dropped his Mehkar title. They couldn't have, as they didn't know it.

Which meant someone at the Gila airport had contacted the palace, and the king had ordered the welcome.

Dal frowned, his chest as heavy as his gut.

His grandfather knew he was here, aware that Dal had not just come home, but had once again shut him out, choosing to retreat to the mountain palace rather than attempt any form of reconciliation.

Dal didn't know why he was treating his grandfather the same way his father had—with callous contempt and utter disregard. What was wrong with him? Why couldn't he be kind to the one man who'd always been kind to him?

Dal planned on accomplishing two things before he left Mehkar: he'd be married, and he'd finally make peace with his grandfather.

CHAPTER SIX

POPPY SETTLED DOWN to work at the desk in the library on the main floor. The room had a soaring, dark-beamed ceiling, arched windows and walls the color of deep red rubies. The beamed ceiling had been stenciled in gold, and the big light fixtures were gold, and then there were the floor-to-ceiling shelves filled with leather-bound books that looked to be hundreds of years old.

Poppy had discovered the room earlier this morning and couldn't wait to return. She opened her laptop, checked the internet and was pleased to see that it worked just as well here as it did at home. It wasn't long before she had accessed all her files through the cloud storage system on the laptop. All of Dal's companies used the same cloud storage, making it easy to use any computer, anywhere.

She checked her email, and then scanned BBC's news and then reached out by email to several prominent employment agencies, sharing the details about the secretarial position to be filled, and how they were hoping to fill the job as soon as possible.

She received a reply from each almost immediately. One wanted her to fill out a more complete questionnaire, while the other promised to begin forwarding résumés later that afternoon.

With no résumés to review yet, Poppy wasn't quite sure what to do with her time next.

And then she thought of Sophie. Where was she? And how was she?

Poppy opened her email and sent Sophie a quick message.

I'm with Dal in Mehkar. Where are you? How are you? Fill me in, please!

And then, because her curiosity was getting the best of her, she went back online and studied Florrie and Seraphina's social media accounts.

Florrie had shared a photograph taken outside Langston House before the wedding had begun. She was with Seraphina and several other beautiful girls and they were all smiling for the camera.

Seraphina was a dark brunette and Florrie was a golden blonde. They were both gorgeous and glamorous, and they knew how to wear clothes well.

But that didn't make them good matches for Dal.

Poppy was staring at the photo hard, so hard, she didn't hear Dal enter the library.

"Are you trying to decide which one is better for me?" he asked, leaning over her desk chair to get a better look at the photo of four smiling women.

She closed the computer quickly. "What are you doing here?"

"Checking on your progress. Any good résumés yet?"

"One agency asked me to fill out a questionnaire, while the other has promised to begin forwarding résumés straightaway."

"Was the questionnaire complicated?"

"No." She wiggled in her chair, not willing to admit that she'd somehow managed to forget all about completing the form. She didn't know how she could forget.

"So you are all done with everything right now?"

"I'm caught up for the moment, if that's what you're asking."

"Yes. Great. I'd like your help in my search." He lifted a hand to stop her when she started to protest. "And I know you don't want to. Sophie was your friend and you're very loyal to her, but Sophie is no longer in the picture and I need a wife."

"But how can I help you when you won't even help yourself?"

"What does that mean?"

"You can't treat your next fiancé the way you treated Sophie. It was criminal. You were the King of Cold, the Master of Remote." She shrugged at his frown. "It's true, Dal. I'm telling you the truth. Please don't propose to another woman without being willing to give her more."

Dal couldn't believe they were back to discussing this intangible "more" again. It was beyond infuriating.

It was also beyond infuriating to have to play this game with her. He wasn't even considering Florrie or Seraphina as a future wife. There was only one woman on his list and that was Poppy. But if he told Poppy that, she'd have a nervous breakdown, and they didn't need that. He had to get married, but he preferred marrying someone stable. And most days Poppy was stable. She was also dependable, and someone he trusted. Perhaps Sophie had done him a huge favor.

"I'm not sure I know how to go about demanding more," he said flatly, battling to hide his irritation. "I am not sure I even know what this 'more' would look like."

"More is just more, Dal. More companionship. More conversation. More laughter. Possibly more tears—"

"Not that, please."

She sighed, but continued on. "More would also be more friendship, and more support, more encouragement, more happiness."

"That's a great deal of more."

"Yes, it requires some thought and effort, but that's how you develop a relationship. It's how people get to know you, and you would get to know them. It takes time, too." Her wide brown eyes met his. "And it's not something money can buy. So you can't throw money at it. If anything, money makes it worse."

"How so?"

Her brows pulled, her expression troubled. "Money is power, and power thrives on inequality. True friendship, just like true love, doesn't care about position, or prestige. It wants what is best for the other person."

Her words grated on his nerves, putting an uncomfortable knot in his chest. He didn't know why her thoughts bothered him so much, but it took every bit of his control not to retort sharply, mockingly. He didn't like the world of feelings and emotions. He didn't enjoy the company of emotional people. Poppy was the sole exception, and maybe that was because at work he could normally steer her in a different direction, and she'd oblige him. But here, here was proving to be a different matter.

"Please don't make me lose all respect for you," he said with a hard, sardonic smile. "Feelings are massively overrated."

"But I didn't specifically say *feelings*," she answered quietly. "I was very careful not to use the word *feelings*. Apparently, that's all you heard, though."

"I think I stopped listening when you said I couldn't solve the problem by throwing money at it."

"You can make all the jokes you want, but you can't change the truth, and the truth is, you have to open up more, and give more and be present in the lives of those who love you."

He shot her a wry glance. "You make me sound like an ass."

"Well, you can be intolerable at times."

"And yet you're still fighting to save me."

"Just for another two weeks."

"So altruistic, then, trying to whip me into shape for the next secretary."

"I'm more concerned about the next fiancée. She's the one that would get the short end of the stick because she will expect a relationship. The secretary won't."

"Have you always been so pragmatic?"

"Charity girls can't afford to wear rose-colored glasses."

And yet Poppy did. Poppy was the least practical, most idealistic woman he'd ever met. He functioned best when his world was cool, precise and analytical...the complete opposite of the world Poppy inhabited.

"Perhaps you didn't get the memo," he answered, aware that she'd had a difficult past. Poppy had lost her mother to cancer and then her father died ten years later, leaving Poppy all alone. Or, she would have been alone if it wasn't for Sophie. "You love your fairy tales and rainbows."

"You forgot lemon drops and fireworks. I love those, too." Then she shrugged. "I know it's hard for you to stomach, but my parents met in school, fell in love and never dated anyone else. They were totally devoted to each other, as well as really happy together...despite Mum's cancer, and the creditors constantly calling."

Her shoulders shifted. "And then when they were both gone, Sophie gave me a second home. She looked after me and showed me what real friendship is. I learned that love isn't just a romantic thing. Love is kindness and commitment and doing what's best for the other person. And that's what I want for you. I want you to have a kind wife. A woman who will commit to you and do what's best for you, and in return, you would be kind to her, and loyal to her and put her needs first, too."

"If you care so much about my happiness, why not just marry me? Wouldn't that be the simplest thing to do?"

For a long moment she said nothing, and then her throat worked and her voice sounded low and rough. "I've never had much in life in terms of material things, but I was loved, dearly, by my parents, and if I ever marry, it will be for love. A marriage without love is doomed from the start."

By the time Poppy made it back to her room, she was absolutely worn out.

These intense conversations with Dal drained her, and part of her wanted to just give up on him and stop trying to help, but the only way she could handle the idea of leaving him was by thinking she was leaving him better off than he was now.

The man didn't need more money. The man didn't need more people to bow and scrape. What Dal needed was honesty. He needed someone to care enough about him to tell him the truth. He needed to be pushed to try harder and give more and be more…and she knew he could, because during the past four years she'd seen a softer side of him. She'd experienced his kindness and patience firsthand. He knew how to talk and be good company, too. But she also knew that it had to be his choice, on his terms, or he'd just shut you out and become that remote, unfeeling ice man that Sophie dreaded.

Poppy showered and then wrapped a cotton robe around her and headed to the wardrobe to see what she'd wear for dinner.

Poppy knew from this morning that the wardrobe was full of long tunics in every color of the rainbow. She'd stroked the vivid fabrics, pausing at a brilliant green gown with gold embellishments from the plunging neckline all the way down the gauzy fabric, and then an ivory one, and another ivory one this time with hot pink fringe all around the sleeves and edges of the long, narrow skirt. The dresses were like art, each unique but stylish and impossibly pretty. Poppy didn't know how she was supposed to choose just one to wear when they were all so beautiful.

She now flipped through all the dresses again, this time stopping at a rich gold dress with full three-quarter sleeves. The sleeves were dotted with a graphic black-and-white sunburst pattern, with black-and-white trim down the front, and along the hem of the straight gold skirt.

But Poppy's favorite part of the dress were the two playful black-and-white fringe pom-poms that hung from the V-neckline.

"Would be beautiful on you, my lady," a soft voice said from behind her in slow, broken English.

Poppy turned around and smiled as she spotted Izba in the doorway.

"These gowns are exquisite," Poppy said.

Izba stepped into the room and closed the door behind her. "His Highness Talal's mother designed them," she said, crossing to the wardrobe and reaching into the closet to draw out a white lace kaftan with coral-red embroidery on the shoulders and vibrant coral-red fringe at the sleeves and hem. "She thought clothes should make a woman happy."

Izba spoke with a quiet sincerity that put a lump in Poppy's throat. "Talal's mother was very talented," Poppy answered huskily.

The elderly woman's dark brown eyes shone and she carefully hung the white lace gown up. "She was most beautiful woman in Mehkar, but with the most beautiful heart in the world." She turned around to look at Poppy. "Which dress you wish to wear for tonight?"

"I don't know which one to pick. What do you think I should wear?"

Izba's lips pursed and her dark gaze swept Poppy before she faced the closet again. She studied the rack for a long moment, cheeks puffing, until she reached in and lifted out a dark cherry gown with big cheerful silver flowers embroidered across the bodice before becoming delicate trailing flowers down the skirt. The sleeves were plain except for a thick silver bank of embroidery at the cuff.

"These are poppies," Izba said in her careful, stilted English. "Just like your name, yes?"

Poppy didn't know why she wanted to cry. Instead, she nodded and smiled. "That's perfect."

"Perfect," Izba echoed carefully, smiling affectionately. "Once you are dressed, I will fix your hair."

"Oh, I don't need help with my hair."

"His Highness expects us to help you."

"Yes, but his—" Poppy broke off, unable to call Randall anything remotely like His Highness, and she searched for the right words. "His...your Prince Talal...knows I am accustomed to taking care of myself. I prefer taking care of myself."

Izba's already wrinkled brow creased further. "But as his wife—"

"Oh! No. *No.* I think there's been a mistake, and I understand the confusion, but I'm not his wife. I work for Talal. I'm his secretary."

Izba stared at her, dark eyes assessing. "You are not just friend. You are to marry the prince."

"No! Oh, Izba, no." Poppy swallowed hard, thinking this was incredibly uncomfortable but she had to make the older woman understand. "Believe me, I am not marrying Prince Talal. I serve as his secretary, nothing more." She drew a quick breath. "I've agreed to help him find a wife, but Izba, it's not me."

Before they came to Jolie, Dal would have described Poppy as pretty, in a fresh, wholesome, no-nonsense sort of way with her thick, shoulder-length brown hair and large, brown eyes and a serious little chin.

But as Poppy entered the dining room with its glossy white ceiling and dark purple walls, she looked anything but wholesome and no-nonsense.

She was wearing a silk gown the color of cherries, delicately embroidered with silver threads, and instead of her usual ponytail or chignon, her dark hair was down, and long, elegant chandelier earrings dangled from her ears. As she walked, the semi-sheer kaftan molded to her curves, highlighting her full, firm breasts and swell of hips.

"It seems I've been keeping you waiting," she said, her voice pitched lower than usual and slightly breathless. "Izba insisted on all this," she added, gesturing up toward her face.

At first Dal thought she was referring to the ornate silver earrings that were catching and reflecting the light, but once she was seated across from him he realized her eyes had been rimmed with kohl and her lips had been outlined and filled in with a soft plum-pink gloss. "You're wearing makeup."

"Quite a lot of it, too." She grimaced. "I tried to explain to Izba that this wasn't me, but she's very determined once she makes her mind up about something and apparently, dinner with you requires me to look like a tart."

Dal checked his smile. "You don't look like a tart. Unless it's the kind of tart one wants to eat."

Color flooded Poppy's cheeks and she glanced away, suddenly shy, and he didn't know if it was her shyness or the shimmering dress that clung to her curves, outlining her high, full breasts, but he didn't think any woman could be more beautiful, or desirable than Poppy right now. "You look lovely," he said quietly. "But I don't want you uncomfortable all through dinner. If you'd rather go remove the makeup I'm happy to wait."

She looked at him closely as if doubting his sincerity. "It's fun to dress up, but I'm worried Izba has the wrong idea about me."

"And what is that?"

"She seems to think you're going to...marry...me."

When he said nothing, she added, "I know I'm not on your 'list' anymore, and so I'm not suggesting you're encouraging her, but it's awkward trying to convince her that I'm not going to be your new wife."

"I'll have a word with her," he said, and he would have a word with Izba, but not about this. The fact was, Poppy would be his wife. She was going to marry him. He knew exactly how to get her acquiescence. Women thought they needed words. But even more than language, they needed touch.

He was trying to hold off on seduction, though. He didn't want to trick her into being his wife, nor did he want to use her body against her. But she would capitulate, if he seduced her. She was already his even without a single touch.

His goal was to get her to think marriage was her idea. It was far better to let her believe the idea was hers. She'd be a far happier, and more malleable bride that way.

"Thank you." She glanced down, fingertips grazing the silver beadwork near her shoulder. "Did you know this is your mother's design?"

"What do you mean?"

"Every dress in the wardrobe in my room was designed by your mother. Izba said she was an aspiring fashion designer when she married your father."

"I didn't know," he said after a long moment. "I had no idea." He frowned at the candle on the table, surprised that such a little detail should knock him off guard, but it did. It might be a small thing, but it said so much about who she was, and the dreams she'd had.

"She had tremendous style," he said gruffly. "I always knew she was different from other mums, but I don't think I appreciated the differences until it was too late."

"I wish I'd had the chance to meet her. She sounds so lovely."

"She was." And then because he found the memories unbearable, he smashed the past, making the memories vanish. As the memories faded, so did the ache. The ache didn't completely disappear, but at least it was manageable.

He signaled to one of the stewards standing in the corner. "Let's eat."

Dinner was a feast, with salad after salad, followed by warm, fragrant pilaf and delicious pan-seared salmon, and of course there was dessert, the waiter tempting Poppy with the description of the honey and mint syrup cake served with a small scoop of spiced vanilla ice cream on the side.

Poppy was full from dinner and was going to reluctantly pass on the cake, until Dal suggested she skip the ice cream and try a slice. He said the cake had just been baked; he'd smelled it earlier in the oven and it was his favorite cake because it was topped with a thick, crunchy layer of slivered honey-glazed almonds.

Poppy couldn't resist the description and the cake was even better than Dal described. She ate her slice, and had just popped a stray slivered almond into her mouth when Dal leaned back in his chair and told her he'd spoken with Seraphina earlier.

Poppy almost choked on the almond. She coughed to clear her throat. "You called her?"

"I did," he said casually as if this was no big deal.

"When?"

"This afternoon." His broad shoulders shifted carelessly. "She was surprised to hear from me, but she quickly warmed up. It seems she and her new boyfriend had a fight on the drive home from the wedding." He looked at her, lashes lowering, concealing the gold of his eyes. "She's not sure if it's going to work out between them."

Poppy's heart fell. She didn't know why she felt such a rush of disappointment. She should want this for him. He needed a wife. Quickly. If tall, slim, Sloane Ranger Seraphina could fit the bill, why shouldn't he marry her?

"That's good," she said faintly, struggling to smile. Many would consider Seraphina an excellent substitution for Sophie. Seraphina's family was far wealthier than the Carmichael-Joneses, and Seraphina was wildly popular, always in the press, photographed at all the right events, and big parties and fashion shows.

The fact that she was as shallow as a plate was only problematic if one wanted a wife with emotions...

"You don't sound very convincing," he said, reaching for his wineglass. "I thought you'd be pleased. I'd much rather narrow down my list to just one and focus on courting her, rather than jumping back and forth between two women."

"You don't want to even give Florrie a chance?"

"I was under the impression that you didn't think Florrie would be a suitable match."

"I never said anything against her."

"But you implied she's one of those horsey girls, always at a polo match."

"Did I? I don't remember."

"I ride, but I'm not by any means an equestrian. If polo is her passion, she wouldn't be happy with me."

"And Seraphina is a clothes horse, always seen in the front row of some fashion show or other."

"Yes, but I wouldn't be expected to attend the fashion shows with her. That's something she could do on her own, and no one would think twice about her being in Paris or Milan or New York without me."

"Don't you want to be with your wife?"

"No."

"Dal!"

"Don't you want your wife to want to be with you?"

"Not really. I enjoy my own company. Besides, if Seraphina is currently disgruntled with the new boyfriend, she'll welcome my attention and it shouldn't take much effort to close the deal with her."

"I've never heard a worse proposal."

"I'm not a romantic man."

"That might be why you lost Sophie."

He gave her a look that wasn't pleasant. Clearly, he didn't appreciate her honesty, but honesty is what he needed. "Women aren't things to park on shelves or in closets. They want and need time and attention."

"The *more* you're constantly harping on."

"Or in your case, some. *Some* time. *Some* attention." She was angry now, and she didn't even try to hide her irritation. "Never mind a token of affection, because I know you gave Sophie almost none."

"Sophie didn't like being touched."

"Sophie *craved* affection. You're the one that rejected her."

"She recoiled every time I reached for her."

"But did you talk to her before you reached for her? Did you take her to dinner? Did you send her flowers? Did you plan anything fun? No. It was strictly business, and cold as hell."

"And you've thought this all these years?"

"Yes."

"Why didn't you say something?"

"Because it wasn't my place, and she didn't complain, not until this last year, and then she wasn't complaining as much as…panicking. I thought maybe the sheer size of the wedding was overwhelming her, but clearly it wasn't the wedding. It was you."

"Of course you'll be Team Sophie until the bitter end."

"I'm on your team, too. That's why I'm spoiling my delicious dessert, trying to make you understand that it takes two to make a marriage. You can't just put a ring on some-one's finger and be done with it."

"I did care about Sophie. I cared a great deal. But the fact is, I couldn't seem to make her happy. It was as if she didn't want to be happy with me—"

"You're just saying that now."

"You wanted honesty. I'm being honest. She didn't want to marry me. But she couldn't stand up to her parents."

"And when did you realize this? Five and a half years ago?"

"No. This past year. I tried to plan several special oc-casions for us—theater, shopping, dinner. She agreed to each and looked beautiful every time we stepped out, but there was no…conversation. There was no…warmth. Even her smiles looked forced as if she was suffering and barely tolerating my company."

"Martyred for the cause," Poppy muttered.

Dal glanced at her, eyes narrowed. "What did you say?"

She was so annoyed with him, and all of them. Money and power changed people, inflating their sense of worth, and bringing out the worst in them. "Your fathers shouldn't have arranged the marriage, not against your wishes."

"I didn't protest very much. It was easier just to make him happy. Less conflict, and honestly, I didn't care who I married."

"Why not?"

"I don't feel emotions like you. I don't feel love, and I wouldn't have ever married for love."

"Well, Sophie did, and she tried to fight it." Poppy saw Dal's startled expression. "I overheard them once, Sophie and her parents. It was a terrible row. They said terrible things to her, squashing her completely." She swallowed hard. "I think that's why she stuck up for me, from early on. Because she never had anyone who stuck up for her."

And this was why Poppy did what she did, sending newspaper clippings to Renzo Crisanti.

She wanted Sophie to have a chance at happiness. She wanted Sophie to have more.

Just as she still wanted Dal to have more.

"You're making me feel like the devil," Dal said roughly.

"That's not my intention."

He shifted at the table, features tight, jaw jutting. "I had no idea she'd been pressured to marry me. It disgusts me to think that she was being forced into a marriage with me."

"You both deserved better."

He rose from the table and crossed the room, hands in his trouser pockets. "No wonder you looked elated when Crisanti showed up. You were thrilled she'd escaped the marriage. You were thrilled she was escaping marrying me."

"Yes," she answered. "I was. No woman should be forced into marriage with a man. Not even if it's in marriage to you."

"Thanks…?"

"You know I mean it in the nicest, sincerest way, because you're aware of how I feel about you. I have that… soft spot. I see all the good things in you that Sophie couldn't see."

"Really? What did you fall in love with, since it clearly wasn't my title and wealth?"

"You give to others, constantly, generously. You provide leadership to developing countries. You donate money to developing businesses, particularly businesses headed by women. But you don't just give money, you give time, and wisdom, and you listen to these people. You truly care."

"So why did you take yourself off my list?"

"Because you care about everyone but yourself. You don't love yourself. You barely like yourself, and it would be difficult, if not impossible, being your wife when I know you'd never love me—"

"But I'd want you."

"Not the same thing."

"Physical pleasure can be incredibly satisfying."

"But it's not love, and I want true love, and I'm holding out for a man who will move the moon and stars for me."

He made a rough, mocking sound. "I understand that I expect too little from marriage, but you, my darling Poppy, expect too much."

"Maybe. But I'd rather believe in happy-ever-after then be bitter, cold and cynical."

"Like me?"

"I think you're cynical because it's easier than trying to muddle through with emotions. Far better to be coldly intellectual than a flesh and blood human being—"

"Just because I don't believe in romantic love doesn't mean I don't bleed when cut."

"I've never seen you bleed, or grieve. You lost your fiancée yesterday and yet you never shed a tear."

"Maybe because she wasn't the right one for me. Maybe because I'm relieved that I have an unexpected opportunity to find the right woman and make this work."

"You're not acquiring a company, Dal. You're talking about marrying a woman!"

"And I think you're angry because you'd like to be that woman, only you're too afraid to allow your dreams to become reality—"

"A life with you isn't my dream. You would never, ever be able to give me what I need!"

He crossed the room, walking toward her with such deliberate intention that it made her heart race. "That's just another excuse. You are full of them today. Why don't you stop acting like a little girl and fight for what you want?"

She backed up a panicked step. "You're not what I want!"

"Bullshit." And then he trapped her against the wall, wrapped an arm low around her waist and pulled her close.

Poppy knew a split second before his head dropped that he was going to kiss her, and she stiffened, shocked, surprised, but also curious.

And then his mouth covered hers and she felt an electric jolt shoot through her. He was right about her fantasies. She'd imagined this for years. She'd had a few dates here and there but she was essentially an inexperienced, twenty-six-year-old virgin. It had been easy remaining a virgin, too, because Dal was the only man she wanted, and how could any other man measure up to him? No one was as handsome. No one as intelligent. No one as powerful.

And now he was holding her, kissing her and tremor after tremor coursed through her. The kiss felt like a claiming. There was nothing tentative in the way his mouth slanted over hers, his mouth warm, his breath cool. Her senses felt flooded and her brain struggled to take it all in…his smell, his warmth and then there was that delicious pressure of his body so hard and lean against her, his chest a wall of muscles.

His head finally lifted and he stared deep into her eyes. "Tell me you didn't want that to happen."

"Do you enjoy humiliating women?"

"I wanted it to happen." His narrowed gaze examined every inch of her face. "Because I've spent years trying not to imagine that kiss."

It was true, too. Dal would have never kissed her while engaged, or married. He would have never acted on any kind of impulse—there would be no impulse—if he wasn't single, but he was single now and she was single, and she was more than available. When she looked at him, she practically offered herself up to him. The sacrificial maiden, the innocent virgin—

He stopped himself, brow furrowing as he glanced at her. "Are you a virgin?"

Her cheeks burned with color. Her eyes flashed dangerously. "That is none of your business."

"So it's a yes," he answered, fascinated by the bloom in her cheeks and the bruised pink of her lips. Emotion darkened her eyes now, making her wonder what she'd look like after she'd shattered with pleasure.

"There is no need for you to be horrible," she protested breathlessly.

She was aroused but fighting it.

He respected her more for fighting it. "Not trying to be horrible," he said, thinking she needed another kiss, as did he. "Just trying to figure out why you still want to fight the attraction. There's no reason. Sophie is gone. I'm single. You're single."

"You are so incredibly unromantic."

"Lust isn't always romantic, but it's real."

"Well, I don't lust for you. I have feelings for you. A huge difference."

"But that's where you're wrong. You might have feelings for me, but you also desire me. I can prove it."

Her eyes had clung to his as he spoke, her wide, dark eyes showing every single thing she was feeling. She was aroused and curious but also remarkably shy and innocent. Holding her against him, he could feel how her slim body hummed with tension, as well as the wild beating of her heart. She was as soft as he was hard, as warm as he was cold, and as he gazed down into her lovely expressive eyes, he thought Sophie had indeed done him a favor.

Dal could imagine Poppy as his wife. A sweet, kind, warm wife. The kind of woman who'd be a sweet, kind, warm mother, too.

"Let's revisit the subject of lust," he said, just before his head dipped and his mouth covered hers to part her full, soft lips and plunder the inside of her hot, sweet mouth. His tongue teased hers, stirring her senses, making her clutch at his arms and whimper against his mouth.

He pressed her closer, shaping her to him, his hand settling on her pert, round derriere. He cupped her bottom, caressing the generous curve, and she shuddered and arched against him, her entire body trembling as if he'd set her on fire.

He shifted around so that he could lean back against the wall while he positioned her between his thighs. He felt hard and savage as he drew her hips against his hips, letting her feel the heavy length of his erection.

She sighed against his mouth, and her breasts peaked against his chest. He relished the feel of her tight nipples and he stroked up, from her hips over the small of her waist to caress the side of her full breast.

She shivered again and made soft, incoherent sounds that heated his blood and made him want to rip her dress off and devour her here.

It had been so long since he'd been with anyone, and forever since he'd felt this way. He'd forgotten what desire felt like. He'd forgotten the insistent throb of need, and the need to claim. And he didn't want just anyone, he wanted her, all of her, and the more she gave, the more he wanted to take. His thumb found her breast, her nipple pebbled tight, pressing through the thin silk of her kaftan. He rubbed the tip, pinching it, just to hear her gasp and feel her hips twist against his.

He ached, and his erection throbbed and he felt more alive than he had in years. Not just years. But decades.

He stroked Poppy's full, round breast again, and beneath her breast, before palming the fullness, savoring the shape and weight. He loved her curves, and her sensual nature, amazed that she'd hidden both all these years with her ugly practical wardrobe and shy, retiring smile.

Poppy was not shy or retiring at all.

Poppy was a goddess and he could not wait to take her to bed.

She was exactly what he needed. And he would have her. It wasn't a matter of if, but when.

Reluctantly, he lifted his head. Her dark eyes were cloudy and her gaze unfocused. She swayed in his arms, off balance.

"We'll marry end of this week," he said tightly, reining in his hunger so that he could attempt to be logical and rational. "I don't know if you want to stay here for a honeymoon, or if you'd want to travel somewhere else."

She blinked up at him, still dazed. *"What?"*

"It will just be a very simple ceremony. A civil ceremony. And then with formalities done, we can do what we want. Honeymoon here, or travel to someplace you've never been."

She gave him a shove, freeing herself. "I'm not marrying you!"

"You are, and you want to. Stop fighting the inevitable."

Her face flushed pink. "Excuse me, but what planet are you living on? I never agreed to marry you, and just because I kissed you doesn't mean we're suddenly a couple."

"We should be."

"Because I kissed you back? Ha!" She took another quick step back, arms folding over her chest. "I have kissed dozens of men and I've never married any of them!"

"I don't care if you kissed three hundred. You're a virgin. You want me. You belong to me."

"Ahem. I don't belong to you, or with you. In fact, I gave notice that I'm leaving you. So, maybe you need to go out there and find someone you can actually date, and court and hopefully marry before you lose your precious earldom and your historic Langston House!"

Poppy practically fled back to her room, nearly bumping into Imma as she threw open her door.

Poppy wished Imma a good night and then once alone, began to pace her floor before flinging herself on her bed, replaying the entire scene with Dal in her head. What a scene it was! The words he'd said, those obnoxious, arrogant words, and then the kiss...

Oh, the kiss...

But no, she wouldn't think about the kiss. That was the most impossible thing of all, too much like the fairy tales she'd loved as a girl because those stories about good and evil, lightness and darkness, helped explain the world and the things that had happened in her world—the financial struggles, her mother's prolonged battle with cancer, a battle they'd thought she'd won, *twice*, only to relapse and die just after Poppy's thirteenth birthday. It had just gotten worse after that. Her father couldn't juggle his job and fatherhood and on the advice of friends, had found a boarding school that offered scholarships to promising young women in need.

She was in need, but poverty was the least of her woes.

She missed her mother and her father and what she'd thought of as family.

But just when she didn't think she could take any more, there was Sophie, lovely, strong Sophie, who took Poppy under her wing, becoming her champion when Poppy was at her lowest.

Sophie had given Poppy her hope back, and hope was everything. Hope made one look forward. Hope helped one to focus on what lay ahead rather than what was behind. Hope made all things possible, and had more than once lifted her from despair.

Hope also meant that she could dream of happy endings, if not for her, then for Sophie, which is why Poppy had written to Renzo in the first place. Poppy had wanted to save Sophie from a loveless marriage. She wanted Sophie to have the life she deserved, which meant true love. Passionate love. Forever love.

The kind of love Poppy's parents had. Poppy's father had dearly loved her mother, taking her to every chemo and radiation treatment and staying with her after.

His love had been fierce and unwavering even to the bitter end.

The love and tenderness he'd shown her mother allowed her mother to say, even after she'd been taken to hospice, that she'd met her prince and had lived happily-ever-after. Their relationship hadn't been one of lust but trust and respect, and that was the marriage Poppy wanted. That was truly the ultimate fairy tale. Dal's idea of marriage made her ill, which is why she would never, ever agree to marry him, or to even be a candidate on his "list." She didn't even believe in lists. Or candidates. She believed in love, real love, true love.

And yet his kiss, that kiss, pure magic…

So unbelievably—

No.

No. She wouldn't think about it, not anymore.

Poppy jumped off her bed, unable to remain inside her bedroom a moment longer but not sure where to go, and then glancing out one of her windows, she spotted the enormous lap pool, gleaming with all the pool lights on.

She rifled through her wardrobe until she found the drawer with the swimsuits and grabbed the black bikini with the gold beads on the straps and hips. She topped the suit with a feather-light green gauze tunic and headed downstairs to the long lap pool illuminated for the evening.

Thankfully, there was no one outside, and she could commandeer any one of the dozen lounge chairs.

She picked a chair in the corner and kicked off her leather sandals and peeled off her tunic, dropping them onto the chair before diving into the pool.

She swam under water as far as she could before she had to surface to get air. Turning onto her back she floated for a moment, feeling some of the tension melt away.

And then from beneath her lashes, she spotted a shadowy figure on one of the terraces above, and she knew from the width of the shoulders who it was.

Poppy turned over onto her stomach and dove back down, swimming below the surface as if she could hide from him.

Maybe he didn't see her.

Maybe he'd ignore her.

Somehow she doubted it. There was too much unsettled between them. And that kiss had been so explosive. She'd always wanted to kiss him but that kiss…that hadn't been what she'd ever imagined.

That kiss had been pure sex, pure sin, and if she hadn't fled when she did, she would have given herself up to him.

Dal watched Poppy swim in the glowing pool below.

She looked beautiful and sensual floating in the water, her dark hair glistening in the light of the pool. He very much wanted to go down and dive in and draw her toward him, continuing what they started.

She'd feel warm and soft, and slick in the water. He could imagine cupping her full breasts and then her rounded derriere.

She was almost naked. He wanted her naked. He wanted her stripped and exposed so that he could drink her in.

She was lush and ripe and unbearably sweet. Her kisses earlier had driven him half-mad. They were ardent and innocent at the same time, and her passionate response had woken a hunger and even now, a half hour later, he still burned.

Everything in him wanted to go down to the pool and take her, and claim her. But he wasn't going to just seduce her. That would be too easy. He wanted her to want him, and want to be with him, but not just for one night. For all nights. Forever.

She needed to marry him. She needed to agree to be his wife.

As his wife, he would spoil her and shower her with gifts and things, endless beautiful things. He'd also give her security and stability. As well as pleasure.

Always pleasure.

But first, the wedding ceremony.

There would be no sex, not until he had his ring on her finger.

CHAPTER SEVEN

POPPY SPENT THE next morning going through the various
résumés and applications that had been forwarded, reject-
ing the ones that would not be a good fit, and then setting
aside the possibilities. She even followed up on the references of two different women who'd stood out.

After finishing with the applications, she answered new
emails that had come in during the night. There were a few
from concerned associates, as well as three very bold inqui-
ries from one member of the press. The reporter was with
an American tabloid and asked if Poppy could jump on the
phone with her for a quick call, and if that wasn't possible,
perhaps Poppy would send a few words…maybe a quote?
The online magazine was also quite happy to cite her as an
anonymous source, and they did pay, too…all very hush-
hush to ensure that the earl would feel no embarrassment.

Poppy deleted the emails from the reporter immediately,
determined not to say a word about them to Dal and was
just about to close her laptop when an email popped into
her inbox from Florrie.

Had such a lovely message from Dal this morning, but
having difficulty reaching him on his phone. He said he
has tickets for Royal Box for the Gila Open in Mehkar. Beyond excited. Send me deets, please! And the poor darling! How is our gorgeous earl holding up?

Poppy read the email twice, unable to believe her eyes.

Dal had been in contact with Florrie now, too. And he
hadn't just checked in with her, he'd dangled VIP polo
tickets to a woman who was completely mad about ponies.

It was a brilliant move—Dal was nothing if not shrewd—but also utterly infuriating because just last night Dal had been seducing her!

Livid, Poppy marched up the flights of stairs, rapped on his door before entering his room, laptop tucked beneath her arm. "I hope you're dressed," she said curtly, "because we have work to do."

Dal was lying stretched out on the couch in the living room, reading, one arm propped behind his head. He looked up from the book, a black eyebrow lifting. "What work would that be?"

"Your work. I get emails about your business affairs all the time. People still think I'm your secretary."

"That's because you are." He sat up, stretching, which just made the soft knit fabric of his shirt pull tighter across the hard planes of his chest. "So what is so urgent?"

She stared at him baffled by his nonchalance. "I have never seen you lie down in the middle of the day and read."

"I was focused all morning. Why not take a break before lunch and get caught up on this book I've been wanting to read?"

"Indeed?"

"You seem quite tense. Is everything all right?"

"I've just been working for you. That's all."

"Good. Since you're still on the payroll."

She bit her tongue to say something she might regret. And then she had to wait another ten seconds to get her racing pulse to slow. Finally, when she trusted herself to speak and not shout, she said, "I've made good progress on finding my replacement. How is it going finding the replacement for Sophie?"

"Better than I hoped."

"Really?" She decided she'd play dumb. Let him be the one to tell her about his clever invitation to Florrie. "Any exciting developments?"

"Well, I kissed you last night—"

"That's not an exciting development."

The corner of his mouth curled. "It was for me."

"How is it going with the other two on your list?"

"I haven't kissed them, but that's probably due to the lack of proximity and other logistics."

"Would you kiss all three of us if you could?"

"Absolutely."

She hated hearing him say that, she did. Poppy clenched her hands into fists. "Why?"

"Because as you so kindly pointed out, physical attraction is part of marriage—"

"I did not point that out. I said nothing about attraction or sex."

"You did infer that compatibility is important, and part of the 'more' relationships needed."

"Successful relationships."

"Right, and that's what I'm to want for myself because I deserve it. I deserve that elusive 'more.'"

She hated that he kept quoting her, and doing it literally word for word. "'More' is not elusive."

"Isn't it? It's an intangible, something one cannot easily quantify when making an offer, or proposing marriage."

"You should stop talking. You're making me hate you."

"And yet you were the one that told me to communicate. I'm trying to communicate."

"I think you're trying to annoy me."

"Why would I do that?"

"I'm not sure. I haven't figured that part out yet."

"Well, when you do figure it out, let me know. I hate having you upset with me when we only have thirteen days left together."

And just like that she felt her heart mash and fall. She ground her teeth together to keep from making a sound.

"You will be missed," he added kindly. "More than you know."

Poppy smiled to hide how much his reminder hurt. He made her feel crazy, but at least she was able to be crazy and near him. "So you don't need me today? There's nothing you want me to do?"

"Why don't you take the afternoon off? Have some time for yourself. Read or swim or feel free to explore the estate." He was smiling up at her, the smile of a man who acted as if he genuinely cared about her best interests.

He didn't, though. Because if he did, he wouldn't have kissed her like that last night. He wouldn't have held her so firmly, his hands low on her hips, making the inside of her melt and ache, while making the rest of her shiver and tingle. She'd felt his desire, but most of all, she'd become painfully aware of her own. She wanted him…almost desperately. She'd always wanted him, but it had been a cerebral thing, not a body thing, but last night had woken her up and set her body on fire.

Poppy headed for the door, her sandals making a light tapping sound against the marble floor, the tapping echoing the hard, uncomfortable thudding of her heart.

All these years she'd wondered what it would be like to kiss him, and now she knew.

And now she'd never forget.

She paused in the doorway to look back at him. "Oh! Before I forget, Florrie emailed me. She'd love those tickets to the polo match in Gila and is eager for all the *deets*."

And then, flashing him a great, wide, *furious* smile, she walked out.

Dal listened to Poppy's footsteps retreat.

Gone was his tidy, buttoned-up secretary with the tight chignons and conservative skirts and blouses. In her place was this passionate, fierce, fresh-faced beauty who didn't hesitate to give him her opinion. He'd always enjoyed work-ing with Poppy, even when she had her mini meltdowns and crises of confidence, because she was fundamentally one of the best people he'd ever known, but now he enjoyed looking at her. And teasing her. And making her blush.

And shiver and arch in his arms.

She'd been impossibly appealing last night; so appeal-ing that he'd barely been able to sleep, his body heavy and aroused for far too much of the night. Which is why he'd deliberately kept her at arm's length this morning. It had been an endless night and he wasn't ready to be tempted.

But clearly, she didn't like that he'd kept his distance, and she definitely didn't like the email from Florrie.

His lips twisted. Poor Poppy. He'd told Florrie that Poppy would be the one to help her get the tickets because he knew Poppy wouldn't like it.

His smile deepened, remembering her extreme vexation. He wasn't a nice man, but he was good at getting what he wanted, and he wanted Poppy, fierce, passionate, beautiful Poppy, who wasn't afraid to stand up to him, and talk to him and make him feel like a man, not a machine.

Poppy took a bath before dinner feeling incredibly con-flicted about the night ahead. At any other time in her life she would have been thrilled at the idea of having a lovely, long evening with him, where it would be just the two of them, but her fantasy Randall was nothing like Sheikh Talal, who did what he wanted and kissed her when he felt like and generally ignored all the rules for polite behavior.

Poppy towel-dried and stepped into the bedroom where Imma had placed a variety of kaftans on the bed for her to choose from.

She wasn't in the mood for the navy or green one, even though both were lovely, and the black looked far too de-pressing even with all the silver and blue beadwork. She reached for the plum gown with the gold and cream and quickly dressed. She tried drawing her hair into a ponytail but it didn't look right with the formality of the gown. Sighing, Poppy released her hair, combed it hard, hating the thick waves, but left it down.

Imma told her dinner would be on the rooftop and directed her up the three flights of stairs in the central tower. Poppy stepped out of the dim, cool tower into the golden light of dusk, thinking she had never seen a more magical setting for a meal. It was a rooftop dining room, open to the sky. It was heading toward twilight now, but it'd be dark within the hour. The walled patio already gleamed with candlelight, pillars of candles along the waist-high walls, while glittering silver lanterns dotted the side tables.

Stewards stood at attention, one with a tray of cocktails, another with appetizers. A third gentleman held a folded silk pashmina should she become cold later.

It wasn't just luxurious, but wildly romantic, although she'd never tell that to Dal. He was already powerful and overbearing. She didn't need to feed his ego, or his ridiculous marriage plans.

She was not going to marry him. Nor was she on his list. She'd never be on a *list*.

Dal emerged from the opposite tower just a minute after she did. He was wearing elegant black trousers and a fitted black dress shirt open at the collar. He wore no tie and his black hair was combed but he hadn't shaved before dinner, giving him a hint of a shadow on his strong jaw and a wicked glint in his golden eyes.

She hated the shiver that raced down her back, as well as the bubbly, giddy sensation she got when he lifted two glasses from the silver tray, carrying one of the pretty icy-pink cocktails to her. "The Kasbah Jolie signature drink."

"What is it?" she asked warily, taking the frosty glass rimmed in sugar.

"I have no idea. There is a new chef and he seems to be having a great deal of fun naming everything Kasbah this, and Kasbah that."

It seemed that tonight Dal was determined to be charming and she couldn't help smiling. "Cheers to the innovative chefs." And then she clinked her glass to his and sipped the drink, and the icy-cold pink martini-style cocktail was absolutely delicious. She could taste pomegranate juice, grapefruit juice plus vodka and something else. "Compliments to the chef."

"Come this way," he said, taking her elbow and steering her across the enormous roof to a private alcove facing the mountains.

Screened by a hedge of jasmine, he set down his drink and reached into his pocket and drew out a small black velvet box.

Poppy's breath caught in her throat as she spotted what looked like a jeweler's box. This wasn't…it couldn't be…

"I haven't showered you with gifts. I thought it was time," he said. "I hope you like them, and I think you should put them on now."

Like them. Put them on now.

Obviously, it wasn't a ring, then, and she didn't know why she felt a stab of disappointment. She didn't want to marry him. She didn't want to be wooed by him. So why did she care that he was giving her some pretty trinket instead of a diamond ring?

She hated herself for feeling like crying as she cracked open the lid, and catching a sparkle of white fire, she popped the lid open all the way. More glints of light and fire. "Oh, Dal." Nestled in black velvet was a pair of large gold and diamond chandelier earrings, dazzling earrings, the kind that only movie stars and princesses wore. Without even meaning to count, she added up all the diamonds sparkling up at her, with eight large oval diamonds in each earring, with dozens of smaller diamonds covering the gold setting. "I am praying these are not real diamonds," she said.

He looked scandalized. "I have never bought anyone fake stones."

"But these must be a fortune."

"I can afford a fortune." He took one out of the box and loosened the back. "And you deserve a fortune."

"I don't."

"Let's see what they look like on you," he said as though she hadn't spoken. "You're not wearing anything tonight."

"The silver earrings Izba had for me last night wouldn't have looked right with this gown."

"I know. I told her to make sure you couldn't wear the silver earrings tonight."

"You're awfully bossy."

"That shouldn't be news to you," he said, stepping closer so that he put the diamond chandelier on her. His fingertips felt deliciously warm and her ear felt deliciously sensitive. She suppressed a shudder of pleasure as he twisted the back to keep the heavy earring from falling out.

"Now the other ear," he said.

More tingling sensations as he attached the second earring and then gave her head a little shake, hearing the stones click, and feeling the earrings move. "How do they look?"

"You look beautiful."

"I'm afraid this is far too extravagant. I'll wear them tonight, but I can't keep them."

"Don't say things like that. It's not polite."

"You can't give me gifts that cost hundreds of thousands of pounds."

"You're supposed to love them, not argue with me."

"Maybe Florrie and Seraphina like presents like this—"

"Oh, they most definitely do. They wouldn't dream of refusing a token of my affection."

"I'd rather have your real affection."

"You do. You had proof of that last night."

"You're making me very angry," she said.

"Don't be angry. It's a lovely night. Just look at the sunset."

She turned to look out over the valley. The setting sun had painted the red mountains rose, lavender and gold. "It is beyond breathtaking," she said after a moment.

"It is quite spectacular," he agreed. "I wish I hadn't waited so long to return. It's good to be back."

She glanced up at him. "Did you think it wouldn't?"

In the elegant black evening shirt, his skin looked more olive and his eyes appeared an even lighter gold. It was funny how she'd always thought of him as so very English, and yet here in Mehkar, he exuded heat and mystery, as well as an overwhelming sensuality.

"I was worried," he admitted after a moment. "I was worried about what it'd be like here without Andrew and my mother. I'd never been here without them, but you've made it easy for me."

"Are you going to see your grandfather while we're here?"

"I should, but haven't made any plans to do so yet."

"Tell me about your relationship with him."

"There's not much to understand. I live in England. He lives in Mehkar."

"And yet you're here in Mehkar, and we were in Gila, albeit briefly."

"It's complicated," he said brusquely.

"That's your code for you don't want to discuss it."

"It really is complicated. I don't even know how to talk about it. One day this place was my home. It was my favorite place in the world. And then suddenly it wasn't part of my life anymore, and the people here were cut off, too. It was bad enough losing my mum and brother, but to lose your grandparents and cousins and aunts and uncles? It hurt more than I can say. It's still not easy to talk about."

"Who cut them off? Your father or your grandfather?"

He shoved a hand through his black hair, rifling it. "Does it matter?"

She looked down into the shimmering pink of her cocktail, the color so very similar to the walls of the Kasbah. "I guess I have this crazy idea that if I understand your past, then maybe I'll understand you."

He gave her a look she couldn't decipher. "I've spent all these years burying the memories. I don't know that it's wise to dig them all up."

"Buried memories mean buried emotions—"

"My favorite kind," he said darkly.

"Don't you want to feel anything?"

"No. But apparently, you do." He finished his drink and set the glass down on the wall next to his hip. "It was June eleventh. We'd just finished the school term and were out on holiday. Mum came to pick us up, as she always did. We were on our way to the airport to come here when the accident happened." He paused before saying slowly, clearly. "The accident that killed my mother and Andrew."

It took her a moment to piece it together. "You were on your way here? To Jolie?"

"We always flew here straightaway on our last day of school. It was our tradition. We couldn't wait to come. At least I couldn't wait. Andrew had wanted to stay home that summer with Father but Mother insisted. Grandfather wanted to see Andrew." He frowned, brows flattening. "Andrew was the oldest of my grandfather's grandchildren, important to both sides of the family."

He looked up right into her eyes, expression still intense. "Until that day, I'd had a very different childhood from Andrew. He was the heir. I was just a boy...a free-spirited, rather sensitive, second son."

She didn't know what to say, so she didn't try to speak.

Dal added after a moment, "It wasn't ever the same after that. Not in Winchester. Not here."

"It wouldn't be, would it?" she said sympathetically before adding, "So you chose not to come back?"

"It was my father's decision to cut contact with my mother's family. After the funerals, I didn't see or hear from anyone from Mehkar for ten years."

"Why?"

"My father blamed my mother for the accident, and so by extension, he blamed her family."

"Was she at fault?"

"No. The other driver was distracted. They said he was on the phone, ran a red light and smashed into our car head-on."

"Mother died immediately. Andrew died at the hospital. And I survived with just cuts and bruises."

"Your poor grandfather," she sighed. "It must have been devastating to lose his daughter and his eldest grandson on the very day they were to return home."

"I'm sure it wasn't easy for him. My grandmother, his wife, had died just months before in an accident. He'd been eager to have my mother return for the summer."

"So your grandfather has never reached out to you since your mother's funeral. If you were eleven that has been nearly twenty-four years!"

"No. He reached out. I was rude. I rebuffed him, and even though I was at fault, I have chosen not to apologize or make amends."

"Why?"

"I don't know."

"I don't believe that. I think you do know. And I'd like to know."

"So you can have additional proof of what a cool, unfeeling ass I am?"

She gave him a reproving look. "I already know who you are, and what you are, which is why I want to know why you—someone I know does have feelings, only you keep them very deeply buried—would rebuff someone you apparently once loved very much?"

His shoulders shifted impatiently. "Because I did love him. And I didn't understand why he left me there, in England. I hated England. I hated my father—" He broke off, jaw grinding, shadows darkening his eyes. "It doesn't matter, and I shouldn't admit that I hated my father. My father had problems. He couldn't help himself."

"But you can help yourself. Reach out to your grandfather. See him. Apologize. Make amends."

"I can't."

"You *can*. Don't be stupid and proud. Tell him you're sorry, because one day he won't be here and then it'll be too late."

Dal didn't say anything for the longest time. He finished his drink and she finished hers and they watched the shadows swaddle the mountains, the rose and gold light fading to lavender and gray.

After a long silence Dal glanced at her, lips curving. "You're the only person that ever tries to tell me what to do."

"You could be a really, truly lovely man if you tried."

"That sounds terribly dull."

"I like dull men. I'm looking for a dull man, someone who will cuddle with me on the sofa while we watch our favorite program on the telly."

"You would hate that after a while."

"Not if it was a good program."

"You almost make watching television sound fun."

Fun. In all her years of working for him, she'd never once heard him the use the word *fun*. Discipline, duty, responsibility, yes. But fun? Never. "You have changed," she said. "You're already very different from just a few days ago."

"It seems I had to. Randall Grant was an arse."

"Is Dal better?"

"He's trying."

She glanced at him from beneath her lashes and felt a little shiver as he looked right back at her, his golden gaze locking with hers and holding. He didn't look away, not even when one of the stewards invited them to the dinner table.

"Why didn't you try before?" she asked softly. "Why didn't you try for Sophie?"

"I don't know. Maybe because she didn't bring out the best in me. Not like you."

"I bring out the best in you?"

His dense black lashes dropped, his lovely mouth curving. "Perhaps I should say you bring out the *better*."

Her chest squeezed, her insides wobbly. He made her feel so much and it wasn't fair. When he dropped his guard and had a real conversation she felt close to him. Connected. *Too connected.* How was she to leave him when he felt like hers?

One of the stewards approached them and spoke quietly in Arabic to Dal. Dal answered and then turned to Poppy. "I have a phone call I must take. It won't take long, just a couple minutes. Please have another drink and I'll meet you at the table."

True to his word, he was gone less than ten minutes, and when he returned she was waiting at the beautiful table with the rose-pink tablecloth and the gleaming white candles.

"I tried to make it quick," he said, sitting down at the table with her.

"Is everything okay?"

"It was Florrie."

Poppy's chest squeezed tight. "Oh?"

"She's heading to Gila for the polo tournament and she had some questions about the tournament and packing and appropriate dress for the royal box."

"I didn't realize you were a fashion consultant."

He leaned back in his chair, his lips quirking. "You're jealous."

"I'm not."

"No, you shouldn't be. I've asked you to marry me—"

"You've never asked. You told me we were to marry. That's not a proper proposal."

"So is that all that's keeping you from saying yes? Are you wanting romance? Flowers? Candlelight?"

She became very aware of the romantic dinner under the stars, and the fragrant roses on the table, along with the candles glimmering everywhere.

"You threw your list together," she said. "There was very little thought put into it, and I wish you would have considered more possibilities. Women who are not Sophie's friends. Women who might actually want to stay at home with you and have dinner with you, or maybe grab a book and read in the evening near you—"

"I don't need a nanny, Poppy."

"No, you just need a woman with hips and a womb."

When he didn't contradict her, she felt her temper spike. "You are so infuriating! You know you haven't tried hard to find a great wife. You're simply settling—"

"Not settling at all. You're on the list."

"At the number three position, which makes me think that the names on your list are there by default. I'd hazard to guess that all three names made it because that's all you could remember in a pinch."

He grinned at her, a sexy, powerful, masculine smile. "Your name was not added because I was in a pinch. *You* were added because we suit each other—"

"So annoying," she muttered under her breath.

"Why can't you accept a compliment?"

"Because I know you. You don't compliment people, and you most certainly don't compliment *me*."

"Let me put it another way. I can barely tolerate most people but I haven't just tolerated your company for the past four years. I've enjoyed it."

"And you wonder why I have absolutely no desire to marry you!"

"It wouldn't hurt for you to be a little more logical and a lot less fanciful."

"How about we focus on the two women still on your list? You can't court both Florrie and Seraphina at the same time. It's not practical when you're down to fourteen days, and so I recommend at this point in time you focus on one. With Florrie en route to Gila, just settle on her and be done with it. I am sure once she learns that you're not just the Earl of Langston but Prince Talal she'll jump through the hoops and marry you right away."

"I had no idea Florrie was your clear favorite."

"She's not my favorite. In fact, of the two, she's my least favorite."

"Is she? Why?"

"She's—" *The least monogamous woman I know.* But Poppy bit back the words, uncomfortable with the truth. "She just doesn't seem quite ready to settle down."

"I don't know. Maybe she hasn't yet met the right person."

"Maybe," Poppy answered sourly.

"What else do you know about them? Who would I enjoy more? No. Scratch that. Which one would be a more natural mother?"

Poppy shuddered. "Neither. They are both too self-absorbed."

"You're sounding very catty right now, Poppy. It's not attractive. I thought these were your friends."

"Sophie's friends."

"Is there nothing positive you can say about either?"

Poppy ground her teeth together and lifted her chin. "Seraphina loves fashion and clothes. She spends twenty thousand or more each season on new clothes."

"You're supposed to be giving me positives."

"That is a positive. She's always beautifully dressed. Oh. And she keeps herself very slender. Very, very slender."

"Is that your way of saying she has an eating disorder?"

"No. It's my way of saying she just doesn't eat. She has a liquid diet. Mostly green drinks and cleansers. Things like that."

"I'm sure she'd indulge in cheese plates and chocolate now and then."

Poppy frowned, trying to remember when she'd ever seen Seraphina actually eat anything. She nearly always had a bottle in her hand, or purse, filled with one of those drinks that smelled of lemon and parsley, cucumber and ginger. "I've never actually seen her eat anything sweet. Or anything with carbs. Or any kind of meat."

"So she won't share a steak and kidney pie with me?"

"Oh, no. Never. The crust alone would make her faint."

"What about Florrie? Would she eat a steak and kidney pie?"

"Probably."

"That's good news."

"Yes." But Poppy couldn't feign enthusiasm. Florrie would not be a good wife for Dal. She wasn't even a good girlfriend. She didn't understand the meaning of faithful, juggling her polo player lovers with disconcerting ease.

"Now, come on, Poppy. What's wrong with Florrie? If I didn't know you better, I'd think you were jealous and wanted to be my countess."

He was right, of course. She was jealous, but she'd never

let him know that. "Fortunately, you do know me better and know I've absolutely zero desire to be your countess."

"Why?"

"I hate that you dangle money and possessions and make it sound as if those material things are the basis for a good marriage, when we both know that nothing is more important than affection, kindness and respect."

"If I wasn't the Earl of Langston, but a vicar in a Cotswold parish, would you consider my proposal?"

Her cheeks burned with embarrassment but she held his gaze. "If you were a vicar in the Cotswold, would you love me?"

"I don't know how to answer because I don't believe in love. It's a fantasy concocted in the twentieth century by advertising giants to sell more things to more people."

"That is such rubbish."

"But I do believe passion and desire are real."

"And I believe that passion without love is just sex. And I wouldn't ever marry a man just to have sex. I could have sex *now* if that's what I wanted."

"Sex with whom?"

She lifted her chin, absolutely brazen. "You."

Her words stole his breath. And all rational thought. Her eyes shone with light while her cheeks glowed with color and her expression was nothing short of defiant.

Who was this woman? When had she become so confident and provocative?

It didn't help that the lush outline of Poppy's breast was playing havoc with his control.

He'd managed his physical side for five and a half years, clamping down tightly on all needs or wants, shutting himself down so that he could be the elegant, chivalrous man Sophie desired.

But with Sophie gone, and Poppy here, he felt anything but elegant and chivalrous.

What he felt was ravenous, his carnal side awake and hungry. After years of not feeling or wanting or needing, he needed now. He needed her. And his body ached morning, noon and night with desire.

Just watching her bite her full lower lip now made him want to kiss that tender lip, and then lick the seam of her lips so that she'd open for him and let him have his way with her.

His tongue in her mouth.

His tongue on her breasts.

His tongue between her legs, lathing her clit.

Dal hardened all over again, his skin so tight he felt like he'd explode.

"You have no idea what I want to do to you," he said huskily, picturing stripping her naked so that her full breasts were bared, her nipples peaked. He'd work her nipples, pinching, teasing, sucking, until she was wet for him and arching, hips lifting, begging.

He wanted to be between her thighs.

He wanted to clasp her hips and hold her still while he devoured her.

He wanted to feel her shattering and hear her cry and know that she was his, and only his.

"Not interested," she said. "I don't want to sleep with you, or marry you. You're not my type—"

"You don't have a type, Poppy. You haven't dated once in all the years you've worked for me."

"Not true. I had a boyfriend three years ago—"

"A boyfriend?"

"Yes. A boyfriend. He was lovely, too, until well, he wasn't so lovely anymore."

"And just how long was he your boyfriend?"

"I don't remember."

"That means he wasn't around long enough to truly signify."

"That's not what it means. It just means I decided to move forward and put the past behind me."

"I have a feeling he was your boyfriend for all of three weeks."

"It's not really any of your business whether he was my boyfriend for three minutes or three years. What matters is that I don't want to be your girlfriend, or your wife, or anything at all because your values are not my values. You don't want what I want in life. We'd be a disaster together."

"Even though you like how I can make you feel?"

Color stormed her cheeks and her eyes snapped fire. "You must be confusing me with someone else on your list because I care about you, and yes, I enjoyed kissing you last night, but I'm not going to give up my freedom and future just because I felt a twinge of lust!"

CHAPTER EIGHT

BACK IN HER ROOM, Poppy allowed Imma to help her ease the stunning plum kaftan off her head. While Imma hung the gorgeous gown back up, Poppy removed her dangling gold and diamond earrings, tucking them into a drawer next to her bed before taking off her makeup.

But even a half hour after changing into her pajamas, she felt hot and riled up. Dal was beyond annoying. He was the worst. The absolute worst.

Poppy stripped off her nightgown and put on her swimsuit and cover-up, and headed for the pool.

She swam a lap under water, and then another lap under water before surfacing to float on her back.

The warm water soothed her, relaxing her tense muscles, while the gentle lap of water against her skin made her feel buoyant and free.

She heard a scraping sound and opened her eyes to discover Dal sitting down on the foot of her lounge chair.

He was still dressed for dinner, which reassured her somewhat because that meant he wasn't planning on swimming. Maybe if she closed her eyes and ignored him, he'd leave soon.

She flipped over onto her stomach and did a slow, easy breaststroke toward the opposite end of the pool. She pretended she was alone, without a care in the world, even though she could feel his eyes, his gaze, following her every kick and stroke.

At the far end she reached for the wall and turned around, facing him.

He looked at her, his handsome face expressionless.

She almost wished for one of his small, mocking smiles.

The smiles and ironic laughter were easier than this tension between them now.

"What do you want?" she called, even as she stretched her arms out along the tiled pool edge, and leaned back so her legs could float up.

"You."

"But I don't want you."

"Liar."

The low, husky pitch of his voice sent shivers racing through her, making her tummy clench and her knees press tight.

She couldn't engage, couldn't encourage him; it would be disastrous to provoke him at this late hour.

Poppy forced herself to relax. She closed her eyes, let herself float where she was, and as she breathed in and out, she pictured him getting up and walking away. In fact, she willed him to leave, pouring all her concentration into making him disappear, but when she opened her eyes, he was still there.

"I can prove it to you," he said.

"We're not children. There's no need to prove anything to anyone."

"You can't hide forever from the truth."

"But I can get some laps in, can't I?"

"I'll wait."

"I have a lot of laps."

"I'll count them for you."

She shot him a frosty look, not comfortable with this game.

She dove under water and swam half the length of the pool before needing to surface for a breath. When she glanced over her shoulder toward the lounge chair where she'd left her things, she realized he was gone. For a split second she felt relief, and then she noticed the pile of clothes set next to her tunic on the lounge chair.

He'd undressed.

Poppy spun in the pool, discovering him behind her. "What are you doing?" she demanded breathlessly.

"Joining you for a swim."

"Are you...naked?" she asked, afraid to look down.

"Have you never gone skinny-dipping?"

"No." Her voice came out strangled. "So you are naked."

"Would you feel better if I told you I was wearing briefs?"

"Yes."

"Then I'm wearing briefs," he answered, reaching for her and drawing her toward him with the assurance of a man who knew exactly what he was doing. He drew her through the water until her breasts brushed his chest.

His body was so large and warm, and it felt unbelievably good to be pressed to him, skin to skin. Her breath caught when his large hands circled her waist, drawing her hips even closer to his.

He wasn't naked. But he was hard...very thick and very erect. Her eyes widened as he rubbed her across him, the tip of his shaft finding the apex of her thighs and all the sensitive nerves there.

Her lips parted. She made a soft hiss of sound.

He lifted an eyebrow. "Did you say something?"

"This isn't a good idea," she choked, even as he did it again, and the thick blunt tip against her core made her want to swoon.

Maybe he wasn't wearing briefs after all...

"I don't think this is a good idea," she said hoarsely, even as her pulse raced and her skin felt exquisitely sensitive.

"We're just playing," he said.

She stared at him, mesmerized, at the gleam of water on his shadowed jaw, and the way the pool light reflected onto the hard features of his face. "But this kind of play is dangerous."

"You're safe with me."

"I don't think that's true at all." In fact, she knew it wasn't true, and yet it was hard to move away from him when everything in her wanted this with every fiber of her being.

But that didn't make it right, a tiny part of her brain shrieked. Sugar is delicious, but too much will make you sick.

And he most definitely wasn't sugar.

He was spice, wicked, sexy spice and beyond addictive.

"You want danger," he murmured, his lips brushing her ear, and then finding the hollow below.

Pleasure shrieked through her and she gasped, lips pressing to the warm wall of his chest.

"But you want danger that won't destroy you," he added, his teeth catching at her earlobe and giving it a tug. "And you know I would never destroy you. I'd just teach you all the things you've always wanted to know."

"Like what?"

"This," he answered, his head dropping so that his mouth covered hers in a light, teasing kiss. Last night's kiss had been fierce and hot, but this kiss was tender and light and unbearably erotic.

His lips brushed hers, and then again, sending ripples of pleasure from her lips into her breasts and belly and beyond.

The fleeting caress seemed to wake nerve endings she didn't even know she had and she lifted her mouth to his, wanting more.

She felt his smile as he kissed her, his lips just barely parting hers, and the tip of his tongue lightly touching the inside of her lower lip.

Oh, that felt so good. Goose bumps covered her arm and made the fine damp hair at her nape rise. Her breasts swelled, aching, too.

"One more of those," she pleaded.

The soft, warm kiss flooded her with heat, and then as his tongue did a slow, lazy exploration of her mouth she pressed herself closer, thinking it was just a kiss and yet so much more.

She wanted so much more.

And when his hand moved to her breast, playing with the taut nipple through her wet suit, she nearly groaned at the pleasure. His hand felt so good on her, and the way he touched her sensitive nipple made her tummy tighten and her lower back prickle as she felt close to popping out of her skin.

"And you say desire isn't important," Dal said, lifting his head to look into her eyes.

She blushed and tried not to squirm as he tugged and kneaded her nipple, each small pull creating more tension inside her and adding to the heat between her thighs. "Desire is important," she whispered breathlessly as he pinched and played with her, the sensation so new and erotic that she couldn't focus properly.

"So you agree."

"I agree it's part of love."

"You can desire someone you do not love."

"Well, I couldn't," she answered, gasping as he pushed the scrap of fabric covering her breast away, exposing her nipple.

She saw his eyes darken in appreciation, his hard jaw jutting just before he bent his head and took the tender pebbled peak in his mouth.

His mouth felt surprisingly cool against her warm skin, and then as he suckled her she grew hot and wet in a way that had nothing to do with the pool or the warm, cloudless night. She clung more tightly to him, her fingers biting into his shoulders as her body came to life, shivering and shuddering from the intense sensation streaking through her.

She strained to be closer, seeking more contact and more

friction. As he drew on her nipple, she pressed her hips to him, wanting the rough rasp of his chest hair and the thick press of his erection.

He wrapped her legs around his waist, securing her ankles behind his back. "Don't move," he commanded.

"You're not in charge—" she began to protest but then broke off as his fingers slipped inside her bikini bottoms, finding the cleft where she was so wet and hot.

She shuddered as he stroked her there, finding her tender nub and then down and circling back again. He then drew his fingers away, and he looked down at her, a black brow lifting.

Her hips rocked helplessly. She felt beyond bereft, her core clenching, her body straining for touch, for relief.

"Are you in charge, then?" he asked quietly, silkily, combing her dark, wet hair back from her face.

Her cheeks burned. She burned. She felt as if he'd set her on fire and was now watching her incinerate.

"Maybe I spoke too soon," she said faintly.

"Louder?"

"You are in charge. There. Happy?"

"Not yet. But I will be, soon."

And then he slipped his hand back beneath the elastic of her bikini panty, stroking between her thighs, learning the shape of her. It was all very nice but she wanted him to do what he'd done before. Touch her there, at that place where all the nerve endings seemed to be.

She opened her thighs wider, pressing her hips at him, unable to ask for what she wanted, but he didn't seem in a hurry to caress the nub. Instead, he traced the outer lips and then inner lips before slipping the tip of his finger inside her. She hissed a breath, lips parting as he withdrew and then did it again, just touching her with the tip, making her shudder, making her want to press his finger deeper.

"It will sting when I possess you on our wedding night,"

he said, kissing the side of her neck, finding more sensitive spots she didn't know existed. "But it will only hurt that first night."

"We're not marrying," she breathed, twitching as he found her nub and gave it a caress.

"You should give up now," he said, stroking the nub again, making her tighten and dance against him. "You won't win."

"You can't buy me, and you can't seduce me," she choked.

"Maybe I can't buy you, but I can seduce you. I am seducing you." And then as he caressed her clit, he slipped the fingertip back inside her, making her whimper.

He deftly stroked both, and she didn't know which pleasure to focus on. Both sensations felt so good, the bright, sharp pleasure at the top of her thighs, or the sensitive shivers from teasing her below.

She felt her body try to tighten around his finger, the sensations so new and exciting but also overwhelming.

He kissed her then, and she wrapped her arms more tightly around his neck, kissing him back. He sucked her tongue into his mouth, drawing on her tongue in a tight, hot, erotic rhythm that had her hips rotating. She felt like she was on fire, sensation flooding her. It was hard to focus on any one pleasure when it all felt so good together—her tongue in his mouth, his hand between her thighs, stroking her. She felt the pressure build and tighten, everything in her tensing, and then he slipped a finger inside her even as his thumb played across her nub and suddenly she couldn't control the pleasure, couldn't keep it together, and she cried out against his mouth, shattering in her first climax ever.

For long moments after, she was breathless and dazed. She felt boneless and weak and she rested her head against his chest as he rearranged her in his arms, letting her legs settle and her body relax. Another few moments later, she felt sufficiently recovered to push away, needing distance now, uncomfortable with what had just happened.

"Do you have a preference for the kind of ring you'd like?" he asked.

Poppy blinked, her brain still fuzzy and disconnected from the pleasure. "Ring?"

"I'll give you the ring tomorrow, and we'll marry a week from today. That gives us a full week before my birthday. I don't want to leave it to the last minute this time."

"That is surely the least romantic proposal I have ever heard of in my life."

"I gave you romance at dinner. I just proved we have chemistry. And there is a great deal of it between us. Now we just need to finalize the details so we can move forward with our lives—"

"You're mad," she interrupted, floating farther away.

"Possibly. It runs in the family."

"Don't say that. It's not funny." Poppy had first learned of Randall's father's illness from the housekeeper at Langston House years ago. The housekeeper had wanted Poppy to understand why control was so important to the Sixth Earl of Langston. It seemed that the Fifth Earl had none.

"I'm entirely serious. My father was quite ill."

"I know."

"Sophie told you?"

"I don't think Sophie knows."

"But you do?"

"Mrs. Holmes told me."

"Why would she do that?"

"It was the day after your father's funeral. You'd told me to return to London and she asked me not to go."

"Why? Was she afraid I'd hurt myself?"

Poppy flinched. "No. She just didn't want you alone. She thought you needed a friend with you."

"And you were my friend?"

She lifted her chin, unwilling to let him see he'd hurt her. "I was the only one there. You'd managed to scare everyone else off."

"You make me sound like a monster."

She heard the bruised note in his voice. She glanced away, over the sparkling surface of the water, trying to think of something to say.

"Sophie used to call me the Ice Monster." His voice had grown even deeper. "You used to laugh."

"It was that or cry," she flashed, glancing down at her hands skimming back and forth just below the surface of the water. "But I'm no Belle, and you're no Beast and I can't save you—"

"Not asking you to save me. I'm asking you to marry me."

"In your case, it's one and the same, isn't it? You don't want me. You don't even want to marry. You're just trying to protect your title and lands."

When he didn't answer, she persisted. "Is it really so terrible to lose the earldom and estates?"

"Yes."

"Why? You don't need the money. And you don't seem to care at all for the title. If you have all this here in Mehkar, why do you need Langston House and the rest? Most of your investments aren't tied to the property, and the title is just a title."

Good for Poppy for asking the question. But then, he would have been surprised if she'd hadn't eventually asked it.

He certainly would have asked it if he were her, because she was right. The income wasn't significant, and Dal wasn't attached to the title, but the house was his home and then there was the real issue, the issue of duty. The issue of commitment and honor. Responsibility.

Duty and responsibility had been drummed into him every single day following his mother and brother's funeral.

His brother Andrew had understood duty. His brother, Viscount Andrew Ulrich Mansur Grant, was to have been the Sixth Earl of Langston, and Andrew loved everything about being the firstborn. He understood the responsibility but he didn't find it crushing. He knew he'd one day marry someone who benefited the estate, rather than someone he fancied. He would have been an excellent earl, too.

Dal had not been a good replacement for his brother. He was hapless—the Fifth Earl's description—and overly intellectual, so his father had been forced to shape Dal into a proper heir, even if it broke both of them.

And it had nearly broken both of them.

"From the time I was eleven, I understood my sole life mission was to marry and have children. Not just an heir and a spare, but numerous spares in the event something awful happened." He lifted his head, his gaze finding Poppy's. "Because awful things did happen. Cars crashed and mothers died and older brothers die in hospitals during surgery."

"Heirs and spares," he added mockingly, bitingly, "were not children to be loved, but insurance policies. Annoying but essential."

Wives were not to be cherished, either. They were brood mares, and income. The Grants of Langston had filled their coffers for the past hundred and fifty years by marrying foreign heiresses: Greek, American, German and in the case of Randall's mother, Arab. The wife didn't have to be beautiful, or even accomplished. According to the Fifth Earl of Langston, Randall's wife needed to be healthy—to bear those heirs—and wealthy. Her dowry was the most important thing she brought to the marriage.

Randall had been shocked and disgusted as a boy, but the years of lectures and discipline had numbed him to all but duty. Duty was the only thing that mattered, because once he fulfilled his duty, he would be free, no longer haunted by the fact that it was Andrew who should have been the Sixth Earl, not he.

"Who I am in Mehkar has no bearing on who I am in England, nor does it change my duty. My duty is to marry and continue the Grant family. It's my sole responsibility. I've known since my mother and brother's funeral that I have no other reason for being alive."

"That is probably the vilest thing I have ever heard you say."

He shrugged. "I will fulfill the promise made to my father, not to save the land or pocket the income, but because I am determined to get this monkey off my back."

"It's not a monkey, it's a curse!"

"I won't let it be a curse in the future. I'm a different man than my father and I'll make different choices." He hesitated. "You have no idea how different I want the future to be, and with you, it will be a new future. With you, I can move on."

"I hear about what you need, but what about what I need? Or do women not matter in your world? Are we just things…property and possessions?"

"You want security in life, and I'm offering it to you."

"You're not offering security. You're taking my freedom and the opportunities before me."

"I can take you places, show you the world."

"I don't want the world. I want a comfortable little house and a garden where I can plant my flowers."

"And in that house there will be a couch, and a telly and a husband that will kiss and cuddle you."

"Yes."

"You have not spent the past four years working for me to sit with some fat, balding bloke who only wants to watch football—"

"He's not going to be fat, or balding, and he's most definitely not going to be obsessed with football." Her chin jerked up. "He will be obsessed with me."

"Right."

"I'm serious."

"It will never happen."

"Why not?"

"Because you're going to marry me, and be my wife, and we're going to have the life you wanted…the life we wanted…the life where you insisted we have more!"

"Marrying you would not be more. Marrying you would be less."

"Coward!"

"Your idea of marriage makes my skin crawl."

"Liar."

"Listen to me. Listen, Randall Michael Talal Grant, Earl of Langston, Sheikh of Mehkar, I have no desire to be your countess, or your princess. I fancied you, yes. I had a crush on you, yes. But I never once wanted to trade places with Sophie because I knew then what I still know now. You will never love anyone but yourself. You can't. You don't know how."

CHAPTER NINE

SHE HEARD THE helicopter early, just after dawn. Poppy left her bed to stumble to the window arriving just in time to see the black helicopter with the gold emblem rise from the gardens, lifting straight up.

She saw the pilot, and then she spotted Dal in the back-seat.

She felt a shaft of pain. Where was he going? And why was he leaving her here?

She struggled to breathe as the helicopter flew away, her chest unnaturally tight.

It had been an awful night. She hadn't been able to sleep, not after the terrible fight with Dal in the pool.

She'd said hurtful things to him, and she'd regretted them immediately. She'd spent much of the night lying awake, wanting to go to him and apologize, but pride and self-preservation kept her in her bed.

If she went to him, she'd apologize and then possibly kiss him, and if she kissed him, then she'd want him to touch her, and hold her and then it would be all over.

He'd win. And she couldn't let him win. This wasn't a business deal. This wasn't a financial transaction. This was about her life and her future. It was about all the values she held dear: love, and hope and faith.

Love, hope, faith and family.

He'd give her the children but he couldn't give her the other things she craved.

And so she'd forced herself to stay in her bed, aware that Dal was upset, but it wasn't her problem. She cared about him—oh, so very much—but she couldn't allow him to just ride roughshod all over her.

But oh, last night…

She tipped her head to the glass and closed her eyes. His proposal had been so incredibly uncomfortable. And her furious refusal, that was even more uncomfortable.

So where had he gone today? What was he thinking? What was he doing?

Poppy dressed and went to her living room and rang for coffee. It was Izba who came to the door, not Imma or Hayek.

"Where did Talal go?" Poppy asked her.

"Gila."

"Gila," Poppy repeated numbly. "Did he say how long he'd be gone?"

The old woman's face creased. "Three days. Maybe four. He said there is a big tournament in the city. Polo, I think he said." She tipped her head, expression curious. "You don't like polo, Miss Poppy?"

Poppy felt a lump fill her throat. "No," she answered huskily. "Not as much as some women I know."

So he'd gone to Gila. Gone to Gila to see Florrie.

Poppy felt ill, so ill that she stripped off her clothes and climbed back into bed.

She heard the helicopter late on the third night after he'd gone. Poppy glanced at the small clock next to her bed. Nearly midnight.

Relief filled her. Relief followed by pain.

He'd left her three days ago and he hadn't said goodbye. He hadn't emailed her, either, even though she'd checked her inbox obsessively.

But now he was back home.

And then she realized what she'd thought. Home.

She turned on her side, pulling the cover up over her shoulder as if she could tuck herself in. But even beneath the covers she was cold. And scared. Had he proposed to

Florrie? Or God help her, had he married Florrie while he was there?

She tried to make herself fall back asleep but she couldn't. She lay in bed, heart pounding, stomach knotting, so anxious. So heartsick.

A half hour passed, and then another. It was close to one in the morning now but she was wide awake and close to tears.

Unable to endure another moment of misery, she left her bed and pulled on a pale green cotton robe and headed for Dal's suite one floor above hers.

She knocked on the door. There was no answer. She gently turned the handle and it opened. She entered the living room, crossing soundlessly the long narrow living room to his bedroom. The door there was open and she stepped inside his bedroom, her gaze going to his bed. It was empty, the bed made. A lamp was burning on a corner table and the sliding glass door was open.

"Dal?" she whispered.

She saw a shadow move on the balcony and then he appeared in the doorway.

"What's wrong?" he asked.

"I couldn't sleep. I was worried about you."

"As you can see I'm fine."

She reached for the sash on her robe, giving it an anxious tug. "How was Gila?"

"Good."

"What did you do there?"

"I saw a lot of family. I think I forgot just how big the family is."

"Were you able to spend time with your grandfather?"

"Yes."

"Did you attend the polo match?"

"I went for a little while."

He just went for part of the match? What else did he

do, then? And did he see Florrie? Did he take her out on a date? Did he kiss—?

Poppy stopped herself there, not wanting to imagine all the possibilities. Not even wanting to know if there had been a date. Too much could happen, and the details would just make her feel half-mad.

"You were gone for three days," she said, hearing the hurt and accusation in her voice but it was too late to take the words back.

He shrugged. "I had things to take care of. Arrangements to make."

For his wedding.

He hadn't said the words, but she was sure of it. Pain exploded inside her chest, and she balled her hands, her nails digging into her fists. "Is there anything I can help with?"

"No, you're doing what I needed you to do. You've given me five strong résumés. Someone from HR in the London office will call the five, interview and then rank them for me, and then hire the one they think is the strongest."

As her eyes adjusted to the night, she could see he was leaning on the frame of the glass door, his shoulder at an angle, muscular arms crossed over his bare chest. He was wearing dark, loose pajama bottoms. He had such a big, hard, gorgeous body and his mind was brilliant—sharp, swift, incisive. She'd loved working with him, and learning from him and hearing his ideas. He was bold and brave, conscientious and fair. His new secretary was going to be very lucky to have him as a boss. "Sounds as if my job is nearly done."

"Indeed. We will probably have someone hired by the end of this week."

She swallowed around the lump in her throat. "It's all coming to an end so fast now."

"It seems everything is working out."

"Does that include your search for a new bride?"

"Yes."

"You must be relieved."

"I'll be relieved when the wedding is over."

"Do you have a date set?"

"I don't want to leave it to the last moment."

"You have nine days until your birthday."

"Yes, so probably three or four days from now." His big shoulders shifted. "Something like that."

So soon.

"That's wonderful," she said even as she found herself wishing she hadn't come here, to his room. She should have waited until morning to ask about his trip. She could have waited to hear this news.

She hated his news. It broke her heart. "Was it good to speak to your grandfather?"

"Yes. Just seeing him again has made the trip here worthwhile."

"I'm glad." She swallowed again, fighting the prickle and sting of tears in the backs of her eyes. "Did you tell your grandfather about your plans to marry?"

"Yes."

"What did he say?"

"He said that he respected me for fulfilling the promise I made my father, and hoped that my future wife will bring honor to the family and the people of Mehkar."

"Have you introduced her to him yet?"

"No, and I won't. Not before the ceremony. This is my choice, not his, and I'm not looking for his approval."

She was silent a moment, trying to imagine Dal with his grandfather, the king. "What is he like? Your grandfather?"

"Perceptive. Powerful. Quiet. Dignified."

"Easy to talk to?"

He laughed softly. "He wasn't at first, but by the time I left, it was better. He has aged. He has worries." He straightened and entered the room. "I suppose we all do."

She watched him cross the floor and take a seat on the side of his bed. "What are you worrying about?"

"My worries are mostly behind me. I've done what I needed to do. Now I can breathe easier." He looked at her. "I'm just sorry you lost sleep over me. That must have been truly aggravating."

"Don't be angry with me."

"I'm not. I'm not angry with you, or anyone. I think for the first time in years, I'm finally at peace."

She wanted to ask him why. She wanted to know if Florrie was wearing his engagement ring. She wanted to know so many things but knew she didn't have the right to ask anymore. She'd essentially found her replacement. She wouldn't be working for him soon. He'd be married to Florrie—

"I hated you leaving the way you did," she whispered. "And then you didn't even email me once."

"I was busy."

"You were punishing me."

"If there is to be no future together, we need to create distance. I left to give us distance, and allow us both to take a step back."

"Is that why you're at peace?"

"I'm at peace because I know, no matter what happens in the next week, I have the answers I need." He reached up to drag a hand through his thick hair, ruffling it. "In Gila, my grandfather and I talked quite a lot about my father. My grandfather had offered to bring my mother home from England more than once, wanting to rescue her from her difficult marriage. She refused. She believed my father needed her, and that it wouldn't be fair to take the children away from him, and so she stayed."

"Your poor mother."

"That is what I always thought, but my grandfather said my mother loved him. Apparently, she was the only one who could manage him." He smiled grimly. "Rather like you with me."

"You're not a monster."

"He didn't want to be, either."

"Don't compare yourself to him! You're not your father. He had struggles you don't have. His mood swings, and mania, that was his illness. It's not yours."

"Emotions make me uncomfortable."

"Because of him."

"His emotions were out of control, so I trained myself never to lose control."

All of a sudden she understood. "You're not him, Dal. You're not ever going to be him. And you didn't inherit the illness, either."

"But my children could."

She felt another sharp stab of pain. My God. She'd never thought of that, or imagined that he'd harbor secret fears that his children could. "Or not," she said quietly, evenly, finally seeing what she'd never seen before.

"I spent my twenties waiting for the disease to strike. I kept waiting for signs or symptoms…highs, lows, anger, despair. But I felt nothing. All those years, and I felt absolutely nothing. I was numb. Even at my father's funeral. And I thought that was good."

"Being numb can't feel that good."

"But at least I had dignity."

"Is that what you call shutting everyone out?"

"It's how I survived. I can't apologize for being me. It's the only way I knew how to get through the grief, and the pressure and the unbearable responsibility."

"You have had tremendous pressure," she said. "But you're not alone. You have people who care for you. Deeply."

For a long, agonizing moment there was only silence.

Poppy's heart pounded. She felt as if she'd been running a very long, hard race.

His lashes slowly lifted and his light gaze skewered her. "No games," he said quietly.

"No games," she agreed breathlessly.

"Tell me why you came to me tonight. I want the truth."

She couldn't look away from his burning gaze, couldn't think of anything but him, and wanting him, and needing him and needing to be there for him.

"Don't marry Florrie," she whispered.

And still he said nothing, just looked at her with his intense, penetrating gaze, the one that had always made her feel as if he could see straight through her.

"I don't know if it's too late," she added, breathing in short, shallow, painful gulps of air. "But I want you to have options, and I should be an option. I shouldn't have taken myself off your list. If anyone believes in you, it's me."

"You weren't going to marry without love."

Her eyes burned and the almost overwhelming emotion in her chest put a lump in her throat. "But I'm not marrying without love. We both know I have always loved you."

CHAPTER TEN

POPPY HAD FINISHED dressing an hour ago and was now waiting for Dal to appear. Her gown was quite simply the most beautiful thing she'd ever seen, high necked with a thick gold collar and then gold starburst embellishments and embroidery down the bodice. The long, wide sleeves reminded her of a royal cape, and the soft silk and chiffon dress was fitted through the hips, the skirt straight and sleek, making her feel like a queen. There was more of the exquisite gold starbursts down the front of each sleeve.

Her hair had been pinned up with gold strands twisted in the loose curls. Her hair glittered, and heavy gold diamond earrings swung from her ears.

Looking in the mirror, she didn't even know who she was anymore.

Poppy turned away from her reflection, uneasy with her image. She didn't feel beautiful or regal, and yet the woman in white and gold looked every inch a princess.

How had this happened? How had any of this happened?

If she didn't love Dal so much, she'd pack her bags and run. She didn't know where she'd go, only that she was terrified of losing herself.

Poppy tried not to pace her private courtyard, but it was hard to just sit still when she felt wound so tight.

It had been three days since she'd agreed to marry him, and since then she'd been filled with anxiety and excitement, hope and dread.

She loved him, yes, but at the same time she feared a future where she'd give, give, give and he'd…what?

Would he ever love her? Would attraction and physical desire be enough?

Hopefully, making love would give her the closeness she craved, but not knowing made everything harder.

She couldn't help thinking that it would have been better if they'd made love before today. It would have been better to know more before the ceremony, just so she'd know how to manage her heart.

The wedding was a very simple service. There was no music or fanfare. There was little but the ring ceremony and exchanging of vows.

The paperwork that followed took far more time than the ceremony.

Poppy felt painfully overdressed for such a business-like ceremony. She told herself that she wouldn't cry, and so she didn't cry. It was her own fault for having any sort of expectations in the first place.

Dal had never said he cared for her. Today's ceremony was about convenience, and the brevity of the ceremony reflected the business nature of their union.

This was strictly business.

He'd married her because he'd run out of time. He'd married her to keep his title and lands.

And she? She'd agreed because she hadn't wanted to lose him. And yet, she'd never had him; at least, she didn't have what she wanted from him. His heart. His love.

His gaze narrowed on her face. "From your expression you'd think we had just attended a funeral instead of a wedding."

"I'm sorry. I'll try to look more celebratory. And maybe I will feel more celebratory once all the paperwork is finished."

"There is always paperwork after a wedding."

"But my impression is that there is considerable more after ours."

"You agreed to this, Poppy. You understood what we were doing today."

"Yes, I did agree. But I could have done this in T-shirt and jeans. I would have probably been happier in a T-shirt and jeans. I know Izba wanted me to look attractive for you, but the dress, shoes and jewelry was overkill."

"She dressed you as if we were marrying at the palace in Gila."

"I wish you had spoken to her."

"I did. I asked her to help you get ready. If you don't like the dress, blame me. I suggested it. It was my mother's wedding dress. The earrings were my mother's, too."

Poppy felt awful. Her eyes suddenly stung and she pressed her nails to her palms. "I didn't know."

"We could have married in Gila. The palace is impressive. There would have been a great deal of pomp and fuss. My family would have preferred we hold the ceremony there, but I didn't want to make this about the family. I wanted this to be about us. I wanted to spend the day with you. After the circus of Langston House, I thought you'd agree. I realize now I was wrong."

"You married me because you had no other choice."

"I married you because you were my first choice."

She bit into her lower lip to keep it from trembling. "You don't have to try to make me feel better—"

"Open and honest communication, remember? I'm telling you the truth. Whether or not you want to believe me is up to you."

It seemed impossible that he would actually want her. She had worked closely with him all these years and he had never been anything but professional and polite. She'd been the one to have feelings for him, not the other way around. But in the end, it didn't really matter about first choice or third choice; hierarchies and rankings were insignificant now that they exchanged their vows and signed the paperwork. They were married. He was her husband and she his wife and he'd fulfilled the terms of the trust with a week to spare.

"Now what?" she asked him. "A game of pool or ping-pong? Or are you going to get back to work?"

He regarded her steadily for a moment before smiling. "You are really upset."

"Yes, I am, and you can turn it into a joke but—"

He silenced her by taking her in his arms, his mouth covering hers. Heat surged through her, heat and longing, the longing so intense that it made her heart ache.

She'd wanted him forever and she'd married him to protect him, but in marrying him, she'd left herself so vulnerable.

He would have access to all of her now—not just her mind and emotions, but her body. And while she craved his touch, she feared it, too. She feared that once he took her to his bed, he'd see the side of her that she worked so hard to hide.

That she was afraid she wasn't enough.

That she was afraid she'd disappoint him.

That she was afraid he'd regret marrying her when he could have married almost any other woman in the world.

"Stop thinking," he murmured against his mouth, pulling her even closer to him, his hand sliding down her back, a caress to soothe, but the caress inflamed as his palm slid over her rump.

The heat in her veins made her sensitive everywhere, and as he stroked her hip, his tongue parted her lips, claiming her mouth with an urgency that she felt all the way through. Her belly clenched and her thighs trembled and she leaned into him, aroused, so aroused, and yet also so worried that she wouldn't keep his interest.

Little kept the Earl of Langston's interest.

Tears filled her eyes, slipping beneath her closed lashes.

Dal lifted his head, brow furrowing as he stroked her damp cheek. "Why the tears, my watering pot?"

She sniffed and tried to smile, but failed. "I have so many emotions and they're not listening to me today."

He gently wiped away the second tear. A glint of humor warmed his golden eyes. "I don't think your emotions ever listen to you. They're not very obedient, I'm afraid."

He elicited a smile, and her lips wobbled but it was a real smile. "You're making me laugh."

"As if laughter is tragic."

She felt another bubble of reluctant laughter. "Why aren't you falling apart?"

"Because it'd be unmanly to cry on my wedding day."

Poppy snorted.

He smiled down at her. "That's better. No more tears. Izba won't forgive me if we ruin your makeup before the *zaffa*."

"*Zaffa?* What is that?"

"It's the wedding ma—" He broke off at the distant sound of drums.

Poppy stilled, listening to the drums. They were loud and growing louder, and then it wasn't just drums but bagpipes and horns.

She looked up at Dal, confused. "Wedding what?"

"Wedding march." He smiled into her eyes. "I hope you weren't expecting an exciting game of ping-pong, because the festivities are just beginning. After the *zaffa* there will be a party and dinner. It could be a late night."

Somehow Dal had managed to get fifty of his closest Mehkar family members to the Kasbah without her knowing.

She found out later that he'd had them flown to a nearby town and then they had bused in. He had also bused in the musicians and belly dancers and the fierce-looking men carrying flaming swords.

While she'd been dressing and having her hair and makeup done, dozens of Dal's staff had transformed the huge lawn into the site for the Arabic wedding and party. The *zaffa* swept them from the house, down the external stairs, to the grounds below. There was another ceremony after the noisy, colorful, chaotic march. Dal and Poppy had been led up an elevated platform, or *kosha*, to two plush, decorated chairs. Once seated, glasses were passed to all the guests and everyone toasted them, drinking to their health.

After the toast, the royal family's Iman spoke to them about the importance of honoring and respecting each other, and then she and Dal switched rings from their right hand to the left index finger before they were pulled to their feet to dance their first dance ever When the band struck up the second song, the dance floor filled with Dal's family.

Poppy was introduced to so many people, and pulled into so many hugs and kisses, she couldn't keep the guests straight, although Poppy remembered two—the cousin who'd greeted Dal at the Gila airport, and then the tall, somber patriarch of the family, Dal's grandfather, the King of Mehkar.

She'd dropped to a deep curtsy before the king, unfamiliar with proper protocol but also profoundly honored that the king would choose to join them today. It couldn't have been an easy trip for a man in his mid-to late-eighties.

The king drew her to her feet, and then lifted her face to his to scrutinize her thoroughly. She blushed beneath his careful inspection, even as it crossed her mind that the king had the same beautiful golden eyes that Dal did.

Dal, she thought, would look like this when he was older, and suddenly she couldn't help but smile at the king.

Dal's grandfather's stern expression eased, and while he didn't quite smile at her, there was warmth and kindness in his eyes as he murmured words in Arabic before kissing each of her cheeks.

"My grandfather welcomes you to the family. He said you will bring us many blessings and much joy."

And then the king moved away and the dancing continued, only interrupted for the cutting of the cake and then again when Dal invited his family and guests to the supper.

It was later in the evening when Dal took her hand and lifted it to his mouth, kissing her fingers. "In our culture the bride and groom always leave before the guests. It is their job to continue the party for us."

And then just like that, they were walking away, hand in hand, as the assembled guests cheered and the drummers drummed and the horns sounded.

A lump filled Poppy's throat at the joyous noise. She glanced back over her shoulder and blinked, not wanting Dal to see that she was crying again on their wedding day. "That was amazing," she whispered. "Beyond anything I could have imagined." She looked up at him and then away, eyes still stinging with tears. "Thank you."

His fingers tightened around hers. "You didn't think I would let our day go without a celebration?"

"I don't know. Maybe I did."

He stopped her then, on the stairs in the shadows, and drew her into his arms for a slow, bone-melting kiss. A shiver of pleasure coursed through her as heat and desire filled her, the warmth sapping her strength so that when his tongue stroked the seam of her lips, she felt weak and breathless. Senses flooded, she opened her mouth to him, giving herself to him, wanting to feel everything she could possibly feel on such a beautiful night.

Below them, laughter and music rose up from the garden where the band continued to play and Dal's family talked and danced inside the colorful tents. And then far above their heads came a crackle and pop, and then another loud pop and fizz.

Poppy opened her eyes to see fireworks fill the dark

sky with brilliant crimson and gold, green and silver light.
The inky sky came alive with the shooting, exploding sparkling light.

Poppy's breath caught at the unexpected beauty. But then
everything about today was unexpected. The simple, practical civil ceremony this afternoon, followed by the exotic,
thrilling Arab ceremony and party and now this: gorgeous,
spectacular fireworks. She absolutely adored fireworks, too.

"Is this another tradition in your culture?" she asked,
gaze riveted to the brilliant display above them.

"No. It's something I did for you. You once told me fireworks made you happy. I wanted you to feel happy."

Her eyes burned and her throat ached, a lump making
it impossible to speak. All she could do was nod and blink
and try to keep from falling apart.

He'd thought of her. He'd wanted her happy. Even though
he didn't say the words she wanted to hear, he'd tried to
make today special for her.

"Thank you," she whispered, standing on tiptoe to kiss
him before turning in his arms to watch the fireworks shoot
into the sky and explode.

When it was all over, the guests gathered on the lawn
cheered and Poppy applauded and Dal grinned, looking
handsome and boyish and impossibly pleased with himself.

He should be, she thought, running up the stairs with
him, heading now for his room, which he'd told her would
be their room. He stopped her on the terrace before they
reached the tall glass doors, and picked her up, swinging
her into his arms, carrying her over the threshold into his
darkened bedroom, which had been filled with dozens of
flickering candles.

Dal could feel Poppy stiffen as he carried her into the bedroom, her heart racing so hard he could feel it pounding
in her rib cage.

"Don't be scared," he said, placing her on her feet. "Nothing terrible is going to happen."

He saw her nervous glance at the bed and he reached out to stroke her warm, flushed cheek. "That won't be terrible, either, but we're not going to bed yet. I thought we should change and have some champagne and dessert. We left the party before the dessert was served."

She gave a half nod, her expression still wary. He didn't blame her. It had been an overwhelming day and he'd known what would happen today.

He'd kept the *zaffa* and party secret from her, wanting to surprise her, but maybe it would have been better to let her in on the plans so that she wouldn't have been so sad earlier after the civil ceremony. He'd hated the shadows that had darkened her eyes when she'd thought the civil ceremony was all that had been planned. It had made him realize how sensitive she really was, and how much she'd need emotionally. But that would be the problem.

He could give her things, and place credit cards without limits in her hands, but he'd never give her the intimacy and emotional closeness she craved, but God help him, he would try.

"I'll open the champagne while you change," he said. "I believe Izba is waiting in the bedroom to help you out of your bridal gown and into a more comfortable dressing gown."

Dressing gown was overstating things, Poppy thought, inspecting herself in the mirror. Dressing gown implied weight and coverage, but this sheer ivory kaftan with the scattered circles of diamonds and gold beads hid nothing. Oh, there was fabric all right; the gown was wildly romantic with shirred shoulders and a plunging neckline that went nearly down to her waist, but if it wasn't for the strategic draping Dal would be able to see absolutely everything.

As it was she had a hard time keeping her nipples from popping through the fabric, never mind the dark curls at the apex of her thighs.

"Izba, I can't go to him like this," Poppy muttered, blushing. "I'm practically naked."

"It's your wedding night," Izba answered soothingly. "And you look so beautiful."

"Beautifully naked." She frowned as she walked, aware that any light shining behind her would give away everything. "Was this another of his mother's gowns?"

"No. His Highness brought this one back from Gila for you. It was custom made." She gave Poppy a pat on the back. "Go to him. Don't be shy. He loves you very much—"

"He doesn't love me, Izba."

"Nonsense."

"He doesn't. He told me so." Poppy's voice suddenly broke. "But I knew it. I've known it. And I'm not going to cry about it. I'm not crying today."

"He wouldn't marry you if he didn't love you."

"He married me because he *had* to be married. He needed a wife by his thirty-fifth birthday."

"His Highness can have any woman. Many women would marry him. But you are the one he wanted."

Poppy wanted to explain that he hadn't had real choices, nor the time to explore all his options. Sophie disappearing from Langston Chapel had put him in a bind, and so Dal had settled...he'd settled for her. "It's more complicated than that," she said faintly. "His Highness had tremendous pressure on him—"

"Stop making excuses for him. He's a man. And he wouldn't have married you if this isn't what he wanted, not just for him, but also, to be the mother of his children."

The ever-important heirs and spares, Poppy thought with a panicked gulp.

She shot Izba a quick, nervous smile and then exited the bedroom before she lost her courage altogether.

Dal had dimmed the lights while she was gone, and he was waiting for her on his grand terrace. He gestured for her to come to him and she hesitated, suddenly shy, aware that she was next to naked.

His gaze met hers and held.

He gestured again, a masculine gesture of power and ownership.

She didn't want to go to him, but at the same time, she couldn't resist. She walked slowly, self-consciously, aware of the way he watched her, a hot, possessive light heating the gold of his eyes.

The soft chiffon and silk gown floated around her ankles as she crossed the floor. Izba had unpinned her hair, taking out the gold beads, and she could feel her hair brushing her shoulders.

"Why are you looking at me like that?" she breathed.

"Because you're gorgeous and you're mine."

Her tummy did a flip. "I think I need that champagne."

He carried their glasses to the low couch and sat down. He placed one glass on the table and then patted the cushion next to him with his free hand. "I have your glass here. You just have to come to me to get it."

"You like being in control, don't you?"

The corner of his mouth lifted. "No. I love being in control."

"So what are your plans for me?"

"Come here, and I'll tell you."

It seemed like it took her forever to reach his side, but at last she was there, heart racing, her mouth so dry. As she carefully sat down next to him she held out her hand for the champagne. He handed her the flute and she took a hasty sip, the cold, tart bubbles warming and fizzing all the way down. She took another sip for courage and then another to help her relax.

Dal reached out and removed the glass from her trembling fingers. "Easy," he cautioned. "You don't want to get sick."

"It's just champagne."

"Exactly."

She drew a quick breath, wondering how this would go, and what it'd be like to consummate the marriage. "You said it will sting."

"It's what I've been told."

"Will it be bad?"

He reached out and pushed her heavy hair back from her face. "I am not an expert in virgins. The whole idea of deflowering a woman has never appealed to me."

"I thought men loved the idea of being the first."

"I think those must be very insecure men."

"You wouldn't care if I'd been with other men?"

"Do you care that I've been with other women?"

"Yes."

His eyes flashed fire, and his head dropped, his mouth covering hers. The kiss was hot and slow, and so incredibly sensual it made her head spin.

She reached for him, holding on to his shoulders, pulling herself closer, needing more of his warmth, and strength and skin. She remembered the night in the pool and how he'd felt against her, and she wanted that pressure and pleasure now.

"Please take your shirt off," she murmured. "Let me feel you."

"If you want it off, you take it off," he answered, his deep voice pitched low.

She felt a frisson of nervous excitement at the hungry, predatory gleam in his eyes as she rose up on her knees to better reach the middle button on his shirt since the top ones were already undone.

When she struggled to get the button unfastened he lifted her off her knees and placed her on his lap, so that she was straddling him, her sheer gown floating out on either side as if they were wings of a jeweled butterfly. Poppy could feel the hard press of his arousal through his trousers. She was wearing nothing beneath her delicate gown and his thick, blunt head pressed against her core.

He was hard, and hot and she shuddered as he shifted his hips, his length rubbing against her where she was open and sensitive.

"My shirt?" he drawled, leaning back to watch her at her task.

Her hands shook as she struggled to unfasten one button and then another. Again, he shifted his hips, the rocking motion deliberate, and this time she pressed down on him, welcoming the feel of his thick tip pressing between her folds, nudging her bud, flooding her with pleasure.

Poppy glanced up into his face. His black lashes had dropped over his eyes, concealing his expression, and yet the sensual set of his full, firm mouth sent twin shots of lust and adrenaline through her.

He was so beautiful. So incredibly handsome and physical.

She'd never met any man half so appealing. Had never met any man she'd wanted the way she wanted him. She'd fought her attraction for years, but there was no more fighting her desire, or him. She just wanted to be his. She wanted to belong to him.

"Are we going to just leave the shirt on?" he asked, arching a brow. He didn't sound annoyed, or impatient. If anything, he sounded very pleased with himself, and her and all of this.

"Focusing now," she answered, forcing herself to finish

with the unbuttoning of the shirt, even though she could barely focus thanks to the heat of his thighs and the way the hard length of him seemed to be making her melt.

And then at last his shirt was open and she leaned forward, her breasts brushing his chest, to push the smooth fabric off his shoulders and then down each arm until his arms were free and his muscular torso was beautifully bare. Her breasts brushed against him again as she reached for the shirt and tossed it away.

"You are a tease," he growled.

"Me? You're the one making me do all the work," she answered, even as she flashed him a shy, breathless smile.

The air practically crackled and hummed with desire. Dal had to fight to keep his hands at his sides and not touch Poppy as she finished stripping the shirt off his arms.

Her full breasts had swayed and bounced beneath the sheer ivory chiffon fabric, her dark pink nipples teasing the hell out of him, the tips pebbled tight. It didn't help that she was impossibly hot and wet. He wanted to bury himself inside her, thrusting hard and deep, but she was inexperienced and even though it had been years since he'd made love, he wasn't going to rush their first night. He wanted her to see herself as he saw her—seductive, stunning, powerful, feminine. Perfect.

He reached up to touch her, finding her breast through her sheer beaded gown. Her nipple puckered tighter at the touch and she gasped a little as he pinched the tender peak. He watched her face as he stroked her and then took her breast into his mouth.

She groaned as he sucked and kneaded the warm, sensitive peak with his tongue and lips. He reached up to cup her other breast while he continued sucking. She rocked against him, hot and damp and aching for relief, and it crossed his mind that he'd never seen anything half as erotic as Poppy rocking on his lap.

He wanted so badly to be inside her. He wanted to feel her tight heat wrap his length, and when his control threatened to snap, he swung her into his arms and carried her into the bedroom, placing her in the middle of the bed.

She fell backward with a soft sigh onto the sheets. She was still breathing hard, her beautiful, dark eyes wide and luminous, her cheeks flushed, her luscious lips parted and pink. He leaned over her, drinking her in, thinking she was the most beautiful woman he'd ever known.

Poppy.

His wife.

His pleasure.

Poppy reached for him, bringing his head down to hers so he'd kiss her again. She loved the way he kissed. She loved the way he touched her. He was touching her now, caressing her breast through the filmy gown and then lower, stroking her flat stomach, across her hip and down the outside of her thigh.

Her legs trembled as he slid his hand between her thighs, parting them.

"Don't be nervous," he said.

"I'm not," she lied.

He dipped his head to hers, his mouth covering hers in a slow, hot, dizzying kiss. She relaxed as he caressed the inside of her thigh, stroking down to the back of her knee, and then up again.

She could feel his fingers trailing over the inside of her thigh again, so very close that his knuckles brushed her dark curls. Her breath caught as his knuckles lightly trailed across her mound, the light, teasing caress sliding the delicate gown across her, as well.

She was ready to have his hands on her, skin against

skin, ready to feel him touch her as he had in the pool, with his clever expert fingers against her where she was aching and wet.

"You're torturing me," she complained when his knuckles brushed over her again, the sensation too light to bring relief and yet too firm to be ignored.

"I don't want to rush you."

"I've been aroused for hours."

"Not hours," he answered, his fingertips trailing over her, pressing the now beaded chiffon over her tender folds and then holding it against her core. "Maybe a half hour."

She felt herself throbbing as he cupped her, his palm capturing her heat and dampness. She could feel her moisture on his hand.

Dal reached for the filmy hem of her gown and lifted it up, drawing it up over her knees, and then her thighs and then over her head, leaving her naked.

She felt his gaze as it took her in. He was studying her so intently she felt as if he was memorizing her. And then his hand returned to her knee, skimming down her shin to her ankle, and then back over her calf.

He caressed her leg until she relaxed and he opened her legs wider, and leaning over her hips, he placed at kiss just above her pelvic bone, and then another one lower, in the middle of her curls.

She shivered at the warmth of his breath and then shivered again when he parted her curls, exposing her tender skin and slick inner folds before placing a kiss right to the heart of her.

His mouth felt cool where she burned, his tongue flicking her and curling around her, toying with the delicate skin, stirring every nerve, making her feel wanton and desperate and yet also empty.

She reached for his belt, tugging it free. He lifted his head, and she nodded. "Please lose the trousers."

He did, very quickly, and with the trousers removed his heavy shaft sprang free.

"I don't think that will fit," she said hoarsely.

"It will. You'll see," he answered, lowering himself over her, kissing her, his tongue stroking the seam of her lips and then the inside of her mouth before catching the tip of her tongue, making her squirm.

With his knee he pressed her legs apart, making room to settle his hips between her thighs. She felt his shaft rub against her as he positioned himself near her core, the tip gliding across her wet entrance, making her feel delicious things.

He didn't try to enter her, instead focusing on kissing and touching her neck, her earlobe, the sensitive skin beneath her breast. She liked the feel of his strong thighs between hers, his legs hard with muscle and slightly rough with hair. Little by little his powerful thighs opened her wider, and the smooth, thick head of his shaft settled at her core, pressing in.

Dal lifted his head. "Look at me," he said quietly. "It's just me and you, and it will only sting this once."

And then he was pressing into her, a slow, steady thrust that made her eyes water and her breath catch, from the fullness and pressure of him filling her. It was a lot of sensation. It felt like too much sensation. The stretching was no longer remotely comfortable.

"Breathe," he murmured, kissing her lips. "That's it, breathe."

As she breathed in, he thrust deeper, breaking through the resistance. It hurt. It did. She blinked rapidly at the burn, and then the strange fullness of him lodged so deep inside her.

It wasn't what she'd imagined.

It was more than she'd imagined.

More pressure, more warmth, more fullness, more pain.

"Breathe," he said again.

She struggled to smile. "Don't worry, I'm not going to faint."

"It will feel better when I move. Let me move. It'll help ease the tightness."

"If I didn't like you so much I'd hate you."

He kissed the corner of her lips, and then her full lower lip, and then pressing up so that his weight was on his arms, he pulled out of her and then gently thrust back in. He did it again, and then again, and he was right; she wasn't as uncomfortable anymore. In fact, as he moved she began to feel something that rather resembled pleasure.

She closed her eyes to concentrate on the sensation and yes, it was a nice sensation, better then nice, as with each of Dal's deep, slow thrusts she felt heat grow and sensation coil, and she reached for him, hands sliding up his lean chiseled torso, fingers spreading wide across his warm satin skin. She could feel the hard, taut muscles beneath his skin and the way they tightened with every thrust of his hips.

Every time he buried himself in her, he stroked a sensitive spot inside, and it made her breath catch and want to press up against him to hold him there. "Yes," he said hoarsely, "just like that," as she rocked her hips again.

The next time he stroked down into her she rocked up and the pleasure was even more intense. She clenched him with her inner muscles, trying to hold him. He growled with pleasure. Poppy felt a thrill like nothing she'd ever felt better.

It was, she thought, rather amazing how their bodies came together, his hardness buried deep in her wet, slick heat, and this simple joining could make her never want to let him go. She wrapped her arms around him, holding tighter, his tempo quickening, stroking her faster and harder. The feel of him in her was maddening and delicious. Her body burned and glowed and she arched up as he pressed deep, her heels digging into the bed to give herself traction.

"Can you come?" he asked.

"I don't know," she said, because there was so much pressure and tension and desire but she couldn't focus on anything but the hard, silky feel of him filling her.

Suddenly, his hand was there between their bodies, and his fingers found her nub and he stroked the sensitive spot as he thrust deeply. The sensation felt so perfect; everything about this was perfect, and as he filled her and touched her, she felt overwhelming love.

He was everything to her. He was the very center of her world.

His deep thrusts were sending her over the edge. She couldn't fight the building sensation anymore. With a cry, she shattered, the climax stunning and intense. He thrust into her one more time, burying himself so deeply that she felt his muscles tighten and contract as his orgasm followed hers.

For several moments after, Poppy didn't know where she was, or who she was. She'd felt thrown to the stars and she'd somehow floated back.

Slowly, reality returned and she turned her head to look at Dal, who was lying on his back next to her.

He was the most beautiful person in the world. There was no one more dear or special to her.

Her eyes filled with tears. She blinked hard, trying to keep them from falling. "I love you," she whispered. "I love you so much it hurts my heart."

He gazed back at her, his golden gaze shuttered.

She held her breath, waiting to hear what he would say. But he just looked at her for a long moment, then leaned over, kissed her. "I hope today was special."

"It was," she answered, trying not to feel empty after feeling so incredibly much. He wasn't being cold, she told herself. This was just him. Dal wasn't good at expressing emotion. He'd never say the words she wanted to hear. "It was magical."

He kissed her again and pulled her close to his side and he was soon asleep. Exhausted, Poppy lay next to him, emotions unhinged, thoughts racing, still too wound up to sleep.

Everything had changed in one day.

She'd done what she'd intended to do. She'd protected Dal, but she'd left herself completely open and vulnerable.

This life with Dal would not be easy on her heart.

Sunlight pierced the gap between the heavy drapes that had been drawn across the windows. Poppy rolled onto her back, stretching and yawning.

She winced a little as she rolled onto her back, feeling a new soreness between her thighs. She flashed back to the intense lovemaking and blushed, remembering his mouth and lips on her, exploring her, and then the way he'd filled her, burying himself in her, making her feel more connected to him than she'd ever been with anyone.

Poppy reached out to see if Dal was still with her, but he was gone.

She turned to look at the place he should have been, and could still see an indentation from his big frame.

She stroked the sheet in his spot. It was cool. He'd been gone a long time.

Poppy slowly sat up, drawing the covers with her. Last night had been a revelation. She hadn't expected the closeness, nor had she realized that a man's body could feel like that...the sinewy pressure of Dal's thighs, and the warm, hard planes of his chest. She could still remember how she'd clung to him, arms wrapped tightly, feeling as if she'd never get close enough. Poppy didn't know if this was how everyone felt when they made love, but the intensity of it had been shattering. She'd anticipated pleasure, and she'd expected new sensations, but she hadn't expected that the desire would become pure emotion.

When he'd filled her, and held her and thrust so deeply into her, she'd wanted to burst out of her skin and crawl into his.

She wanted him, all of him, his mind, body and soul.

It was why she'd told him she loved him. She wanted to be part of his heart, and safe in his heart and feel secure forever.

But she didn't feel secure.

If anything, making love had made her feel more alone and isolated than before.

It was late afternoon before Poppy saw Dal. He found her down by the pool, reading beneath an umbrella. He leaned over her, kissed her and then sat down on the chair, apologizing for being gone all day, explaining that he'd spent much of the day making sure his family returned safely to Gila, and then a problem had come up in the London office and he'd been on conference calls ever since.

It wasn't until he sat down next to her that she realized he was wearing the traditional white robe of his people.

"Where has Randall Grant gone?" she asked, and she wasn't just referring to the clean, elegant lines of the robe, but the gradual transformation that had taken place since they flew out of Winchester. In England he'd been so private and contained. He wasn't just more open here; his personality was warmer, too. He smiled here, and made jokes and teased her. And made love to her. Her cheeks heated remembering last night.

"Do you want him back?"

"Not necessarily. Although he is the you I know best."

"There is just one of me. But the me here is more relaxed. Happier, too," he added, leaning forward to kiss her, a hot, erotic kiss that made her tummy tighten and her breasts peak. She was breathless when he pulled away.

"Are you happy here?" he added.

"It's beautiful but very remote."

He studied her face for a moment. "Was it not a good day?"

"It was a rather long day. I got lonely."

"I'm sorry. I expected to be free sooner." He pressed another lingering kiss to her lips before rising. "I'm going to go shower and change. Join me soon. I've asked for some drinks and a light meal to be sent to our room since I haven't eaten anything today."

She reached for his hand, catching his fingers, preventing him from leaving. "What's happening at the office?"

"A problem, not an emergency. Nothing you need to worry about."

"Is there anything I can do?"

He squeezed her hand and then let it go. "I have one of the administrative assistants in the office taking care of some things for me and soon we'll have your replacement. It's just a temporary stress, nothing to trouble you."

And then he was gone, striding toward the Kasbah, his long white robe swirling, reminding her of a powerful desert warlord just returning home while she very much felt like a concubine with no purpose other than being available to please her master.

She grimaced, frustrated, not wanting to be shut out from his life, or his business. She'd worked with him for years and had enjoyed the partnership. What were her responsibilities in this new role of hers?

Poppy pushed off the chair and went to her room to shower and change before going on upstairs.

"Where did you change?" Dal asked her when she entered his suite of rooms.

"My room."

"This is your room now," he said. "I expected you would have the staff move your things today."

"You never said anything."

"You are my wife. This is the master bedroom suite. This is where you belong."

"How do I know if you don't tell me?"

"I'm telling you now."

Poppy compressed her lips, not liking his autocratic tone. "This is all new to me, Dal. You're going to have to communicate a little bit."

"You're upset with me?"

She fought to keep her voice steady, not wanting to sound hysterical on their second day of married life. "You were gone when I woke up. You didn't leave a note, or tell me when you'd return."

"I didn't know myself."

"In England you communicated far better."

"In England you were my secretary."

"Maybe I liked being your secretary better than your wife!"

He gave her an intense, brooding look. "Really?"

Her pulse quickened, her chest tightening. "I don't want to be shut out of your life."

"You're not. You are the very center of my world now." And then as if to prove his point, he swept her into his arms, carrying her to the bed where he tossed her, pinned her down and kissed her fiercely, deeply, the scorching kiss torching her senses.

As he kissed her, he slid a hand between her legs, caressing her thighs until she opened them for him. He leaned over and kissed the top of her thigh, and then the inside of her thigh and she trembled.

"I'm not sure I can handle *this*," she murmured unsteadily as she felt his fingers slide over her, lightly tracing her folds and then lightly, lightly parting her before placing a kiss on her, and then another kiss, followed by a flick of his tongue across her clit.

She gasped as sharp, delicious sensation shot through her and when he covered her there with his mouth and sucked, her hips jerked up of their own accord. Dal shifted his weight, clamped an arm across her pelvis, holding her open and still while he kissed, sucked and licked her to an orgasm so powerful she dug her nails into his shoulders and screamed his name.

The orgasm was so intense she felt almost broken. The intensity of the sensation made her feel emotional and undone. Flushed, spent, she felt him stretch out next to her and pull her to his side. He left his arm around her, his palm covering her breast.

"I want to be in you," he said, "but I don't want to hurt you. Maybe tomorrow."

She nodded, glad he couldn't see the tears filling her eyes.

She hadn't thought sex would feel like this…physical and carnal but then afterward, painfully empty.

It was hard to love someone who didn't love you back.

"Poppy?" he asked, shifting her so that she lay on her back. He pushed her thick hair from her face and then untangled a strand still clinging to her damp cheek. "What's wrong?"

"Nothing."

"Something is. You're far too quiet."

She looked up at him, seeing his strong brow and the high, hard lines of his cheekbones. She loved his face. It was so very beautiful and familiar. But the rest of this…it was new and overwhelming. In bed, he was overwhelming. The sex was overwhelming. His body was so big, and powerful and sexual. He was so very sexual. But then after all the physical intimacy there was no emotional intimacy. If anything, after sex, she felt even further from him than before.

"Is this what you thought marriage would be like?" she asked carefully.

"No. It's better." He smiled crookedly. "You're not just my friend, but now you're my lover."

"So you're satisfied? Happy you married me?"

"No regrets." He rolled onto his back and pulled her toward him so that she was lying against his side, her cheek on his chest. "And you? Regrets, my sweet Poppy?"

It took her a moment to answer. "No regrets," she said unsteadily. "But I think I may be a little homesick. We've been gone a long time."

His hand stroked her hair and then trailed down her spine. "What do you miss most? Winchester? London?"

"My flat."

His hand stilled in the small of her back. "Why your flat?"

"It was cozy and familiar. I felt...safe...there."

"But Poppy, your home is with me now. I have promised to take care of you, and I will. You must know you are safe with me."

She nodded, eyes closing, holding back the hot emotion, because despite his words, she didn't feel safe. She didn't feel secure. She didn't have what she needed—love.

Sex was good and fine, and pleasure was definitely nice, but what she needed most in the world was to be truly needed, to be truly special, to be truly loved.

CHAPTER ELEVEN

THEY FELL INTO a pattern over the next week, a pattern Poppy did not enjoy. Dal would be sequestered in his office working while she drifted around the Kasbah trying to find ways to occupy herself. She'd asked if she could work with him, or assist him like she used to, but he curtly reminded her she was his wife now, not an employee.

After that he seemed to withdraw even more, at least during the day when he was distant and unavailable. But then in the evening he emerged from his office and was warm and charming and always he'd make love to her. The sex was incredibly hot, and he never failed to make sure she climaxed, but the long days of being alone followed by the carnal lovemaking was breaking her heart.

He'd take her body, and pleasure her body, but that was all he wanted from her.

And that was also all he'd give her.

"We will leave here soon for Gila," he said on the ninth night of their honeymoon, in that quiet aftermath that followed their lovemaking. "I thought perhaps we could look for our home in Gila together. Would you enjoy that?"

Her brow creased. "Are we going to live in Gila?"

"I'd like to have a home in the capital. Maybe something modern, or if you prefer classical architecture—"

"What about England? What about our home there?"

"My intention is to divide our time between the two. I want my children to know Mehkar and be comfortable in both places."

"They would be my children, too," she said in a small voice.

"Of course. I meant our children."

She wasn't so sure he did.

Poppy couldn't sleep that night, but she didn't lie awake tossing and turning. No, she spent the long, quiet hours of the night making a brutal but necessary decision.

She'd given Dal what he'd needed. She'd protected his lands and title. But now it was time she protected herself.

In the morning she would leave, and she wouldn't go in tears. She was going to leave strong and proud and focused on her future for a change, not his.

He was at his desk when she entered his office. He didn't even look up for a minute, so engrossed in the document he was reading.

She watched him read, feeling a pang of love and regret, recognizing the Randall Grant focus.

No one could compartmentalize like Dal.

She shifted the hands holding her purse and worn travel bag but made no other sound. Finally, he glanced up at her, his strong black brows flattening over his light eyes.

"What's happening?" he said brusquely.

She didn't take offense. She knew it was his tone when concentrating. His sharpness wasn't aimed at her but rather the annoyance of breaking his focus. He wouldn't like what she had to say, but it was time, and she'd made her mind up. "I'd like to leave now."

For a moment there was just silence and then he slowly rose. "What did you say?"

"You told me when you found a new secretary, you'd put me on a plane. You have a new secretary. I know she's working in the London office right now, but she replaced me a week ago."

"You're my wife, Poppy, not an employee."

"Please have your helicopter come and take me to Gila. I intend to sleep tonight in my own bed, at home."

"I don't understand."

"I know you don't, and I don't expect you will, but this marriage helped you, but it's not good for me. Please do the right thing for me, and let me go. If you care for me at all, you'll send me home now."

He moved away from the desk, walking slowly toward her. "I won't send you back to England like this—"

"So you don't care for me."

"I won't send you because I do."

"Then you're not listening. I'm not happy here. I'm not happy living like this. I don't regret marrying you, and I won't call it a mistake, because I gave you what you needed…the title, the house, the estates…so please give me now what I need. My freedom."

Dal was grateful for twenty years of lessons in control and discipline because it allowed him to keep his expression mercifully blank. He was stunned, though. Inwardly reeling.

"I am listening," he said casually, calmly, as he approached her. "I always listen to you, even when you think I'm sleeping. I am there in bed with you, hearing you breathe, hearing you weep—"

"If you've heard me cry at night, why didn't you say something, or do something? Why just let me cry myself to sleep?"

"Marriage is new, and an adjustment. I thought you needed time."

"No, I didn't need time. I needed *you*." She nearly backed up a step as he closed the distance, stopping just a foot in front of her. Her chin lifted, her dark eyes bright with anger and pain. "*You*, Dal," she repeated fiercely, "not time. All I've had here is time."

"But you have me. I sleep with you every night. I hold

you through the night. I am not far during the day, and when you need me, you can find me. Just as you found me today."

Silence greeted his words. Her eyes narrowed a fraction and then her lips curved but there was no warmth in her eyes. "This you," she said at last, nodding at him, "the one you're offering, the one you're giving, it's not enough. I'm sorry if it hurts, but it's the truth."

He'd never seen this side of her. He didn't know what to make of her anger. "People are not perfect. They will inevitably let you down. I'm sorry if I've disappointed you—"

"There are small disappointments, life's little irritations and then there are tragedies. I can handle the irritations. I expect the irritations and annoyances. But me marrying a man who doesn't love me...that borders on tragedy."

She'd stunned him again. He couldn't think of a single appropriate thing to say. Poppy, for her part, was so still and pale she reminded him of a wax figure.

"Please put me on the plane—"

"No. Absolutely not."

"So you don't care for me. I am just another of your toys and possessions."

"I don't know where this is coming from, and I don't know what has made you feel so insecure—"

"You have, Dal! You with your lack of words and lack of emotion. You only make room for me in bed. But out of bed, there is no place for me in your life!"

"You are bordering on hysteria."

"Of course you'll mock me and shame my emotions, but at least I have emotions! At least I feel, and at least I'm able to be honest about what I need. I need a man who will love me. I need a man who will share with me and sacrifice for me." Her voice cracked, broke. "But from the beginning it's been about you, and as long as I stay here, it will only be about you, and I was wrong to think I could do this…live like this. So let me go now while we both have some dignity."

"I'd rather lose my dignity than you."

"You've already lost me."

"No, I haven't. You're hurt and angry, but we can fix this."

"It's impossible to fix us. We can't be fixed. You can't be fixed—"

"I am not a machine! I have feelings—" he broke off, grinding his teeth together, trying to hold the blistering pain. "And maybe it shocks you, but your words hurt. Your words wound. But I'll take the words and the wounds if it will allow us to grow stronger together."

She averted her head, lips quivering. "I don't want us to be together. Not anymore."

"I don't believe you. I can't believe you. After four years—"

"I didn't know the real you! I didn't know us."

He felt like he was in quicksand and sinking fast. Emotions were not his strength. Tears and sadness and grief and need…they baffled him. He'd never been allowed to feel or grieve, and he'd learned to survive by being numb. But he wasn't numb right now. His chest burned. His body hurt. She might as well have poured petrol on him and then struck a match. "Perhaps what you should be saying," he said tightly, "is that you didn't know you."

She looked at him then, tears in her eyes. "But I did know me. I knew what I needed. And every time I refused your proposal it was because I knew what I needed…and that was love."

"Poppy, I am trying, with everything I am———"

"It's not enough." Her chin lifted, eyes glittering with tears. "Call for the helicopter. I'll be downstairs in the garden, waiting."

* * *

Poppy walked away then, quickly, her heels clicking on the marble, her eyes scalding.

That was beyond brutal. That was awful, so very awful. She'd said hard, harsh things, not to hurt him, but to make him understand that this wasn't a game. She was done. She felt broken. He had to let her go.

She sat in the garden on a bench waiting for the helicopter, her bags at her feet. She would stay in the garden until the helicopter arrived, too. It might take days, but eventually he'd know she was serious.

Thirty minutes later Dal emerged from the Kasbah with his large black suitcase. She watched him cross the lawn and then he squeezed onto the bench next to her. She refused to make eye contact. This wasn't an act. It wasn't a game. She was leaving him today.

"The helicopter should be here in the next five to ten minutes," he said, breaking the silence.

"Good."

"The jet has been fueled and is ready in Gila."

"Thank you."

"I needed to file a flight plan and I told them London."

"That's correct."

"Good. Glad to know I've done something right."

She shot him a furious glance. "I don't feel sorry for you. You're a grown man, a very successful man. You have extensive experience in mergers and acquisitions. You're accustomed to the bumps and disappointments. You'll bounce back in no time."

He met her gaze and held it. "You're not a merger, or an acquisition. You are my wife, and you're hurt, and I'm sorry. Your happiness means everything to me."

"Those are just words."

"But isn't that what you wanted? Words? Tender words? Affectionate words?"

"You can't even say them!"

"Love, you mean?" His black eyebrow arched. "I do love you, Poppy, and yet I find the word hard to say, but that doesn't mean I don't feel it."

"Huh!"

He caught her jaw, turned her face to him. "I'm not a machine. I feel emotions. In fact, I feel them so intensely they scare me. I have spent my entire life trying to contain my emotions, determined that they wouldn't dictate my future. And every time I said I wanted you, I meant it. I wanted you then, and I want you now."

"Sexually," she said, bitterly.

"Sexually, emotionally, spiritually. I want you as my partner, my best friend—"

"Your *only* friend."

"The mother of my children," he continued calmly.

She gave her head a toss. "For the all-important heirs."

"Not heirs," he corrected, "but us, our family. You'll be an incredible mother. And I'd like to be a father, although I'm not sure I'll be good at it in the beginning. I'll have to learn, but I can."

"You never talked about family before. You and Sophie—"

"Because I couldn't imagine raising a family with Sophie. I couldn't imagine a life with her. But I can with you. I can imagine everything, and I want everything, and I do mean everything. You, Poppy, have made me want more."

She bit her lip and looked away, tears in her eyes. "It's too little, too late, Dal. You've hurt me—"

"I did. I know I did, and I'm sorry. Poppy, I am an arse. I'm ruthless and relentless but none of this should surprise you. You know me. And you married me, knowing me."

"True, and I've realized you haven't changed. You'll never change. I'm not going to change, either. I will always want more and you will want less."

"If I wanted less, why did I marry you? If I wanted less, why didn't I pick one of those silly party girls who would have been grateful for my wealth and position, instead of throwing it in my face? If I wanted less, why did I choose the woman who wanted *more*? Who demands more? Who insists I demand more, too? If less was my future, then why have I struggled to grow and change for you?"

She said nothing.

Frustration filled him. "Poppy, who would I be without you?" And then he fell silent, his question hanging there between them for what felt like forever.

Finally unable to bear the silence a moment longer, she said, "You are the Earl of Langston and the Prince of Mehkar."

"Actually, I'm not the Earl of Langston anymore."

She looked at him, aghast.

He shrugged. "You're not the only one who can make grand gestures. I can, too, and I've chosen to walk away from the title and the house and everything it entails. It was a bit more complicated than I imagined, but it's done now. It's what I've been working on since our wedding."

"The problem in London?"

He nodded.

"But you married me to secure—"

"You. I married you because I couldn't imagine going through life without you. Poppy, I don't care about titles and houses. I don't need anything but you."

"Then why the rush? Why the pressure?"

"I wanted to keep the promise I made to my father. And I did. And now I'm free."

She looked away, blinking back tears.

"I am not good with words, my sweet Poppy, but you

are my other half. You are my heart and my soul. You are my family and my future. Please don't leave, and if you're determined to go, then plan on taking me."

She brushed away her tears. "You won't like my crowded, untidy little flat."

"I will if that's where you want to be. If that's what feels like home."

"The flat's so small there's barely room for me, never mind you."

"We'll downsize."

She spluttered on laughter. "You have no idea what you're saying. You're accustomed to huge houses and servants and people bowing and scraping."

"Not anymore. I've given it up."

"What about here in Mehkar? Are you still Prince Talal, or have you dispensed with that, too?"

"No, I'm still Prince Talal." He grimaced. "And I should probably tell you something that I ought to have told you long ago."

"Oh, no." She looked at him, immediately wary. "I don't know if I want to hear this." She looked into his eyes, worried. "What is it? What else have you done?"

"I haven't done anything yet. You see, I am my grandfather's heir. When he dies, I will be king."

"Oh, Dal."

"I know it's a lot to process—"

"He's healthy, though, isn't he? At least he seemed relatively fit and strong when he was here for the wedding."

"He's as healthy as an eighty-four-year-old man can be."

"That's good."

He regarded her a moment, the corners of his mouth curving. "You took that better than I expected."

"You must know I don't really wish to be a queen. I just want a cozy little house in the Cotswolds—"

"With a couch and a telly." He smiled and kissed her.

"I promise you'll have the house you've always dreamed about. And the television set, too."

"Are you making fun of me?"

"Absolutely not. I'm just trying to reassure you that I'm listening and attentive to your needs."

She groaned and rolled her eyes. "You are impossible."

"Yes, I know. But isn't that what you always liked about me?"

EPILOGUE

TALAL'S CORONATION WAS nearly ten years to the day of their wedding at Kasbah Jolie.

It was early July and impossibly hot. The Gila palace was air-conditioned but with so many guests crowded into the reception room, the air conditioner couldn't quite do its job.

Poppy was miserable in her gold gown and heels. Not because the kaftan was tight; if anything it was made of the lightest, softest silk imaginable, but she was very pregnant, nine months pregnant, and her ankles were swelling and she was desperate to be off her feet.

Thank goodness she knew what to expect. This was her fourth pregnancy and she always felt irritable at this stage, ready for the bump to be gone and the baby to be in her arms. She was always anxious as the due date grew closer, worried about any number of things that could go wrong. Fortunately, the first three deliveries went without a hitch and all three were really good children, and very excited about the new one, because finally the three boys would have a baby sister.

Poppy struggled to not fidget as Dal accepted his new crown, and the duties it entailed.

But it was hard to stand perfectly still with the odd contractions. They were false contractions, she was sure. She'd had them with the last two pregnancies and she knew now not to be alarmed.

She pressed her elbow to her side, pressing against the tension that wrapped her abdomen.

She must be overly hot and overly tired because that one felt like the real thing.

And then her water broke and Poppy's head jerked up.

Dal was suddenly looking at her and she didn't remember speaking, or making a sound, but suddenly he was there, at her side, his arm around her.

"What's happening?"

"My water just broke," she whispered, aware that all two hundred plus people in the reception room were watching. "But it's too early. She's not due for another couple of weeks."

"Apparently, no one told her that," he said, smiling warmly into her eyes.

Poppy's heart turned over. Ten years of marriage and he still made her melt. "I'm sorry we're disrupting the ceremony."

"I'm not. I can't wait to meet her. You know how much I've wanted a daughter."

Another contraction hit and Poppy gasped and squeezed his arm. "It seems she's in a rush to meet you, too!"

"I'm not surprised. If she's anything like her mother, she's going to be fierce and loyal and impossibly loving." He wrapped his arm around her waist, supporting her. "I love you, Queen Poppy, completely and madly, you know."

"What has happened to my safe, predictable Englishman?"

"Gone, I'm afraid."

She gripped his arm as another contraction hit.

"And so are we," he added, swinging her into his arms. "Because I don't trust our little princess not to make an appearance here and now."

* * * * *

COMING SOON!

We really hope you enjoyed reading this book. If you're looking for more romance, be sure to head to the shops when new books are available on

Thursday
14th June

To see which titles are coming soon, please visit
millsandboon.co.uk

MILLS & BOON

Coming next month

THE BRIDE'S BABY OF SHAME
Caitlin Crews

"I can see you are not asleep," came a familiar voice from much too close. "It is best to stop pretending, Sophie."

It was a voice that should not have been anywhere near her, not here.

Not in Langston House where, in a few short hours, she would become the latest in a long line of unenthused countesses.

Sophie took her time turning over in her bed. And still, no matter how long she stared or blinked, she couldn't make Renzo disappear.

"What are you doing here?" she asked, her voice barely more than a whisper.

"It turns out we have more to discuss."

She didn't like the way he said that, dark and something like lethal.

And Renzo was *here*.

Right *here*, in this bedroom Sophie had been installed in as the future Countess of Langston. It was all tapestries, priceless art, and frothy antique chairs that looked too fragile to sit in.

"I don't know what you mean," she said, her lips too dry and her throat not much better.

"I think you do." Renzo stood at the foot of her bed, one hand looped around one of the posts in a lazy, easy sort of grip that did absolutely nothing to calm Sophie's nerves. "I think you came to tell me something last night but let my temper scare you off. Or perhaps it would be more accurate to say you used my temper as an excuse to keep from telling me, would it not?"

Sophie found her hands covering her belly again, there beneath her comforter. Worse, Renzo's dark gaze followed the movement, as if he could see straight through the pile of soft linen to the truth.

"I would like you to leave," she told him, fighting to keep her voice calm. "I don't know what showing up here, hours before I'm meant to marry, could possibly accomplish. Or is this a punishment?"

Renzo's lips quirked into something no sane person would call a smile. He didn't move and yet he seemed to loom there, growing larger by the second and consuming all the air in the bedchamber.

He made it hard to breathe. Or see straight.

"We will get to punishments in a moment," Renzo said. His dark amber gaze raked over her, bold and harsh. His sensual mouth, the one she'd felt on every inch of her skin and woke in the night yearning for again, flattened. His gaze bored into her, so hard and deep she was sure he left marks. "Are you with child, Sophie?"

Continue reading
THE BRIDE'S BABY OF SHAME
Caitlin Crews

Available next month
www.millsandboon.co.uk

LET'S TALK
Romance

For exclusive extracts, competitions
and special offers, find us online:

📘 facebook.com/millsandboon

📷 @millsandboonuk

🐦 @millsandboon

Or get in touch on 0844 844 1351*

For all the latest titles coming soon, visit
millsandboon.co.uk/nextmonth

Want even more
ROMANCE?

Join our bookclub today!

'Mills & Boon books, the perfect way to escape for an hour or so.'

Miss W. Dyer

'Excellent service, promptly delivered and very good subscription choices.'

Miss A. Pearson

'You get fantastic special offers and the chance to get books before they hit the shops'

Mrs V. Hall

Visit millsandbook.co.uk/Bookclub
and save on brand new books.

MILLS & BOON